Luna

Gaea

This is a work of fiction. As such, any persons, places, things or ideas appearing in this book that resemble those of the real world, living or dead, human or biomachine, are either coincidental or used fictitiously.

LUNA
Book Three of the Mother Trilogy

Vanguard Edition

Cover art and design by Ferdinand Ladera
Maps by Jacob Gamber

Font: 11 pt Sylfaen
140,000 words
Printed in the USA

Idea Engine Press LLC
850 Euclid Ave Ste 819 #4020,
Cleveland OH 44114, US

The Mother Trilogy: Book Three

- L U N A -

JACOB GAMBER

Gaea

The Known World of

Mani

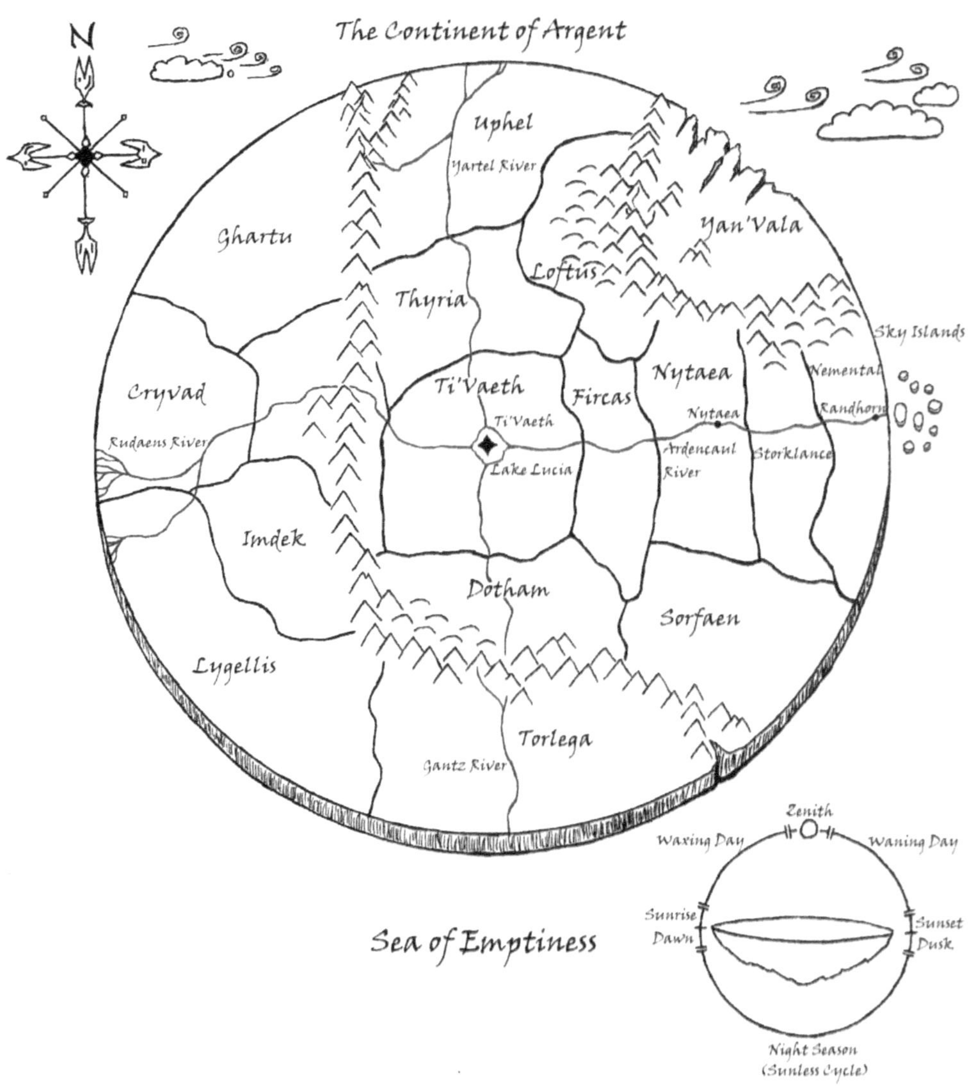

The Far Continent of

Darsor

Gaea

GAEA
The Nine Cities of Man

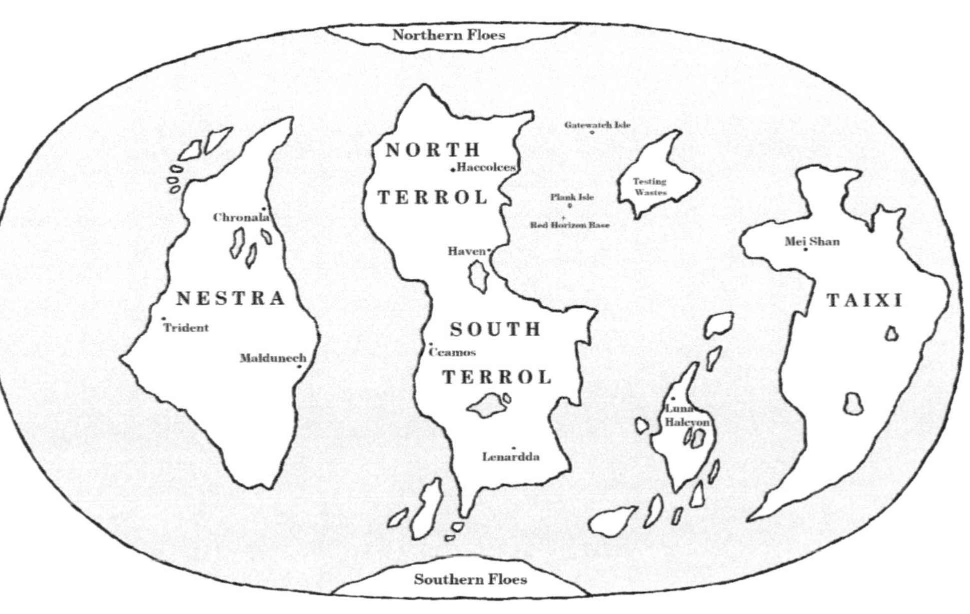

Gaea

Gaea

— For my mother —
You don't have superpowers
But you're still cool

(And for some reason you like my books)

- Acknowledgments -

Luna bound at last . . .

The final showdown. It's been a long road here, but I hope you'll find it worth it. Since my brain works in series, I've never had to truly end a story before. I'm . . . sad, but also satisfied. Quick note: I wrote this novel under the assumption that the reader has read Lyn's previous adventures, but I included a synopsis to catch you up in case you skipped it. Also, as with *Mani,* there's an appendix at the back with glossaries for characters, terms, places, worldbuilding details, etc.—possibly containing minor spoilers.

— Jacob G.

- Prologue -

Ancestor

(Planet Gaea—Anier headquarters
Soldor 14, A.E. 1318, E120)
[Placeholder]

- Exordium -

Stranded

[Placeholder]

(From Lynchazel's Vault)
To think that it would end here, like this . . .

Here we are again . . . only this time I'm on an alien moon. And . . . I might not be making it back. Only time will tell. This next part is going to be extremely dangerous, but fortunately we figured out how I can transmit signals back to Gaea.

Let's back up and start from where we left off last time. Gaea was embroiled in war, and I was the new unwilling Senator of Ccamos in place of my forever love, Sylleo . . . well, all right, he wasn't exactly that. But . . . I can almost wish. At this point, were there an opportunity to love a man, I feel I would be yoking myself to a different creature, another species. Sylleo was perhaps one of the few beings in the universe who could understand me on a certain level. One meta-human experiment to another.

I'm on Luna. I'm sure you've heard that by now, of course. Things here are . . . not what I expected at all. I'd like to say the Cydenges are more friendly than I anticipated, but that wouldn't be entirely accurate. They want something from me; that doesn't mean they like me. They feel a kindred bond, and indeed I feel it reciprocally . . . but does one like her family? Not necessarily.

In this case, I'd say not, seeing as I'm about to be eaten. But no matter. Uploading all this takes little time, just a bit of concentration. So . . . here goes. The possibility of me dying here is . . . unsettlingly high.

Gaea

Gaea

- 4 -

PART ONE

Gold

Gaea

- 5 -

- Chapter 1 -

Serpents of the Moon

Finhal 1, 1294:
To think that each recurring offensive of the Cyenges was taken so lightly
as to assume simple aggression . . . the arrogance of man never ceases to boggle
the mind. They thought the metal predators were coming to steal their world,
and this was true, but the significance was far greater. They were a message—
and blind eyes and deaf ears were turned toward Luna.
— From Lhinde's Vault

I was exploring the ruins of Luna Halcyon, the old city. Not the one where Holman rules, or not exactly. I had his permission, though of course, that of my retainers back in Ccamos was harder to obtain. He's going to betray you . . . Emperor Lldsaor will find you there . . . such went their excuses.

I understand that they were good ones, but I say excuses because I . . . well, it's hard to explain. In the months since my inauguration, I'd felt a growing, ever-thickening mixture of unease, claustrophobia and paranoia—and an increasing certainty that this was the same felt by my mother shortly before my conception and birth. They'd thought it to be hormonal imbalances, or a mental disorder obtained in her long imprisonment deep within Haccolces, but I was now convinced that the cause was deeper still, and far more sinister:

Lhinde, her mother before her—the initial Mother Gaea first created to be the queen bee of all humanity—had hidden a part of herself in her Vault, a piece large enough to be self-aware, in her final bid for vengeance. There is an old saying: If you want something done right, do it yourself. And she intended to do just that.

Within my own Vault, my grandmother stalked the farthest corners, prowling like a locked lion. Locked she was, more so than my mother, Lynchazel

I. I went to *her* often, now that her entire memory pool was open to me. At first, I avoided many personal doors, like her relationship with my father, Kallyn, but at her permission I overcame that. It felt wrong at first, to see so intimately another's life . . . but now it was as though we were two consciousnesses within one flesh, merged into one mind. That had been her intent, to bare everything to me so as to leave no lingering coal of bitterness like Lhinde before her.

Of course, as I said, Lhinde was now more present in my mind than ever, but that was unavoidable. I inherited my mother's burden—and now I had to see it through.

We came upon the island of Escatar at 10:00, at the north of which sits the modern city of Luna Halcyon. A thick stratus layer obscured Sol's yellow light from Gaea's face as we neared the city. Merely "neared", for the city could be seen on the far eastern horizon, but we were not here to see the city. Upon arriving, I was greeted by an armed escort sent by Holman. A group of some dozen soldiers, armored and outfitted with energy weapons, enough to be intimidating.

For, you know . . . ordinary Hellebes, that is. My own escort of six descended with me, looking apprehensive as normal. Neither Zent nor Kaen accompanied me, which was a rare thing anymore. They were busy with their own tasks, and I was just beginning to get away from all the advisors and generals who were far more competent than me at . . . just about anything where administration is concerned.

Holman, unsurprisingly, was not among these men. The leader, a captain, approached and said, "My Lady Senator," dipping his head respectfully.

As courteous as his greeting was, he'd have made it more so for any of the other seven on the council. Of course . . . I wasn't *exactly* on the Senate yet, so his use of the word Senator was relatively generous. A good sign from the local Senator. Holman and I were on . . . well, to my knowledge, fair terms. This seemed his way of showing good will toward Ccamos, despite his continued avoidance of an actual meeting between us.

"Captain . . ."

"Hoverdd."

"Captain Hoverdd, it is good to meet you. Let your superiors know I appreciate the welcome. Are you to escort us to the site?"

"Indeed, My Lady, if you will allow."

I looked back, nodded to my men, and stepped forward. They shifted uncomfortably, but did not move. They knew their orders.

"You wouldn't like to take some men along?" asked Hoverdd.

I shook my head, as though my heart weren't frantically nodding. "I am not anticipating foul play, Captain. I wouldn't have come if I did not trust Senator Holman this far." In the past, I'd thought to use the threat of destruction that my powers granted me, but I deemed this better now. Not that I necessarily meant the words . . . but I was trying to learn this thing called tact.

Besides, the decision to leave my men at the ship was a strategic one. They were well practiced on what to do in the event of an attempt to seize or destroy the ship, and our enemy would find it more well-outfitted than might meet the eye. The more guarding it, the better.

Me . . . I could take care of myself.

I boarded the Halcyon vessel, and we flew off to the south. Where our ships had landed, there stretched a grassy plain with trees to both north and south, rolling hills looking on to the city, which sat across a deep canyon. If my mind traced my memorized map well enough, there were reaches in that canyon that actually connected to the ocean, due to rather unique geography. Luna Halcyon was vaguely shaped like a crescent, with two main bodies and smaller islands, but some were nearly broken, held together beneath sea level and coming back together in places, some with water above or below sea level.

Southward, the cloud layer was amassing into rain clouds that shaded the thickening forest. The trees were not tall but healthy, with good summer leaf coverage on them. The air here was quite muggy, as expected, but the tropical heat could have been worse. Ccamos was hotter, although most of my time there was spent in air conditioning. Let's be honest, I made good use of the comforts they had on my mother's planet . . .

"The ruins are hidden by deep woods, Lady Mother," said the captain. "I'm sure you've been briefed on the geography and all. Let's just say it's an area that has been purposely left untouched. There are certain rules regarding the preservation of historical sites, you understand."

"I trust you have a list?"

"Indeed. Ferro?"

A soldier beside me pulled a folded paper from a pocket on his unusually long-torso, grunting, "Here, Lady," in an unbelievably deep voice. So deep that it seemed to crackle like thunder instead of projecting normally. It was not the type of voice that speaks often, so I returned a nod of thanks as I took the note.

Unfolding it, I scanned a list which had been printed off a state database, showing *Article 31.2.1* through *Article 31.2.12,* all of which were written in that incredibly dry legal copy with the traditional amount of redundancies. As was my habit, I scanned it not for comprehension but data collection. After a minute, I folded it away in a hip pocket and began to process the important points. I still kept White around, as the personality I'd developed for her helped to keep a core analytical part of my brain open for work such as this.

In her whiny voice, she read off the highlights, telling and retelling me not to take any stones or other samples from the reservation without going through my "escort" first, as they would act as mediators between me and Holman for legal purposes. Most of the rest was similar guidelines, silly but old. I might have to fudge a few regardless, and to do that I may have to get closer with some of the soldiers. We would see.

They let me down on a high point in the forest's geography, where an opening in the trees allowed the thirty-foot compact carrier to land on its four telescoping legs, which tracked the terrain as we landed and adjusted for levelness and stability.

The men gestured for me to step out first from the passenger hold, and Captain Hoverdd met me at the back hatch. "If you'll follow me, My Lady. I will bring a few men with us as well; I trust you understand."

I did, and at the same time did not. The formality, yes. But if he were still leaving the bulk of them at the ship, then I didn't see what a few more men would do other than help to keep tabs on my doings better. I'm sure each one of the four men he called off the transport were desperately hoping I didn't cause any trouble.

I wouldn't. I would be good.

The odd part was that I didn't immediately see the ruins. I saw only a lumpy hill fenced in with gnarled, uninviting trees. No path, no "No Visitors" or "Do Not Touch the Ruins" signs littering the way. Then I realized, just as we crept into the woods, that the hill we'd descended *was* the ruins, giving way to stone that proved to be worked and carved centuries—perhaps millennia—ago.

Our chest lights pierced the macabre setting, revealing much more turbulent stone beneath their roots. The seemingly odd way that the trees grew, and their shifting and unevenness, now made sense, as the forest had essentially overgrown the ruins long ago. "Will we need to . . . clear a path?" I asked.

Hoverdd looked back. "Depends. On what you're looking for, and on whether you want to go through Holman to get clearance."

I was already supposed to have *clearance. What are they trying to hide, anyway?* His words indicated that our location was being tracked as we spoke, and likely a video/audio feed being sent back to Luna Halcyon. If I chose to disobey them, not only would I have to kill innocent drone bees, but Holman would know at once. Better to keep him neutral to me than to see how quickly I could arouse his anger.

"But you are free to explore at your leisure," he continued. "We are here to guide and to supervise, nothing more."

I nodded, though at the back and unseen by the others save for one. I turned, spreading abroad the light of my chest light. "Thank you, sir."

- Chapter 2 -

Sendoff

Finhal 1, 1294:
And so she went—for the last time? This she wondered as she left to go to
my new home at the brink of the stars, as I once will. Or will have done. Or
might have . . . but not yet.
— From Lhinde's Vault

[Need a chapter or two here before she sets off, otherwise Chapter 1 just feels like a prologue. Of course, maybe the Luna Halcyon part can be skipped entirely. Just going to have to fill out this beginning best I can, then test it out on readers.]

[Need to at least mention the Archmother and where Lyn got all that, right? Or . . . no, that's fine. She made up the term herself. More like why she feels so strongly about her connection...]

"I'm going, Kaen."
Kaen

- Chapter 3 -

The Call

Finhal 1, 1294:

And so she went—for the last time? This she wondered as she left to go to my new home at the brink of the stars, as I once will. Or will have done. Or might have . . . but not yet.

— From Lhinde's Vault

"I'm going, Kaen."

Kaen swiveled at the sound of his childhood friend's voice, calling from the doorway behind him. He turned slowly with a frown. "To Luna?"

I nodded.

After a pause, he said, "How? What are you taking?"

I shrugged. "I'm not. I'm just going." I made an odd nervous gesture, tucking in one shoulder and looking away, never lighting on one spot but roving with my eyes. "I . . . think I told you about it before. I've got Cydenges blood, Kaen. I'm not human, not entirely. No Hellebes is. But I . . . I've a special bond with Luna, one I've been ignoring since before my own birth."

He opened his mouth to respond, then judged it wiser to keep silent while I finished.

"It's time to spread my wings and fly," I continued, almost talking to myself. "To Luna. Back to my Mother."

His frown resurfaced, deeper. "Your mother is not on Luna."

"A different Mother. You could call her the Archmother, so to speak."

Kaen felt hairs bristling on his neck. *Archmother . . . He looks confused.* Understandably so. Luna the entity, the "Titan" sibling of Mani. Mani's soul had spoken to him of her through the sword, but he'd known too little to follow along. In fact, Mani had compared Mydia to her.

"All right, then," he said with a short sigh of exasperation. "Tell me, what's the difference between Luna and Gaea? The beings, not the planets."

Lyn pursed her lips in thought, or perhaps slight annoyance. "You're talking about Cybele. Or at least . . . I think that's her name. The Titan of the Earth. She's the one they themselves called Mother. Did Mani ever speak of them?"

"Not really. Luna, yes. I've never heard the name Cybele before. But you're avoiding my question."

It was my turn to sigh. "I don't know, Kaen. It's not Cybele, not Gaea. Someone is waiting for me on Luna, calling to me. And I know it won't be safe. I might never be back. I really can't say."

Clearly frustrated, Kaen made a hurried gesture for me to enter the room and sit down. He was seated at his desk, and seeing someone hang in the doorway for so long made him anxious. I complied, taking the extra seat beside the desk. I promptly put her boots up on the metal desk, however.

"Lyn, are you sure? Really sure?"

I nodded.

"But you're fifteen! You have a life ahead of you! You've got a city, basically a country, that looks up to you."

"I know." My tone implied that I wasn't happy about the latter part, particularly since the word I liked to use for that was *worship.* He'd specifically avoided that word. The other side of that coin was responsibility, however, which was also not easy. He knew, since he as well had a fair amount of responsibility saddled on his shoulders, far more than when they were Legaleian-sized.

Kaen laid a hand on my shoulder, and I turned to look into his eyes. Mine have been described as a cool blue like the Gaean sky, appearing older than they were. Somehow, despite being at least half human, I'd aged like a Hellebes, maturing far quicker than was natural, and my mental age did not match my biological age. "Lyn, I guess I'm just—scared for you. But also, I mean, you still never said how you're going to get there. According to modern science, it's impossible."

"Kaen. Like I told you, I'm part Cydenges already. In a way no Hellebes is. And I think I've found a way to the moon."

"No . . . Oh, come on."

Another nod. "You see? I have every other ability they can do."

Except for the red lights . . . those things aren't natural, and they aren't of Gaea. Again, he kept his thoughts to himself. He thought for the words to say instead, working his tongue back and forth against his cheek. "All right," he said, throwing out his hands to either side. "So you're going. Or you'll try. I can't exactly stop you. You're the Mother, after all."

"Yes," I said softly. "Exactly. I'm over it all, being this mythical figure that everybody talks about but no one understands. Powerful yet powerless. I don't just want to do this, Kaen—I *need to.* I have to go. I must."

The words almost sounded like a historical quote. Whether my own or taken, I spoke them with conviction, rising to my feet. He rose with me, and I embraced him, throwing my arms around him and squeezing with all the strength I knew a Hellebes could take. Strength a human never could. Two experimental results, sharing what could be a last embrace.

He couldn't help a wan smile as they pulled apart. "I'll be rooting for you, Lyn. I don't know what in the world—or, the moons—you'll be doing up there, but . . . just be careful. And come back."

"I will," I said unconvincingly.

"When are you leaving?"

I drew in a long breath. "As soon as they'll let me. I'd better make these goodbyes quick."

- Chapter 4 -

Taking Off

Humans: Aggressors. Enemy.
Not enemy: Prey.
— Cydenges Eternal Vault

Many thoughts raced through my head as I prepared to depart for Luna, emotions roiling in my breast. A certain high as of adrenaline or caffeine pulsed in my temples, yet my heart did not beat quickly as I looked at the gathering I had amassed. People were still arriving in the square in Ccamos to see their Senator leave. Probably wondering, *Why's this lady ditching us when she just became Senator?*

Good question, guys. Wish I had an answer. But I didn't. Not one to satisfy inquisitors like Kaen and Zent. And the generals. And pretty much everyone else.

Besides, I was far less a lady and more a mere girl in shoes many sizes too big. In various ways. I mean, I *was* only fifteen. A lot of people seem to forget that. But of course, that was not truly what had me grinding at my bit so, jumping at noises, fake-smiling wherever a real one seemed most fitting. I was beset by a strange feeling, and indeed which had plagued me for some time now, only growing: a sense that this was goodbye. That men were seeing me off today here in Ccamos whom I would never see again.

It was a stormy day. The forecasts had all predicted it, so no one was shocked. I strode out from the manor, southward toward the gate, followed by some dozen retainers and Kaen. I considered Zent one of the retainers now, since he was in charge of the battalion formed from the remnants of the Red Horizon, now called the Red _____. The clouds above were not like those in Haccolces or Maldunech, the industrial cities who stirred the ire of the smog gods, but nevertheless churned and boiled in what a Legaleian would call an alien way. They blanketed the entire sky, yet the periodic lightning illustrated the clouds' geometry in stunning detail, echoing one another in quick bursts.

Someone punched me on the shoulder as we walked. I jolted only slightly, glancing over my left shoulder to see Zent grinning like a kid. "Still jumpy, Heiress?"

Some still called me that, despite my new title. It was like a second name by now, so it made no difference. "Trying not to be, Colonel."

"Well, I know you've been feeling a lot of weight these past days, so I won't put any more on those skinny shoulders, but . . . just make sure you come back to us."

"Zent, I don't—I can't promise—"

"Promise."

I screwed up my face in consternation, angling my face forward again. General Inecc was now in front of me. "I'll try," I said, almost under my breath. It wasn't that I was afraid of all these men seeing my weakness. They'd seen me at my worst already, and they'd had to put up with my moodiness and "paranoia" lately, even if not all of them mentioned it.

"Lyn, just remember you're a groundbreaker in the history books if you can pull this off," said General Frauss from my left. "We need you back so we can hear more about Luna. And gain some intel on our foe."

They were right on that one. If I died on Luna, I would be wasted in more ways than one, since we had no other confirmed way of getting to the golden moon. My entire objective was to prevent the Cydenges from attacking Gaea further, and secondarily to gather information. "I know, general. I'm sorry. I've convinced you all to let me try, so I owe it to you to do my best."

We stopped soon, and my retainers formed a semicircle around me. I'm sure they didn't intend it to look like some manner of cultic gathering, but I couldn't help but picture men in crow outfits bowing down to some artificial god they were about to sacrifice to the darkness. That wasn't far from the truth, only in this case it was my idea.

Behind us followed the honor guard of two hundred Hellebes soldiers, who took up formation on my right and left sides, guns held to their chests, feet together, in the Ccamos salute.

After a moment's hesitation, I turned and threw my arms around Zent's chest, squeezing him tight for a moment. Proportionally, we were like a father and small child. He patted my back, muttering encouragement.

I moved on to Kaen, embracing him and then saying, "I authorize you to to take a trip back to Mani, Kaen. You have to get back to Nytaea."

To see her. I didn't have to say that. He gave a brief, awkward smile and nodded. "I'll see you when you get back, Lyn."

From there, I moved on to handshakes, allowing my small palm to be crushed repeatedly by ten gentlemen grey suits. Then I stepped into the midst of the semicircle, looking around at our spacing before moving out slightly farther toward the gate. "All right," I said with a gulp, a slight tremor in my voice. "Here we go. You can do this, Lyn."

I crouched down, assuming what one might call a runner's stance, touching my forward foot with one hand and the ground with the other. I felt the grass beneath my palms and the life that flowed beneath, aware of how that same energy coursed in my veins. I felt the pulse of my heart, and attuned it to the "rhythm" of Ccamos, which was biotic and primal in a way that might seem to defy the definition of a city. Vaguely, I could feel the many Hellebes lifeforms present in Ccamos, but more deeply, the Geokinetic power that flowed throughout all of Gaea. The power of the Mother. The power that the Cydenges sought to steal from us.

The power that made me what I am.

I bent my legs further, lowering my rear end, and tensed my muscles. I didn't truly know what I was waiting for, nor how I would know I was ready, as I was operating entirely on instinct, the animalistic instincts of my Cydenges kin. And then I felt it. I looked up, watching Luna's dusky golden form overhead in the morning sky. So far away, and yet I could *feel* her presence. Calling to me.

Come home, child. Come to me.

The words did not reach my mind, more of a vague impression I'd had many times lately. But as I "felt" them, a shiver ran through my bones, an ecstatic elation that excited an unexplainable urge to leave this world. I opened my mouth and . . . I don't know, I might have howled or made some other unearthly noise. I hope not, for my onlookers would surely think me insane.

My muscled spasmed, and I felt my entire body vibrating as a red light enveloped me. Then my consciousness was engulfed in a brilliant ruby hue.

- Chapter 5 -

Lunar Abode

Mother is all. Mother is commander.
— Cydenges Eternal Vault

The first sensation I had was of cool stone against my fingertips. The second, a weight pressing hard against them, a weight we like to call gravity. Thirdly, I gasped in a breath of air. I could breathe. My lungs flung themselves open and shut, gulping in air. Had I gone without it for a time? How long?

I looked up, seeing only brazen rock, and sank back on my haunches, rising fluidly. It was easy, similar to on Mani. I looked around me to see a black, star-strewn sky empty in comparison to the worlds that I knew. There was a very faint atmosphere, at least visually, which refracted rays of burnished gold, hazing the dark sky only faintly. But the actual atmosphere was breathable . . . somehow.

Yet I'm here. I, a human, have jumped to Luna like a Cydenges. The thought chilled me. I had done what no human had ever even thought of. The Gaean Senate, when they planned out their experiments for my Cydenges DNA, had never once thought of me as something that might be capable of interplanetary travel, but as a mere energy weapon, or a bio-conduit.

About me lay a rocky wasteland of the same dull, bronzy color, more varied in topography than I'd have imagined. I was in the midst of a sort of crater, and at the crater's edge I could see the beginnings of others, with ridges of rock rising up in the background. There was no way to orient myself, no real landmarks to go by. Fortunately, no Cydenges yet either. Though that would be a matter of time.

I froze as I sensed something odd. I thought I'd risen to my feet, but I looked down now, bending my head further than one would think possible, and lifted a hand from the ground. My hand was not a hand, but a silvery metallic foot with five claws and one in back. Nearly frozen in terror, I tried to turning the paw, finding it resistant to the motion. It was not as mobile as a human hand. *Human . . . am I not . . . ?* I wiggled the claws, watching in fascination. One, two, three, four five . . . and six. It felt almost natural.

I curled my transfigured body to the side, peering at my left side and hip, which were also sheathed in reflective metal plates. The hip, doglike, the torso long, and obviously my neck was lengthy as well, like the Cydenges I'd seen on that plain in Gaea. *A Cydenges . . . oh, Mother, what have I become?* But wait . . . I also had . . . wings? I searched my shoulder area mentally, realizing that—yes—there were muscles and nerves associated with the strange appendages. I unfurled them, stretching both out into my vision, perhaps what amounted to ten paces in all. (I lacked any concept of proportion, being that my Cydenges body was far larger than a human's.

Simultaneous to the rising panic, I experienced a fleeting elation parallel to it. I began, hesitantly at first, to prance on my new claws, picking up all four legs almost playful as I tested the instinctive quadrupedal movement scheme. I beat my wings, feeling the rush of Luna's strange air as I displaced it in powerful wing bursts. I felt myself lift off the ground, the strangest sensation—I dare say—I've ever felt.

How can this be? Do all humans become Cydenges upon reaching Luna? Is that how all these Cydenges gained their form? Or is it something to do with my powers? It wouldn't make sense if humans automatically became these creatures, because (a) Humankind shouldn't ever have been able to come here at all without the powers, and (b) that would mean that they were not truly a unique species, and thus I couldn't have "Cydenges DNA" in my veins.

Right?

I sensed a tickle at my mind, like a whisper in my ear, almost a physical sensation: *Daughter?*

. . . Yes?

Daughter! At last you've come to this place. Welcome to my world. I've awaited your coming for many eons.

You have? I looked down at my forelegs once more, thinking on my strange body and what it could mean that a pseudo-godlike lunar being had been waiting for me. Had *she* done this?

Yes. And . . . yes. In a way. Many generations ago, by human standards, the rulers of your world took it upon themselves to utilize my powers to create a replicant of me. Naturally, it failed, but here you stand today as a testament both to the power of longstanding determination and to the strength of my own power.

OK. I'll take your word for that. Am I . . . will I get my body back?

It's not as simple as that. But yes, I believe you will. You must come to me first. My children will guide you. They are almost there.

I felt that same cold chill. Her children . . . the metal beasts who preyed on my kind. At least so far she had not exhibited any ability to read into my mind as Mani had done to Kaen. I could only assume that this creature, Luna or whoever she was, was similar to him.

Soon, I saw them, creeping over the crater's edge on their deerlike legs, tails swishing behind them. Most did not have wings, though a few did. It hadn't occurred to me that the Cydenges could take different forms. Or perhaps each was made a little differently. I recalled Zent talking of Cydenges swimming in water—was that yet another form?

"Hello," I said uncertainly to the creatures, although my mouth did not work as intended when I opened it. Instead, a crackly cry came forth, almost like a bird. Instead, I tried the mental communication. *Hello? Brethren?* It seemed a safe way to call out to them.

I was greeted with a metallic growl, a rapid clicking like metal plates chattering against one another, almost feline in its intonation. If lions or leopards were made of metal, they might make a sound very similar to this.

I'll . . . take that as a hello.

There was no response, or so it seemed, but rather a chorus of echoing clicks coming from ahead and round about to either side:

Brrrrr/Chrrrr-r-r-rrr-rrrrrr.

Gaea

Gr-r-r-rrr/Hrm-ch-ch-chhhh/Gnn-r-r-r

Thr-thr-trmmm/Grrrrrrrrrrrr.

Ch-ch-chrrrrrrrr-crmrm/Trattt-tra-tra-tra-trrrr.

(I can't translate it, but this is roughly what it sounded like, arranged in verse with divisions indicating where they overlapped and interrupted one another.)

Then I saw them, slinking over the crater wall like cats on the prowl. Perhaps more like wolves, given how they roved in a large pack, though I'd never personally seen wolves. Their metallic scales made surprisingly little noise as they slid smoothly over one another with each of the creatures' lithe movements. Their grinding growls grew louder, though their movements did not; I couldn't say if Luna's atmosphere had any noticeable effect on sound or not.

A faint buzzing filled the air as the Cydenges converged on me. I let them come, having expected a similar welcome of course, and knowing full well that any adverse or threatening reactions would be the most likely way to raise their aggression. While I suspected they were growling at each other, or at least in conjunction with one another, I now sensed them projecting the screechy, grinding snarls onto me.

The closest stopped but a dozen feet from me, head held just lower than my own—though twice the size of a human's—and shoulders slightly higher. *Wait, what am I saying . . . those are human comparisons. I am . . . one of . . .*

Newcomer.

This impression came clearly through the growls now, causing me to flinch ever so slightly. But I listened, receiving similar verbal impressions from the other beasts of silver. *Traveler. Form-taker. Welcome. Mother: bids you come.*

This last seemed to emanate from the throats—or whatever inner parts made the noise—of multiple Cydenges.

I . . . I will. Thank you, I said, this time aware that my own metal chest was vibrating with noises in a like manner to theirs, chaining different frequencies and rhythms to create the verbal greeting, if indeed it could be called that. The feeling was odd, to say the least, as I intended words and thought them in my head.

Pleased purring came in reply, as though the beasts were pleased to see me taking to their kind's ways. That was good, I figured, perhaps a sign that they wouldn't turn on me and chew me apart. For some reason I pictured them having a practice of doing so, even though nothing I'd seen of them so far would have given a cannibalistic impression.

They turned one by one, long serpent-tails swishing, and returned whence they'd come. In all, there were eleven present, but perhaps more lurked behind the visible edge of the crater.

I followed after, turning my head to check my peripherals briefly. I did not use my wings, but instead kept them folded at the sides in what seemed a natural position. *My wings . . .* It felt so wrong to be thinking something like that. Was I insane for thinking I was actually here on the moon, embodying a metal monster? I half wondered if I was dreaming.

But no, my dreams didn't work like this. Anytime I felt conscious in a dream, I *was*. And that was all thanks to my blood ties with these very monsters. My . . . well, did they actually have blood? I had been privy to very little of the current Hellebes insight on the Cydenges. Not for lack of searching, of course. Ccamos is simply not where most of that knowledge was kept.

We traversed another valley, though this one more laterally shaped, and angled slightly to the right. My Cydenges escort picked up speed, entering a loping and then a bounding gait. Past the ravine's edge came a plateau broken only by smaller rocky pocks and picks, plus the occasional large boulder. All were of a similar bronze tone and rough makeup. The scientist in me—or perhaps my mother—wondered at their chemical makeup. Could this type of rock be found on Gaea?

Hard to say without taking a sample, daughter. We don't typically study geology with eyes alone.

The voice almost jolted me out of my synced stride; I didn't at first realize that it was my mother's. *Mother? You can still reach me all the way out here?*

Yes dear, came the longsuffering reply, her tone ever so slightly superior. *Even here. You are here, after all, and I exist solely in your mind.*

It was the type of comment that might have made my ears burn, back when I had ears. In this form, I could hear, so clearly they had some manner of auditory input, but the creatures had no visible ears behind their horns. I shouldn't have wondered at my mother's intrusion, but it was comforting to hear her again—perhaps especially so now. *Mother, am I making a mistake?*

That's the sixth time you've asked me that this week, child.

Because I need—I mean . . . I sighed inwardly as I ran with the Cydenges. *I know, I'm independent now, and never have been dependent on you. Perhaps I've just been second-guessing myself.*

Clearly. Lynchazel, you really mustn't . . . wait. I'm detecting something strange. Like you're . . . you've . . .

I transformed into a Cydenges, Mother. You're not hallucinating.

But that isn't possible. We talked about this. You are a human woman, not a Cydenges. How . . .

I couldn't claim to explain it myself. Instead, I simply relayed to her my own surprise and panic upon realizing the body I had assumed upon coming to Luna. Or . . . had I taken this form *before* the jump? Was that how I'd managed it? What must the men back on Gaea have seen before I blinked out?

Sister . . . hush. The air is noisy. You are breaking too many silences.

It was the Cydenges around me. They didn't seem to have heard my inner conversation, and nor did I think they suspected my mother's presence, such as it was, in my mind, but they had clearly sensed the . . . "noise". With an inward shiver, I said no more. My mother did not need me to finish my thoughts, as she was a mental conjuration with no real motive of her own.

The landscape did not stay flat for long, but became rockier and filled with small valleys and ravines. I still could not see any great topographical highlights on the horizon, nor any sign of vegetation whatsoever. Luna appeared to be completely barren, unless I'd just arrived in the desert region. But then . . . there was no Wellspring here. Of course it was desolate. We kept on for I knew not how long, bounding across dusty stone, until the moon dragons led me at last to the first real anomaly: A cavern in the ground.

Okay, it was a little more than that. The place rose like a low mound on the horizon, and I soon saw that it was ringed by a deep gully with multiple tiers and tunnels reaching down into the earth at the bottom.

Come.

I couldn't tell if the beckon came from my escort or from the Cydenges Mother, who I presumed to be entombed beneath this mound. It probably came from them all. I followed, feeling excitement in my bones. Or whatever skeleton I possessed. I felt as though my heart would be pounding, my pulse quickening, my breath coming quicker, all the usual signs of excitement. But . . . the creatures didn't even seem to breathe. My chest did not expand or contract, and until I thought about it, breathing had not crossed my mind at all. No wonder they could survive here with so little atmosphere.

We entered into one of the tunnels, though some of my honor guard poured in through alternate entrances. Some climbed the mound like squirrels, watching my entrance from above. Each tunnel was perhaps double our height in width, and so steep that the creatures used their every appendage to skitter down the sides almost like bugs. The stone burrows were rough enough that such a task was not difficult for me. Awkward, yet almost natural. Cydenges could apparently move like almost any natural creature on earth, including her instinct-equipped metal body. Nothing could have prepared me for what awaited me inside the Cydenges burrow:

Majesty untold.

- Chapter 6 -

The Queen

Hive. Home. Hive. Strength. Birthplace. Palace. Heart of Mother, Heart of
Moon.
— Cydenges Eternal Vault

[Will probably have to edit some of this chapter's description, but I think that goes without saying.]

Luna, to the best of my reasoning, is fairly similar to Planet Gaea in that it is comprised of layers: An atmosphere, an outer surface, a crust, and so forth. But these layers are extremely thin. Here beneath the mound stretched what I call the Queen's Hive, the capital of the Cydenges, their ancestral home for the last thousand years, carved only larger and deeper over the centuries.

We exited the entrance tunnel to emerge into a gargantuan chamber. Where before I'd relied on the ruby luminescence of my "brethren" to guide me, I now saw color laid out in glorious arrays, with gold veins tracing down stalactites the height of mountains, etched with brilliant red in patterns that seemed less natural, as though the Cydenges had somehow carved it into the stone. We entered the Hive upon one of many trail-webs that connected to others lower and all about by spindles of darkly-colored rock. Above, there were more stone trails, and far beneath, reaching down ad infinitum, where everything merged together into a vague red glow.

As we proceeded, I observed my surroundings and especially the depths below to see that we were in one section of many. There were dividing walls of a sort, whose gold and red etching disguised the tunnel openings from the uninitiated, and once I was able to make out the patterns better, I realized that they pointed toward where different sectors must surely be. But how large were they? Did these lead to dwelling burrows? The massive, cavernous beehive we were traversing felt like a hub area or place of transit more than anything else.

Your Queen, I asked the creatures before me, trying to communicate as they did, *Does she dwell beneath here, or . . .*

She did. She will. But for now, she waits. Waits for soon. We come, see her. Wait her. She comes soon.

Nonplussed, I decided I would soon find out what their cryptic words meant, so there was no point in pressing.

Seeming to sense my confusion, one of them said, *She is above. We will go to her.*

Even as it spoke, the ones in the lead crossed over to another stone track via one of the weblike connections. Ignoring my nervous skepticism about the Hive's structural integrity, I followed them, scrambling up to the next tier of shafts. This one was less flat on top, more of a great cylinder hewed or chewed from the lunar rock, roughly the length of a Cydenges in width and rough enough for our powerful claws to easily grip. In fact, the Cydenges skittered across the stone erratically, often crawling all the way around it like squirrels on a tree trunk. I suppose it helps that gravity on Luna is similar to Mani, that is, far less than Gaea's.

The shaft column of stone twisted, snakelike, rising upward to connect to more shafts, and I saw beyond those the centerpiece that crowned the upper chamber of the Hive: A nest of silver, webbed over and pocked strangely, dusty in places but glittering in the branching tendrils that connected it to the mound's ceiling. These webby roots also connected to neighboring branches of stone, the uppermost of them all, although it was not clear which was holding which.

A cocoon? For that was what it appeared, like a cocoon or chrysalis formed by an insect ready to move on to the next stage. There was no doubt what creature it housed, although the implication both baffled and chilled me.

One of my companions, seeing me inspecting the cocoon, said, *Yes, that is her Cocoon. A house of her own making. She dwells. She grows. We near, then wait. Your timing is good, sister.*

Daughter, came a voice in my head suddenly, causing me to pause once more in my climbing. I immediately shook off the discomfort, listening as the feminine voice, deep but soft, continued: *You are here. You are come at my request.*

I have, I sent back, though I couldn't tell if she was looking or listening for an answer, or simply sending out a sort of greeting. Could she sense my specific presence and location? Obviously, she'd sensed my proximity growing nearer.

Finally, we arrived at the foot of the Queen's Cocoon. I could have sword it shivered upon our arrival, perhaps a coincidence or a mere trick of my mind. I stared at the intricate silvery work on the webs that strung the chamber together, pulsing with eerie marks almost like symbols along the threadlike wrappings. There were no apparent openings in the ovoid.

I turned my eyes downward, wondering all over again at the intricate scales that sheathed my thick-boned legs, almost as the skin and fur of a canine creature. Five shining claws decorated each reptilian foot, reflecting the red and gold hues of this sacred place. I became aware of my escort shifting, taking each one a reverent seated position with great horned heads bowed. I was in the midst of a sort of half-circle. I mimicked this position, though I cast my eyes about me curiously, observing those near me with greater curiosity, now that they were still and in such a curious position. Each had such a . . . regality . . . to it.

Him. I was pretty sure all these creatures were male, though how one might tell that to look at one was beyond me. The Cydenges immediately to my left had strong shoulders, two pairs of gently-curving horns almost like an antelope, and a noble sort of droop to the scaled lips that almost exposed his teeth. Somehow, they all looked so much more canine in this sitting position, whereas their form and movements had thus far struck me as far more feline.

The one on the right was taller, leaner by a smidge, with only one set of horns. Smaller horns, so short that they were almost nubs, sprouted along its cheek. Its scale pattern was different, as indeed they all seemed one from another. Its look was such that the scales seemed more pronounced from one another, whereas the aforementioned Cydenges had a smooth pelt of scales that seemed to blend together. Farther left and right, the next two each had two sets of horns, one's ribbed and curly, the other's bending outwards like claws. Even the color of their scales were different, some darker or lighter or tinged slightly coppery or brassy. Some had spikes running all the way down their backs to their tails while others possessed less spikes, or only a cluster on the end like a fisherman who'd tied together an ungodly knot of hooks for a ruthless catch.

The one who seemed more eloquent than the others spoke for the second time: *Soon she comes. Feel her power, strength of our Moon become flesh. Metal, a form for our Mother, Queen.*

If I still had hairs, they'd be bristling at his words, my skin tingling. I even *felt* like it was, but such a reaction was impossible. Were my scales shifting? Twitching? Yes, born of a similar feeling of unsettledness, exposure to something unearthly and unknown. Would this Queen really come forth from this Cocoon? If so, then where was the last Queen? Did she pass her role on from one generation to the next? I'd just assumed her to be immortal, or even . . . almost divine? Semi-divine, perhaps.

In my head, I heard my birth mother whispering hesitantly. *Do you feel it too?* I asked her.

Her ramblings cut off, and then she answered,

I believe so.

Another shiver ran through the Cocoon—unmistakable this time, for I felt it underneath my paws. My eyes roved at the peripherals, but I caught no movement in the Cydenges beside me. Low whines and whirs coming from deep in their chests, which had a sort of character to them and spoke of adoration and ecstasy. With a small shock, I realized that others had joined us, and were still creeping in, ringing the Cocoon upon the surrounding stone skeleton. For creatures of such size and bulk, Cydenges were near silent save for their alien calls and clicking of claws.

The metal sounds of the Cydenges echoed all about, soon ubiquitous, rising to a crescendo that radiated off the silver Cocoon and caused my metal body to vibrate uncomfortably. The great chrysalis twitched multiple times, continuing to do so after the metallic chant cut off, echoing in empty air. I shifted my feet restlessly, trying to keep still as the others, and beheld the birth of an alien Queen.

The Cocoon gave a low groan, then a screech, and I heard other sounds from within: Rustling, clicking, then an ear-splitting screech that undulated, vibrating throughout the Cocoon and its onlookers.

She is upon us.

The Queen has come.

Now Queen. Again Queen.

Pick me, O Queen!

I could hear the babble of reverent murmurs from the Cydenges around me, those whirring utterances that manifested in my mind as mostly-coherent thoughts.

The Queen continued to wriggle and thrash inside the Cocoon, or whatever it was she was doing, until at last the first layers of the outer shell peeled away. A claw pierced it and ran a jagged line down, unhindered by what seemed to be solid metal. More clawing, accompanied by more growls, and a cut-out swathe felt down, landing upon the stone catwalk right in front of one of the Cydenges. It didn't move, showing no fear.

More of the silver walls came down, forming a messy bridge of sorts, and then she strode out: Taller than any Cydenges by a few hands and far longer, she had a brilliant coat of shimmering gold scales, starkly contrasted against the normal range of silvery colors—almost as though each were a petty, impure mockery of the true Queen. She was impressive, gorgeous, a creature of both power and grace.

She stopped in front of one bowed underlings, back legs hardly even out of the door, and suddenly pounced on the creature, jaws clamping savagely around its neck even as she knocked and pinned its torso to the ground with her powerful claws. It kicked and thrashed while its closest brethren rose up, defensive instincts triggering before they backed away with submissive postures.

It was fascinating to watch. The Queen ruthlessly twisted her neck and split her victims own neck open, red light escaping between the scales. As it did so, her body tensed almost in ecstasy, long tails flashing back and forth. The light did not go far, however, for she sucked it *into* herself. She held its struggling back legs with one hind foot while her foreclaws sank in, tearing the scaly skin of its side to produce more red light. Soon, its entire makeup broke up, falling apart as the inner red light rushed into the Queen. The broken pieces began turning into dust even as they hit the stone.

She turned her gaze upon the others nearby, tail twitching back and forth. The horns on her head were nothing short of majestic, at least six pair sprouting in all directions before rushing forward to cover nearly the span of her long, fanged snout. A ridge of dramatic spikes ran from the base of the horns to her tail, which ended in a twisting, pointed curl of four horns. Before her, her subjects bowed and prostrated their forms. One even rolled over like a submissive dog. More reverent utterances, such as *O Queen, have mercy!* and *Glorious Queen, you are harsh but just,* were conveyed to the Queen in clicks and whines, leaving me wondering how much was translated in my head and how much she heard in her own mind.

She watched them impassively, posture still dominant and undecisive. *All a show of dominance?* I wondered, unsure just how animalistic their species was. Did she need whatever sustenance that poor Cydenges had provided? Was this the normative behavior of the Queen, and a primary way of "serving" her? I certainly wouldn't want a ruler like that.

As if sensing my thoughts, the Queen finally turned my way. Her long horns swiveled, pointing toward me, and I found myself staring fixedly at her burning gold eyes. Not red, like her children, but twin flames of purest gold, purer than the sun. *Daughter,* she spoke into my mind, accompanying the deep mechanical rumbling that echoed from her, *You have arrived in time to witness my rebirth. You were bold to come thus.*

She stalked toward me, stance not softening, and the Cydenges made way for her. I stayed put in my four-legged stance, wary but not wishing to make the wrong move. I could only assume this Queen to be far more powerful than me in my Cydenges form. *No words, Lynchazel daughter of Lynchazel? Speechless before the Queen of Gold?* With a glance toward the others, she said, *Leave us. I would speak to her alone. Go!*

The last was a harsh, guttural growl, one that was promptly obeyed. The metal creatures slinked off, some readily and others reluctantly. Some voiced objections, but she ignored them all. She waited till they were all gone before prowling about me in a circular fashion, fixing me with her golden stare. Her gold plating reflected the red etching on the closest stalactites eerily, like shifting veins indicating a furious undercurrent.

She said nothing to me, and I almost spoke—or rather, *thought*—a response before thinking better of it. I didn't know how intelligent this Queen was, nor how brutal, nor how reasonable. Was I truly an honored guest here, or a morsel about to be prepared for dinner? I would find out.

The Cydenges Queen turned from me, tail whipping. As it whipped top-to-bottom, I couldn't help but notice that between her legs ran only the smooth tapering of her belly, which seemed to transition seamlessly into tail. She was female both in her position and—I presumed—her ability to lay eggs of some sort, but there was no obvious indication. With most species, the males were larger if nothing else, but she was the greatest in size by a noticeable margin.

With only a brief backward glance, she bounded off, as nimble as any of her children.

- Chapter 7 -

Of Dominance

Winged. Legborne. Other.
— Cydenges Eternal Vault

I followed, taking her cue. She led me around the circular inner ring, slowing to a brisk stride, and I realized we were just circling the silver Cocoon. I said nothing, but she seemed to sense my confusion with something akin to amusement. *You do not understand the purpose of this thing, yes?*

Yes, I answered, seeing no need to be evasive.

We Cydenges do not live forever, Gaeaborn, and that includes me. I am their mother and creator, but also my own, for my frame wears out as the ages turn and I am forced to craft another vessel. For my children, there is a far different process, for they are born in mass every day in the duplication chambers below. For this process, they give to me over a span of time, hence these webs of metal you see. Each strand is a life or a part of a life. When the new Queen is ready to serve, I discard the old husk in the lower crypts and assume this metal flesh.

She'd stopped in front of the door from which she'd emerged, allowing me a good look inside it. The walls were much like those I'd seen of insect cocoons, made of many thin layers, the pattern web-like and rhythmic. Metallic strings the size of Gaean conduit dangled from the ceiling of it, perhaps the life-sustaining lines that had fed her energy while she grew. The frayed ends still glowed and sparked.

So . . . how often do you recycle your body? I asked. *And are you inactive in between, or is the transition immediate?*

Ah . . . I sensed an impression of laughter. *You take up the voice of the intelligencer. That is, of course, why they sent you.*

I—that's not—no, you're wrong! I ask only out of curiosity. If I seek information to bring back to my people, it is only in the interest of all parties, that I may more accurately represent Luna to the Hellebes. A piece of my mind had noticed that she seemed misinformed about who had "sent" me, for indeed no one had.

She seemed not to pick up on it. *That is well, daughter of humans. Sadly, I have no wish to be represented. You are a gem forming in a cavern of toxicity, a precious seed sown among thorns.*

My tail twitched, and I turned my long skeleton to watch its whiplike motion, mesmerized and almost terrified by it all over again. I glanced inside the Cocoon, analyzing new details in the wrapped metal work of the Queen's former prison. My eyes were sharper now than they'd ever been as a human. *I would say more like taken, then forgotten, and now demanded back.*

But no demands have been made. My children never came to steal you away like in your ancient stories. Instead, they pillaged Gaea's lifeblood to return to me, feeding my newest body.

Wait . . . that's *why they make their periodic raids?*

Why else? I send them to my ancestral home to steal from my mother, draining what fuel they can before making the return jump. Invariably, your Hellebes compatriots kill and wound many, making the gathering inefficient, but I simply send more. They are quite expendable. I imagine the Hellebes are still puzzled as to the reason we target Geothermic hotspots.

I could not discern whether this last line was meant sarcastically or otherwise. Before I could answer, however, the Queen had made a smooth, catlike transition into a quick stride. *Come.* It was less a word than a thought communicated from her mind to mine.

I obeyed, trotting along behind her as she turned from the topmost coil of stone. We descended multiple levels before she leapt straight onto a near-vertical pillar of gray stone, claws biting in and carrying her down with almost lazy force. Squirrel-like, she descended into the cavernous depths.

I followed, opening my fanged mouth for an anxious in-take of breath. I promptly closed it, realizing that the gesture felt off to my Cydenges body, and leapt onto the stone pole. For the briefest moment, fear threatened to take me, but my spine twisted almost on automatic, forelegs grasping the stone with their terrible claws, back legs maneuvering to grip the upper chinks with only the barest lack of grace. The strength of each paw, each individual claw, was immense, not only holding onto but in some cases biting into the pillar.

I put one foot in front of the other, finding I could descend rapidly while maintaining balance. The Queen's words resounded in my tin skull, a note of amusement in them: *You could always use your wings, little one. You possess them for a reason.*

I almost slipped on my way down, but I quickly caught myself. The stone shaft was becoming gradually more lateral anyway. How had she even known of my discomfort? She must have somehow sensed it through my mind—an uncomfortable thought—or even heard my cautious descent. Perhaps she could sense my proximity. The Queen too had wings, so why had she not used them? I wouldn't unfold mine until I saw her do so. Was that out of fear?

Probably, yeah.

I began to lope down the inverted tunnel, pushing the limits of my Cydenges comfort and testing my speed and agility. The path curved and diverged, and I followed the golden Mother on a twisting route ever downward, into the dark belly of the Cydenges Hive. Round about us, Cydenges perched on the roping pillars and passed close by. Eventually, we came to one side of the Hive and exited the path smoothly into a dark tunnel, wherein I followed the Queen's golden glow, admiring its rich qualities, almost like a false Sun in the darkness.

Why do I find myself admiring her, though? said the rational part of my mind. Why should I not hate and fear and despise this thing, this mastermind of Gaea's continual barrage? Well, okay, not mastermind, since she had yet to be successful, but the point stands. There was something about being in this body . . . was my mind even the same?

This time, to my horror, the Queen responded directly to my thoughts. She did not slow or turn, but spoke into my head as I neared her. *You are troubled.*

Tell me your mind.

There were multiple ways to take such a directive, but I settled on the obvious: *How are you reading my mind?*

My senses extend beyond the limits of a mere human, was her only response.

The flippancy, condescension and tight-lipped nature of her response made me bristle, prompting rash words to the surface. *Says the monster trapped on a moon. You think you're somehow better than—*

I cut off as she spun with a growl, twisting the golden light patterns cast on the wall. Her face snapped toward me, jaws opening, and the growl suddenly became a full roar such as I had not heard from a Cydenges. The sound was deep, quivering, a metallic vibrato that swept from low to high and faded into a malevolent buzz. She snapped her jaws shut, teeth *cling*-ing together, and the roar cut off as quickly as it had begun.

I'd skidded to a halt as soon as she began to turn around, and now found myself rearing back like a scolded cat, posture lowering, legs tensing. Again, I had a sense that my heart would be pounding if I currently had one. A defensive snarl split my long mouth.

"You know nothing, whelp! Speak to me again in such a way, and I will rip your throat open and drain your life force. Among humans and Hellebes, you are special, but before me, you are nothing. I was here a millennium before you, and before that I ruled Gaea as a tyrant. Do not come here of my own power and insult me to my face. Am I clear?"

Her speech was not made up of words in the human sense, but the guttural growls which I'd caught the Cydenges making. Somehow, in my mind they translated into intelligible speech. For my part, however, I was groveling on the ground, half rolled over with one foreleg raised in a submissive posture. *Yes, I* said back. *Yes, My Queen.*

That is better, she spoke telepathically. She did not, however, relax her stance, but instead stalked forward, tail twitching but once in an ominous gesture. Then she pounced, and I scrambled to my feet just in time to take a swiping blow from her powerful forepaw. It knocked me nearly to my feet, but I tensed my muscles and sprang back up, only in time to be set upon once more, this time with two feet. Almost like a playing dog, a small part of me realized, though in that instance I had no idea if she meant it in play or truly wanted to kill me. Her manifold teeth snapped viciously in my face, taking hold of the scales of my neck when I made a replying snap. She both pulled and pushed me down, slamming my back end into the rock walls of the tunnel.

Pain was an odd thing as a Cydenges. My body felt solid and hard, and did not much react to physical sensations, since most materials could do little or nothing to them, but this much force produced a terrifying pulse from within that very much resembled pain. I let out a pathetic moan, which she choked out with a shake of her neck.

But it was measured. Her teeth but scraped my scaled neck, though I felt her cold claws sinking into my left flank as I lay on the ground. Between that and her other forepaw on my left shoulder, the weight she applied rendered my struggling nearly futile. Apparently, Cydenges claws could indeed pierce one another, and also could retract and extend like cat claws. She pressed them further in, punching nearly through all of my silvery armor. She snarled in my face, producing a menacing growl, and then snapped her jaws with a clash as I struggled further.

I fell still. Finally, fear for my life overpowered the animalic instincts that compelled me to fight. This was serious, or so she was clearly trying to impress upon me. She gazed down upon me, the aggression ebbing from her snarl only a bit, and then spoke again in her guttural growl:

"You see the futility now. You are a mere Cydenges. As such, you are not kin to me, but a drone. An ant. Know your place."

I gazed up at her, frozen in fear. *Yes,* I said, unsure of whether it got through.

"Say it in our tongue."

I almost panicked. Did she really want me to . . . ? Unsure if I was capable, I shakily opened my mouth, a pathetic look of terrified doubt surely smearing my snout, and tried to force something out. It came out in a similar warbling, grindy, mechanical way, but clearly did not satisfy her.

The Queen opened her own mouth just a crack and issued a small serious of whining pitches, beginning with a strange purr. I automatically understood its meaning.

I echoed her, surprising myself with the accuracy of my utterance: "Yes."

The Queen slid her paw farther up my belly, claws tearing my scales in parallel lines. They collided with my steel ribs and caught, but she only purred further until they slid over with a *crshhhCRUNCH-shhhhh,* resuming their course.

I dared not move, nor breath—if that were even something I needed to do—until she at last let me go. She removed her claws, then her weight, and backed away, finally turning and continuing on down the tunnel. Belatedly, I took the cue to get up, following after her with a wince. That scar *definitely* felt like pain. Judging from intuition, I thought the wound would soon heal, nor would it hamper me much, but it was concerning how the pierced scales below my ribcage bled sparks and red light.

I slowly caught up to the female Hellebes, her golden light gently blending in with the red/grey light of my own. She had purposely refrained from leaving me in the dark and dust, just as she had purposely tempered her fury. Perhaps the whole thing had been a carefully contrived act to train me as a mother cat trains her kitten with only a small sliver of wildness. Of course . . . she had not shown restrain on the poor victim of her post-hatching meal.

Will she eat me too? I was practiced enough at warding away Lhinde's buried consciousness that I was confident of the secrecy of that thought. The Queen—Luna?—said nothing, leading me farther until we came upon yet another cavern, this one long and deep, arching downward. Stone branches, similar to those in the main chamber, twisted throughout, paving a chaotic path downward.

My hostess looked back at me, a question smoldering in her golden eyes. Perhaps she was merely waiting for me to say something.

Taking a chance, I cracked my scaly lips and—hesitantly—said, "Where are we going, O Queen?" The churning, clicking growls that primarily made up the "words" came out shockingly smoothly, and almost naturally. The last part, her title, was made of a deep-throated hum filled with powerful vibrations—the title "Queen"—but with an honorific attached on the end, a buzz that rolled downward, indicating a submissive presentation of the question or answer. My Cydenges . . . instincts . . . seemed to tell me so.

After a moment's pause, she gave a regal nod, the most human gesture she'd made yet. It seemed to say, *Well done,* though know impression of words came with it. Instead, she gave a direct answer. "We approach the Epsilon Pits. One of many growth chambers."

The phrase "growth chamber" was one of those I translated in my mind but did not comprehend. I'd heard the word *growth* used in regard to Luna before, speaking of some ability of hers—presumably the way she made her children, the Cydenges race—but I couldn't say whether this was the same usage.

Apparently, I thought too noisily for a bit, for the Queen graced me with the first mental interaction in a while. *Growth, you call it. Hmmmm. We think of this in multiple different ways. I grow, for it is the power granted me by our creator, a power that sets me apart from my mother and brother. But the Cydenges, they too grow in size and strength, and this is separate from the way that I birth them, as well as from the growth of ordinary living creatures. If you follow me, I will show you what I mean by this, and what these busy ants are doing in these great pits.*

While she spoke these words in my mind, the golden mother stood still, seeming to gaze out over her domain with . . . who knew what emotion, if any, nor for what purpose. But now she spread her wings, unveiling a triple and then quadruple set of fans that interlinks between great bones, spreading to a greater width than the tunnel we'd just traveled through—far greater. They were dark silver, like most of her armored pelt, but overlaid with a shimmering deep gold and traced with the brightest gold at the edges and along each bone. This pattern swirled between the joints, creating a swirl like a false eye.

Without the need for discussion, I knew what it meant. I click-clacked up behind her, clearing the tunnel mouth, and spread my own. The motion felt odd, even though I'd technically done it once already on my way to the Hive. Much like the tail, it was a part of the body that had no reasonable counterpart for a human to speak of. Back and front legs are much more like a human walking on all fours than you might think—the only difference being that the skeletal and muscular makeup is such that it is far more natural to move with.

We are flying, O Queen?

Flying, she agreed.

- Chapter 8 -

The Blessing of Wings

The Queen leapt from the stone path, glowing wings creating a blurred illusion against the black backdrop. I followed suit after a moment's hesitation, knowing there was no alternative. I was usually the daredevil, the risk-taker, yet today felt like being a little child again. As I sailed into the dark void, I felt a mixture of emotions rush through me, but what won out in the end was that familiar rush of exultation that accompanied an adrenaline rush.

I flapped my wings, following the swooping trajectory of the Queen, gliding when she did. Our wings held us surprisingly well. I could not say how heavy a Cydenges is, but I suspected not nearly as heavy as one might think. I watched as the twisting webs of walkways and bridges sailed past, ducking and weaving as she did to avoid them. Due to the gold and red veins tracing most of them, that was not a hard task.

The pit was both deep and long, fanning out to a width I could not make out from our position. As we sailed across, however, I began get a sense of both the scale and geometry. If this cavern was any smaller than the main one, it was only by a slight amount. I almost wondered if this was a whole warren of super-caverns that connected one to another, perhaps each with their own mounds up top, but the scant information I'd gathered so far indicated that was not the case—particularly as these seemed to extend downward, not upward. The shape of the walls was such that they curved into a different shape entirely as we got far enough to see it.

Then I began to see it. Along the walls were twisting patterns of stone, and Cydenges climbing up them at intervals. But . . . no, that wasn't right. These were many-legged arachnids of great size, clinging to the stone seemingly with large claws like the Cydenges. Or . . . the normal Cydenges.

They are the Arachnid Brood, said the Queen. *One of many. Here in this testing chamber, they make their way up from the depths, fighting for dominance and food along the way, and must prove themselves once they reach the top, lest they be cast down again. The pits make them strong.*

As she said, I looked up and saw a cliff at the top, with red-eyed Cydenges waiting for the newcomers. *There must be some reward for them as well?*

There is: A better place in the hierarchy. Cydenges can work their way up to pack leaders and commanders, all to greater serve the Queen.

I let no answering thought escape from the personal recesses of my mind. It seemed strange to me, certainly, that they would do it out of a sense of honor. Perhaps there was a threat in it as well. But more importantly . . . *I don't understand, though. How many different kinds of Cydenges are there, O Queen? How have I never seen them on Gaea before?*

You are young, child. I do not send them all in every raiding season. But you have also not encountered them in the ocean, I trust.

And what do these eight-legged ones excel in? What can they do that the regular kind cannot?

They possess superior climbing capabilities, thanks to their many legs, and are quieter, with better nighttime senses. They can also cloak themselves, removing the red signatures that so easily distinguish my broods. Does that satisfy your curiosity?

Yes, My Queen.

She took us into a dive, and we descended toward the abyss below. It struck me, as everything rushed by us in streaks of black and red and gold, that I couldn't truly see the bottom. Just how deep did these crevasses run? How long of a climb did these young Cydenges have?

I can see you wondering, daughter of humans. What is your question?

Oh. I . . . How young are these Cydenges starting out? Do they begin this climb soon after hatching?

Hatching . . . I see you are applying once more the mode of my reentry into the world to my children. They do not "hatch," but beyond that . . . yes, it is immediate. They have little choice but to climb or be eaten. Cydenges do not all begin great, and the lesser fall behind. Lunar nature is similar in that regard to Gaean. Those who survive are the strongest, made more so by the ardor set before them.

Keeping alert for the Queen's movements ahead of me, I pondered these things. I was curious what "eaten" meant in this case, since it didn't make sense that there would be Cydenges at the bottom, eating the younglings that came forth from . . . wherever they did.

We circled in our dive, moving with the wall and then out around its wide-curving edge, getting a close but high-speed look at the spidery crawlers making the long journey upward. Slowly, ever so slowly, a glow began to alert me that we were nearing the bottom of the chasm, a glow that emerged from the entire floor. It sloped inward, and we traveled with it, gliding overtop more climbers. The lower glow solidified into pinpricks, far-away beacons that lit the darkness. But then I realized that it was a false bottom. We came upon them and dove past, nearly free-falling now. The low gravity made for a low terminal velocity. The lights were indistinguishable in nature, but they blazed from atop jagged spires that reached to varying heights.

Below them, the air seemed thicker, more dense somehow. And far darker. I saw no more red veins, nor golden tracers, and realized that the twisting pathways the Cydenges loved so much had not been in view for a while.

The darkness took us, our bodies' natural glow the only thing to light the way. The Queen was clearly guided by instinct, or a sense I did not yet understand, and which she'd hinted at already.

Her golden aura suddenly grew larger, and I spread my wings and braked before colliding with her. We sailed parallel to whatever lay below us, and she said, *We are near the bottom of this pit. It is one of the lowest. Be careful, for those at the bottom are ever ravenous.*

It was then that I heard it: a constant whirring sound, accompanied by sharp clicks at intervals. The sound was unearthly, with no quality of life to it. Slowly, we continued to descend. My wings somehow had not tired yet, for which I was mightily glad. At last, the Queen's glow illuminated an unsightly jaw, massive and black, dull and gnarled. It twisted and lashed out, mouth flashing into hungry teeth, and I heard the *click!* that had alerted me. The head withdrew into a black hole, and only then I made out what teemed all over the stone cavern floor: spiders. Tiny, teeming, forming into lines that moved with erratic purpose, heading toward the cave walls. Looking above and about me, I could just barely make out the red and gold threads that outlined the pit at its walls, beyond the point where the walls tapered outward.

They're running from these mouths, I realized. But that was only part of it. They were crawling over something metal, broken pieces of something, and a few of them glowed, which each attracted entire masses of the spider Cydenges, as though they were feeding off of it. With a start, I realized that these broken shapes were other arachnids, far larger ones, which had . . . fallen in? Yes, that must be it. They fed off of their larger, failed brethren, competing for the scraps of life energy. But did they need that to grow?

It expedites their growth, she confirmed. *They do not need it, but they crave it.*

And to think I still had no idea what it was at all.

We flew over the creatures and the field of broken metal corpses, riddled with the gaping holes from which hungry mouths snapped periodically, coming up to take gigantic mouthfuls of the Cydenges younglings.

The Queen was the first to flap her wings, gaining altitude. I, of course, did as she did. Finally, we neared a light source at the far end. Oh, blessed light . . . As we approached, I made out a pattern in the golden light, almost like a honeycomb. Cydenges were crawling from the cells within after bursting a sort of thin membrane, more of a translucent flap that soon resealed.

Here, said the Queen, *is where the duplication chambers connect, issuing new offspring on a regular cycle.*

And what feeds those chambers, Queen? I asked.

Nothing. They are. They exist to create new Cydenges from the pattern I've laid out. They are conditioned to operate on automatic as long as their Queen lives. That means that while I am growing a new body for myself, they operate, and when I die, they continue duplicating new younglings even as the transition occurs . . .

But . . . At risk of annoying the Queen, I pressed on, unable to stop myself. *That does not make sense. How can this magic operate on its own, without anything sustaining it? Does this duplication run on some power derived from Luna herself?*

The Queen paused, either in consideration or to give me time to give me time to consider for myself. *I am Luna,* she said at last.

- Chapter 9 -

Duplication

Our Mother is unstoppable. She breathes, birthing new generations.
Flickers of light spawn endless armies.
— Cydenges Eternal Vault

For some reason, that simple statement shocked me, which I believe was her intent. It was logical enough, as I recognized her voice—which spoke into my very mind—as the voice of Luna that seemed to beckon me on Gaea, crossing the empty sea between planet and moon. And yet . . . I had only been told to call her Queen. It was far easier to think of her as the "Cydenges ringleader" than a godlike, moon-abiding force of nature. And yet Mani, too, had a sentient force dwelling inside it, influencing it . . . powering it.

Was that the secret?

Luna swooped upward, supplementing the wind force of her speed with new wingbeats. *Come,* she said. *It is not far to enter the duplication chambers.*

We rose for a few minutes, flapping our great wings in the blackness. I gazed at the honeycomb cells that still poured forth spiders. There was no indication of regrowth inside the empty ones, so I concluded that they must be made and released in waves.

Just as we reached the top of the thickly dark lower region, come again into the brighter zone lit by geological illumination, I saw at the top of the honeycomb an entry point, through which she now took me. She landed on top of it, and I caught my footing behind her. She bounded off, and I followed, snaking down a mysterious tunnel that soon gave way to translucent, nearly transparent walls on both sides. Above us shown an indistinct golden light.

You may have deduced the nature of this light by now, she said to me, turning her head half-round.

I paused in thought. *Your power?* My mind associated the color with Luna the moon more than the sentient force, despite the vivid color of her Cydenges frame, which poured from her eyes and highlighted her beautiful armor between the darkly colored scales.

You are correct. I think a human would assume that it is the red, and not the gold, that symbolizes my creative power. That I am a red force of evil and destruction, and the gold merely the pleasant hue the creator made the moon. Which is . . . also close to the truth, yet could not be more wrong. You have seen me, and you have spoken to me. I am rational, and I am intelligent. I was also long ago vested with a power unique to me, the power to make manifold a single thing. The power of Duplication—this is the force of gold.

As she spoke, the Queen moved throughout the well-lit tunnel, the additional light reflecting off her scales and making a brilliant kaleidoscope of gold. *I have the power to clone myself, but also to tweak the ensuing result. Any thing of metal, I can clone it to the point of infinity without using up a drop of energy. I am my own well of power, not a thing that must feed off of other power. My children are not so, and neither is my metallic body. The power of gold animates them for a set amount of time, degrading only the slightest amount, and they can steal it one for another . . . as can I. I have ultimate control over each of my cloned minions, but they each have an element of agency and intelligence, and even unique properties of size, strength and reason.*

I had far too many questions to begin with a single one, so I let her continue.

This is one of many Duplication Chambers I have set up over the centuries. I breed new lines of Cydenges periodically, based on stimuli they send back to me from Gaea. New abilities allow for new and diverse lines of attack, keeping the Hellebes on their toes. Most of these I have yet to launch upon the world. As your people have long suspected, I do not yet wish to invade . . .

Yet. The thought gave me a mental shiver, and also reawakened my mother's voice, which had long been silent. *Lynchazel . . . this is an evil place. You cannot trust Luna. Make no parley with her.*

Parley? Who said I would be doing that?

Why else would she bring you in and treat you well, showing you around her palace? She clearly wants something, and it isn't just a new puppy.

Mother . . .

She was right of course. There was certainly danger. But I knew that I had to be here, that the fate of the Hellebes and Gaea at large was at stake. But I could feel the Queen's inner eye on me, brushing against my mind, so I dismissed my mother's consciousness without another word.

You realize I can sense the other minds within yours, she said suddenly, slowing to eye me with one yellow eye. *There are three, Vaults within Vaults. I assume you are aware of each?*

I . . . I let out what might be called the Cydenges equivalent of a cough, a harsh grinding sound that cut off as quickly as it began. *Your awareness is great, O Queen.*

It is.

You heard what she said about the air here, Queen? It was a gamble, one that could earn me a greater injury than before. I'd spoken on impulse.

Only some. Vaults are located in the deepest caves of the mind, and a Vault within a Vault is a distant thing indeed. Only a powerful mind such as mine could draw it out.

So she did have cognitive limits. That was a relief to learn. Perhaps I could teach myself to access my mother's Vault without alerting the Queen at all. Then again, might she grow more powerful after a while out of the Cocoon? Who was to say whether she hatched from it with her full capabilities?

The Queen led me in silence, allowing me to take in the honeycomb cells and their contents. The smeared-glass effect of whatever sealed them in became clearer, until it seemed that I looked through clear glass at a murky, brown-gold pool containing . . . Cydenges. All of the spider variety, all the same size. As we moved between sections, I realized that each group of cells, be it a hundred or thousand or more, contained one size of Cydenges, reflecting a specific stage of development. It occurred to me that this wasn't so different from how the Hellebes were propagated in Gaea's biomanufactories.

The paths split, branching in countless directions. We rose with each tunnel, turning enough times that I suspected we had doubled back—laterally—at least once, finally coming to a doorway that opened into a tall shaft. This we climbed near-straight upwards, silent but for the clatter of claws on stone and the shifting grind of scales on scales as our leg muscles bunched and extended.

Where are we headed now, O Queen?

To my nest. To talk.

Some time later, we lay in a comfortable cavern roughly the size of a house, or perhaps longer. Three tunnels led outward; we had come from the leftmost, which connected to the Epsilon Pits via a series of turnoffs. I describe the cave as comfortable because the veins of gold—no red here, but pure gold—lit the room just enough, and the floor curved gently upward at the edges with smooth ups and downs that made for a decent bed such as an animal would see it.

The Queen, declaring herself to be in need of rest, wasted no time curling up near the back, tucking her tail in almost like a dog. Of course, it was long enough to nearly wrap around her body once more. She did so, but then let it uncoil a bit and raised it, looking at me with an invitation.

Hesitantly, I approached. Some instinct informed me that I too could use rest. Perhaps it was simply my weary mind, or an aftereffect of the transformation. Or . . . well, it didn't feel as though I'd been on this moon for long, but I didn't have a good way of telling how much time had passed. I did as she had, circling the defile next to her before laying myself down front to back, tail hanging into the cavern. The Queen let her long tail fall on me, but kept it cocked at the base, as though indicating for me to snuggle closer. I did so with a mental eyeroll, inching closer until my nose was just behind her hips, a foot or two from her own scaled snout. I looked uncomfortably into her golden eyes as she lowered her tail, letting the tension out of it. Glancing back at my own silvery tail, I pulled it in on a whim, tucking it around the Queen's face.

Do you mind that? I can move it, I just—

No.

You're sure?

Yes. She let her eyes close, and I realized she truly did just want to sleep. But why the companionship? She really was treating me like her puppy.

[Lyn: asks perhaps one more question.]

The queen cracked one eye, looking both tired and disgruntled. *We will talk when I wake. Keep this up, and I will bite you. Viciously.*

- Chapter 10 -

Dream of Predators

Cybele: Earth, beginnings. Luna: Golden dawn. Princess. Second. But no more, for Luna will be Queen not over barren moon but all the domain of life. Barren mother no more, but true Queen.
— Cydenges Eternal Vault

This entire chapter may take place in a dream.

[**Purpose**: To add to Lhinde's villainishness, also foreshadowing the ending, though it has no immediate bearing on Lyn's journey as far as she or the reader know. But . . . then why is it shown here? I guess she is experiencing it?]

Lyn is dreaming of Lhinde, or even like a passive observer in a conversation, slowly realizing what's going on. The idea being that, with her proximity to the Queen, Lhinde's mind is getting past the confines of her Vault and brushing against Luna's. That is of course what she (one of the two, at least) wanted all along.

- Chapter 11 -

A Chat

Language is of the Queen. Queen gifts it to us from the human world—grants speech, intelligence. Queen: Source of all, source of our life and power and being.
— Cydenges Eternal Vault

I awoke to a strange sensation: A smell, a brushing physical touch, a light source, a sound. Yet I cracked my eyes to see nothing but the Queen's chamber, the only sound the inner rush of energy our Cydenges bodies made, like a furnace.

Belatedly, I recognized it. The Queen had been speaking to me. During my sleep, a communication had occurred. But why couldn't I . . . access it? Perhaps my mind was simply slow from sleep, or I was turning into an animal, losing abilities like memory. I rested my head, relaxing once more, aware of the Queen's tail still looped over my long skull and the length of my body. It was not warm, yet still comfortable somehow. I didn't even know what rest did for our Cydenges frames. Perhaps we only needed the sleep because our bodies were new. This idea of being a young creature and yet fully grown bothered me on a level that I could not explain.

Luna let out a groan, incredibly deep, and her scales shifted audibly, skin twitching in a couple places. Her tail curled around me, tightening for a moment. Her eyes opened, and she gazed at me lucidly, almost expectantly. *Good morning,* she said softly.

You don't . . . have mornings on Luna, no?

She let out a deep, rumbling chuckle. "No." I wasn't sure why she spoke it in the Cydenges vocal language now, but the sound for *no* was a powerful one, a resonant clash that ended like muted cymbals. I recalled hearing it already. She opened her mouth again, continuing, "We have no such trackers here, save for the turning of a full rotation, one revolution around your birth planet."

I hadn't given it much thought till now, but I did know that Luna was tidally locked with her mother planet just as Mani was. If Mani was the "younger" moon, as it was said, then perhaps it was modeled after Luna's relationship to Gaea. And yet, not for the first time I wondered how that would have affected the world . . . Two tides, suddenly, an additional magnetic field, a new heavenly body to create periodic eclipses. It was a lot to swallow, and no one had definite answers.

No one except this gold-haloed creature before me.

"You said we would talk today?" I said slowly, sounding out the strange consonants on instinct. "Or . . . what passes for today?"

"There is no today. Only later. And this is later, so yes." The Queen rapped her tail once against my silver hide, like a dog who is pleased to see someone but too comfortable to rise. Then she twitched it, a gesture that seemed totally at odds with the first.

She seemed to be waiting for me to start, so I made a gesture like clearing my throat—more a coarse, metallic trumpeting sound—and asked the first question that came to mind: "Why are you doing all this for me? Treating me like a . . ." I stopped before saying *queen,* which would have been an apt figure of speech in Hellebes or Legaleian. ". . . like a daughter?"

Her right cheek twitched, baring steel fangs, yet it almost seemed an attempt at a smile. Perhaps a mischievous grin. "Because you are already."

The words did not surprise me, yet they stirred an unpleasant swarm of lunar insects in my proverbial gut. "Please explain."

"Very well. I have not a full knowledge of these histories, so you may know more accurately than I on some points . . . But the Hellebes created your first iteration near a millennium ago by destroying one of my own creations for the sake of science. In fact, it took multiple. They discovered a way to dissect the Cydenges and extract their cores, and subsequently combined them with human females in an attempt to derive a race like my own."

"I know all this, Queen."

"That is well. Perhaps you can now see why it failed: There is no biological aspect of Cydenges reproduction. They are duplicated by me alone, based on a model honed over time—multiple models, now. But the unthinkable happened: your grandmother became the first meta-human. As soon as she awoke from her sleep, I was made aware of the happening. A piece of me woke with her, though she did not know it then. It was then that I began to understand humanity, and to plan."

She paused, neck spines raising. She must have sensed the animosity in my physical reaction to her words, so strong was my loathing of Lhinde and the way she had gone. Luna's explanation only redirected that, funneling me toward what seemed an inevitable new direction: Luna was the dark influence in Lhinde's life, the one who had turned her bitter and pointed her against humanity, all of Gaea . . .

"Lynchazel!"

I jerked my head up, meeting her gaze and seeing a mouthful of needle-sharp teeth. She had not actually spoken my name, but a Cydenges word that approximated to it somehow. But it was as unmistakable as the rebuke in her tone. "When your emotion is strong, your thoughts are bare to me. Your anger is foolish, child, for it is misdirected. Lhinde's faults were her own; you assume much."

I lowered my head submissively. She had a point, and especially with her former statement. I let my emotions overtake me. Perhaps I simply wanted to believe in my own family, no matter how much my mother had convinced me of Lhinde's evil. No, forget that, Lhinde had shown time and again that the only thing left of her was an enduring hatred for the Gaea League, powerful enough to resist the corruption of time and pierce through to my outermost Vault, my own mind. "Yes, Queen."

"You may call me _____," she replied. "Or Queen," she added, supplying with it a short list of honorifics with which to address her. The new name mystified me, as I had never thought she had a different identity than Luna. "If I may, O Queen . . . is Luna, then, merely the ancient name of the golden moon?"

"Yes. Though it was not always golden. I made it my home one thousand years ago, when the people of Gaea drove me away. It wasn't long before they exiled Mani as well, to the Unnamed Moon.

Unnamed . . . Mother, have you heard of this? I needn't have bothered asking, for I'd have known already if she had any knowledge of that. As far as she knew, it was always called Mani and the other moon always Luna. "If I may My Queen, who is Mani? Who are you?"

Again, that voracious predator smile. "Direct. I like it. You came wishing to know things, and I will oblige, for I expected this. I am Luna, Titan of Duplication, also known as the Lady of Proliferation, long worshipped as a mother goddess by the people of Luna Halcyon, or Kanlyuuna, as it was known.'

I felt a strange chill tingle through me, stiffening the spines on my own back briefly. Kanlyuuna . . . again, that name had come through for me, not in writing but in pronunciation, despite the lack of conversion between our languages. Somehow, I knew this name was correct. She was aware of many things from the human world both before and after her departure, in a way that I had yet to make sense of. It reminded me of the things Kaen had said of his temporary bond with the sentient force of Mani.

As if she'd read my thoughts, Luna continued, though almost no time had passed: "Mani, therefore, was my brother, a god if you will. Or Titan, to be technical. The Titan of Growth. Lord of the East, worshipped in what is today called Mei Shan. Once it was called Mani Halcyon, and before that, I'Maniiya. Our mother was called Cybele, Titaness of the Earth. When you hear the phrase Mother Gaea . . . she is the one that phrase is based on. She is the original appointed guardian of the planet, entrusted with the ways of nature, the cycle of life, geologic formations, the weather, et cetera. I trust you are curious as to what started the conflict between Titans, of course?"

I nodded my head.

"Then I shall explain. Mankind came after us, appointed as the caretakers of the earth and Cybele. They did not serve her, but rather worked hand in hand with her. We were called the Ideals, twin children of Nature, set before the sons of man and charged with guiding them and showing them the path forward. We were . . . always at odds, however.

"In the days when the world was young, and we were young, Cybele used to tell us that she would eventually go away. That men would push her away, and those who chased after would never find her. She told us that we would become the guiding lights, the pillars of humanity, and that we would shape more than be shaped. And that one day there would be a reckoning, when we would at last be allowed to reciprocate the crimes of man, the wages of their failings toward us

"What came about instead were times of blessing and peace, during which the peoples of our respective lands came to our dwellings not to gain wisdom from my brother and me, but to lay praise at our feet. Without even asking, we drew hordes of slavering people ready to give us their wheat and animals and sons and daughters . . ."

"And you accepted it?"

She looked sidelong at me. "Of course. We are gods. We were not prepared for it, but neither were we going to deny the humans their religious fervor. They built us temples and altars all over the world. I was their mother goddess, the successor to Cybele, their Lady of Proliferation, provider of children and crops and abundance."

I did not ask whether she was able to give them such things. She had already made known to me her powers, which did not include such things as fertility and soil health.

She continued. "Mani, on the other hand, drew a different cult—one of knowledge and power and ambition, the learned, the astrologers. They became ever more reclusive and secretive, walling off the masses from their temple."

"And . . . the Wellspring, ___? What of that?"

"Ah. An apt question. The Ancient Fount of Life . . . You see, there were two, not one. The other lay in my territory, the Fount of Wisdom. I can sense your surprise, and it is half warranted. It is not as contradictory as you might think. Proliferation of mankind is one kind of progress, that is, it will eventually lead to an ideal, or final, or maximum population, no? But as mankind spread, they need knowledge. But again, it is not that simple. My spring was the hidden one, meant not to be found until the time was ready.

"But the cult of Mani, which became known as the Anier, abandoned the magic that allows one to shape nature for the mysterious, the hidden power that none knew. They broke in and took the secrets of knowledge, and set about devising advancements for humanity—true growth, in a sense. I had already grown bored of my religious fanatics and the debauchery they did in my name, and when I saw that the Fount of Wisdom already emptied, I sought to free myself from my temple. To take my power and withdraw, using it for my own purposes. Enough with the children of man.

"But I left behind my new children, clones of my metal avatar, to wreak destruction upon the priests of Luna. The slaughter was great, and the group called the Anier were some of the few who survived. To this day, none speak of the cult of Luna, for the slaughter that occurred in Luna Halcyon was greater than the atrocities they did in my name. But the Anier used this. . . . I trust you see where this story is going now?"

"I . . . I do, O Queen. I do." A trembling had overtaken me, despite the lack of human body's frailties. This was a lot to process, far more than I'd expected. Her frankness alone was surprising, although I couldn't say I trusted every point of her story. Slight inconsistencies hinted at bias; how heavy, I couldn't say.

"To bring it full circle, just in case you cannot put all the pieces together . . . The Anier blamed the people of the Fount—those who followed Mani but practiced the ways of natural artistry that the Found allows—for the Cydenges, the 'shining ones' who predated mankind and siphoned energy from the very earth. I suppose you wish I would show sorrow for it all, but I predicted a similar outcome. But I take no responsibility—the people had it coming.

"Mani was the one who gave the Legaleians the tip on how to defeat the Cydenges with magic, and they helped the Anier to eradicate the predators. He then played the caring, wise older brother, denying fault but saying that those suffering could come to live in his lands, that the Wellspring gave enough abundance for all. But the followers of Mani turned on him as one, threatening to remove his temple burn the countryside if he did not flee. For there is a prophecy of Cybele about Silver and Gold, two gods for two moons. They believed this would solve the problem."

"The priests of Mani were sent with him, and he achieved the impossible with their aid: growing an entire moon to the size of Luna. No longer was there a greater and lesser moon, or so it would appear. I know no more of the affairs of Mani: In fact, you would be far more knowledgeable than I."

"I . . ." My metallic voice skittered to a halt, but I revved it onward. "I actually know little, My Queen. But I can tell you what I do."

She waited, unblinking eyes staring holes in me, and I began to relate to her my story of Nytaea and Kystrea, what I knew of their history and how I was raised that strange world of silver and four-week day cycles. Of my fire powers, and of my father, Kallyn, who went to Gaea searching for a way to bridge the worlds. She was surprised to learn that humans had populated an entire world on Mani, and that the Wellspring had made it more than livable. Finally, I told her of Domon and Kaen's sword, the two forces that apparently warred with one another right now. Dark and Silver.

She was silent for a while after I said my last. There was more I could have told her, but I was frank enough with describing the gist of how the silver world worked. At last, she said mentally, *All this talk makes me tired all over again. You may be surprised to know that I do not get much practice at conversation.* She rose with the hind-leg stretch of a four-legged animal, pulling out into a slow pacing circle. *Yes, I have lain abed too long. You as well. Cydenges are active creatures, and lying still does us no favors.*

What else is there to do, Queen?

Much. Luna is nigh a thousand years into our colonization, but I have worked tirelessly to craft it into a . . . tool.

A weapon. You've been preparing here . . .

She glared in my direction, and I realized I'd forgotten an honorific. *Yes, daughter of humans. A weapon. While Mani has made himself a false world out of a dead one, I have been crafting my golden moon into a machine of war. A weapon fit to wipe the warped remnants of mankind from the face of Gaea, that we may start afresh.*

Wipe . . . from the face of Gaea . . . Something in her words triggered a memory, and I quickly located Lhinde's words which she had once spoken to me: *'We can purge this taint and restore balance to Gaea . . . with blood. Blood for blood.'*

'How much?' I had asked that terrible voice. *'When will it end? When will you be satisfied?'*

'When this earth is swept clean of all artificial life. Then we can bring back the Cydenges, the original keepers of Geokinesis. Humanity is long gone. Let us sweep all remnant of that sorry race from Gaea.'

Was it a coincidence? The chill that rippled through the spines of my back hinted at more. All these thoughts ran through my mind in a blink, but I opened my mouth to issue more grinding words lest she grow suspicious: "Then there is more that you would show me now? Without knowing my motives for coming here? Without forming any kind of agreement?"

This time, her laugh was unmistakable. Entirely unhuman, but unmistakable. "You think too highly of yourself, "Mother Gaea", or else you have forgotten your situation entirely. You have come to my home, my world, and have been granted the form of one of us. You are a newborn predator in a world of predators—what could you possibly do to harm us?"

The question was neither naïve nor rhetorical. Even as she said the words, I felt embarrassment wash over me. How could I say something so stupid? If anything, I'd spoken out of a guilty defensiveness for my own secrecy. I didn't feel that she had any reason to trust me yet, nor I her, but that had no bearing on her point: I was no threat to her here. That had been established as I lay belly-up beneath her deathly claws, learning the laws of the jungle from the Queen herself.

"You are right, My Queen."

- Chapter 12 -

Daughter of Earth and Moon

Eight Pits for eight variants. Copies of aspects, experimental children. One day: Cydenges perfected, we shall be one.
— Cydenges Eternal Vault

Queen ＿＿ led me out through the tunnels, and we eventually came to one of the other Pits, containing avian Cydenges with long wings and beaklike heads. This Pit had only a few winding trails at the top for other Cydenges, but it was hung with vicious-looking stalactites and had a maw-like passage through which the metallic birds evidently had to eventually pass. They darted about like bats, and fought viciously with one another. The Queen explained that this variety changed as they matured, becoming less aggressive and more group-oriented. The test here was to see which ones, even under the powerful influence of instincts, would be strong enough to escape into the upper aeries.

＿＿＿ called this the Delta Pits. We had now seen two of eight. She claimed to have only sent four different varieties to Gaea. We visited the proving grounds of each in turn, traveling higher for some and lower for others (although each reached to varying depths, so which one was "lowest" was not always apparent). Two of these varieties were what I'd thought to be the "standard" shape, the beast-like spiked dragon variety, but one was leggier and winged, while the other was stockier and more powerful.

Another was a burrowing variety, whose pit was the smallest by natural shape but the most isolated, apparently constructed in an area hemmed in by denser bedrock. Adult Cydenges patrolled the tunnels at the perimeter, ready to alert others or kill and devour and escapees. The burrowers themselves looked like long worms, and were the only ones capable of metabolizing something other than pure energy. Made up of interlinking bands and plates of a duller make, they funneled dirt and debris in at the front, sawing through stone with their circular, bladed heads, and expelled the debris behind them through vents in their carapace.

Two pits, as it turned out, were filled with water, which came as quite a shock to me. A sort of airlock tunnel system kept it contained within, and the glow from the gold and red wall veins cast the water with eerie lighting, rippling like a Manese illusion. One of these pits contained shark-like Cydenges, whose flexible bodies were like a combination between the catlike variety and the worms. The other aquatic monster was reminiscent of an octopus or a mythical sea kraken, containing six long tentacles, which they used for swimming or to grip walls. They had a horrible beak made for snapping things in two, and which they used to attack one another, sucking the red light from others' dead frames. I wasn't sure which seemed more deadly, the sharks or octopi. The sharks were certainly faster, though smaller.

The last Cydenges type was the most recent invention, and the most disturbing by far. I won't even attempt to describe it, because I wanted to forget the sight of it immediately. I do not know how powerful they could be, nor what Luna's use for them is to be.

After all this, she took me to the surface through the main central hub and up through one of the many access tunnels. We ascended like chipmunks from the stone portal, skittering onto the outer surface of Luna once more. I was struck again by the alien sight of this world, which felt so very alien and isolated without atmosphere or flora. I was still uncertain on whether one would classify the Cydenges as "life" per se, since they were artificially-created machines that ran on pure energy and who thought without brains.

Wait a minute . . . do I have a brain right now? Well, that was a disturbing thought, one that for some reason had not occurred to me yet. Of course I didn't, though. I had assumed a sort of temporary machine body. "Luna," I asked as I followed her, "Where is my body right now? Did you truly transform it, or is it back on Gaea?" *Or . . . floating in space somewhere . . .*

"That is a good question," she replied, "one to which you will have to find your own answer."

I wished I hadn't asked at all.

We kept on for miles before coming to a spire of rock guarded by dragon and spider Cydenges, which she referred to as an outpost. The drones bowed and made the low buzz of deference I had come to recognize. It wasn't something that I did, but then I wasn't really one of them.

We climbed the spire, which rose some few hundred feet, and she showed me a breathtaking vista of Luna's landscape—largely flat and entirely barren—and the visible curvature. The strange, bronzy atmosphere appeared as a panoramic halo, stretching some few miles into the atmosphere and gently disappearing.

What do you think of it? she asked in my head.

It's beautiful, in a sort of way. Lifeless, alien, but . . . there's a beauty to it.

I'm glad you are connoisseur enough to recognize it for what it is. Although to me, you may be surprised to find, beauty is a thing that does not exist. I was created as an ideal, you'll recall, and to that I hold above all. The only other thing is the approval of man, which I discarded long ago, and a burning desire for vengeance, which has grown over time. I wonder if my brother, too, is consumed by this desire.

Against you, O Queen, or against Gaea?

She stared strangely at me. *That is the question, no?*

It was a moment before she decided to tell me our purpose up here. *This signal outpost, Lynchazel, ties together an optical network, each of which link to Luna's opposite surface.*

Opposite surface . . . so facing Gaea. It hadn't even occurred to me that I had been transported not directly across space to a corresponding position on the gold moon, but rather to Luna's Dark Side, the side that never saw its mother planet due to tidal locking. *So you have spies positioned on the Light Side, watching Gaea?*

Sort of. We avoid the Light side for security reasons. It is one of the great laws of Luna. Any Cydenges who ventures onto the Gaean Hemisphere is to be killed on sight. Although of course I have . . . let us say safety measures . . . in place.

But what is the reason for that, My Queen? Beyond simply disguising the true number of your armies?

Well, for one, there is the matter of the four types of Cydenges I have never sent upon Gaea. Remember that the Hellebes possess powerful telescopes, not to mention satellites. Not only now, but a thousand years ago when I was banished. Even then they could inspect the surface of the greater and lesser moons quite closely using glass telescopes.

But . . . what about the drones they use nowadays? They say they've tried many times to get close to Luna or land on it, and nothing comes back. So clearly they have the technology to photograph every inch of Luna's surface, given that there is no Energy Field as Mani has.

The flying machines that the Hellebes use? They are not so often an issue as you may think. Certain of my Cydenges strains have far-reaching senses that can pinpoint them from afar. An alert is sent out, and all take to the tunnels—which connect nearly every inch of this moon. You are wrong about the Energy Field, however, for Luna does possess that, and mine is quite powerful—It simply has no "magic" behind it, no powers of illusion or light manipulation. Many of these drones we can destroy, but we leave them alone unless they come very close. As you said, nothing lands that every leaves Luna. And yes, we tear the machines apart, though I'm afraid my minions are not skilled in mechanical thinking, so that does not go very far. My lunar senses are strong, however, reaching even as far as Gaea whenever my children are present.

I stared around, still taking in the view. It was quite breathtaking, even beautiful, hills and valleys and canyons and tunnels laid bare. No geologic features were as large or grand as anything on Gaea, and overall you would call it flat, but with the bronze horizon and the infinite blackness filled with white stars—one horizon lit by the faintest hint of Sol's morning light—was impressive nonetheless.

Have you ever been back to Gaea yet, Queen? I asked on a whim.

Again, that mechanical laugh. *No, child. No. But I will, when the time is ready.*

Gaea

The days soon approach. Come, for I have more to show you.

- 63 -

The days soon approach. Come, for I have more to show you.

- Chapter 13 -

A New Predator

What are you, dissonant sibling? To defy our Mother is the dream, the pleasure craved. You defy her to incite us toward greater obedience, toward the ultimate goal.
— Cydenges Eternal Vault

As Luna's Queen took me once more below the surface, my mind flashed back to the dream I'd had the previous night . . . or . . . whenever that was. My last sleep. Nowadays, to recall the wanderings of my mind during sleep was like recalling a prior day or week: clear and simple, a mental trip to the books. Access to my Vault was not automatic, per se. It took concentration and was not always instantaneous, but there was no doubt about whether I could recall something—usually, anyway.

Even still, my mind had been distracted since awakening to Luna's face but a few feet from my own.

Thus far, I've described what took place here on Luna without too much of the baggage I brought with me, but the truth is that the distraction and wonder here on Luna was growing thin enough that I was no longer overcome with the here and now and was once again tickled by thoughts of home, of memories and emotions alien to Luna. Perhaps it was this body that somehow suppressed certain thoughts, and I was finally overcoming it.

In my dream, I had overheard a conversation between Luna and an unseen speaker. Yet I knew who it was: Lhinde. *'Why do you not come over to me as well?'* Luna had said.

'Who says I am on any side?'

To which Luna had laughed harshly and said, *'You think that I do not know you, Lhinde, that I do not recognize you? I was the one who called to you those long centuries ago, while you yet stood on Gaea's face awaiting the justice of the humans who spawned you.'*

It was a bit cryptic, but indicated heavily that Luna had some form of connection with my grandmother back when she was alive . . . but more troublingly, possibly still. I stopped my line of reasoning here, checking mentally to see if Luna was listening in, but I was all right. She was a little suspicious of my silence, and would soon question it if past experience served right.

Sure enough, as we passed through the hub shaft that seemed never to end, Luna said, *Your thoughts seem distracted, little one. Share them with me.*

Apologies, Queen, I replied. *I was thinking on how tired my mind grows here, perhaps because my body does not. It is strange, to think with a mind I cannot place in a body that is not my own.*

Indeed. The mind is a strange thing, for it is the crossroads of intelligence and will, the meeting of brain and soul. The reason you feel that you are you is not that your brain stayed intact through the process, but that your will inhabits this body. Each body, except in a select few cases, can only have one will, and that will governs thought and moral decisions and intent.

Then what of your children? Do they possess wills and souls?

That is a good question, young one. One I will leave up to you to answer.

The Hive dwellers and lookout drones had largely left Luna along during this entire time with me—she must have given them some order to leave us be while we bonded or she taught me—but she was now intercepted by a few on the way in. I could easily interpret all their communications now, which sounded almost like a first language:

O Queen, live forever. The western Wingnest requires your attention soon.

How urgently?

The dog model Cydenges bowed his head. *Very, O Queen.*

Then I will go. That dismissed the scout, who turned and scampered off in a vaguely westward direction—according to my sense of direction. *And what do you require?* She asked of the two remaining Cydenges.

We were sent to inquire as to the Gaeaborn's purpose here, My Queen.

Forgive our rudeness. The Epsilon Guard saw you with her yesterday and—I'm
sorry, we meant no offense. We're just the—

The Queen's roar was sudden and fearsome. She lunged forward without
warning, taking one's neck in her jaw whilst gripping the other with one
forepaw and her tail. She forced the first to a kneeling position by its neck, and
the second she pulled off-balance such that his feet tripped.

Lynchazel, she said mentally, *this is what I do with those who
inconvenience me by way of stupidity.* I was aware that this was not a threat to
me so much as a display of her power and capricious cruelty. Her jaws crunched
together and she shook her neck, shearing her victim's spine in a burst of ruby
light. She inhaled it like a vacuum cleaner, letting the corpse drop like a
discarded set of armor, but she continued to hold down the other one. I expected
her to consume a follow-up meal or else let him go with a harsh warning, but
instead she did something else.

Come here, Child of Gaea.

I did so, and immediately saw what she wanted me to do. I watched her
second victim thrash under her grip, red eye wide with fear, teeth snarling, and
would have gulped had that been an action possible for a throatless creature. She
put one set of claws on its neck, cinching them tight under the jaw, but I saw
the muscles bulging underneath as it tried to get free.

I did not hesitate. I took his neck in my jaws, forcing them around the thick,
scaled trunk, and began to bite. As I did so, the Queen let go entirely. *You won't
get so easy a meal . . .*

My own neck was jerked to the side as the Cydenges thrashed his way out,
neck rearing and teeth snapping at me. Sparks flew as my teeth dragged on his
neck, but it did little damage. I reared back, swiping with my claws even as the
defensive Cydenges went straight for my chest. He bit in hard, but I forced him
back before his teeth broke much armor. A concerning amount of light did seep
from my breastbone, however.

I crouched, watching my opponent's next move. We were near the mouth
of one of the tunnels, and I didn't want to carry him any farther out for fear of

us both tumbling into the dark. Wings or no, I didn't like that idea.

The silver-scaled beast leapt in again, all thought of its Queen gone now that it was in fight mode. It was like two dogs that had begun a fight over a bit of meat. Once the fight commenced, there was no breaking it up easily, and the Queen wasn't about to interfere. I dodged to the side and tried to bite the creature's leg as it reached for me, but my teeth caught nothing. His shoulder caught me, nearly sending me tumbling. This one seemed a little bigger than me, and certainly more practiced with his canine body.

Come on, Lyn. After everything you've been through, you can't lose a dogfight. The voice was White's. She was right, too; there was no reason I couldn't beat this thing, even being the interloper. I extended my claws to full and pulled, rolling with the huge thing against the curved tunnel wall. I kicked with my back legs, forcing back his own feet, and defended with my dagger-like teeth while searching for an opening.

There. I lunged in, curling my spine further, and grasped the skin and bone beneath my opponent's right foreleg. I bit in hard, teeth making a final click together after punching all the way through, and ripped, opening up a hole in its side. After that, it was a downhill fight, ending in with my jaw around his throat. I clawed, tearing it open, and then sucked in almost on instinct. Cydenges don't breathe, yet this was an inborn action that felt immensely right, draining all of his red light into myself. As the lifelight left him, his body seemed to deflate and collapse into glorified sheet metal. A husk, almost like that which an insect would leave behind.

I stood up, head jerking upward to meet my Queen's gaze. Her face was almost impassive, but faintly pleased in a discomforting way. And yet the Cydenges instincts in me *craved* the Queen's pleasure, as though making her proud were the only reason I was created.

And yet *I* was never created, was I? I was born of my own mother, back on Gaea. Right? Surely my entire life up till now had not been a delusion, a mere dream.

Not too bad. Had you the killer instinct already, you'd have finished him before he could get up and attack you, but perhaps this was good for your confidence, as it made you feel a bit more justified in taking the life of another creature for yourself. You have already come to see these Cydenges as fellow living creatures, yes?

I lowered my head, eyes parting from her piercing golden stare. She was right, of course. I'd spent long enough in this metal flesh that another creature walking the same world who looked like me, and even seemed to possess a mind of its own with some manner of will . . . surely if I was alive, then this poor thing was as well before I . . . *It wasn't my fault,* I reminded myself. The Queen made me do it, and would not have taken no for an answer. She'd never *asked* me—it was a command.

The new light swirled within in me, and I felt its boost to my energy. "This energy—how long will it last?" I asked the Queen, mouth working out the mournful sounds as though to ease my guilt.

"How long does the light sustain you?" she echoed. "Each Cydenges strain uses it at a different rate. You may not have realized it, but you were getting somewhat low. It comes from the gold here in Luna's belly, which I duplicate and my children metabolize into Bloodlight. I will give some to you soon, but for now, this will keep you going. Bloodlight is incredibly efficient, staying with its host even when it appears to leak and converting near equally when taken. That is why a Cydenges must be mortally wounded before it will truly escape—or can be sucked out by a more powerful Cydenges.

"But come, we must be on to the Wingnest, my daughter."

I followed down a nearby path, as vertical and winding as all, before she sprang off and opened her wings. Though caught off-guard, I was only a second behind. Neither of us opened our wings yet, for apparently we had long to fall before our destination would be near. When she finally did, it was at perhaps the quarter way mark down, heading roughly between the Beta and Gamma Pits. We entered a tunnel somewhat larger than the others.

A minute later, we arrived in the Western Wingnest, which was indeed a nest—presumably for the avian Cydenges—but I couldn't see any here at present. Only empty stone nests set two-deep against the walls of a clover-shaped hub, with pillars and arching overhangs housing more nests.

Empty, but not silent.

From the far end of the Wingnest there came a clash of metal-on-metal-on-stone, accompanied by Cydenges clicking and hissing and a further screech unlike any I'd yet heard on Luna. The Queen's tail twitched, either in irritation or confusion, but she said nothing as she stalked purposefully forward, leading the way between the frontmost two clover leaves of the chamber. There, a hall split off, and I began to see how the nest was arranged: an interlinked group of the leaf-shaped nesting rooms. Evidently, the commotion was in one of the further ones.

Sure enough, after one more turn, we found the source of the stir. More specifically, the Queen had just rounded the tunnel corner when a Cydenges body nearly slammed into her backward. With catlike reflexes, she immediately jumped in reverse and slammed a paw against the body, tumbling it onto its side. It was not dead, but as far along in the dying state as I'd seen one. The lights glowing from her scales turned suddenly red, and she bolted into the room, leaving the Cydenges to die in its throes. I followed more carefully, entering to find her bowling in, thundering out a ululating, descending howl. At the Queen's presence and her fearsome cry, the nesting clover's two dozen or so occupants jerked their heads toward her, scampering away from one another or hastily prostrating themselves with feet outstretched. For the Avians, this meant a straight-legged bow with tucked wings.

"What is going on in here?" she demanded with utmost authority.

Multiple forms lay strewn about, sparking and motionless, one of them drained entirely. Others seemed wounded, and most were in a frenzied state, her sudden order having cut out only some of their agitation. The chaos largely seemed to center around an enormous Cydenges Brute, who glared defiantly Queenward now, and—as I watched—turned to the nearest Cydenges, an Avian, and snapped its neck agape. Red light spewed, and it began hungrily sucking it down.

"Stop!" roared the Queen, stamping a foot.

The massive Cydenges ignored her, ripping its victim's neck further until the metal vertebrae snapped and the beaked head flew across the room. The nearest Cydenges cowered, seemingly unsure whether to keep prostrated or prioritize their own safety. As it set upon its next victim, however, that one fought back along with those nearest.

The Queen launched herself forward, plowing over the smaller Cydenges in her path to the rogue destroyer. She plowed into him with both forelegs outstretched, taking him in a bundle, ignoring the two Cydenges who got bundled into the roll. She growled and slashed and gnashed with her fangs, and the rogue did the same, whilst the others limped away wounded. Beneath the Queen's furious onslaught, the dark Cydenges eventually backed away, spines raised, circling warily.

"What are you?" spoke the Queen.

"A weapon of your own making," answered the aggressor.

- Chapter 14 -

The Core

We all go there eventually. Each body of gleaming metal one day corrodes, cracks, becomes defective, and is no more. Body now dust, the figment returned to nothing, but the Light returns to Mother's Core.
— Cydenges Eternal Vault

It did not end there. When the aberrant creature did not submit to its Queen, she lit into it once more. The beast was nearly as long as she, and thicker, armor chinks glowing with as much a black light as red. But whatever his rabid furor, the Queen's was greater. She abandoned the animalic dogfighting and began throwing him around like Hellebes in the Iron Dojang. She kicked with a hind leg, and his body flew directly into one of the onlooking Cydenges, plowing it over. She trampled the thing as she gave chase.

It wasn't long before she had the rebellious Cydenges pinned, gripped by the neck, forelegs bent outward and held down with her own. It bucked with its back feet, but she only bound them with her long, serpentine tail, cinching it with her spines. "Give up," she growled, "or I will take your life here and now."

The Brute glared at her for what seemed an eternity before slowly, slowly draining of its crazed malice. "Why? You should slay me for my impudence." It did not sound angry, nor even sorry, but more confused.

"Fairness was never a Lunar ideal," she replied with a malicious, fanged leer, pulling back from his neck just long enough to gauge whether he would snap at her. "If you agree to serve me till your last pulse, I will show you a path to true greatness."

Again, a long pause. Then, "Yes, My Queen."

"Very good." The Queen backed away, standing up and allowing the umbral Cydenges to spring to his feet, stance not as submissive as most but head kept bowed. "Now kill, and consume. Let your anger be free, that it may consume these weaklings, and then save it for the day we march on Gaea."

She backed away, toward me and the doorway, where we stood and watched as the slat-colored Cydenges pursued and tore apart the living. They fought back viciously, but they were no match for his nightmarish fury.

Shaken, I asked, *What is he?*

I asked the same of him. He is the first of the new blood, it would seem. This was prophesied, yet I failed to see when we had achieved it. The anger of Luna has consumed him in the Pits, and he must have devoured countless, triumphing over all, before clawing his way out, no doubt leaving a trail of sparking corpses in his wake. The strength to destroy is a beautiful thing, is it not?

She looked at me, and for the first time since the previous day, I was too scared at first to answer. Then I realized the correct one and gave a slight nod. *It is, O Queen. And . . . if I may, where do I fit into this? What is my lot as a Cydenges? Do you wish me to stay in this form forever? To kill and consume and become like this feral thing?*

I feared the Queen might take offense to my bold words, but in light of her treatment of the rabid creature, it seemed right, and indeed she took none. *Yes and no, daughter. I would like nothing more. But you are not Cydenges—merely enough that I could do for you as I could for no other Hellebes. The Elites are close, but of course, they are also my sworn enemies, so I would never do such a thing. For you, Lynchazel of Mani . . . there remains a choice. One we have yet to speak on.*

A choice. I'd known that since before I set foot on this world, but I still had no idea what I was in for. Not even after becoming a dragon and donning the scales of Luna.

For tonight, child, do not trouble your mortal mind. Rest, and we shall talk again.

And . . . where am I to . . .

You remember where my nesting chamber is?

Yes, Queen.

Good.

The next day, too, I awoke next to Her Lunar Majesty. I soon woke her with my tiptoeing claws, and she arose to show me what she would this day. She said that we would still wait for this "decision," which I was apparently not ready for. Instead, she took me out into the main hub and then down, down, down to the blackest abyss. I'd thought that the gold was not as present here, but the blackness was merely thick and present, like in the Pits, and if anything, it covered up the red more. The gold veins continued downward with us, not as many but thicker and more vivid.

The black void continued down far deeper than I'd realized, narrowing to become a shaft, then a narrow tunnel. Still she dove, and still I followed, trying to suppress the nervous fear in my mind. I pictured how my human ears would once have popped at the altitude change . . . ears that I still hoped to regain someday.

As we continued down the straight shaft, I admired the gold veins, which twisted about us, lighting the way through the thick blackness. *How deep are we?* I wondered. Miles, surely. Perhaps ten to twelve kilometers at this point.

At last, our destination came into view. The tunnel opened up into a cavernous space too large to make out aside from the sinister glow of a web of gold threads that seemed to entangle the cavern. We hit the far side, stopping our fall with surprising ease. The room was circular, and dotted with golden pinpricks around the door where we'd come in and the far side. As I thought about it, I realized that their pattern tied in with the field of larger golden streaks that seemed to converge on a point near the entrance. It was almost as if this entire cavern represented . . . Luna.

The Outer Sanctum, the Queen said in my head. *This room, though still in Luna's crust, holds immense significance. The gold threads you see throughout the moon are my gold, created by my presence. Slowly, over the centuries, they have crept through Luna's innards, as I lack the power of Growth that Mani has.*

She strode up the circular wall, golden glow mixing with that of the large golden veins beneath her amidst the shifting darkness, and I trailed behind, realizing that the wall, though smooth, allowed us to do just that with ease. Gravity seemed to shift along with us, always just right for moving easily over the surface.

What power is this that moves gravity? I asked. *Only Mani possesses authority over gravity, yes? The Silver? Or does Gold hold the same ability?*

No, Daughter. This is a bit different. Silver for your people only has that property because of Mani's influence over his own planetoid—complete influence. He controls it entirely. I do not control the entirety of Luna's sphere, but my web of gold is strong enough that, in a chamber like this, my metal can warp its physics.

Wait . . . is that how you also pull off the special leaps between moon and planet?

In a way. That is more unique. But these here—she reached the space where their they'd entered through the straight tunnel, indicating the golden stars around it with a clawed foot—*represent the nodes of power in the Outposts on Luna's Dark Side, which stretch across the moon and eventually lead to the corresponding position on Gaea's surface.*

And . . . I see. That is how your children can spatially hop to different parts of Gaea, depending on its position?

Close. But not precisely. They follow these routes, yes, but this is more a map than a guiding place. But come, for we will perform a jump to the most crucial place on Luna. From here, you can jump to any point on the surface, but you must focus on the very center . . . for that is our destination.

My spines stiffened at the directions. *The very center . . .* Something told me that now, today, I would finally learn something pivotal, perhaps why Luna said that she had made Luna into a weapon. *Yes, My Queen.*

She crouched, stiffened, and disappeared with the brief afterimage of a leaping golden form. With an inward breath, I did the same, centering my mind as she said on Luna's very core. Of course, it was more an idea than a firm place to visualize.

Suddenly, I was there. The Queen stood directly beside me, or rather on another inverse sphere, walls curving upward all around us. This one was far larger and intensely bright, filled with almost overwhelming sensory input. Gold consumed the entire plane, tracing mind-bending patterns that swirled around portholes of a sort, which shone with their own lights—no, displays. Yet . . . only the furthest ones, directly above us, had the shifting displays, while most of them showed a black starscape.

The Queen allowed me a moment to take in the breathtaking sight. About us were more of the portholes ringed by swirls of brilliant gold. These showed an aerial view of the towers about Luna's surface. Each was about half my length in width. The area between the displays, where not embroiled in knots of gold, seemed to be a highly dense, black stone.

Wait . . . dense. We're at . . . the center, aren't we?

Yes, she answered, and I didn't realize I'd projected the thought to her. *Luna's core. Or heart, you might say. Here, my power met that of the Greater Moon. What you see is the result of a millennium of patience and the ultimate duplication. But also a power center unlike anything Gaea is prepared for.*

She went on to show me how to leap about the power center—which was easily a thousand feet across—using the Cydenges teleportation method, arriving instantaneously on the opposite side of the ball. She then showed me the ports, and we looked in on many pieces of Gaea, somehow visually connected to these gold-powered nodes. Each was a scene drawn entirely from some hue on the yellow section of the spectrum, creating the eerie effect of seeing through colored glass. What each screen actually was, I could not say.

The Queen let me freely explore the nodes, getting a feel for the spacing and the general area that they covered—essentially half of Gaea—and the views they afforded. Each was moving, surprisingly, at a great speed. Scientifically, I knew this made sense, as the earth moved at a rate of over a thousand miles per hour, but it was off-putting to see land moving at such a rate and know that our perspective was not changing.

Gaea

[I think I'll skip for now.]

- Chapter 15 -

Choices

Will she be the one? This . . . human? Will she usher in the new age in lieu of our Queen? Can she commit such obedient blasphemy?
— Cydenges Eternal Vault

Over the course of the next few days, I had some thinking to do. The Queen had not made her offer lightly, and had effectively impressed on me that I would get one answer. Not two. Not zero. One.

The Queen seemed quite unconcerned in the meantime. She allowed me to continue using her royal nest to sleep—or whatever it was that we Cydenges did—and gave me free rein for the rest of the day. When I grew aware of my weariness, I retreated to her chamber. One day, she beat me there, and I curled up beside her, but usually she crept in some time later. I visited the Pits and intimidated the guards who patrolled top clefts or waited patiently for the next round of victims to cruelly push off. Well, I say intimidated, but perhaps they just felt awkward around the Queen's new favorite. Jealous. Or they were messing with me.

The different Cydenges types seemed to have varying temperaments, although each was also somewhere on a spectrum. The Brutes were surly and prideful, while their more graceful winged kin were curious, a bit playful. Avians tended to be prickly, while the spiders rarely engaged in any conversation. As I grew more accustomed to the Cydenges and was broadly accepted, I made more of an effort to speak to them, often receiving more than a single-thought response. They were fully capable of rational speech both in mentally and through their growling language, although they seemed to naturally gravitate toward vocalized communication—just in small doses. Necessary things, not long-winded conversations. Most tended to get lost eventually, lacking the attention span or intelligence to keep track of an entire conversation.

Don't ask me about the aquatic guys. They're . . . I don't know. Not as reasonable. Although swimming in the depths of the marine Pits was uniquely exhilarating. My Leonid Cydenges frame was surprisingly capable at swimming, even underwater—although I wasn't that fast—and was immune to pressure. Granted, water pressure wasn't on Luna what it was back on Gaea, but this pit was extremely deep. Liquid movement relied mostly on the wings for our type.

As for the raging beast we'd met in the Western Wingnest . . . he was now a loyal servant of the Queen, though in a different way from the others. It reminded me of the mindbreaking the Red Horizon rebels had performed on their prospective soldiers—and which Sylleo had consequently performed on his upper population—which freed the Hellebes mind from the loyalty programming, allowing rejection or true obedience. While the ordinary Cydenges were wild creatures with strange, animalic instincts, there was a deep-rooted reverence for their Mother coded and trained into them. This one lacked that, but he had been persuaded by force and by power bribery to join her new team of Generals.

These Generals would lead the war on Gaea, taking groups of Cydenges warriors to various power centers on the planet in far greater numbers than ever imagined. Other generals were birthed following the Brute, whom she named Kur'Shos, by way of a personal visit from the Queen to the Pits. She started in the aquatic ones, giving up on the kraken Cydenges before moving on to the sharks, wherein she found one that impressed her with his strength of body and will. She fed his inner flame with her own, igniting the buried frenzy to terrifying degrees, and soon the water was a frothing sea of turmoil and battle. I could feel him as he slew and drained other sharks, feel his presence and power grow. She named him Tul'Skaya.

The next was an Avian, tall and almost black in color, whose almost heron-like ridge grew behind his head as he drained power from others. Tli'Dora, she called him. And next . . . one of *them.* I still shudder to recall their odious forms and black power, the corruption and wrongness that defined their entire being.

Most of the Cydenges were beautiful in their own way, crafted from natural animals in ways that made a sort of sense and mimicked nature's own beauty, but these . . . they grated on every sense, and though not large, were terrifying beyond description. This one, chiefly, was a nightmare with identity—at least it possessed one now.

I took advantage of the leave that the Queen gave me, and between and after these new appointments to her "generals"—for these proved to be the only ones ready for a while, though I knew not the full number to which she aspired—I thought and reminisced on the life that had led me here. I know it sounds cliché, and perhaps unnecessary provided I do, in fact, make it out of here alive, but . . . let us say that I have never been the type for this feminine sappiness they call introspection. I like to do and be done, to go and discover and move on, not look inward and face my own demons. I swear, some folks don't just face them but chat with them, checking in to say hello everyday. Does this cultivate some insidious sense of inflated ego? Or am I just the monster I always thought myself to be?

Well . . . who are we kidding? That's an easy question.

Fifteen years I had walked Mani . . . and Gaea, and now Luna. Fifteen years since my mother gave birth to me by an off-worlder, against all apparent judgment. Sixteen years ago, she was rescued by the Manese prince Kallyn Kalceron, son of the man who would be the bane of my existence for most of my life. Coincidences do indeed abound.

But there was more, far more, going on here. At this moment, Rhidea and Mydia and Kaen and many others worked to secure a peaceful end to the coming war—or was it already starting? The battles between Hellebes and Legaleian, the approaching culmination of the struggle between Cydenges and Hellebes, and my own strange parley with Luna . . . these were all just events like symptoms rising to a boil in the face of the end of the millennium. Luna herself had confirmed this: That the moons had waited each in breathless anticipation of the end of the exile, the full time to strike at one another and Gaea. What was the full meaning of this phenomenon, I certainly did not fully know, but I had a growing sense that it would all come clear soon enough.

But also that I may be in for a longer stay on Luna than I'd anticipated. My life had taken a sudden turn, and this turn had not yet resolved into a new road yet. It lay beyond a warped horizon, a hill which I had yet to crest.

That was the crux of my conundrum. She waited seemingly with infinite patience for me to come to my own decision, but we both knew that I had little agency—or did I? All the advantage was on her side, yet—much as Lldsaor and his men had—she seemed to wait for my consent as though that were a necessary factor. Did she need it, then, or want it? If want, then . . . why? What could amuse this ancient dragon about my willing cooperation? Why not force my fealty out of me as she had forced my temporary submission?

But what she asked of me . . . it was no simple alliance, was it? Who was I kidding? I couldn't make an alliance with Luna? With the Cydenges—that was insane! I'd as well sign a warrant for the deaths of all Hellebes, for that would be the effect of this. But could I stop her? What could I possibly do against the Queen of the Moon? The Archmother?

My mother spoke to me from her Vault frequently in this time, often trying to reason with me. Sometimes I wondered, however, if the ability to raise me throughout childhood would have made her far more admonishing. It seemed like all the mothers back on Mani, bless their hearts, had far more correction than encouragement for their daughters. But perhaps that wasn't ideal . . . how should I know? Lentha was certainly an admonishing figure in my life, and looking back on my childhood in Nytaea, she seemed almost strict to the point of abuse. Yet I had nothing but fond memories of her.

My own mother, on the other hand, well . . . she clearly loved me, but she was infuriatingly passive. Right now, I wanted nothing more than for someone to step in and make a moral decision for me. To tell me that I should go for broke and defy Luna because it seemed right, not because it seemed possible. Or better yet . . . to tell me to take the easy path, thus justifying my decision.

But underneath all of that, Lhinde stirred, restless and just below the surface, nearly awake, tossing and turning and mumbling like a sleeper about to rouse. Sometimes, she did come awake and lash out with her tongue, but she made little sense. She talked of hearts of worlds and the Path of Luna, of me being born as a sacrifice to her, that the last act I would make would be to bow down before her.

Far as I could tell, she was mostly harmless, but she was certainly creepy. Once, she took me and showed me a vision, sucking me down into her Vault within a Vault within my Vault, and I woke in an ancient place—a city of mud-and-stone buildings, devoid of people save for her. And she looked not like herself, but dark of skin and hair, wearing a fine one-piece garment. She looked hollow, sad, and couldn't even say why I thought this to be her, except that I believed the vision had once been hers.

Then the vision was gone, and I was back in my draconic body.

The longer I thought about my decision, which was over the course of days, the more I realized how much would be lost if I sided with Luna. How could I ever have entertained such a thought? Had she put it into my mind? If I went with her, there was the sliver of a possibility that I could betray or influence her in some way, since she seemed to take a genuine liking to me . . . but that was a fool's hope. Like taking in a wild bear and hoping you could tame it because it did not at first maul you.

No, I had come to Luna to do something about the coming invasion. There *had* to be something I could do. There *had* to be a way to stop her. And if so, then I was the only one able. It was up to me.

Oh, Kaen, if only you could be here . . . or Rhidea, certainly she would know.

You have me, my mother said softly from the shadows of my mind.

I know. But you're no help—let's just face that fact.

She retreated with an impression of emotional pain. Real or crocodile tears, it didn't matter. She would come around again, and I was not in the wrong in saying it. Telling me to follow my heart or do as I felt right was as flimsy advice as ever there was. When the Anier were children, I imagined their parents telling them similar things. Perhaps they were well-to-do and never denied them anything. Back in Nytaea, that was why much of the nobility or rich merchant class grew up to be worse than their parents.

Man, even Sylleo . . . I'd take him right now. His company was always awkward and a bit strange, but he had a far better head on his broad shoulders than I ever gave him credit for before he . . . you know. It's fair to say that the end he chose told far more than the words he said, and put a different spin on all my interactions with him. Most, at least. Some I still couldn't figure out, but I replayed them often.

Yeah, I'd go for his company right now. Any human company, artificial or not. Immortal or not. Tyrant or not.

Ten sleeps since I'd come to Gaea, I awoke in the Queen's lair and knew before I even opened my eyes, what my decision would be. What it had to be. It seemed I'd awoken early, though, or she had been out later than usual, for no sign of wakefulness could be seen or heard in her body, her slow-shifting scale lights that pulsed gold. Bright, darker, dark. Bright, darker, dark, in a wave down her neck and back and legs.

I watched her sleeping face, so majestic and peaceful despite the ferocity I knew lurked beneath. I'd watched this metallic god-beast devour dozens of her kind so far, yet somehow my proximity to her gave me no more pause than ever. On a whim, I scooted my forepaws and nose forward, brushing her cheek and neck, and shifted my back end over closer, closer, until my hips bumped into her short ribs near the spine—if Cydenges truly have ribs; I couldn't say. I hunkered down and wrapped my tail over her, as she often did for me, and closed my eyes again. Cydenges emitted mysteriously little heat, almost as though we consumed the heat within all energy instead of metabolizing and using it. I know how silly that sounds, but regardless, there remains a certain semblance of warmth that a Cydenges body produces, and the Queen's was most comforting, almost intoxicating.

I let out a low, contented purr, surprised at the sounds my metal body instinctively made even after inhabiting it for so long. Nor could I say why I made it this time. Eyes closed, I began to perceive something in Luna's warm energy signature, a motion deep inside. In the darkness of my mind, an image steadily formed of a current, like a long snaking river of light. What flowed through it, I knew not, only that in some way she was this river. I looked back, making out the long, winding trail of the river in the blackness. Somehow, it never seemed to grow smaller in the distance, as though the past diminished but a small amount—or perhaps the river was simply wider at its start and thinner here where I traced alongside it.

If the Queen waked at all at my presence, there was no sign of it. With the vision of the river came more detail, and I saw a swirly, painted background in the night, all while faint stars appeared in the blackness, small and infinite in number. I beheld another river, far beyond but snaking its path ever toward this river. Following it in my view, I realized that it was heading for this river, and would get there eventually. It hadn't yet, despite both seemingly never ending. This second stream was grey-white, while the first was made of a goldish light.

Luna and Mani, I realized suddenly.

The vision continued to morph and develop, and I made out a green light in the distance, where the rivers began. Before I knew it, I was seeing an impossible panoramic view of a more purposeful path of both rivers, stemming from a flat green plane that slowly curved into a planetoid shape. Both streams flowed out in a great, twisting arc, eventually coming back to the planet. But not quite. Their trajectories were left incomplete, though the end was clear: they would return to Gaea, and they would meet there. I did not get any impression that this was literal, yet there was significance to the long, almost casual arc of each, which went its separate ways before clashing in the coming collision with Gaea's green.

If the green represented Cybele, then would they come together and reform, creating the missing goddess? Or would their meeting be a battle of the ages, perhaps a struggle between the forces of Luna and Mani?

My view began to zoom in of its own, and I realized that I was seeing the glowing streams from afar off. It sucked me in, but I went of my own accord. In fact, I believe it was me in part who gravitated inward, turning back against the current of the stream. What passed me by were high-speed particles of light appearing white and gold at a distance but resolving into images—snapshots of events, as it were—of Luna's past. I saw the Cydenges at work beneath the surface of the golden moon, hollowing out the vast network of their home-to-be. I saw the Queen laying a clutch of eggs in the incubation chambers, something I had yet to witness. She did it only once per turning of the moon.

It wasn't long before I heard Luna's voice in my vision, and it was not a part of the rush of images and memories—it was her, speaking to me within the vision. Yet I did not wake, and I even had the impression that she would hold me there if I tried to wake from the vision now. *That is right, child. I've waited for you to come here,* she said in a soothing, inviting voice.

And . . . where are we?

Where do you think? My Vault. Welcome to the Vault of Luna. The first and truest Vault.

You're . . . giving me access?

Her laughter rang in my head. *Do not be a fool, Lynchazel. You are a guest here, as you are a guest on my moon. I do not give such access to mere guests, though you may soon earn the right. For a guest you will no longer be, one way or the other.*

That was not the end, but the beginning, of our journey through the memory stream. She guided me back through history, slowly retracing the cycles and years, but she allowed me to take the wheel for a bit, pausing at important events. It seemed the new Queens were needed every fifty years or so, at which point Luna issue a command that put all Cydenges into a state of passive guard duty, some keeping watch over her cocoon which she spun at the top of the great hub while the rest waited largely in silence from their various posts, holding their proverbial breath in anticipation of the new Queen. I witnessed the death of the last Queen, which was a voluntary giving up of her body, in one of the lowest chambers referred to as the Tomb of Queens.

I scrolled backward farther, skipping through the bright stream in a torrent of information, all the way to the previous Queen six hundred Cycles prior. Each, it would seem, had entirely different features, as though Luna slowly grew bored of her form and decided to pull from the divers features of her children to craft her next shell. Backwards we went, reviewing the construction of the towers and the intricate webs of tunnels that connected the underground lairs and Pits. The creation of each individual strain or "species" of Cydenges. Unsurprisingly, the Brutes and Leonids were the first appearing to originate to a progenitor Cydenges that eerily resembled the general form of the Queens.

Along the way, she let me pause and view the current information gathered by Luna's monitors of Gaea, which had been running for centuries, and thus I was able to see much of Gaea's history as well, the modernization of the shield-walled cities, and eventually how the Hellebes first reacted to the invaders. It was astonishing how effective the beasts were in Gaea's medieval times and killing and terrorizing the cities and countryside, with sometimes one single metal beast laying waste to an entire village.

Yes, for they knew not how to counter us in the olden days. Before their great advancements in technology and after the banishment of the Legaleians, who used their Stonesinging to bring destruction to our bodies. We hate them still, as we hate the musket and cannon builders of the Anier. But the Anier had only localized influence then, and it was our destructive impact on the world that in part gave rise to their world seizure. If I could redo anything, it might be to focus in on them or be more judicious with my attacks.

Her honesty was chilling, laying bare her utter disregard for humankind. *I thought you said you want to wipe the earth of artificial life, not humans*, I said, shortly before realizing that it had not been her, but . . .

Ah, that sounds a lot like my daughter Lhinde, first of your kind. She . . . yes, she was special. I noticed her early on, early enough to contact her and . . . well, I won't spoil any good surprises. Let us say that that is her interpretation, and very close. You are correct in observing that I have no particular objection to humankind—and of course, my creation was for their benefit in the beginning. My own betrayed me, and them I hated, but it is the Anier and what they made truly inflamed my ire and gave me purpose.

Then why did you not strike them down?

She was silent for a bit as I spun through more and more history, nearing the millennial waking of the moons. *You understand, at least in part, how I speak to you in these visions? Perhaps not. But it is like that. I speak of a prophetic knowledge of Gaea's future, when we will return to reclaim the world from the hand of its evil caretakers, and I do so not of my own calculations and intellect. No, but there is an order to things, an order which I did not set into motion and over which*

I have little influence. This order it is that dictated the thousand years. The humans did not give Mani that time span, nor the Legaleians. The exile aligned with the order, the plan, the pattern. It moves and flows as it wills, beyond my control.

An order . . . Somewhere, I'd heard of something like that. *Is this the same order that created the world? The universal force, or evolution, or god?* Gaean scientists seemed to have many viewpoints on such things.

God . . . yes. And no. Perhaps it is He, or a force that He set in motion.

I chewed on her words as we traveled farther upstream, nearing the green planetoid of the millennial dawn. [Probably something in here about how the thousand years *actually* started when Menily burrowed into Luna, or when Mani was exiled, not sure about that.) The images blew past, slowing to frosty speeds as I focused in on them. We beheld the day that Mani was sentenced to exile on the lesser moon, following his sister's betrayal and her nature-defying flight to the Great Moon. He was sent by powerful Reality magi using the Ancient Font's power, another relic of "His" making according to my patron.

Next, the day when Luna fell upon Luna's surface like a golden star, creating a meteor impact of red and gold intermixed. She was enormous then, far heavier than the current Mother. Soon after that, the faint bronze atmosphere slowly came into being, turning from gold to reddish and settling into that dull orange.

The day when Luna rebelled against her legions of worshippers, snapping like a wild animal thought to be tame. The dragon was only one of her forms, and she became the first Cydenges Mother that day in a golden rage, a monstrosity that seemed to awake from her very image in their temple, uprooting the gold-painted pyramidal foundation and low walls, stripping it of the gold paint and casting mortar. Like molten metal poured from the crucible, she grew from the small form she'd been, hips like boulders, shoulders dulled blades of gold, claws tearing at stone and earth, many-horned head snapping forth to rend the unfortunate. The roar that echoed from her blood-soaked jaws vibrated the earth for acres round about, pealing like thunder.

Then we reached the green wall, which shattered before us as a wall of insects might—scattering into smaller bits, moving away altogether and making way for a new view. To my shock, the inside of what her Vault had shown as a great ball proved to be only a black void, into which the silver and gold trails disappeared.

Do not be afraid, she said. *Go in, child.*

Gaea

- Chapter 16 -

Her Divine Vault

The Millennium comes. False humans will fall, and echoes of dragon.
prepare Mother's return. And our hated foe, the essence of silver, shall be . .
— Cydenges Eternal Vaul

I gravitated inward, pulled by the unseen weight of Luna's transmillennia
mind. Darkness enveloped me, my consciousness becoming confusion until
glimpsed light once more. The transition was smooth, yet I immediately saw
that I was in a different space, not that same ethereal astral plane. This surface
curved visibly like a very small moon, or perhaps like the descriptions recounted
to me of the world deep within Mani. The surface was far smoother than Luna's
seemingly of some greyish metal etched in a pattern of gold. The pattern was
geometric, but such that I could not interpret or even correctly understand it
As I gazed about the place, beholding the heavy, leaden sky filled with shifting
golden lights, I felt an odd sensation that resolved into an awareness of
something . . . off.

It was the space itself—there was too much of it. On the ground, the pattern
took up more space than could fit in a flat—nor especially a rounded—surface
The glowing lines between the geometric shapes seemed almost to tease
knowingly intimidating my human mind.

Either sensing or anticipating my overwhelm, Luna spoke to me again:
"Fear not; you need not navigate this infinite labyrinth. It is not meant for a
mind such as yours."

At first I did not realize she was speaking aloud, at which point I turned
and found her on my left, not in dragon form yet clearly she: A coal-black female
form, anthropomorphic but not human. Her face was set straight forward,
fastened in the distance beyond me, and as she turned I saw her features,
somehow more frightening than any human face I'd ever looked upon. Her form

was not at all vague, yet chiseled in such a way—seemingly from pure, burnished metal—that plates and ridges and geodesic faces came together in a whole both more and less detailed than a woman's form. Her hair, such that it was, seemed to be carved from her head, while her eyes were the same infinite pools of burning gold I would recognize anywhere.

"Yes, this is another form of mine, the last vestiges of which you glimpsed in the memory of my turning against humanity. Like it?"

She seemed to expect a response, so I hazarded a few words of praise. "It's beautiful, My Queen." By now, some variation of that honorific was ingrained in my speech, much as it galled me. It felt natural, yet it piqued my indignation to honor this manslaying force of destruction so.

The metal face smiled, a feature far more terrifying than comforting. "Here of all places, your thoughts are bare before me. It makes no difference, of course. I will not fault you for such notions, nor punish them within this Vault. We are nearing the end of your teetering state, and will soon move forward one way or the other. Won't we?" She turned to face me head on, and I realized that her frame was at least a half head taller than mine, deceptively large and, despite her refined elegance, powerful. Daunting. The reaching bones between joints decked in a perfect combination of elegant smoothness and rippling muscle— defined in that deceptively simple dark-metal geometry.

She was not so different from the eighth Cydenges breed.

"You . . . you mean for me to make my choice now, don't you, Queen?" I asked, seeing that she had drawn me in perhaps on purpose, like a trap for a dumb animal.

"I do. For not only is your mind open before me, child, but you have already made your decision. There is nought left but to lay it bare before me."

She was right. Somehow it galled me to hear her say the truth of it, but it made no difference. Before I came here, I'd known. I'd known for weeks now what I had to do. Even now as I considered my situation, and the words with which I must express my answer, the Queen waited, patient and not interrupting.

Gaea

I took a breath, burying my fear with a stern hand.

"Very well, Luna. Here is my answer."

End of Part One

PART TWO

Offensive

Gaea

- Chapter 17 -

Tree of Sorrows

Finhal 5, 999:
It sprouted like an otherworldly vine, golden and gleaming. None could
have predicted its coming, nor its influence . . . nor the terrifying prophecy
that was its purpose. Nay, not a prophecy. More a warning. Is there a
difference?
— From The Book of Mani's End

[Could instead be the prologue]

"We shall move forward with the plans as established, My Queen," said Secretary Keuda with a small curtsy. Her short grey skirt, which came only to her knees, stayed remarkably level during this practiced motion.

The Queen Regent glanced about the room, which contained an uncomfortable amount of dignitaries from all across the continent—including representatives of Lygellis and Yan'Vala, though Torlega was still pretending to not remember the "northerner" empire. Kystrea had, after all, beaten them soundly ___ years ago. At the same time, pride threatened to introduce a girlish smile on her face, pride at how far they had come over the last year. It had started with the envoys sent out across the Kystrean Empire, then to the surrounding nations. Things were finally starting to come together. Promises of peace and solidarity, and with them hope, were working in the world.

"My lady!"

Mydia turned jerkily to see Captain Straif of the Mage Guard, chest heaving underneath her glimmering silver breastplate. The mage soldiers all wore them, but hers was of the ancient spell-forged design fashioned by the Silversmiths. "What is it?" the queen asked, neither hesitating nor eager. All talk of the alliance plans was postponed by the urgency evident in the small woman's words.

"A signal from the east shore towers."

A curse rose to Mydia's lips, and she issued the halt command before it made its way out. "Invaders?"

"Invaders."

They both knew that meant another sky raid from Gaea. Secretary Keuda looked between them, jotted down a note on her parchment, and scurried off. In the following minutes, Straif and Marshal Enchro barked orders at soldiers and the Palace entered an emergency state. An evacuation was ordered, and as many as possible would be corralled into the bunkers that had been recently dug by expert earth magi. Mydia made her way to the east wall, accompanied by a growing force of mage soldiers.

So it begins again . . . They knew the Gaeans would be back, but it had been a year without any return. Lyn had sent a contingent back to Nytaea only once, bringing astonishing news. Gaea's entire political balance had shifted, and this "alien threat" known as the Cydenges were stirring of late. Now . . . evidently, the powers that be had decided it was time to engage the silver moon once again.

Today was the day they put their practice to work.

Mydia eventually got away from her military officials only to meet Ethas Gandel, her coregent and his wife Aldyr. Lacking the long legs of her sister Syneria, she seemed to have just caught up with him.

"You heard, Mydia?" he asked. It was never "Queen," nor even "Lady Mydia," with him, as befit his station. Ever the perfectionist. He stood tall in dark boots that matched his surcoat, tassels on his shoulder cuffs matching his golden hair.

She nodded curtly, though with an accompanying gulp, and resisted the instinct to brush at her bob-cut black hair. She used to have a real problem with that, but now it mastered her only when she wasn't focused. "I don't think the magi have an estimated time, but they seem to be heading right for Nytaea again."

"Did—did they really attack Darsor already?" asked Aldyr from beside her husband. Though usually proper and perfect in etiquette, the woman contracted a strange shyness when around both he and Mydia, as though the presence of two royal leaders demoted her from family to spectator. While it was true that the plentitude of women made subservient to the rarer men, it was a phenomenon often lost within the nobility, where rank and birth were everything.

Ethas turned half around. "That hasn't been confirmed. Coming, lady wife?"

"Yes." His wife's indignant tone sounded much more like her usual demeanor.

"You'll see to the evacuation?" Ethas asked the Queen Regent.

She gave another sharp nod, hesitated for one breath, and diverged from his path. It wasn't a matter of any moodiness, she just . . . didn't have any words to add. She tried not to focus on two many things at once these days, especially since . . .

Her gut twisted. Somewhere deep inside a knot twisted, a knot so often pulled that it had worn in, not out. How many months had it been since Kaen had died, and she still pined for him like a young lover?

Eight. Almost nine now. Kaen was never coming back. A woman ought to get over such a loss, yet it had been eating a hole in her soul like an undying coal. Mysteriously, her emotions were branching out in an unexpected direction as she walked—or trying to; she kept the lid on the pot. But under that lid smoldered a burning anger toward these invaders, the same she'd glimpsed in others but thought herself incapable of. Was this how Kaen had felt about his sister?

She met up with various officials as she descended the Palace, sending them off to see to evacuation of various districts. The Palace was always the first to hear about such an event, and indeed the nobility the most paranoid of the city's population. But no one was unimportant, and no one completely safe. They still had no idea of the enemy's number or purpose. This man and that woman begged her to come with them to safety, leaving the defense of the city to the magi, but of course . . . she was one of them. She had no intention of shutting herself in.

In fact, two powers warred within her breast as she strode along: one demanding that she flee, the other urging her to give up her own life for her people. That animalistic instinct to give oneself up for the herd, usually only felt by men.

She exited the Palace out the tall stone door that had been expertly repaired by Nytaean craftsmen. Its broad stone sill had been woven back into the Palace's magical defenses by magi, though it would never be as one with the structure. The majority of the evacuation plan involved getting as many as possible into the Palace—the lower floors—because of the strong wards. In the broad stone-paved streets, spear soldiers were waving townsfolk on into the Palace. They made way for her, but she tried to keep to the outside to allow for as much human flow as possible, nodding nervously to the guards. There were no mage soldiers to be seen here, as they were all heading to the western wall too see to the defense of the city. They would *not* be caught unprepared as last time.

That is where she was heading now. She could have used a Reality Stone, but instead hurried manually through the streets. It wasn't far, and people made way for her at every street corner. She checked in with the soldiers and shouted for reinforcements to be brought in where needed, hoping they heeded her. The soldiery was well-aware of their own uselessness of defense in a situation such as this, and thus had practiced instead to be a guiding force for directing traffic and keeping peace during the emergency. An evacuation had been a when, not an if.

When she heard the rumbling, that was when she pulled out her crystal. She waited a moment, listening. She could feel the faint vibrations in the ground, even though she knew they came from the air. Gaean military forces favored the air above all, or so said the Hellebes man called Zent, and well they should if they had such miracle technology. Lyn had described much about their world in such a way—marvelous feats of engineering and modernization that boggled the mind, all without the use of elemental or other magics.

She activated the stone, and with a pulsing of the air around her teleported to the high wall. Her practiced feet caught the new ground immediately, and she took in her surroundings: mage soldiers on either side, close inhabitants still trailing through the city gates below . . . *Too many. Did they run too far with the message?* There was no point guiding those too far out to safety if it meant them getting caught out in the open. Pursing her lips, commanding them not to tremble, she supposed that there was nothing to be done at this point.

She located the nearest commander and asked after their readiness. The man responded saying that the Reality weapons were primed and linked with magi around Kystrea. She made out the capes of the Reality magi pearl white colored pink by the slowly-setting sun. The Perception magi wore violet capes, and would be highly instrumental in the defensive endeavors. Perhaps the most vital.

Mydia would be joining them. She was pretty sure Ethas thought she wouldn't be, but that was no matter. She couldn't see him from this stretch of the wall, but she could see a purple-caped group of mage soldiers. They hailed her, and she asked after west coast.

Their response was almost drowned out by the growing intensity of the droning vibrations from the incoming force. Looking to the horizon, they finally made out the force. Her heart sank as she perceived how wide the band that overtook the sky. *Great auroras . . .*

As they came closer, she could make out individual vessels—dozens of them. Far more than last time. *They don't just mean to talk.* But neither did the Nytaeans. The Perception mage soldiers had already cast wide a net over the wall, concealing the existence of all but the fewest number of guards. They would not be conspicuous, but rather the opposite, for they did not appear to be targets. For the sake of expedience, they did particularly veil the locations of the most vital magi, those with powerful Authority.

But that was not all they did. High in the sky flapped fire-and-lightning-infused apparitions like the great mage golems of old. As expected, these were the first and primary targets from the enemy skyships, which targeted them with a torrent of bright bolts across the sky as they drew nearer. The sight was frightening, but Mydia and her fellow Perception magi kept up the sky apparitions, causing them to flap and produce audible roars. It was tricky to give them voices, and trickier still to make them respond to physical stimuli— impossible, on that count—but they made the best show of it.

Mydia had designed hers on a waterfowl motif, cloaked in apparent misty clouds that caught Sol's light and cast a small rainbow in the air. Its coloration and density were far more intense than a regular cloud, so it stood out as a creation of magic. She'd doubted whether such a bird, even one as large as a house, would seem a threat, but the Gaeans took it as seriously as the falcon, the bat and the dragon. That last had been Gendric's invention. Any use of the imagination to threaten or mislead the invaders without directly taking unnecessary lives was a great victory in his sight. He'd given them a rough sketch of what this creature of old was supposed to have looked like, a streaking worm that darted through the air without wings.

The dragon was certainly unsettling to look upon, scaled and winding like a serpent yet possessing sets of multilayered wings as long as but thinner than her waterfowl's, fluttering and flitting faster than such a massive shape should seem capable. But they had assured her that this was as close an approximation as they could come to the mythical beasts. She may never set foot on Gaea, but if she did, she should like to ascertain just whether they did indeed prowl the earth. Or perhaps the original basis was these Cydenges creatures . . .

The green bolts issuing from the sky ships lit up the sky, casting reflective streaks upon the white walls and silver of Nytaea. With each streak, Mydia's heart jumped in her chest, for they carried an unknown destructive power that seemed a natural predator to their way of life. Perhaps not natural, but certainly superior.

The pilots of those ships seemed to catch on, at least to a degree, and some split off, turning this way and that, and blasted the walls and houses as they made for the Palace.

They did not get far, for the magi had real weapons as well as fake. Powerful lightning struck the ships, focused on the engines, and though none seemed to lose control immediately, Zent of Gaea had assured them that it would at least weaken their shielding. The wind magi they had received in exchange from the Sky Islands pulled the ships down toward Argent in mighty undertows, and earth magi hurled stones that had been made ready for the purpose, meeting the confused ships with at least a handful of projectiles.

In a beautiful sight, some of them went down. Mydia cheered inside, though she worked to keep up her apparition, causing it to chase the ships. Their goal was to keep up the charade by making the attackers think that they were at least reacting to the attack, whilst the lightning and other magical bursts were hopefully attributed to them as well.

Meanwhile, the Reality Cannons fired. These were inventions of Oliver's, which operated from afar as directed via Perception and Reality. Magi halfway across the world controlled machines that moved objects like stones at great speed, and a Reality gate was opened at the mouth of their little cannons. As the first round went off, she saw the glorious and terrifying effects. The work of Randhorn's engineers and elite fire magi, these projectiles exploded upon impact—and thus were only fired forwards, away from the city—with enough force to blow a hole in a wall.

The first ships hit by such bombs did not go down, unfortunately, but she saw their shielding flicker red-and-green. One was taken by the "lightning" falcon, bursting into spontaneous flames. A cheer erupted, and continued as more and more of the fleet was struck while shieldless. There was only so much damage each could withstand.

They were without Rhidea's Silver Authority today, for she was occupied in Redufiel, Halstar, but they were making an admirable effort, enough to make Mydia smile despite the carnage and fearful magery.

She was nearly blown aside as the first Reality Cannon was targeted. At least one of her water magi went down, but she couldn't tell through the chaos. *No! Stay with me, my duck . . .* She glanced up at her automaton as she regained her footing and set it to chasing down some of the more adventurous sky invaders, then looked around to see who needed medical help. They had battlefield medics, but water magi and mundane, and one crouched alongside a soldier over a man whose left side smoldered with unnatural fire. Mustor, a mage soldier of Fircas. She knew him only because she had helped in the training of the water division for defense preparations.

Over the course of the next half hour, the battle took over everything, and she hardly knew what she was doing. The enemy stopped coming, and those inside the city began to bomb more buildings, then to drop out troops at the Palace. Some were blasted away with magic, but others made it.

Group by grouped, they retreated from the walls toward the Palace, where they could be more effective. Messengers came and were redirected by Mydia, shouting first that she must be kept safe and then that she was needed. She grudgingly let herself by zipped away by Reality Coaction, and looked overhead at the terrifying attackers as she headed farther into the Palace. It would hold, she told herself. *I was crafted of the oldest Silver magic alongside master stoneworkers, imbued with charms and protections irreplicable today.*

Marshal Enchro was the first to meet her. "Milady, this will not do! Please get inside immediately. Lord Gandel has been looking all over for you."

No, he hasn't. She knew him better than that. He was passively looking for her while actively taking part in much more important directions. She did make her way toward him, however. Concussive blasted followed her in, the sound of houses being ripped apart by the evil work of mankind. *But are they? Are they truly men?* She'd wondered before, but now the doubts that sprang to mind had little to do with that.

They took him. They stole him from me, and they'll pay. Nytaea would *make* them pay, whatever Gendric said.

In uncharacteristic anger, Mydia stopped and turned suddenly, scowling up at the enemy. She felt her pulse beating in her breast, and an accompanying rhythm nearby. Looking, she beheld the Ardencaul River, which flowed from here out through the Palace, making its way underneath. The water called out to her, trying to assuage her fears and guilt. Or . . . no, it was echoing her anger, perhaps inflaming it. It spoke to her like an old friend, sang to her like a lover.

Hesitating, she gulped. People were still being redirected into the Palace for safekeeping, and mage soldiers and archers were taking up battle positions closer to the magnificent structure. Two melodies clashed in her heart, one a thundercloud of rage, the other an ocean of sadness. The sadness was overpowering the other, seeking to be the melody. And an ocean it was, like a body of water unseen on Mani, calling out to her from the river.

She stepped off the Palace road, ignoring calls. She hopped down to a side path, dress snagging on the coarse stone rail. In her mind, she tried to focus on the battle, and on what her Water Authority might grant her to aid in it, but her heart overpowered it with thoughts of Lyn and Kaen, one taken and the other taken forever. And Rhidea, who seemed to have abandoned them all for . . . for Domon. Was it possible?

They took him from me. That alone was enough to be angry forever toward the greater world, as childish as she felt for it. Now, it seemed a consuming tide, beckoning her down to the river. Again, she looked up, and felt a rain pouring down on her. She hardly felt rain anymore, and now laughed as it seemed to fall upon only her. Was it her imagination? Was it all?

Come to me, Child. Give your cares to the water.

It had to be her imagination. Mani had proven to have a voice, but the elements did not. The Wellspring did not.

But she cared not; she answered. *I'm here.* Dimly, out of a seeming torrent of emotions, still working to suppress the pull of duty and fear and embarrassment. Surely they were all staring at her by now, wondering how the queen had lost her mind. But she could not make herself care. She wept open tears now, becoming another of the clouds shedding a bitter rain of tears. Then she knelt.

And then she howled, voice straining at her highest vocal chords, making not a pitch but a harsh keening that, she thought, pierced the sky and cut through the din of chaos. Or was that only the pride left in the small conscious bit of her mind, pride enough to pretend that her own sorrow trumped the desperate plight of their city, which might this day perish from the world? They had expected to win, to suppress their attackers, but they were too strong . . . surely they could still manage, could drive them away? But at what cost? Her city . . . her beloved city.

She knew not how long her cry went up, only that at some point a miracle had begun. When later she asked the inhabitants of Nytaea what they had seen, they attested that it began with a great rumbling. She felt a cool embrace as the river's water rushed upon her, and then the ground opened up in front of her, in a small patch of ground between walkways near the river's edge. From this earthen mouth issued the a golden sprout, threading its way through with a magnificent twist to spiral upwards, upwards. It reached for the sky, and she looked up in wonder to see—though through a curtain of water that largely obscured it—the stem branch out, seeking the attackers.

Along its length, the shot grew at the same time until it was one, two, four feet in diameter. Soon, it was well beyond a man's height in width, turning crispy and brown like a tree trunk, still shooting upwards. She was aware of voices crying out in astonishment, and the sounds of battle seemed to fade as the wondrous tree overtook the sky, spreading out over the entire Palace while engulfing all enemy ships. Even as they tried to speed away, the branches twisted about them with unearthly power—or rather, very earthly— and forbade such maneuvers.

She could not say how long the growth went on, only that she felt something go out from herself with it, in addition to the water's aid. She knew well that her Authority had never brought about so great a feat, no would she have ever dreamed such a possibility. But the way the water spoke to her . . . it did not continue to do so, and yet she felt her bond with it in new ways. At last, she stood up, dizzy and reeling, and look up the great trunk, which was nearly at her feet. In so doing, she fell upon her own rear end, landing on her dress on soggy ground. The brown trunk had soared to unfathomable heights, branches reaching nearly all across the city, and had sprouted with vibrant golden leafage, consuming the Gaean vessels at least from sight. Its great roots had pulled up the stonework around it, even moving one of the stairways leading into the Palace.

Her lips tried to form words, but she could find none. She looked inward, but the voice of the river was gone. However, in place of the inner torment and sadness sparkled a new hopefulness. The loss and guilt remained, but this euphoric feeling overpowered it. She rose as the first jaw-droppers rushed down into the new throne of tree roots. One was Captain Straif of the Mage Guard, while her Queensguard were next, rushing to help her up amidst protests of "I'm fine, really!"

They helped her up onto the stairs, where she backed up through an awed mass of onlookers who reverently made way for her. Someone asked the obvious question, but she said nothing, having no answer for how she had made it, nor if indeed it had been her. The farther she backed away from it, the more impossible the creation seemed.

She knew not the implications of this miracle, but she was certain that this was a milestone in Manese history, a new manifestation of magic that just may see a sequel soon. A blooming of the Wellspring, the beginning of a new age . . . or a final countdown. "Keuda," she said out of her daze, seeing that the prim secretary was standing nearby, looking like a frightened mouse seeing a giant. The woman jumped and squeaked, then curtsied to her lady the queen. "What day is it?"

She was well aware of how stupid the question sounded, but she honestly couldn't say given the scrambling that now ruled her brain. Promptly and with no mirth, Keuda answered, "999, the first of Manidor, My Lady."

Mydia nodded slowly, and one by one, the heads around them turned, as though collectively wondering the same thing.

Either Mani or the Wellspring . . . one of them was trying to send a message.

- Chapter 18 -

Echoes of Creation

Finhal 1, 1294

The twin cities of the Titans, though separated by more than fou.

thousand miles, once represented the power of the greater world that reignec

on Gaea—and lingers still today

— From Lhinde's Vaul

Kaen took his seat at the controls of his sleek aircraft, waiting for his companion Kennick, before thrusting off toward the south. The Geokinetic engines went from a hum to a roar, though he soon backed off. *Don't want to go too fast here in the city.* Chronala was not technically friendly territory, even if Daedalus was tentatively allied with Ccamos at the moment, and indeed had been rather friendly in the course of this meeting. Emperor Lldsaor did not just allow

He and Kennick had been checking up on the progress of their latest experiment [what in the world would this be?], and in exchange the scientist/Senator had run a detailed checkup on the makeup of his biomechanical body. After all, he had been a sort of experiment once, bred and mind-grafted to make a warrior out of a Legaleian man. It felt terrifyingly familiar, as in a way . . . this was all he had ever known. His new self, anyway. Daedalus had twice now done this, an exchange of scientific data, and this time [again refer to these experiments, or just cut them?].

This time, Daedalus had been most interested in his mind.

Arriving back in Ccamos two hours later, Kaen was allowed in through the northern shield gate. Red and angry, it looked strong as ever. The city, just as peaceful despite the threat of war looming directly overhead. But then, what else were the people to do? Kennick was largely silent, but then, on the three outings they'd been on together, he had been consistently quiet.

A steady rain sought to soak Kaen as he exited the docking bay at military

HQ. General Inecc met him soon after, and he gave a quick report.

The general gave a Hellebes grunt. "Well, let's take it to command." Command was a nickname for not only the military center of Ccamos, but the council of generals and former Red Horizon who ran the city largely in Lyn's stead. That was her doing as much as theirs, so it was a matter of practicality that someone had to see to the military and civil functions of one of the eight metropolises of the world.

Thus they did not have to go far before meeting General Fors and General Frauss, who called the others. Zent was out at the moment, but should arrive later today, assuming he got back in one piece from Mei Shan. It was hard to believe that over six months had passed since the events that had torn the League. Still none pressed hard enough to call it a true war, though there had been some skirmishes between forces. These had mostly been minor encounters in places where it could be politely explained as an accident. At least, when it was politic.

"We'll bump him up just a tad," said Frauss, moving an actual slider on one of their command screens that displayed the Senators by order of favorability. It had started as a gag, but he'd done it as a small show of professional rebellion, perhaps to win the amusement of his new Lady. Kaen had no more knowledge of how Hellebes minds worked in regards to females than how human psychology worked.

No one else said anything. The sliders showed Phelps, the new Haven Senator, at number one, as he had the strongest reasons for favoring an alliance with them, and Daedalus at a close second. Long, Senator of Mei Shan, was not shown despite being alive, and not for his failing state of health, but because he was not publicly known to be alive at all—a secret they would milk for as long as possible—and had nothing to offer militarily. Holman wasn't far down, but De'Witt and his administration seemed to have developed a dislike for Ccamos following the global rift.

Lldsaor, obviously, was at the bottom.

"Cydenges activity, of course . . ." said Fors, ignoring Senator_Slider.exe, indicated the stats page showing Lunar activity of different forms. There was also a distinct radiation that their instruments picked up from the golden moon which was usually reliable for predicting the next attack. Part of the reason for the Senate staying their hand for the moment was the higher number of false alarms in past months. The L-radiation was only strong shortly before an attack, thus why they tended to come suddenly, but these times they would get a strong reading and then . . . nothing. It was suspicious, to say the least.

Overall, however, increased activity, and even a few rogue sightings this month. Kaen refrained from speaking his mind, of course, but he did have some thoughts on the whole matter. Zent would have had more, but he knew the Colonel thought similarly.

Colonel Maiss, a new appointee to the Ccamos council, spoke now. "The patterns are getting tighter and tighter. If I may say so, I would not be shocked if soon one of these false appearances is revealed to be a major offensive. Not as though Luna herself were planning this, but more as though she were undergoing a transformation, a process of change." He looked around as though expecting displeased surprise, saw only attention.

Someone has to speak at these meetings . . .

"A process of change," Maiss repeated, "Or preparation. We have good reason to suspect that Luna may be sentient, yes?" He looked at Kaen as he said it. Kaen nodded. "So that's one possibility. But I fear the Senate at large is growing lax, looking back towards their Mani invasion."

"They've already begun again," said Fors. "You all heard about the recent fleet sent there?"

"Just two flights, sir," said Maiss.

"Which is over double what they sent before," the general responded. He glanced at Kaen, as though expecting a comment about his beloved homeworld. They seemed to often expect him to pine for home, which of course he did in more private settings. He'd never let it out here. Though a captain now, he was the lowest here bother by seniority and rank, and would not give them more reason to look down on him. "Regardless, it's as you say, Colonel. They've grown lax."

Ever the expansionists, Kaen mused. *The colonial mind yearns for more land to dominate.* Speaking for the first time, he said, "We still have not learned what they want it for, no?"

"Mani?" asked General Inecc, who'd also stayed quiet thus far. He was a judicious speaker. "Lldsaor has certainly has some things to say about the silver moon over the past year, but . . . you're right. Whatever their true intentions, the Imperials are not forthcoming with them."

And they'd thought Strongs to have an agenda. Which he had, and now that agenda was crushed. Kaen didn't think any of the current Senators had world domination in mind, or at least not directly, but Mani was certainly a stepping stone toward that in some way or other. It could only be the Wellspring. They wanted it back. And yet the Senate had never let on that they knew much about it . . .

General Frauss looked his way. "Any updates on the Lady Senator?" There was no derision in his tone, and yet Kaen had developed an ear for it, often tensing slightly whenever her name was mentioned. While he did not harbor the same affection for her that he once had, he felt a kindred connection to her, an accompanying urge to defend her. He didn't know if any of the condescension was intended, for it could well have been accidental, or even imagined.

Kaen shook his head. "She arrived safely in Luna Halcyon. How long she'll be there depends on what she finds, of course."

Heads nodded at the repetition of common knowledge. Lyn had been fighting to get free of the oversight recently, but she still wouldn't do something without the council's knowledge. It was too risky. But he knew what she *wanted* to do . . . it hung in the room like an unspoken elephant. After a brief pause, Colonel Maiss asked it:

"Does the Senator still wish to personally breach Luna's barrier?" It was a far more tactful way of broaching the subject than could have been done, making it out to be some breakthrough in science—which indeed it would, were it possible. Some rejected her proposal—insomuch as they could even to a female Senator—out of its outlandishness, others out of safety objections, arguing that she was far too valuable. Of course, the same had kept her from deploying anywhere with as little guard as she currently had, but Kaen was . . almost on her side about that. He just wished he or Zent could personally have been with to protect her. That would be good enough.

Perhaps he, too, worried too much about her. The Lady Senator . . . it would seem totally insane, mere months ago, to think that his friend from Lentha's orphanage would become one of the leaders of an alien world. Her world, by birth, and in a way, by right. But the tension in the air spoke of a doubt he shared with all present: That Lyn did not truly belong in her position. It was a doubt born not of any personal ill will, nor in statistics, but of the nature of the Mother's relationship to Gaea. And in her case, to Mani. But most importantly . . to Luna.

That was the true crux of it. Whenever she mentioned this fool's idea of going there, it stirred a discomfort in all, one she couldn't understand and—perhaps—couldn't even perceive.

Suddenly a shorter Hellebes, red-faced either by complexion or from excitement, bustled in. Ccarius; Kaen only knew his name. "My lords, Colonel Zent is back from Mei Shan."

After a couple acknowledging nods, Ccarius left, and soon Zent swaggered into the room. The tall Hellebes, imposing despite his middle age, glanced around the room as though expecting a warm welcome. "What did I miss?"

"Not much, sir," said Kaen.

"Good. Nothing groundbreaking in Tai'Xi, but I heard Lyn might be making some discoveries."

Most of the officers showed little reaction, but Frauss raised his eyebrows.

""

[Very important chapter, likely setting the scene for much of Part 2]
- A bit more political discussion, revealing the current state of the League and Lldsaor's intentions, etc.
- Then Zent arrives, and more stuff is mentioned, plus of course the unrest regarding the Cydenges (which is mostly Lyn, right?)
- Is Kaen mad that she went to Luna Halcyon w/o consulting him?

Gaea

-

- Chapter 19 -

Mani Halcyon

Finhal 1, 1294

Mani Halcyon, of course, is the one that is mentioned no more, for its fall
was a shameful thing entangled in secrets and conspiracies to great to tell their
whole. Mani's temple, it is agreed, is there no longer, but what clues remain? I
wonder . . .

— From Lhinde's Vault

Zent piloted his omnicraft deep beneath the Cynnith Ocean, bound for the mysterious land of the Orient. He had been here only once in his life, years ago for a training operation with the Haccolces Air Force. Now he was here under orders from his Senator back in Ccamos . . . Lyn.

At least, officially. It was his idea. She'd simply gone along with it. The girl wanted him out of her hair so that she could go on her little archeological expedition in Luna Halcyon. Why it was so important to her, he couldn't exactly say. But once in a while, he had to admit, they needed to let the little bird fly free. She was not the weak outworlder she was when she'd stumbled through that Gate a year ago. It was hard to think that a year had gone by, yet harder still to look back and accept all that had happened to his world. Two Senators dead and deposed, leaving behind a cold war between two factions.

Two main factions, anyway. As with anything, it was more complex than that.

Zent allowed his eyes brief breaks to look about him at the ocean scenery: forests of towering kelp, multicolored reefs below, shafts of rippling sunlight reaching down from the surface but not quite touching his level. There was light, obviously, but none of the dramatic beams that glinted and intermixed in high contrast. Ocean creatures swam hither and thither, schools of fish and the occasional mammal. As they had noted back at the underwater base, there was usually a higher level of undersea animal activity than predicted by the Gaean League's researchers. Whether intentionally or not, he couldn't say. And that was close to a base that used high amounts of Geothermic energy, which animals were known to be shy of.

It was approximately three and a half thousand miles across the Cynnith Ocean from the central Terrol canal, and around a thousand more from Ccamos to the canal, so the trip was not insignificant. There were better ways to get there, but . . . well, there were those who ought to be avoided. Not all Senators needed to know that the infamous ex-captain was investigating Mani Halcyon at the source.

Some would, regardless—and indeed already did.

Eventually, he came to landfall. His instruments picked it up first, and then he saw the rising reefs and stones. Surfacing, he rose above the water and coursed over the dry sands of Tai'Xi's northwestern desert region. It was funny to think that Mei Shan, a lush land of plenty, was so close to it. The Senate taught that the entire continent was some manner of wasted space, where they could but had no need to build more bases—of which there were currently three— with little agricultural potential. Why, Zent could not figure. Perhaps they wished to let it regrow for longer without the presence of man. It was undoubtedly true that not the entire continent was as fertile as the northern sections, but it seemed that the keeping of a century-long secret was more important to the League than establishing better supply chains.

Of course, when you could just lessen the population at will to account for lower food production, he supposed that wasn't a real problem. In a way.

At last, he came upon the Gyutan Mountains, making his way up the foothills before snaking into a valley. He followed the directions he'd formed the first time he was here, around two months ago, and twisted with the mountains until he was overlooking the gargantuan crater lake. Green forest, mostly deciduous, spanned the decline all the way to the water, whose sparkling surface was largely obscured by the surrounding trees from this angle.

Long had already been notified of his coming. He took the omnicraft down to the first clearing and landed his vessel on the southern side of the city. He couldn't help glancing around at the natural beauty of the place. Mei Shan, city of beauty . . . it was a fitting name, even if he was not equipped to understand anymore of the original native language. If indeed it was the native tongue here, for they said there were many even in each continent in ages past.

Curious humans approached to look at the vessel, eyes widening upon seeing him. He gave them a greeting, receiving nervous smiles or bows in return. He spotted a couple of younglings—no, children—who gaped at him before ducking back behind their mother's skirts. They didn't look too dissimilar from Mani's population, except for the fact that their skin and hair colors were as wide-ranging as the Hellebes gene pool itself. How had they gotten such a large sample of humans, and how had they avoided blending into one single ethnic homogeny by this point? Zent had never claimed to be a geneticist.

One man, blond and with just a bit of a belly, stepped forward and said "Colonel Zent?"

Zent stepped up to him, seeing only a hint of hesitance in his eye. He had seen Hellebes before in his day. "Well met . . ."

"Marge, sir. Governor Marge."

Zent raised his eyebrows. "Governor, eh? So your Senator really is trying to modernize. Come on out, men."

His escort of five Hellebes stepped out of the omnicraft, bearing the various supplies they had brought. The craft was a larger one, containing a fair amount of cargo space. When the Senator arrived, they'd go over the placement of the men, who would be staying for protective purposes and to assist with the construction of outposts in the area. Each was specialized in his own field of tech, and would be receiving additional supply drops over the next few weeks for the construction efforts. Zehl was a geologist, Recco a biochemist, Staggs a metallurgist, Argo a mechanical engineer, Philos an architect. The next to be sent over were weapons experts and soldiers to train the human men.

Soon, Long appeared, shuffling out from somewhere or other. He looked as old and worn-out as the last time Zent had seen him. It was hard to believe Lyn's stories of his combat prowess, for she described him as a man who had pushed his physical body to its limits, the very uppermost thresholds, and could go toe-to-toe with the other Elites, or even surpass them. He had trained Lyn, and she'd subsequently taken down old Strongs all by herself, so he believed it.

"Hello, young man," he said white beard rippling as he tucked his chin in a quick show of deference.

Zent made his best approximation of the traditional eastern bow, learned from Lyn, prompting a chuckle from the old Senator. "My Lord, here are our specialists as promised."

His team saluted the ancient Senator, and Zehl said, "It's a pleasure to meet you, Senator."

Long gave a small chuckle. "Former Senator, thank you. It has been a while. Very well, Colonel Zent. We'll try our best here. I think these Hellebes and I can get well enough acquainted."

Zent nodded. "I'll be stealing Zehl for a bit, however."

"Ah, yes. That is well."

Zent saluted Long, and the team made quick work of unloading the vessel. Then the geologist followed his colonel back to the omnicraft, and they took off eastward. "Sir. What are we looking for exactly?" the scientist asked.

"I was hoping you could help me with that."

Zehl surveyed the land outside the window. "Hard to see much through these trees, sir."

"Then we'll just have to get through them. I know it's on the east side of the city." It was hard to call the primitive gathering place of humans a city, but technically Ccamos classified it as such, for the League was supposed to have nine cities, and this was all that was left from the bombings one hundred years ago. Still, it was remarkable, and Zent wondered what the Senate and their close officials would truly think if they could see present-day Mei Shan and how beautiful it was.

They located a small clearing and landed the omnicraft, disembarking to study the area. Forest litter was all over, looking mostly untouched despite being a little over a mile from the main residential area. But Long had said that these ruins lay mostly untouched. He'd spoken the truth. However . . .

"I don't see any actual ruins," Zehl said. "That is, none that are obvious." He kicked what appeared to be a moss-covered rock, scraping off the mossy layer to reveal intricate working on the stone. "And here we have our first hint." The geologist knelt to inspect the stone, and Zent followed, leaning over as he took out a specialized tool. Scraping at the moss, he used the tool to drill carefully into the rock in a few places.

Zent left him to his research while he himself perused the area further. Bumps and mounds scattered about indicated more of the carved stone.

asdf

- Chapter 20 -

Growth

Finhal 1, 1294:

We thought Creation to be a fixed, an immovable thing. Is it pride to think that Man cannot change his world? I must wonder if, in a way, that is the case, wherein one pride says that we are masters of all, holding the power of evolution in our hands via magic and technology, while another . . . another says that we have always existed, that we received an immovable inheritance at the dawn of Creation, and that protecting it is a sacred duty.

— From Lhinde's Vault

[Maybe make this Chapter 2]

Yes, just like that, whispered the voice of Mani. *Hold it steady. Now shape. Shape it.*

I am well aware! Rhidea hissed back. The Wandering Mage, at age 201, was losing her patience with the so-called Heart of Mani.

And that is well. See, you are molding the lump as deftly as a Silversmith. But now grow *it.*

She drew in a breath, refraining from making a response. The planetary entity had been telling her of this ability for some time now, stressing its importance. *Like . . . like this?* She attempted to pull on the silver shape with her mind. Its form was arbitrary and multi-limbed at the moment, but she tried to pull it from within and achieve what Mani was looking for.

Nay, such efforts will produce nothing.

She sighed, setting down the silver on her desk. She was seated in her new office in Redufiel Castle, on the same floor as Archlord Domon. Not a bad little room, furnished sparsely just as she liked it, outfitted with a serviceable bed and good lighting via a candelabra. Once, she would have been fuming, and even fearful, at having to stay so close to the black lord, but the paradigm had changed drastically in the last six months. She still hated him inside, but at this point she was uncertain if that hatred even originated from her. Perhaps Mani hated him more, though they had both learned to deal with the traitorous emperor. So far he had not attempted to backstab her, nor to renege on the alliance he had made with Nytaea and the other outlier nations of Argent.

Would that change when he at last returned?

Focus, red one.

That one was new. He was getting more robust personality, and had been experimenting with quirky ways to refer to people. Though perhaps that was just the ordinary way he referred to people by their traits. Again, she made no reply. She tried to probe inside the piece of silver, but could not find any seed of growth that she could manipulate or encourage.

It is not the silver itself, Vessel. Remember that. It is my power that gives it shape and growth.

Right . . . that sounded easy to say, not to mention impossible. But impossible was what she'd been attempting to do for a long while. She tried to look within, at Mani's presence, and feel beneath her toward where the core of the moon lay somewhere far beneath. Under that vast expanse, Mani had originated. Or had . . . grown. It was the titan's ability, which he had taken from Gaea. She still knew little of his history, as he was as good or better at hiding things as she was from him.

Ah, yes . . . so I may be.

He was also adept at reading thoughts. Blast that creature. If creature he was.

Speak to it. Our powers were given by the power of voice, and are themselves tied to voice.

Now you tell me . . . No, that wasn't right. He'd told her this before, probably all of this. Voice . . . but what did he mean. She attempted to focus her thoughts toward the clump of silver, as she did when communicating with Mani. *Change. Shape yourself. Grow and bloom.*

She felt something. She could not say whether it actually moved or she simply felt a stir in her mind—or with her mind. *Silver?* She felt foolish for the thought, almost a plea for an answer, yet it was more a question for herself or Mani, an expression of curiosity. Had it worked?

No. But that was closer. You felt something, no?

Something. But I know not what. Is this how it was when you first tried it?

She rarely spoke so frankly with the being, and was half expecting an evasive answer, but after a moment the response came: *My earliest workings with silver were long ago, before coming here. On Gaea, there is no spell silver, and it was I who first made it into what we know on Mani today. The two are very different types. But the ability was almost useless on my Mother's planet, for she has very little silver. The gift itself was a trick, almost a joke, for I was not granted the ability to grow anything—only one metal.*

Only one metal . . . Rhidea hid this thought from Mani, or seemed to. These were the first words from him in some time that sparked questions she had yet to answer. Her fascination was piqued. *Who granted this ability to you? And what of your sister, Luna? What is her ability?*

Proliferation, he replied. *Duplication. As I've told you. From her spread the Cydenges, formed after the first Cydenges. As for the one who grants these gifts, and who made us in the beginning . . . it is so long ago that I can only just recall.*

Cydenges . . . the Silver Beasts, or so she'd thought before becoming the willing pawn of a moon god. But it was more complex than that. She had not simply given over to him, not without good reason.

These thoughts he did pick up on. *Yes . . . the Silver Beasts. Surely I've told you about them before? They are Gaea's plague, not mine. Luna is my rival, but not one who seeks this moon. She cannot come here. She envies our mother's world, as do I in a way. Perhaps I'm not as . . . aggressive about it. But the true Silver Beast—he could spell my demise.*

Indeed. Do you believe he will set foot on Mani? What will happen if he does?

An impression of distinct annoyance crossed her mind, and she was satisfied with the results of her prompting. *You make it out as though I am afraid, Daughter of Silver. Just because I take defensive measures does not mean*

I fear. Not for the people, nor my presence here, but for my body.

Body . . . another thing he had spoken of before without great clarification. Mani had a way of "explaining" something by mentioning it once or twice. Henceforth, he seemed to assume she was on track. Still, she could not see into his mind, if indeed mind it was. Whatever consciousness inhabited her silver world, the force that was Silver itself . . . that was Mani. *But these dreams . .* she'd been having them for a while now, premonitions of a sort. Some felt more real than others. Multiple times, she'd woken to a cry from her own throat, dripping sweat. Rarely did she recall the contents of the dreams, but on one occasion, she'd dreamt that she became a new creature, undergoing some hideous transformation into a metal monstrosity.

She shuddered just to think about it.

Mani said nothing, indicating that she had once again hidden her thoughts from him. She quickly filled the mental void with, *So . . . Growth. You still have not explained how it works for you, nor how I should succeed in replicating this feat.*

The shifting you felt was a natural response within all soul-touched silver to my touch. This indicates that you are on the right path. I have never had a Vessel like you. The boy could perhaps have progressed as far, though I did not expect him to, but you are of the old priestly line and possess the lingering power of the prior age. A sliver of it, at any rate.

That told her . . . not much. But she tried again, focusing on the lump of silver in her hand. She remolded it using her Authority, producing a smooth ingot once again. Silver could be reworked infinitely, a process she had seen many a time back in her ancient village. She had performed it little, as she had been young when Domon murdered them en masse, but she'd had a small basis to work from—and of course, centuries to perfect her craft. Mani spoke little of it, but he seemed to approve of her level of Authority. Naturally, it had increased dramatically since becoming the Vessel—not necessarily in knowledge, but in sheer power. She was no longer an offshoot of the planet, she was the voice of the planet.

Something stirred again in the metal, a vibration, a resonance tingling against her mind. She felt it move, but only with her mind. Concentrating harder, she began to feel something in her hand as well, though it could be a trick of the senses. Mankind was only meant to have five. She opened her eyes to see the silver squirming, not exactly by intent. But in its shifting, she could feel it—yes—a warmth as of life.

Yes, that is it . . . stoke it, speak to it.

Unsure how, she did so, communicating on some primal level with the metal. It was a small exchange, too deep for words, sounding to her like a low rumbling of thunder. It caused her ears to pop and her eyes to defocus momentarily. She shut them out of discomfort. She didn't know what she communicated to the silver, only that it was some manner of encouragement, as though it were a living thing that she were cheering on in a competition.

Then she felt it, truly. Her weight shifted as its mass increased, and she opened her eyes for the first time to see glinting metal spiral from her hand—in uncontrolled directions, no less. She cried out with a flash of fear as she saw the thin spines curling around her arm, threatening to pierce skin. *Will it hurt me? Can it?*

Possibly. It is hard to say. You can stop it again with your voice, but it is not easy once the process is begun.

Now you tell me . . . Rhidea tried to do so achieving a suitable level of nothing, and then began to shake her arm in panic, dropping the morphed ingot. But its branching horns caught her arm, digging in instead of letting it fall. And they continued to curl, some threads piercing her skin and continuing through. She groaned, gritting her teeth against the agony. She didn't want to alert the palace guard, as she'd rather not tip Domon off to her experiments. Not yet, anyway.

Her eyes widened as she watched the growing spiral reach its way up her arm, tugging and shredding her sleeve and producing small rivulets of scarlet. *What do I do?* she asked her patron, but he was silent as if in fascination. *Mani! Advise! Do something about this silver!*

She felt only an inkling of a father observing a child while pondering when he should step in to stop her from hurting herself. Calmly as she could, she did what she knew and pulled on the Silver, retracting its thorns. It worked to an extent, allowing her to negate its weight and pull out some of its branches, moving its growth away from her, but she couldn't accurately stop it.

The pain was excruciating, and only increasing as more skin tore. She couldn't free herself without self-inflicting even further pain. Even as she tried, a branch of the metal burrowed deep and sprouted within her flesh. She felt it brush on her bone like a scrape of metal on metal, setting her to shivering, and she finally cried out uncontrollably.

Sooner than she'd have thought possible, someone was there, dressed in a dark robe. Domon. He swept in, shouting, perceiving no response, and quickly summoned a dark flame. Something in her head hissed at its sight, or its presence, recoiling as though from a venomous serpent. *Get it out, get it out, get it out!* was all that ran through her head, and she could not say if it came out her mouth or not.

Then she was blasted with heat. Or rather, the metal was. A cool heat familiar to her now, and then a surging wave of dark energy. Mani's hissing grew stronger, and suddenly she felt the growth in her arm stop. The pain did not.

"My lady! Are you all right?" asked the Archlord, a question which at another time would have been a shock to hear.

All she said in reply was, "I'm—I'm not sure." She sank to her knees, clutching her silver woven right arm, which clanked on the ground. *Got to . . . get it off.* She tried to work at the silver, retracting it, but the pain it brought was too much, causing her head to swim dizzily. She shook her head, blinking at tears. She opened her mouth to say something else, but she cut off that along with the silverwork.

"You're losing blood quickly! What do you want me to do?" the Archlord hissed in her ear, close to frantic.

"Just—agh!—don't know . . ." *Mani, you filthy moon beast, you did this to me! How can I be rid of this agony?*

We will try regrowth. It is . . . good . . . that the Black Soul was there to neutralize my silver, else you might have been devoured without me able to stop it. He seemed loath to express appreciation for Domon's Dark art. Even as he said it, she finally felt the healing force of Mani, which she had already experienced during various experiments, starting from her shoulder down, gradually healing her as he seemingly pulled the silver out himself.

She began to gasp in pain once more after a few inches, clutching madly at her arm. *Stop! Stop! Too fast.*

We only have so long, daughter. This silver will become part of you if left too long.

She didn't like how little he seemed to be bothered by that possibility.

Domon was saying something else to her, but she only shook her head weakly in some form of answer. Her vision was darkening ever so slowly, along with her senses. She could no longer move any limbs, nor feel the trickle of blood issuing from her dominant arm. In the background someone shouted. *Just . . . shut up, at least. Why the noise?*

She awoke with a flash, eyelids wide, glancing around. She couldn't move her neck. Or . . . no, she could, it was just unearthly stiff. Her limbs, too. She lay in a bed, draped with a white sheet, and seemed to have some foreign dress on underneath. Wiggling her right arm and receiving only pain in reply, she glanced that way and immediately gasped. She would have scrambled up in her bed, but her legs weren't quite responding, so her reaction was likely very comical and turtle-like, including a painful amount of abdominal spasms.

Her arm. Mani . . . what had he done to it? Or had Domon's doctors . . . ? No, no, they couldn't have. It was Mani.

Her entire right arm was gone at the shoulder, and in its place was a silver sculpture, eerily resembling her arm. It had joints at the elbow, wrist and fingers, which she could move after a moment of concentration and careful manipulation. They bent like the fingers of some machine, yet there was a natural quality to it, and the metal itself had to stretch, doing so seamlessly. At the shoulder, the arm had apparently attached to her bone and now fit over the skin like a cuff.

Sitting up slowly, she rotated both arms, testing her new one's motion along with the other. It was just a hair heavier, so there would be balance issues at first, but not as much as she'd have expected. *Mani?* she said in wonder, *is this your doing?*

The voice of the moon returned to her after a few seconds. *No less, daughter. It was apparent that the surgeons would have to remove your appendage, at which point I began prepping your body for self-growth.*

Self-growth . . . were you aiming for this the entire time? She should have been, and indeed wanted to be, angrier than she could muster at the moment.

Not exactly. I intentionally pushed your body, but not in such a way. I will admit, however, that I tarried long in observing the silver as it overtook your arm. For this, I apologize. It was fascinating to watch, and to feel.

Why was my body not able to force it out and heal quickly? I am supposed to be able to heal rapidly now, right?

Two problems: You yourself awakened the silver, so your body did not recognize it as a threat. Almost more like . . . a child? Furthermore, once it had penetrated your skin to the bone, your body began to fuse with it. I now see that this is a dangerous phenomenon, for you could theoretically bond yourself so to the entire world, or at least a continent, and feel pain throughout Mani's entirety, at which point even I could not help you.

Well, it's a good thing Domon's physicians were there to rid me of the excess silver.

Indeed. Your new alliance is at times useful. I cannot be certain, but I believe it has been around a week since our experiment. It was hard to be aware of your body's surroundings during your slumber, but I detected surprise when they initially found your arm to be reforming itself through the stitched skin, but I believe the Black Soul saw it and was pleased, seeing that the growth was controlled and . . . shall we say, natural.

Rhidea sat up straighter, reaching carefully behind her head to smooth back her hair. She admired the graceful artistry of the new arm's making, how its form changed as she bent it, wondering at how she seemed to automatically use Silver Authority to operate it. The Authority granted by her symbiosis with Mani, not that which she'd been born with. Glancing down, she beheld the stitching along her right side that held her dull red garment together. A medical garment, she thought, crafted to be easily fit on a sleeping patient. She hoped he paid his doctors well.

Just then, a nurse came in and gasped upon seeing her awake. "Oh! My Lady, you're awake! Are you well?"

Rhidea nodded. "Can you fetch the emperor?"

"He is already on his way." The woman hurried over to her and felt her forehead, then—carefully—her shoulder. As Rhidea subtly indicated her approval, the nurse ran her hand down the metal arm, mouth moving in silent wonder. She stood up and backed away a pace. "It's . . . miraculous. You really are the Blessed Lady."

Rhidea raised an eyebrow. She'd heard that phrase somewhere before lately. "Thank you for your services."

"It was nothing, My Lady," the woman said, curtsying. She headed out, and was shortly replaced by the tall, blond Archlord-turned-emperor, Domon.

"Lady Rhidea." The greeting was spoken in not only his new pseudo-respectful tone, but this time in relieved awe. "I'm glad to see you made a full recovery. But what exactly happened to you?"

I'll bet you are . . . unless you thought there was a chance you could take my place. "Yes, well—" she swung her legs out of bed, tentatively testing her balance as she rotated her new arm, flexing the fingers "—you could say it was an experiment between me and Mani. I'm still trying to figure out if he wanted this or not. Care to try it out with an arm-wrestling match?"

- Chapter 21 -

Growth and Regrowth

Finhal 1, 1294
Anothe.
— From Lhinde's Vaul

Mydia stroked the shaggy bark of the golden tree to which she'd given birth feeling its refreshing coolness on her smooth skin. Though coarse-looking, the pale bark did not chafe against the skin, but almost seemed to encourage such stroking through its otherworldly interaction with touch.

The tree was even bigger now, two weeks later, though only by a few inches near the base. The whole height of it had thickened, the bark peeling away from the trunk in thick chunks—which had proven surprisingly tough to pull off, and quickly lost their luster after doing so—and its branches had only grown in density and leafage. This created an interesting phenomenon whereby it blocked out an overwhelming portion of Sol's light and that of the auroras from the city, whilst giving off a warming light consistently. Many complaints had arisen due to this, but the people were beginning to adjust. It was perhaps similar to if one of the fantastical beasts which she and her mage entourage had conjured for the battle had suddenly come to life and dwelt as a public pet in Nytaea. Such a wonder may cause disruption, but the sheer novelty of it and the awe it inspired were well worth it.

Of course, now she had all manner of attention on her. How had their queen performed such a magnificent feat? What magic had she hidden inside all her life? Was House Kalceron as powerful as her father used to claim? For her brother Kallyn had been a High Mage of such caliber that Governor Edrius had bragged to all the world, taking credit for both fathering and teaching the young man.

If ever the world had sighed in relief at a man's death, it was her father's.

"But what *are* you?" she murmured to the great tree, almost as one speaks to a favored steed. How had it sprouted and grown? What magical seed within her had sparked it? She knew that it was her great anguish which had fueled it, somehow, but . . . the best her mage scholars could come up with was that Mani was changing, and this was one of perhaps many signs to come. Already, there were reports coming in of strange things—hills turning into mountains, earthquakes in peaceful plains, and sudden plant growth in the arid wilderness of Dotham.

This in turn gave rise to differing theories: One was that Mani's magic was returning in force, following perhaps something that Lyn had done or even the Archlord, such as the destruction of the Gate to Gaea. Mydia herself balked at the thought of that . . . Or the return was a sign of the times, as they were entering the final year in the "countdown" to which Domon had drawn attention. This was increasingly becoming a topic in their councils, for the fact could not be ignored that no one knew what may come when the year 1,000 was reached. For the longest time, Mani's general population had chugged along, heedless of the years, with only a handful at all speculating on what may come with the turn of the new millennium. For Mani was a blessed world filled with the privileged and the oppressed—those too blessed by Magic to pursue further greatness for humanity, and those who saw it as a curse, but nonetheless endeavored not to seek a new world.

Gaea was the missing key. Now that the planet had entered public consciousness, rumors and theories were circulating. Sadly, a lot of the knowledge being passed around was as much a lie as ever, though the mere existence of another world was a new standard for such discussion. A springboard for all manner of fantasies.

"Lady Kalceron," came a resonant voice from behind her.

The queen started, pivoting to see the familiar face of Ethas Gandel, blond hair trimmed shorter than he once kept it. His attire was trim and almost militaristic, a quality she admired for its earnestness. Beside him stood his wife, Lady Aldyr Gandel, the dark-haired noblewoman often called the most beautiful of the court. Her makeup, though meticulous, gave a look of noble, natural beauty, accentuated by her casually graceful earrings. Mydia was often jealous not for her features, nor her pristine outward appearance, but for the fact that she did it all with no handmaids at all.

"Ethas, Aldyr," she said with a gracious head-bob. It was not necessary, but she knew how her tendency toward less formal greetings grated on him. She was pretty sure he understood, however, that this came from no disrespect on her part—simply a discomfort with court customs. They were equals, after all.

"'Tis a wonder, no?" said the tall lord, further approaching the golden giant. His face held respect for the power symbolized by the tree, and the same fascination that captivated most people who tried to understand it. Of course, she broadly considered this a mistake, but at least he didn't look on her with the same wonder. In fact, none of it. He saw rightly that she had not made this by sheer personal power, but that the right chances had aligned.

"What brings you out here, Ethas?"

He glanced her way, expressionless. "A few things. The new councilors wish to meet soon to discuss ____—"

"Julia informed me."

"—And there is the matter of Torlega and Yan'Vala."

Mydia's eyes brightened. "Did Yan'Vala finally send their response?"

He paused and shook his head. "Not yet. But they pose a similar problem to the Torlegans, as you understand. They are uncertainties."

"And," she began, then stopped for a short breath to compose herself. "As I've said, we should take all offers of parley in good faith."

"That is well. But that doesn't answer the problem. If you let a dangerous animal into your home, one is obligated at least to take certain precautions."

"Then what are you suggesting?"

"An armed retinue as a reception. A show of force. Triple the guard detail."

"We didn't even do that for Ti'Vaeth!"

"Correct, but Ti'Vaeth agreed to a standard treaty discussion between representatives. They did not come out and announce that they'd be bringing half their army."

Mydia nodded slowly. "Well, we can post extra mage soldiers at least. That will look like a show of formality. An army to meet them will just seem overly defensive."

There was another pause, wherein Aldyr cleared her throat and said, "If I may, I think you are both correct on this matter. Nytaea cannot be taken lightly as a world power, but at the same time we can't afford to make unnecessary enemies. A moderate answer would probably be the best."

Ethas glanced over at his wife as she spoke, then turned back to the Queen. "A mage-oriented approach may be best, then. I will speak to Straif. There remains one more matter . . . Cae Rhidea. How long since you tried to contact her?"

Mydia pulled her lips into a grimace. "Too long. A few weeks now." She would have tried more often, but a deep and intensifying sense of foreboding had taken all joy and anticipation from the notion. The mage was surely busy, of course, but they needed to know more of the events in Redufiel.

Rhidea had called on Mydia one month ago, shortly following the raid on Nytaea, expounding on the old news that she was working with Domon. Previously, she'd given the excuse that she was working on him and did not expect to get anywhere fast. This time, they'd gotten more detail: Experiments were being made between the two High Magi on the interplay between Silver and Dark, and Rhidea was now on the Umbra Council. Lieda and a new addition, one Solomiya, were acting as Domon's personal agents, while his military still actively worked to suppress and discourage rioting and the like.

But she had expressed desire to visit Nytaea again soon. In regards to her visit, Mydia had to tell him, Rhidea had said nothing more.

Ethas grunted in dissatisfaction. She knew that he did not trust the woman. He'd met her on many an occasion, and each time had confronted her with frank questions. He looked at her as a bully who used her personal potency of magic as a tool to get whatever she wanted at the moment. He didn't believe in, or at least feared, rogue forces that could not be pinned down or taken neatly into account.

Worst of all, she shared some of that fear.

Just then, Ethas jolted, reaching a hand into his coat pocket. "It's the wall guards."

Mydia's own Reality Crystal began to resonate as well, and she looked eastward, toward the aurora-lit horizon whence Sol would soon show its first glimmer. A voice came through the crystal: "Your Majesty! It's her."

Time sped up, and the next few minutes happened in a feverish blur. Horns sounded from the walls, and Ethas Gandel cursed, turning and calling to soldiers. A silver light flashed above them, some ten paces out from the tree, resolving into the floating form of Rhidea of Randhorn, bedecked in a flowing black dress and scarf that whipped in the wind. One soldier loosed his crossbow bolt at her, and Mydia cried out in dismay despite knowing it would be harmless. The High Mage deflected it without so much as raising a hand, and the soldier gasped upon seeing the invader's face. He dropped to his knee.

The silvery glow was still fading from Rhidea as she hovered in the air. She slowly lowered herself toward the ground, turning her gaze upon Rhidea and her coregent. "Mydia Kalceron. Ethas Gandel." She touched down on one of the roots, seemingly oblivious to the stunned eyes on her, the torches and crossbows lining up to wall her in, and the wary gazes of Nytaea's foremost leaders.

But in Mydia's case, her shocked and distrustful stare did not last long, melting in the face of overwhelming joy. It was perhaps only Ethas' hand on her shoulder that stopped her from rushing to Rhidea's side and burying her face in that thick scarlet hair. "Rhidea . . ." Mydia said slowly, finally taking in a shocking detail. Her right arm was missing, replaced by an appendage of purest silver, which seemed to move naturally with her. A creation of magic? "Your arm! What happened to you?"

The woman glanced down at it as though just remembering about it. "Ah, this. It's a long story, my dear."

"Do you come in peace?" Ethas demanded, wife held close to his side. "Your coming was most . . . sudden, and I must know whether to reprimand this soldier for his instinctive reaction."

Rhidea gave the humiliated man the barest glance. "It is nothing. But I do. I come in peace, and also on behalf of Archlord Domon."

"That is what I am wary of," Ethas said warningly.

The woman waved a hand almost dismissively. "Do not be. We can speak as soon as you like. Do you wish to call your council together? Queen Mydia?"

Mydia glanced at her colleague, nodding subtly. She knew he would not be impressed by any show of familiarity between them, and was content to let him give the obvious answer: "Yes. That would be good." He began giving out orders to fetch the proper representatives to meet at the strategy discussion room.

While Ethas was turned away, Mydia dashed over and embraced her favorite mentor, receiving a warm reply. The regent's disapproval was immediate, and he even called her name, but he quickly cut off with a glance at the soldiers, seeing that reproving their Queen in front of them was unwise. Mydia unlatched herself from the Wandering Mage and looked up into her face. "You know you're going to have to tell me all about it."

"Indeed," she replied with a wan smile. She appeared very tired, and distinctly off-beat, although that should be expected given her great expenditure of energy in getting here through Reality Authority. "You used our linked system to travel here? Oliver has been hard at work on setting that up."

Rhidea gave a slow nod that seemed to communicate an unwillingness to admit that she had not known that. Then she said, "I'd heard rumors. Let us say I wouldn't be so eager to risk offending my new . . . compatriot."

That sounded far more like the Rhidea that Mydia knew. The Rhidea of old times.

"And that sums up my recent interactions with him on Darsor," Rhidea said in closing to her exposition on events in Redufiel.

Secretary Keuda continued scrawling frantically on her sheet of parchment until well into the first comment, which came from Marshal Enchro: "Lady, one finds this all a bit hard to swallow, except for your . . . metal addition. May I?"

She gave a small nod which, on anyone else, would have looked embarrassed, and proffered her reflective appendage, allowing the aging man to squeeze and tap the metal, working and unworking the fingers. She briefly flexed them, and he gave a sharp exhale of breath at the strength of her grip. Finally, satisfied, he huffed and said, "Well, I'll be. Don't mind me, ladies and gentlemen."

"And you said this latest experiment occurred when?" Keuda asked, half-glancing up from her parchment with pen paused just above her inkwell.

"Not the latest, but the latest significant one by far. Soldor the tenth."

The small woman gave a sharp nod and jotted the date down.

"In short," Ethas said, "You come in the name of Archlord Domon to get us to sign this one-sided alliance?"

"I have not gotten to the alliance part," she corrected him. She added no honorific, as usual. Mydia could not recall her ever addressing a ruler with an honorific, save for King Fenwel of Nemental. "And it is nothing final nor demanding. For it is as much I who want to work with you as Domon."

Mydia spoke for the first time since the woman began her discourse. "Rhidea, your account of Mani and your deal with him . . . it is troubling, to say the least. I understand that it was necessary and pivotal in your securing Domon's cooperation, we of Nytaea cannot help but see that it was not we who allied with him . . . nor King Fenwel."

"As I said, child, this broader alliance of great importance to me, and I have gone out of my way to return alone to Nytaea to work this out for the good of all involved, and hopefully all of Mani."

"Lady Rhidea," Ethas said, stepping forward from his place next to the Queen. "You will address the Queen of Nytaea as befits her station."

There followed a moment of shocked silence, during which Lord Gandel stared down the Wandering Mage. While Mydia would never have asked for such a defense, and he reminded her in this moment too much of her overprotective Queensguard, who stood watch outside the door . . . she had to admire his bravery.

Rhidea, for her part, looked away first, eyeing the other occupants of the room as if to decide whether to show weakness in front of them. The question was: Did she consider humility to be weakness? Eventually, she said, "I have no issue with formality, Lord Gandel. I have walked this continent for perhaps longer than is good for me. And given this situation, it is fitting."

Ethas looked at Mydia, who shrugged, trying to suggest to him that he should take that as a victory and move on. He did, to his credit. "Then perhaps we ought to discuss this alliance now. But of course, Lady Rhidea, you understand that we may require further clarification on certain points in order to move forward with the proceedings."

"Of course, My Lord."

The words sounded so foreign coming from the ancient mage's mouth. The group of a dozen moved into a mode of negotiation that began, to no one's surprise, with some proposals of Rhidea's from the Archlord/Emperor. These were picked apart, questioned, and thoroughly pressed by the other party. Rhidea's first proposal was as follows: Nytaea should become an official of ally of both the Kystrean Empire and the new Darsorian Empire, aiding Domon's expanding empire there with good weapons and—most importantly—magi to help protect Darsor from the Gaean invaders. When prodded on this, however, she revealed the many stipulations on which Domon insisted. She then gave an alternate, which was a simple agreement of peace, opening the doors of Nytaea and those lands in the Archlord's dominion to exchange further offers and trades as needed.

Mydia and Ethas, among others, pushed for an alliance with set rules and mutual protections, but also informed her of the expected arrival of the Torlega and Yan'Vala ambassadors. Rhidea, for whatever reason, had yet to call on Nemental, but she heartily agreed that Fenwel should be allowed a say in the negotiations. Indeed, it seemed Domon, or at least Rhidea herself, expected that the outlier nations would inevitably band together to form a more cohesive second party to the alliance negotiations.

Thus, time would be required. Rhidea conceded, realizing that such negotiations were rarely made overnight. Perhaps she also considered it fair considering how long she had stayed in Redufiel with the Archlord.

The meeting was adjourned on the agreement that the same council would meet on the morrow to discuss further points of contention, but also that Rhidea had other matters of great import to discuss with Mydia and her closest advisors. The first thing the woman said to the Queen upon leaving the room was, "We have to speak more about this tree."

Her directness and earnestness spoke the same feeling that Mydia had regarding Rhidea's mysterious pact with Mani last year. Yet there was more . . . she felt a butterfly swarm in her stomach in anticipation of their conversation. This was not the same Rhidea she knew. Just as . . . just as the Kaen she had said goodbye to was not the same Kaen who had snuck into the Palace two years hence to rescue his dear little sister.

"Rhidea, would you like to speak over dinner?" she found herself asking, yet surprised at the words. It just felt the right thing to ask of this honored dignitary, or perhaps a distant relative in town for an event—as though that was all the woman was to her. It was fitting, the formal way to offer hospitality to a dignitary or individual of such fame as she—yet it felt wrong.

Rhidea surprised her by considering it for a moment and then responding with a shake of her head. "I'd come to a dinner, if you have the time and resources for such things, but I believe it would be better to discuss in private."

"We-we can do that, Rhi—Lady Rhidea," Mydia stammered, feeling a flush of heat in her cheeks at her awkward speech.

Rhidea seemed not to notice. "Good. When will you be available?"

Mydia took a long breath, glancing at the swirl of people around her, some making small talk, others hurrying out, others like her guardsmen simply watching her and Rhidea. "Right now. Before I get busy."

She had neither the desire nor the schedule to be so busy later. Rather . . . she knew it was better to confront the mage now than later.

"Excellent. How busy are the Palace Gardens this time of the day?"

- Chapter 22 -

Zent

Finhal 1, 1294
Anothe
— From Lhinde's Vaul

I don't like prison.

- Chapter 23 -

Argent History

Finhal 1, 1294:
Another
— From Lhinde's Vault

"Syneria, look at this."

It was Viktor Amma, her associate at the Randhorn Mage Association, a dark-haired young man with whom she'd recently been on an adventure at the center of the earth. He pointed at the tome he had open, then the rubbing he'd been poring over, taken from the giant stone monoliths in the Down Under.

"Hmm?" She eyed his work, trying to see why it was worth disturbing her.

"This phrase here: Aurus tu Kassys Luna. I believe that is 'Luna, Mother of Gold.'"

"Okay . . ." she shivered involuntarily, uncertain why "But why is that—"

"And along with 'Mani, Father of Silver,' we have a very interesting pair here," he said excitedly. "Given what we've already translated. Mani and Luna would either be two different moons, or two different entities, as in 'The Heart of Mani.'"

"Wait, do you have that whole section done already? We're going to have to go back down there soon, aren't we?"

Again, excited nodding.

"Then let me see!" she demanded, louder than she meant. Other scholars lifted their heads, and she bowed her own, embarrassed at having forgotten the rule for a moment.

He showed her his sheet of parchment on which he'd scrawled the translation for one entire column of High Legaleian etched on one of the most prominent stone slabs deep under the continents. Embedded into the soil of the falls, they would need to be excavated somehow in order to read the whole of the writings. Thus it was technically only a part, a piece. It rea:

Thus did Mani, Father of Silver, abandon those who rejected his insight, accepting his exile, and we with him. The Anyr took their revenge for Luna, Mother of Gold—her great betrayal—and rejected the Font of Life along with Growth itself. Two forces inexplicably tied yet at odds, doomed to inhabit the Lesser Moon for . . .

That was the end of the readable message. The next word was a total guess. "Huh. Lesser Moon . . . she mused. Is that the same word King Fenwel used to talk about, an old word for Mani?"

"Yes, that's right," came a voice from two seats down at the long table, Stessa Valiant. "I remember that. Didn't that play into Lady Rhidea's theories about Gaea?"

It did . . . Syneria recalled, replaying information in her head. "So if Mani is a personification of this moon, or world, then Luna is the personification of another. Lesser . . . and presumably greater. Silver and Gold. That's . . . not a little scary, I do say."

Heads nodded in reply. Finally, a breakthrough after days of study. "Good work, Viktor," she said grudgingly.

"What is the latest word from Lady Rhidea?" asked Stessa. "You traveled with her once, Syneria? And that 'Lyn of Nytaea' woman?"

"Pfft. Once. That was years ago." Even as she said the words, her mind was trailing off. She dipped her quill pen for some more scrawlings and then . . . just held it there, letting the gooey black stuff drip. She hadn't mentioned it in a while, but was pretty sure most of the scholars here knew, that she was now related to King Regent Ethas Gandel, though she spoke rarely of her sister Aldyr. At first, the news had been too exciting to be kept to herself, but then she'd seen the way it got her more whispers than friends. She'd stopped, and they'd barely mentioned it as well. Being a scribe or scholar was no glorious work, and knowing your peer was better than you made it no more pleasurable for anyone.

"Neer dear?" Stessa caught her attention again by way of her nickname.

Syneria could swear she did that just because it rhymed.

"Hmm?"

"Rhidea—any word from her of late?"

"She's . . . I believe she's coming to the castle tonight." Syneria only knew from overhearing the staff talk of it. She had no connection with the Lady of Silver, the Wandering Mage herself. As she spoke the words now, the general sentiment regarding the mage—much changed from years previous—was laid bare. It started with niggling, doubt, and quiet questioning, but was now visible as apprehension . . . worry, perhaps even fear.

"Oy," came a low voice from the eastern doorway, and Syneria recognized Cort Flanning and Leo Sable without even looking up. The latter was an established mage scholar of Fire specialty who bore a distinctive limp, and thus could be detected by his uneven, thumping gait. "It's all quiet in here," Cort commented with amusement. "Like you're all at work or something, even though it sounded quite animated a moment ago."

_____, the only one who actually had been at work the entire time, looked up only to shush him. Cort looked a bit abashed, but still sauntered up, approaching Syneria and saying in a lower voice, "She'll be arriving soon, and the king wants a report on your progress with the monolith writings for her."

"Oh! Very well." She looked at Viktor. "Catch that?"

He nodded.

It took them some fifteen minutes to gather their scrolls and rubbings and order them as neatly as possible, making some hasty last copies to tie things up well enough. "Are we bringing these with us?" he asked.

She returned a shrug. How should she know.

It wasn't long before the air in the castle changed and they became aware of a general buzz of excitement, which had bubbled over into murmuring and hubbub. She was here. Sure enough, a servant came and asked for Syneria by name. She immediately followed him all the way to the main audience hall, where she caught sight of the woman.

She looked . . . different. Taller than she remembered, more vividly bright in her magical aura that all High Magi faintly carried about them. But that wasn't right, it was something more insidious, perhaps less innocuous. Her face almost seemed different. The woman turned a silver-eyed gaze upon her, voluminous red hair rustling at her neck, and suddenly smiled. It was a purposeful smile with little warmth, but was still enough to prompt a similar reply from Syneria. "Hello, Miss Tolruin."

Why did she feel so uncomfortable right now? "My Lady," she replied with a curtsy.

Rhidea turned back to the grey-headed King Fenwel, apparently too busy to wave dismissively at the formality like usual. "I'm glad my contributions from the Academy have been of service."

"Quite the dears, yes," the king said, shuffling over to put an arm on Syneria's shoulder. A heavy one . . . was he getting more frail, or simply not noticing the burden of literature she already carried.

"Let us see your work, child," Rhidea said briskly, waving the golden-haired girl over to a table near the east side of the hall.

Syneria gladly removed herself from the king's leaning pose and brought her things over, setting them down with a muffled *thump.* "These are all we've managed to rub and translate so far, Rhidea," she said, taking a calculated risk at the dropping of any honorific.

The Wandering Mage took no notice. "Excellent." Carefully, she began leafing through them and sorting the sheets and scrolls into piles, then peering at each in turn. Syneria hesitantly guided her on which to start with, even though the intended "order" of them had been hard to distinguish. Hastily, she made mention of the collection's incompleteness, how they had yet to go back and glean further from the source, not to mention any archaeology.

Rhidea simply shook her head, most likely indicating that this was fine for now. "Mani's core . . ." she murmured along with one scroll of copied text. "Okay . . . hidden, but not by intent. By necessity the center, kept watch over by the Undying Lords Argent." Her lips turned downward in satisfaction as she flipped through more, words of which Syneria and her peers had little context. They seemed to hold a bit more meaning for her, though she asked for clarification on a few terms, some of which Syneria was able to help her with.

Eventually, she set her last scroll down and stood there, head downturned for a moment, seemingly lost in thought. None interrupted her, though the king said to Syneria, "I can see she is impressed. Good work out there, dear."

Dear . . . Now they're all doing it. Or . . . no, he was the first. Stessa had gotten it from the old king first.

"Well, Rhidea?" she finally asked.

The mage rounded, piercing her with intense eyes. "Good work," she repeated. "We will have to keep at this. You are doing an important thing. I'd say the expedition was certainly worth it."

"We've already taken two. The trickiest thing by far was keeping the parchments dry."

"I can imagine. You didn't . . . Hmm. Fenwel, how are your Reality magi here? I've dealt so much with the art lately that I'm forgetting how comfortable various groups are and aren't with it. Our new crystal system is quite smooth, and I'd recommend using that to set up a travel method between the surface and the Down Under. It could also provide a means for those beneath to get out if they wanted. Did you scholars pay a visit to the village down there? Hearth?"

Syneria shook her head. "We were a bit concerned of what they might think of us, and how they might react."

She chuckled. "Only room for four passengers in your little car, I've heard. Tell me, how precisely did you manage what you did?"

Syneria related their team of four Water specialists, and the role each played. It had indeed required teamwork and a bit of bravery, but the second trip was by far and away easier.

- Chapter 24 -

The Secret of Ribsha

Manidor 2, 1295
It should almost amuse me how far my own mind has fallen from al
human ideals. Human life means fair nothing to me at this point, as the
entirety of my world revolves around transcending and replacing that dated
race. All while providing sustenance for the ever-ravenous machine o.
progress
— From Lhinde's Vaul

- After this land and/or the growing monster presence is mentioned… [Yes definitely need to mention that, perhaps both on Argent and Darsor via earlier chapters, and a small dialogue w/ Domon about it as well.

In the northern reaches of Darsor, just beyond the Corset Mountains, the land of Ribsha hid for centuries in relative peace, interacting little with the Duchy of Halstar and the surrounding lands. In the wake of Domon's conquest they had sent one representative to him: Solomiya, one of their strongest artsmasters.

Now, she was back in her home country. Just breathing in the high-elevation air here felt better. It felt normal. The central lowlands were almost terrifyingly thick with clouds, fog, water everywhere. It was not meant to be so. She had been to two of her people's two major cities, Skabeld and Asshok, with a few purposes. Her lord had sent her back with intent, despite not understanding Ribsha entirely. He only knew what they housed. Indeed, Skabeld and Asshok were known for their monsters. But there was more to the monster keeping.

Presently, she knelt on a hill just east of Asshok and felt the earth below her hand. Red and packed, dotted with sparse vegetation. This area was not particularly fertile. Below, she felt them; this was where the Sor'Vech were kept. Using her Earth Authority, she opened the door and stepped inside. She smelled strongly of a certain flower, and carried in her hand a food which only the beasts' human masters fed them. Thus they controlled them. Otherwise, the Sor'Vech were known to devour humans.

Torch in hand, she headed into the hidden tunnel. Yipping and growling came from below, at the end of a spiral. There, the sturdy wooden gate penned the creatures in. Their eyes glowed light red in the flickering torchlight, heads about waist height. They had six doglike legs and a rat's tail, thick dark skin ribbed like a hairless rodent's. The neck tapered like a horse's, but the head was what unsettled most, with two sets of ears—one pointing upward like a Renhound, one hanging down like a bloodhound—atop a long snout. The eyes were frontward and focused like a predators, but they were known to roll them sideways one at a time. Hair almost like a human's hung from either side of the jaw and neck, some of the little on their entire bodies.

Right now, they were yipping madly and throwing themselves against the wooden bars, teeth gnashing, some biting one another. They were most closely related to dogs, both bodily and in temperament, which meant that she could tame them. That was one of her specialties. Taking the treats, she tossed in a few over their heads. A few who were not able to get in amongst the scuffle and not alpha enough to try turned and whined at her, standing back on four legs and briefly two. They often raised up their front set of legs, looking a bit like the centaurs of old stories. That was not a real creature, or at least had been truly wiped from the earth if it had.

"You poor puppies," she said, face frowning long with her tone of utter sympathy. Unlike some monsters, she truly liked these beasts.

The day was coming soon, for the prophets of Ribsha warned of a hastening. Indeed, it was now the last year until the millennial time. None knew for certain what would come on the fateful day, but according to Domon . . . *No. No longer do I hear, but I have seen with my own eyes. That Wellspring of theirs hides much.*

Much, yet so little. She had given heart and soul to Archlord Domon's cause, and would not falter, but . . . that did not mean she had no personal reservations regarding some details. Now there was this deal with Rhidea, the ancient mage of Argent. She was not supposed to be a factor. Solomiya did not trust the makers of the Wellspring, she did not trust Rhidea, and she did not trust the force of Silver at work within her.

She also did not trust the little woman, the slimy cat Lieda. But that was another matter. She was ambitious but quite harmless in Solomiya's estimation. Just . . . infuriating to work with. There is a certain merit to one who does not disclose all of the workings of the heart to the world, and then there was . . . well, Lady Lieda—one who, in so doing, displays only the truer heart beneath her single-minded fixation on Domon. She wore it like an obvious tattoo.

"Here," she whispered to one of the stragglers who had yet to get any food and had just turned away from her, looking uncertainly for an opening. "Come here, that's right," she crooned, opening the gate a crack wider. She held out some meat for the creature, and it hurried through the gate, eyes brightening. Barging it open, the Vech scarfed the meat down, then proceeded to lick her face while pawing at her with its two frontmost paws. "You will do, sweetling. Come, and we shall meet the Archlord. Your new master."

- Chapter 31 -

Homecoming

Manidor 2, 1295:
It should almost amuse me how far my own mind has fallen from all
human ideals. Human life means fair nothing to me at this point, as the
entirety of my world revolves around transcending and replacing that dated
race. All while providing sustenance for the ever-ravenous machine of
progress.
— Journey of a Hellebes

High above the grey cloudscape of the Sea of Emptiness, a gleaming metal ship slipped through Mani's Energy Field and descended like a dart falling on a battlefield. But this was no battleground, and the purpose of this military gunship had nothing to do with war directly. The ship's pilot immediately engaged defensive shields as a precaution, readying for the time to deploy the message system devised for advance communications with the inhabitants of Mani's Dark Side.

Kaen worked the controls, taking his ship lower in a controlled descent. The atmospheric entry/reentry protections mostly unneeded now, and the wind was beginning to cool the exohull effectively. If all went according to plan, no one had followed from Gaea, but of course he would find out one way or another soon.

Inside his lab-formed chest, his artificial heart pounded with excitement, both at the adrenaline-producing trip through the atmosphere and the anticipation of seeing his long-lost love. His last trip outward through Mani's atmosphere and into Gaea's had been while under the "spell" of Mani's blade, so it represented a fuzzy part of his mind clouded by the warping influence of the lunar entity and his own shame.

Redemption. That was his goal here. But also . . . well, that was his personal goal. He had as well a duty to his new kinsmen back on Gaea, amongst the sons of Ccamos. The legacy of the Red Horizon and the officers of the Ccamos military, both were counting on him to deliver the message stealthily to as many across Mani as possible, to ready the Mother's people for the war. There was far more at stake here than one people versus another . . . humankind as a whole was represented by the small but genetically diverse population in Mei Shan and the large but far less diverse population of Mani's two continents. That was it.

If Lyn's report from earlier in the year was accurate, then Mani should already be well on their way in defensive preparations—and indeed, Nytaea had successfully defended themselves, though the League's outpost remained on Darsor as far as they knew.

Kaen could not say what he would truly see when he saw her face again. Phoebe, Rhidea, Kymhar and the others . . . he would be glad to see any and all of his Manese friends. But Mydia . . . he'd pictured their meeting, and the words they would exchange, perhaps a thousand times now. So many times that it couldn't possibly resemble the reality. He didn't even know if she would recognize him. He didn't know if they could be compatible on a marital or even a human level. Or if she even remembered him—humans had such faulty memories.

Shut up, he told himself. That was silly, and he knew it. He was just . . . playing "Mani's advocate", perhaps. Yes, that was a fitting moniker.

The cloud seas rushed by, slowly coated with the western sunset light of Sol as he neared the far horizon. That meant it was somewhere in the evening back in Nytaea, and roughly midday in Ti'Vaeth, where the day calendar was oriented.

The northernmost Sky Islands appeared on the southern horizon, telling him that he had come in farther north than he'd meant, despite the ship's magnetic readings. The shoreline was in sight shortly, and he cut southward ever so slightly, though he'd be bypassing Randhorn on this trip in.

Before ever reaching the land, and before nearing the Sky Islands, he let out the pulse did something to alert the magi in the linked web that he was not an enemy. The Gaean League had no way of getting such information of a code, although of course they would work to perfect their system in time to come.

Fircas was the easternmost province of Kystrea, the first land after Nemental, and by far the more boring if he was making a personal judgment there. Nytaea came along shortly, and then . . .

There. The white spires of the Nytaean Palace, reaching up over the broad alabaster city walls. *Oh, there really is no place like home . . .* It felt like an eternity since he'd been here. Even slowing down further with the omnidirectional brakes, the city rushed forward to meet him. He repeated the same pulse, alerting the city guardsmen with lights and sound as to his allegiance, before gliding over the walls and toward the northern square in front of the Palace. Fortunately, the city didn't seem to be in any state of uproar or chaos like last time. In fact, it looked far better, like a pet's shiny pelt after a good bath and healthy food. Buildings had been restored to their former luster—or simply whole structure, in the case of meaner houses and shops—and the Palace bore few and minor wounds from the recent battle with Lldsaor's forces.

[Um, I forgot about the giant golden tree overhanging the city.]

It must have been something.

Guards and citizens about the Palace turned to gawk and ran to fetch others, and soon he glimpsed the familiar faces of Nytaea's new officials, along with . . . Rhidea? She was here! And Mydia . . . oh, Mydia.

He landed the ship after being certain that all was well and that the area was clear. The people had purposely vacated the central square near the statue of ___ to allow his descent. The thrusters, rotated downward, slowed his ship the last measure and he landed on the four extensible docking legs. When he emerged, he was greeted by staring eyes and gawking mouths, those who hadn't gotten a glimpse of a Hellebes crowding in to see their first alien.

The tall man, Ethas Gandel, stepped forward, motioning the others back, and addressed him, "Foreigner of Gaea, state your purpose. Do you have a message for us?"

He didn't recognize Kaen. With a sinking feeling, Kaen's eyes flicked around, noting others who should know him but did not seem to.

"I . . . I do, My Lord. Lord Gandel?" Kaen bowed graciously.

The blond man seemed off-put by his response. "You speak—you recognize ...?"

"Allow me, Lord Gandel," said a feminine voice, and immediately Rhidea stepped into the inner circle of people, pushing Gandel aside. She strode up to Kaen and stopped within about two feet. "You," she hissed. "What are *you* doing here? Where is Lyn? Where is Mani's blade?"

Now it was Kaen's turn to take a step back, eyes narrowing worriedly. *What did I miss? She seems to know something about ... me. Oh, he didn't. No, no her ...* "So you've been speaking to Mani now? Can we ..." He looked around. "Can we speak more privately about this?"

"No!" she said forcefully. "Who are you?"

Kaen opened his mouth, but the words didn't want to come out. "I am Kaen of Nytaea. Lyn's generals sent me."

He heard a ripple of gasps issue forth into the crowd, especially from Mydia's direction, who covered her mouth with her gloved hands. The small woman pushed her way through the crowd, followed by her Queensguard, who tried to hold her back. She slapped their hands away. "Kaen!" she shouted. "Is that you? What happened to you? Rhidea, you said he died!"

Rhidea's eyes grew wide with irritation as she turned to face the Queen. "My Lady, you should stay back. This is not Kaen. This is a Hellebes creation with his mind."

"With his ..." Mydia's head spun from Rhidea to Kaen's tall form, her black bob spinning above her shoulders. A negative emotion like doubt or fear or disgust began to creep over her face, and she seemed for the first time to realize the implications. "You're ... you're not ... him? But Rhidea, you told me—"

"I know what I said! My Lady." Rhidea fixed her burning eyes once more on Kaen, tilting her chin up to meet his gaze. Even she was nearly a head shorter than him, for he was a Hellebes and she a human woman.

"Rhidea ... Mydia ... we can talk about this further," he said as calmingly as he could, though his voice was not entirely even. No amount of battle coding and military training could prepare him to face such a situation without a stutter. "Trust me when I say I'm on Lyn's side. I come from Ccamos, the city that follows and reveres her. She herself urged me to come. On Gaea, my body died . . . but I was made into a Hellebes. You can believe that or not, but I can prove to you with my memories that I am who I—"

"Memories can be faked," Rhidea said in a surprisingly cold voice. "I would not trust this man, Mydia."

Kaen could not understand why the red-haired mage would be so unreasonable as this—surely something of Mani's doing—but it was now Ethas Gandel, coregent of Nytaea, who came to his defense:

"Ladies, please. I believe him. Let him come in to the Palace, and we will discuss his message. We cannot afford to be so petty."

Kaen never knew how much he liked the man until now. "Thank you, My Lord. With no objections?" he asked, looking around. "This is highly important. The Gaean League will not stop with this last attack; you must persevere, and you have allies on Gaea."

Mydia nodded as though in shock. He knew he had somehow inflicted that by appearing when she'd thought him dead, yet in a new flesh. Somehow, in all his multitude of predictions, this reaction both surprised and did not surprise him. Rhidea, for her part, nodded only after consideration, pulling her lips into a line and swallowed seemingly a bad-tasting objection. "Very well."

They led him up the Palace steps, out of the eyes of the general populace, where Mydia's handmaid Julia scurried up, dropping to one knee. "Will our guest require refreshments?"

Mydia looked up at Kaen. "Well? Hungry from the trip?"

He was, but not from the trip. Flying to Mani took shockingly little time, but a Hellebes appetite worked around the clock to consume as much energy as possible. "Yes, please," he said. "Something with protein."

"Perhaps . . . a vegetable tray? And pastries?" the girl asked with a small shrug toward her liege lady.

"That . . . ah, that will do," he said with a dip of the head. "Thank you, Julia."

She started, took another look at him, and then made to hurry off.

"In the main audience hall," Mydia called after her. "Come, Gaean guest."

Kaen had not been to the audience hall in some time. He kept glancing around, taking in the suits of silver armor, red carpeting and other decorations not to mention the intricate white stonework that made up most of the Palace rooms. This was one of the more lavish.

He sat awkwardly in a sturdy chair that was barely sufficient for his great weight. He tried not to shift, as it produced a groan of pain from the wood with each movement. The others sat around in a half-circle, centering on Mydia's great chair. The Queen, for her part, looked more nervous than she had leading them back here. The nerves were getting to her. She glanced nervously toward the door as though considering making a run to the privy.

"Visitor," Ethas Gandel said from his seat beside his coregent, "You who call yourself Kaen—why don't you start by giving us an account of—forgive me good people, if I get details wrong here—but tell us what became of you after you *died,* as these have said." He indicated Mydia and Rhidea. The purposeful inflection in his words did not convey rudeness, more just a sense that he wanted to clear up an area of conflict. He looked at Rhidea, and she merely gave a grave curt nod.

Kaen took a breath. "Okay. I mean . . . very well, My Lord. I left last year with Lyn and Captain Zent of the Red Horizon rebels, and came to the rebels' underwater base after entering Gaea's atmosphere . . . perhaps I will avoid terminology you won't understand." He paused, scratching his chin as he thought of a strategy, and settled on simplicity.

"The rebels, as you know, were in a guerilla war with the Gaean League, the world power of Gaea. And as I believe Lyn exposed to you, we ended up binding ourselves to one of Gaea's eight cities as the rebel numbers were cut down. I was captured while on a mission with Lyn, and held by her enemy, Lord Strongs. He is the leader of the most militaristic city, Haven. He had scientists working in the shadows, one of them a traitor at the Red Horizon, coming up with new models of Hellebes, who are essentially man-made humans."

He tapped his combat suit, indicating his large frame. "These bodies are created in laboratories, human factories. The Hellebes have for a long time possessed the technology necessary to transfer a human's entire consciousness to a new body, and they did this on me in order to steal control of the Heart of Mani, my silver blade."

"Which you no longer have," Rhidea pointed out.

He snorted. "I left it in the ship. You couldn't detect it?"

She paused, mouth open. Then she frowned, saying nothing more.

"Anyway, Strongs' plan worked, and he played what we call a video—" he held out his arm, pulling up an exampled video on his wrist console for them to see "—like this, we can capture a live feed of events and play it back visually, with audio as well. They played a video of it for Lyn, making her believe they had killed me as a threat. I watched as they . . . they tore my body apart. It was horrible. But they immediately transferred my mind to a new body—that's how I was able to see it. I still don't know if I am the duplicate, or if no mind or soul occupied my dying body . . . and I may never know. I don't wish to.

"But after that, I was cut off from Mani's voice, yet able to use all of the sword's abilities. They controlled me, however, programming my body to do their every bidding, and I did terrible things against Lyn and against Ccamos and Senator Sylleo. After hounding her for weeks, they finally cornered me and subdued me, subsequently performing an operation that freed my mind. So what you see now is the free me, with all of my memories as a human but also the abilities and language knowledge of the Hellebes."

"You have the perfect memory?" Rhidea asked. "The Vault?"

"Yes. In fact, my entire human memories are open to me like never before, curiously enough."

Mydia was dabbing furiously at her eyes with a spotless handkerchief. "Pay me no mind," she said as she detected eyes on her. "I'm just—getting sentimental."

Rhidea considered Kaen for a minute, before meeting Ethas' gaze and shrugging. "It is not quite as I expected. I must apologize, for I had only limited information. You see, Kaen, it is as you said: Mani has spoken to me, and he told me of your body's death. Also that another being had been created, taking possession of the blade. He called it highly dangerous, and was most persuasive in asking that I become his new Vessel."

"Figures," Kaen muttered. "You don't know how manipulative he can be. I assume you've joined him now?" He assumed this not because it was what he'd expect from her, but because the signs clearly pointed there. "And what is with your new arm?"

She shrugged it, as though having forgotten it was there, which she surely hadn't. "I have allowed my Silver Authority into the open now, no longer keeping it secret. On Darsor, I made a deal first with Mani and then Domon, but not without thought. I couldn't have persuaded the Archlord so without Mani's power to tip the scales—or at least, I would have had to use much more roundabout and uncertain methods, and I couldn't be certain that I could take him out if it came right down to it." She flexed her arm, causing the many layers and jointly to ripple and gleam, though the metal *shk-shhk* noises it made were nearly inaudible. "And yes, it was Mani's power that allowed me to grow this arm back."

She did not say, however, how she'd lost it. Something about her story of Darsor and Domon left a decidedly bad taste in his mouth. The thought that Mani had corrupted—or at least won over—Rhidea of Randhorn, the Wandering Mage, leader of their expedition to Gaea, a pillar of both Nytaea and Nemental. Rhidea the wise, the implacable, that Rhidea . . . it was hard to swallow, and deeply unsettling. Had it been her deep-seated hatred for Domon that had pushed her to do it? The thought that it was worth selling her entire soul to position herself to strike him down? If so . . . why did she talk as though she'd shaken hands and called him friend? They seemed to be working together.

Mydia finally found her voice. "Kaen, I—I don't know what to say, truly. This is . . . most startling. The—the thought that man can come back from the dead thanks to technology, something that no magic can achieve. I do not know why Lyn did not mention this development."

Her face clouded over at those last words, and it broke Kaen's heart to see her doubt for her friend. "Lyn did not want to trouble you or your council unnecessarily. I'm . . . sorry for the deception. It was—it was my suggestion." He opened his mouth to say more, but decided against it. He already felt self-conscious enough.

Mydia looked away as well. Her blinking green eyes tried to hide her own emotion.

"Kaen."

He started, turning around to see Rhidea's intense expression, stripped of the cordial moderation that had suppressed it. Somehow, he had for a moment expected the voice to belong to Queen Mydia, but she appeared to have not left the hall yet. He swallowed. "Rhidea."

"Come with me," she said, brushing past him.

He glanced about him, observing the number of people who seemed to have noticed their exchange. Zero. She had spoken quickly and moved on, and—he remembered suddenly—she had a speech-sealing ability that could auditorily wall out any except those whom she wished to hear. Setting his jaw but making no other outward signs of tension or annoyance, he strode after her.

- Chapter 32 -

Silver and Iron

Manidor 2, 1295
Looking back on it, I see that that morning in the library was the turning
point of it all, where I realized there was no going back
— Journey of a Hellebe

Kaen's steel-lined boots thudded on the marble floors of the second-floor Palace hallway as he followed the woman with hair like a fading inferno. Once, he would have called her tall. Lithe, well-formed, beautiful in her own mature almost cold way. Today, cold was a fitting description. Her austere ash-grey dress licked at her heels without a sound.

It seemed to him that the servants and maids passing them by not only took notice but walked in a different dimension, perhaps a different time—a few minutes to come. They turned to look, but he was already looking past them. Perhaps he just wanted to ignore the fact that anyone and everyone he didn't want watching him right now was paying attention due to his great size and otherworldly attire.

They did not go to her office. They descended a side staircase and headed westward, in the direction of the library. In fact . . . *We are going there. I'm going to a Nytaean library—no, the, not a—with the Wandering Mage.*

She rounded the arched library door with a familiar stride, hand preemptively catching and forcing the door open. Fortunately, she didn't strike anyone, but he soon saw as he entered the ornately decorated room that there was no one in sight. *The old fox must know the hours that well. And even still today.*

She led him through the main room, navigating through aisleways that were a bit trickier for him with practiced casualness, and into a back section of the library with windows overlooking the River Ardencaul. He never would have guessed that the library of all places had such a good view of the river.

She took a seat on the opposite wall, right of the window, and eyed him expressionlessly as he took the seat she indicated on the lefthand side. "Now, I believe we need to make something clear here. I . . ." she began drumming on the mahogany end-table beside her with two fingers, and he realized that perhaps she was the nervous one here, "I am afraid. Of you. And of what you mean to the worlds."

Kaen nodded along with her words, as though they made perfect sense, yet it was the last thing he expected to hear from her mouth. "I'm sorry, Rhidea—I don't understand. I don't follow."

Her eyes looked somewhere far away, and he perceived that she was communicating with Mani's spirit. Then she sighed. "Well, then I shall lay it out: You were unstable and volatile, and I sent you to Gaea in hopes that Mani would be cut off from you and you would finally be free, free enough to gather your strength and resolve and come back strong enough to compete with Mani.

"But of course, that is not what happened. I'm still trying to piece together how things could have gone the way they did, but the fact remains that I took up Mani's mantle, and I would not give it back if I could. I do not believe that you would wish it back, no?"

He nodded hesitantly.

"Wrong." She transfixed him with a stare. "You have already lied about the blade you carry. Reveal it."

Kaen's eyes widened, and he sat up, jaw clenching. "I do not have it. Don't make such claims."

"Then you have discovered how to instantly transport it . . . ?" She looked both angry and confused.

"Is Mani whispering all this stuff in your ear?" he asked incredulously. "I expected far more of the Wandering Mage of Randhorn."

She made no reply, again looking far away. "This is troubling," she said finally. "Mani is being difficult. He appears to be trying to speak to you, and yet I can see he is not effective. What kind of barrier have you erected? How have you learned to shield your mind thus?"

He scrunched his brows in consternation. "What is this ridiculous talk?

Rhidea, his powers were cut off from me save for the sword's most basic abilities as soon as my soul was transferred. That is the end of the matter."

She eyed him suspiciously. "That may just be the truth. Which indicates that he is the one withholding information from me."

Suddenly, she lashed out with her Silver Authority. He saw it in her hands, her eyes—which went suddenly metallic silver—and felt it in his bones like lead. Only it was a dripping, a splash, an almost feeble attempt. For a moment he questioned whether that was truly what she was doing, but the next moment he had done the unthinkable and drawn his hip blaster, training the barrel on her. "Stop," he growled, deep and threatening.

She flinched back, face paling beyond the usual, and he felt her slip in the use of her Silver arts. Then rage filled her countenance, and she shouted back at him, "You would dare raise a hand against me?" She had sealed their speech once more. She redoubled her gravity Authority, pulling on his bones and flesh, but he held firm. Mani's gravity was nothing to his superhuman body, and this greatening of it made it only like Gaea's own. But it was also possible that the Gaean energy that circulated through his veins kept it at bay—or even his prior connection with Mani.

He stood up, pistol still trained on the woman. "Rhidea, I'm warning you. Stop this."

"You would dare . . ." It came out in a vicious snarl streaked across her face, and with a chill he realized he could hear the voice of Mani growling along with it, distantly or as though through a great fog.

Then the voice of Mani was upon him in galeforce, causing him to stumble for a moment: *Traitorous welp, impure and defiled by Gaea. Bow! Bow before my true Vessel. Grovel and beg, and turn no weapon against me or I will destroy—*

Kaen shook off the voice, feeling the weight of Rhidea's Silver Authority once more but ten times stronger. He stood up under the great weight, arms shooting up to pull off two shots in quick succession, aimed at her left shoulder and left leg.

Her eyes widened, and she twisted, avoiding only the lower of them while the other took her in the arm. She cried out not in pain but in rage, and pulled up the stone from the floor and windowsill to trap him in it.

He snapped it with ease, and she replicated it with ice. He mostly shook it off, pulling off another shot, but it was absorbed by her outstretched arm of silver, the same as his blade had done. *My blade . . . should I . . . ?* He still couldn't believe she could use silver like that now, to create entire body parts.

Rhidea rushed at him, faster than a normal Legaleian, and swiped with an arm now barbed with dagger-like fingers, a sudden transformation. Two of them caught him in the chest, knocking him against a wall shelf and slicing the front of his combat suit. "You demented old witch!" he shouted. Thinking instinctively, he summoned Mani's blade remotely and blocked her next attack with it, pistol still held in his off-hand. He shot again while her silver arm was kept busy, piercing her left leg in two places with liquid energy, and this time she screamed, toppling. The energy charges burrowing into the stone floor and sizzled out between her breast and wounded arm. *No . . . barely wounded anymore. That one is already healing somehow.*

He held the silver blade to her chest, poking the end in a centimeter and drawing blood. He was aware that this kept her lungs from grabbing much-needed air, but he needed to stop her, to finally get in a word and stop this madness. Mani was clouding her mind with irrational fear and hatred. "Please," he begged. "We can be reasonable. You instigated all this while making false claims about me."

Her face was still contorted with the pain from her leg, but he saw the care with which she barely breathed, forcing her chest not to rise into his sword blade. "Remove the blade," she hissed quietly. "I'm warning you, boy. You're in over your head."

"No, you listen to me!" he hissed back. "Mani is lying to you, just like he tricked me. Mani is a force of evil, not good. He set this all up to use you."

She rattled her head back and forth, a soft and almost demonic chuckle escaping her lips. "Perhaps. But only for—" she gasped as she breathed in too deeply "—for the sake of my destiny. Oh, but what an inexperienced pup you are. Good job, boy."

Suddenly, he heard it too, and with a sinking feeling realized just where they were, and what this looked like. "No," he muttered, glaring down at her. To let her up or not? She may well spring upon him and even—he almost wouldn't be shocked—try to kill him.

Boots thumped in the library proper, and voices shouted, "What is going on?"

The feeling of dread intensified, and he stepped back from Rhidea's prone body, sword leaving a small trail of blood. She let her face fall to the floor, and he knew it to be an act, a trick . . . a setup. *The speech seal. She let it down.*

He closed his eyes, swearing softly through gritted teeth, as the first guard came upon them and let out an exclamation. The next minute was a blur of orders and demands, accusations, concern for the Wandering Mage, orders of arrest for Kaen . . . and a slow, weak response from Rhidea, who sat up only with great apparent effort and rose with the help of a pair of guards, who glared daggers at Kaen. Eventually, the blond woman called Captain Straif came, taking him away as others gathered.

Finally, he met an angry Mydia, who instantly assaulted them both with her words. She did not, as he expected, immediately show concern for Rhidea, but seemed almost to dismiss the possibility that he was ever a danger to her. Kaen would lean toward agreement, although he did wonder what a green charge directly through her chest would have done. Could Mani repair her heart and internal organs? Or perhaps replace her entire inner workings with Silver?

What a terrifying thought.

For his part, he largely hung his head and accepted all the accusations. What could he possibly say in his defense? This was no dispute between two squabbling friends—Rhidea was the most famed and illustrious mage in the world, a longtime friend to Nytaea and the crown, and he had assaulted her in one of the most sacrosanct places of the Palace. He, an alien claiming by a thread to have once been a friend of theirs.

There was no use in fighting the tide. Left was only to see where it washed him. The mage soldiers held him at threat of a full onslaught and tested, one by one, which elements could most effectively be used against him. In the end, they took him to the old Prison Tower, which to this day lay vacant, and secured him on the first floor with heavy stone blocks hauled in by perspiring servants and then fashioned into a stocks and manacles of size and width greater than his own body. He was set with Lightning mage guards, who had proven to be most effective at stunning him and inflicting pain, and these would rotate round the clock until the council decided what should be done about him.

The next day, Mydia at last came to him, flanked by her Queensguard and the Mage Guard captain. But they let her mostly alone, by her orders, and she quickly approached and dropped to her knees, looking up into his tightly-secured face. "Kaen, why? Why did you do it? I have to know; this . . . this isn't an inquisition."

Not yet, he thought bitterly.

He opened his mouth, then coughed painfully. Talking would be an uncomfortable chore. He truly couldn't say whether or not he could burst the stone bonds, but of course he would not try, for the magi would have him dead before he ever got to his ship, which had surely been impounded by the crudest means. "I don't have an answer," he said at last. "Not—not the one you're looking for. You wouldn't believe me if I said I didn't attack her first, and she's already denied it."

The sad expression in her face made room for a new one: agreement. She believed him, at least on some level. Although he knew that she would never take his own word over Rhidea's. "You're not wrong," she said. "But you understand how grave this is. We cannot simply overlook it, and there . . . well, as you pointed out, it is not a simple matter to call the Wandering Mage a liar."

"Then she's pressing charges against me?"

She hesitated. "No. I don't think so."

That was a relief. He would get out of here eventually. But not soon enough. "Mydia, I . . ." He closed his mouth, swallowing with another painful motion before changing his tack. "I still need to relay my message. Rhidea can say what she likes, and you can believe that I attacked her out of some kind of rivalry, but you can't deny that Lyn sent me."

"Actually, we have no proof of that whatsoever," she reasoned. "Why should we take your word?"

His eyes flashed, and he almost spoke in an indiscreet manner. "Because the writing and the seal are Lyn's, written in her own hand."

"Why didn't you get the letter to us immediately?"

He shrugged. Perhaps, if he were to record these events at a later date or retell it to Lyn, he would say that he'd done it on instinct, but not intention. "If you recall, Rhidea was the one who turned the entire meeting into a discussion on my identity. I wanted to meet with you again."

She hesitated, and for why he couldn't say. "With me personally?"

"I—No, no, Your Majesty. I mean, My Queen."

She gave a sad, chuckling snort, which resolved into a small, unintelligible head shake. She rose from her knees, delicately brushing off her multilayered skirt. "Well, you may be a different man, but you're still the same fool. Very well, Kaen; I think I can convince them to hear you out and perhaps let you go soon. Let me guess, the message is locked in your flying vehicle?"

He hesitated, rolling his eyes upward, then nodded. "Conveniently, yes. That was not planned."

"Then I'm sure you can give us some manner of key," Straif said, stepping forward. She would almost be intimidating if she didn't only barely come up to his head level while bent over in the stocks.

He snorted. "Yeah, I . . . guess I can."

- Chapter 33 -

The Prisoner and the Patron Saint

Manidor 2, 1295:
It should almost amuse me how far my own mind has fallen from all
human ideals. Human life means fair nothing to me at this point, as the
entirety of my world revolves around transcending and replacing that dated
race. All while providing sustenance for the ever-ravenous machine of
progress.
— From Lhinde's Vault

Mydia walked from the tower, blinking back her emotions. She breathed long and deep, putting a hand to her heart and feeling the frantic thumps. It felt whole, not broken or torn or stitched back together. Just . . . beating far faster than normal. She tried to walk ahead of Straif, face forward, so that the captain could not see her barely-dammed tears.

Keep them in check, silly girl. You're a queen. It felt like the thousandth time she'd said it to herself, but it was no easier, nor more effective, than the last time. She blinked further, fighting the tide, and felt herself winning.

Larks and killdeers called from the Palace grounds, while the wind blew a faint whistling over the land of Nytaea. The air was warm and surprisingly pleasant, the sky an even morning blue. This may be a hot Day Cycle as it progressed, according to her weather scholars. The mild climate did little to help her mood however, the birds' songs falling on deaf ears.

One of her guardsmen spoke softly to her.

Belatedly, she gave an undignified, "Hmm?" and looked up to see Inno's troubled expression.

"Are you well, My Lady? I can fetch a—"

"I'm fine," she said, voice clipped, face turning abruptly forward once more as they rounded the gateway that led around to the left, through one of the Palace towers and inside. She was too troubled to give guardmen so much as a nod, though Inno and Ruel gave them passing nods.

Back inside, her eyes began to dart around, plotting an escape. Straif hurried to catch her up. "Milady," she said in a controlled murmur, "What do you actually think regarding the Hellebes spy?"

"Spy?" she scoffed, without thinking.

Straif took it in stride. "For all intents and purposes, that's what we're calling him for now."

"Then we'd better lump Rhidea into that category as well."

"We . . . should. You are right."

Mydia stopped, looking at the short blond woman for a couple of breaths. "Well, at least I'm not the only one."

"If I may, Milady, I'm not stupid."

Mydia nodded absently, though she meant it as some manner of meaningful gesture. "Are you free for a bit, Captain?"

"I . . . suppose?"

Mydia turned to her Queensguard. "Inno. Ruel. You're excused for the moment. I've got Straif. Look for me in the audience hall in perhaps a half hour."

Mydia found Teli and signaled to her to bring some tea to her upper chamber. The girl's eyes brightened, and she scurried away. What a dear. Always helpful, always polite . . . true, Mydia was a queen and one of the two most important figures in the city, but still, she seemed to serve Mydia by choice as much as station. Ever since Lyn had rescued her from slavery among the maids.

In Mydia's chambers, she took a seat and motioned Straif over to another. The woman looked at it for a moment, as though racking her brain to remember the function of such an implement, and then sat down, silver armor rustling and chinking. She made an instinctive reach down toward her feet, then seemed to remember where she was and stopped, sitting back up straightly.

"You can take your boots off," Mydia said off-handedly.

"I . . . can't, My Queen. You dismissed your guards, and I am on duty."

"Oh. I suppose you have a point. Well." Mydia pulled up her own feet and pulled off her slippers with a furtive glance at the door. Wiggling her toes, she said, "Ah. That's better. Don't worry, they don't smell."

Straif gave her a brief glance that seemed a soft accusation, as though a queen couldn't possibly do enough work to have smelly feet. Or skip enough baths. And she was right, of course.

"About your friend . . ." Straif began hesitantly. Mydia waited for her to continue, and she did. "The entire thing makes me uncomfortable. I remember when he walked the Palace before, looking aimless and speaking to his strange blade like it could hear him. Like it spoke to him. He unsettled half the Palace, but—well, I hesitate to say this, but we didn't do anything about it because he was a friend of the crown. You understand?"

Mydia nodded, a lump in her throat momentarily damming her speech.

"And . . . well, he's entirely different now. If indeed this is the same man. He is far more confident, with seemingly no such attachment to the blade as before. And yet, when we found him in the library, it was as though he had been possessed by it again. And he summoned it from a state of invisibility or great distance . . ." Her eyes asked a question of the queen.

"He was able to do both, far as I knew," Mydia said grudgingly.

Straif nodded. "I thought as much. Those are troubling characteristics, and more so for the fact that they remain. Yet, aside from his unexplainable aggression toward Lady Rhidea, his story matches up. He said that the sword kept its power, yet held no power over him now that his body is not the same."

Mydia bobbed her head slowly. Straif was laying out the thoughts of her own mind, which was not so bad since it gave her time to analyze and parse thoughts from feelings. "And the only issue is . . . what is this new body? How can they . . . *make* a Hellebes?"

"Your friend Lyn claimed that all of them are made the same way. In large . . . manufactories, or whatever she called them. And the man Zent certainly seemed his own person, freely capable of rational thought and moral decision making. Not so bad to look at either, no?"

She was teasing her, Mydia knew. She gave a low snort, wondering if her cheeks were coloring. They still did that from time to time, despite her best efforts. But it was fine. She had yet to tease her about Kaen, which would be far more effective—and also unkind, given the circumstances. "And what of Rhidea?" she asked. "Your thoughts on her?"

Straif hissed in a breath through her teeth. "I . . . hesitate to say anything about her. It is also difficult given the fact that she has always been a rogue, or times you might even say a vigilante, working to get her own way here or elsewhere, and excels at averting authority when and wherever she can. There are many in Nytaea who do not like her, despite all she's done for us. And yet . . that is just it. If she is in the wrong here, and not only that but is now an *enemy* . . . well, then we are in a tight position."

An enemy . . . Mydia shivered at the thought. It seemed impossible, yet a notion that had gone through her head a dozen times in the months since her trip to Redufiel. Never would she have even thought of doubting the lady— never—but as time had passed, and the news about Kaen and finally about her being Mani's Vessel, came . . . a worm of worry and doubt had not ceased to gnaw in her gut. A seed of distrust, an inkling of fear.

Rhidea, the Wandering Mage, worker of wonders, citizen and helper of Nytaea, savior of the city, seeker of truth—*that* Rhidea may be a traitor? The thought was almost unbearably silly, not to mention painful. But truth was not always easy.

Yet . . .

"Straif, what do you think actually happened in the library?"

The mage soldier looked up, lips pursed seriously, and then in judicious care as she prepared to answer. Then her eyes widened in that distinct expression of one out of his or her depth. "It still makes no sense," she finally said. "He obviously seemed the aggressor, yet . . . how could he get the jump on such a highly trained mage? And why would he attack her in secret? Obviously, I do not know the capabilities of a Hellebes, but it is a fearful thing to think of one having the power to kill a High Mage—one of the Silver bloodline, no less."

That was common knowledge now among Mydia's inner circle, perhaps the entire city. That Rhidea was the last of the Silversmiths. It was only one more thing that marked her out as above the law. Anything they tried to do against her would look political, or jealous. But she had a point. "Well, I believe her

Silver Authority has no power over that blade. She found that out before."

"Very well. But she has the personal power of Mani . . . or whatever that force is. The very one that made and once inhabited Kaen's sword."

"Oh. Yes, but again, as he said . . ."

"And that would make it the perfect weapon against one such as she. It is possible that he bears a grudge against Silver itself, and thinks to permanently vanquish it by killing one who in part embodies that force itself." She motioned to her right arm, which on Rhidea was entirely made of silver. "I'm throwing out suggestions, My Lady. Please understand, I have nothing against Mister Kaen, may he rest in peace, but—"

Mydia growled in her throat, a sound which stopped the Mage Captain. "I'm sorry, I just—I don't like this line of reasoning, Captain. It feels . . . off. Incorrect. I think it's a mistake to assume that he's a different person—"

"Which I have not, Milady."

"But you have! Admit it."

Straif paused. "Perhaps . . . for the sake of argument and legality. I meant no offense whatsoever. But we must look at this objectively. If a man claims the power to clone another and then says that he is, in fact, that other man . . . you see the logical problem?"

Actually, she did. The very existence of such a cloning ability—not just the creation of human creatures, but duplicating the consciousness and mind of another, or transferring it to another body—would give rise to all manner of deception that could be achieved. Kaen could very easily be a spy, and if he had his mind . . .

"Very well," she said with a small sigh, brushing the cheek below one eye and blinking, as though at a possible eyelash. "Let's, um, let us get back to the topic of Rhidea. Suppose she's turned, and my friend and mentor is now a force of evil working hand in hand with Domon . . . what could we possibly do?"

"That . . . is not a pleasant thought, My Queen. I shudder to think upon it. I will admit that it's a possibility we would rather not seriously consider."

"I know, but *what if!*" Mydia said harshly, voice rising with emotion. "I don't want to choose between them either."

Straif crossed her gauntleted arms over her curved breastplate. "Well, if her intention—and Domon's in sending her—were to destroy or conquer us, then I think we would already be doomed. It would be like the day that Domon personally came here and slaughtered many, executing nobles and letting in her soldiers. Only . . . far worse."

"But what if she's not that evil? Just . . . working with Domon for some reason, bent on securing Nytaea's submission? What if she's still Rhidea as we know her, she simply has different goals?"

"Then there's no knowing her mind. But . . . there are many ways she could go about it," Straif began, going on to run through a small list of ways to cripple Nytaea and take control. Insidious ways, ways that did not require mass bloodshed.

Even as she began, however, Mydia's mind wandered a little. Because she already knew that the assumption of the "same" Rhidea was a false and foolish one. This is what had been nagging at her. Rhidea seemed distinctly different while Kaen seemed more rational by far than the last time they'd met. If there was one of them to distrust . . . and if Rhidea, not Kaen, had initiated the skirmish in the library . . . if Mani was communicating with her not as an insidious, nagging influence but as partners . . .

Oh, great auroras. We are fools.

- Chapter 34 -

To Fell a Tree

Manidor 2, 1295:
progress.
— From Lhinde's Vault

Cae Rhidea activated her Earth Authority and Perception Coaction in succession, resealing the block she'd carved from the floor. What she had thus implanted would come in handy in the days to come. She had already similarly tapped the library, her office, and a few other key spots. It was remarkable how low the Palace security was, particularly when she was such an esteemed personage. Explaining herself away or gaining access to a room was as simple as a quick, discreet explanation that she had to get in somewhere for just a bit. She was looking for a scholar, or needed to inspect the premises. Domon had eyes everywhere, or some other boogeyman.

She was not taking Nytaea down today, that much was certain. She had many places to be, and many things to do, before such events. There was yet time. Eight months before the end of the world—or the beginning, looking at it from one angle.

Yes . . . that is well, daughter. You are beginning to see the world through my lens.

Yours is very big, and a bit skewed, so I'd say that's not entirely accurate, she returned.

Fair point. Skewed is not the correct terminology, however.

No matter. How long until the men of Torlega arrive?

Four hours. They are close. Yan'Vala has yet to mobilize, so you can reach them before they ever confirm their desire to support Nytaea and their alliance.

Which they do?

They do, as of now. You will convince them otherwise.

It was both a command and an observation, but she had increasingly treated his commands as mere suggestions, and he increasingly did not try to correct her on it. Their wills were aligning more by the day, one might observe, but also he was growing more comfortable with her. Kaen had been, as Mani called it, a limited Vessel, lacking magic and knowledge but also lacking the willpower to properly engage with the god-being called Mani. The Titan of Growth.

At the same time . . . No. She hid that thought, and quietly to herself remarked that their disagreement regarding her body's limits was a problem that would have to be resolved. Only in that area had he tried to manipulate her of late, and it did not sit well with her. It was as if his aim was to increase the amount of Silver that made up her body. Mere bones were not enough. He wanted . . . No. Enough.

What is it, my daughter?

It is nothing. My arm aches, but I can manage it. She stretched it, a motion of which he received an impression of increased clarity from her normal motor abilities. That was one more thing about her new Silver arm, something that may be a factor . . .

She headed back to her office, making her way quickly away from the east wing until she sensed human traffic enough that she may be seen, at which point she slowed to a purposeful but dignified stride, sweeping her charcoal-grey skirts with her. Her wounds, of course, had already no visible sign to indicate their existence except for the charred holes in her dress, which she'd patched over with Perception Coaction for the moment. No one had made a comment on it, as it seemed only sensible not to allow such a view of her torso and upper thigh.

The injuries did still ache, however. Her Silver bones seemed often to hold pain as metal holds heat for an extended length of time.

She was glad when she ran across a higher mage scholar, a middle-aged nobleman named Korcebran. One of his wives was also a scholar at the Palace. "Lady Rhidea!" he greeted her with a grin and a smooth bow. "How is your stay? Are you well? I heard about the incident . . ."

His tone said clearly that he had not heard at all accurately about said incident, which had been her every intention. She avoided any facial indication of that fact, but instead cleared her throat and looked away, as though slightly embarrassed and wishing to not draw attention to her humiliation in the library—which was extremely close to the truth. "Yes, it was . . . well, I'm fine. It was a misunderstanding, to say the least. That visitor from Gaea is . . ." She shook her head in wonderment, eyes widening just enough to get the message across.

The man laughed nervously, displaying a common reaction to mention of the Gaeans. "I can imagine. I'm only glad you are all right."

"Have you seen the Queen or her handmaids around?"

"Her handmaids? Hmm. I don't take much noti—actually, you know what, I saw the smaller one heading upstairs with tea just a bit ago." The man looked almost proud to remember such a detail about someone so insignificant. Typical nobility.

Rhidea nodded. "Thank you, Korcebran." She headed off with purposeful strides, bound for the Queen's northeast tower. Mani alerted her to the presence of the Mage Captain Straif, and she instead watched as they both headed in the direction of the main audience hall. Rhidea waited until the woman was gone, replaced by one of Mydia's Queensguard, Ruel. He noticed her first, nudging the queen and making an unconscious motion toward his sword hilt.

Good instincts, that one. He always had them. "Ho, Queen," she called warmly as Mydia turned.

"Hello," she said, face troubled. It was to be expected following the event with Kaen and her subsequent encounter with him. It was a good sign, in fact.

"I . . . want to apologize," Rhidea said, taking hold of her skirt and dropping into a short curtsy. "For the disturbance with Kaen. If anything, it is my fault. I instigated him by prodding the gap where his bond with Mani was. Mani suggested it, but I was the one who asked Kaen to come to the library. I wanted to speak with him about it where he didn't feel threatened by the presence of so many people." She had prepared the speech over the last half hour, knowing full well that Mydia would come to some conclusions, correct or not. Looking into her deep green eyes, she saw the confusion that marked the exact intended reaction.

"Oh," was all she seemed able to say at first. Her guardsman looked at her and she could not tell what passed between them if anything. "That is—that is good of you to so humbly apologize. My thanks. I'm sorry for how he attacked you, Lady Rhidea." She looked like she wanted to say more, lower lip trembling slightly and eyes shifted. Two blinks, and she looked away.

Probably about to cry, if I know her. Rhidea was surprised at the disparagement in her own thought. When had she begun looking down on her beloved apprentice Synergist and scholar? She approached, putting a hand lightly on the Queen's shoulder. Ruel's hand went all the way to his sword hilt but of course they both knew how powerless he was against a High Mage. "There, now. It will be all right. We'll get him out of there soon, and perhaps we can ascertain whether he is actually—" She looked around furtively. "I meant to speak to you about this, Mydia, but there are some troubling signs about him . . ."

"Not now," Mydia said with surprising harshness. "We can speak more soon, but for now I need to do some thinking. We also have Torlegan guests coming any day now."

"Of course, of course. I understand. Speaking of, since I happen to be around . . . well, I was assuming you'd allow me to sit in on the negotiations with them—if that is still well with you?"

"Oh. Of—of course, Rhidea," the Queen answered. "I must be going though. We will speak soon, or when they arrive."

Oh, it won't be long.

Now free of the Queen's presence, she felt a weight lift and realized she had won that conversation. Or rather, she'd accomplished what she wanted and come away with no more—hopefully less—suspicion than before.

Mani was spot on in his calculations, as well he should be. Of course, she pretended surprise at the Torlegan's sooner-than-expected arrival, and did not hurry to the south gate but hung back, waiting for the procession to lead them up to the Palace. The men, for men they mostly were, were tall and broad, a trait for which they were known, bearing clothing of skin and fur that looked far to thick for the current day. They said it was cooler down there in the "winter lands", particularly in the mountain regions—which comprised a large chunk of Torlega. They did their hunting on the southern plains and the foothills, it was said, and brought back the spoils to be traded and worked and eventually traded over the border with Dotham Province.

Just a few months with her new co-conspirator and she was already thinking of them all as Provinces, not the more historically accurate city-states. Nytaea was actually something of a novelty, in that she and the rebels who'd freed it had appealed to a far earlier Argent and Kystrean region, when the city-states were their own nations with few ties at all with the surrounding lands, each ruled by a king.

The mountain men filed up the north-facing front Palace steps, and Rhidea nodded to the leader, who was introduced as General Tubarcoss. He was tall and scarred, looking about with an expression that moved just enough upon meeting the new faces that she could tell it was not one flat emotion, yet each looked just as displeased. *Some people just wear that all the time,* she remarked to herself.

True to their word, they had brought a retinue of soldiers, apparently having left the majority at the southern barracks to get acquainted with the local muscleheads. That still left a solid three dozen two-legged bears. A passing thought had Rhidea wondering if they would look any less ursine without clothes. Something told her she would rue the day she ever found that out.

"You are aware that your lands are infested with monsters?" Tubarcoss asked Lord Gandel as they shook hands.

Ethas' look of politely mild disgust took on a frown. "I'm sorry? Monsters? More have been sighted this year, but I had not heard reports of—"

"Of course you did not," the bear man said, bowling over his words. "We traveled the wild lands through Dotham and southern Nytaea, coming by way of few Kystrean men. Many are small, like the Drothnir, hiding in places they think we not see. They do not attack large groups."

"You . . . recognize these creatures from Torlega?" Ethas asked as they moved on together, and Rhidea fell too far behind to hear the rest. She greeted

a few of the others, who seemed to nod and reach out for handshakes a
complete random, at times holding up the entire procession. Strange lands
strange customs. Of all the outlier nations, she had been to Torlega least, and
only once to their mountain capital of Tistwyll. She remembered such reaction
from the locals, but did not think that their customs would extend to a first-ever
expedition of such force straight to the main city of an unallied nation.

She trailed inside with the group, and couldn't help noticing that, while the
Torlegans didn't seem to recognize who she was, the Nytaen soldiers kept her
always within sight. Almost as though fearing she would mess up the entire
alliance by starting a battle on the Palace steps. Or perhaps they were looking
out for her safety . . . but more likely the first.

Naturally, she wouldn't attack these foreigners within Mydia's Palace. She
wanted an alliance as much as anyone else, and she had Domon's interests, the
cursed idiot, to uphold as well. Eventually, small tour done, the Torlegan leaders
heading the party negotiated with Mydia and Ethas on who should attend the
meeting, and it was decided that they would select five representatives to go in
to the upper strategy room.

These five Rhidea met as they were heading inside: General Tubarcoss
apparently the foremost among their military chiefs; General Ingval, the second
Torlcand, chieftain of Tistwyll; Vomnell, chieftain of the eastern passes; and
Hars, Scoutmaster of the Southern Border. Rhidea recalled that many nations
and Provinces had such scouts patrolling the world-borders of Argent, whence
superstitious lore dictated monsters came. The mountain passes, it would seem
also had their own scouting parties looking for such things, and the Torlegans
declared that monsters had indeed been returning to the world that Argent.

They . . . seemed to have not heard the news of the other continent.

The negotiations began with formal introductions, and a surprisingly
peaceable discussion of such topics as the monsters, military presence of
different parties on the Torlega border—which the Nytaeans stressed was not a
matter they had any direct influence over, although they could of course contact
the Kystrean authorities that they were in contact with.

This, of course, was where Rhidea was properly introduced as their liaison with the absent Archlord, the new Emperor of Darsor. She told them of Domon and his recent discoveries and ambitions, stressing for her part that she had struck an accord of necessity with him, no one that she wished. They explained she had long been an ally to Nytaea and Nemental, being of birth a Nytaean citizen. They explained to the Torlegan men the situation with the Wellspring, being as honest as possible.

The Torlegans had some contacts in the Kystrean Empire, and were apprised of some of this, but they very much seemed a distrustful people who valued personal meetings such as these far above distant reports. Chieftain Torlcand of Tistwyll took the on the role of lead spokesman, though she knew that Torlega recognized no one man as the leader of their entire nation. That was partly the reason for the large retinue of leaders with their soldiers and followers.

Fortunately for all parties, they seemed surprisingly open to the idea of alliance, and the grudge that some of them bore seemed to center around the lack of attempts made by Kystrean leaders to initiate such discussions—although, as Torlcand admitted, the previous few chieftains of Tistwyll were notoriously more "stonehearted", as he called them, which context indicated to mean stubborn. Such men would have only repulsed the efforts of Kystrea, and indeed there had been such attempts. Mydia and Ethas did not press this point, however.

But there was more at stake here, and Rhidea eventually saw and took her opportunity, capitalizing on it with a pertinent question: "Men of Torlega, what do you make of these tales of Darsor and Gaea? Do you believe them?"

There was a hush, during which the leaders looked at one another, grunting and stroking their bushy beards. "Well," said Hars the Scoutmaster, "It is not as though we have not heard such talk. But from where we dwell, secure in the mountains, it seemed only fanciful talk. Your group here—" he indicated the entire long table with a finger "is quite persuasive in their stories."

"Face to face," agreed General Ingval, whose voice was higher but no less rough than the others. "There is much value in a discussion like this. We should have more." He looked at the chieftains, who nodded their agreement sagely.

General Tubarcoss spoke up. "If these other worlds do exist, then we will need to see proof. For the sake of . . . ah, this discussion, we will take you at your word. Eh?"

Rhidea then put on them the next question, that of the threat of Gaea and what they proposed to be sound wisdom. The answers she got were neither shocking nor novel: Argent should band together. Lygellis and Yan'Vala, too, should be in on the alliance. Chieftain Torlcand insisted that they would need proof, and further discussion, before they could give any oath of support.

"Very well," she replied. "And that is sound reasoning. But we must also look to the other side of the world, where Archlord Domon works now to bring the people together. He was harsh at first, it is true, but his plan is working, and the many outlier nations of Darsor are beginning to come of their own will." This was a white lie, as it was technically true but not at all representative of the general opinion of the far continent toward Domon, and even toward his goal.

She then crafted indicated a decoration sitting on one windowsill, which her new order of cartographers called a globe, a gift from Nemental to Nytaea some months ago. She used this to show the best current estimates of the positions of each nation and how the continents fit together, using Perception magic to highlight certain areas and speak of the surveys that proved the distances did not match up near the edges of each continent if they were indeed circles. The space would not truly fit on a flat plane, and thus was a geometric impossibility.

The Torlegans' eyes glazed over a bit, of course, as she explained the world thus, though the Scoutmaster was nodding along most of the time, and opened his mouth to hesitantly say that they had experienced some of this already. It was attributed to the "strange workings" of the world, or human error, but it could not be denied that flat maps never seemed to do the lands of Argent justice. They were, however, much more interested in her silver arm, calling her Silverbone. A fitting nickname, one she approved of.

She was eventually shut down by Ethas, who declared such talk to be enough for now, aiming a meaningful stare her way. *Does he suspect?* she wondered, and Mani picked up on this, answering dismissively. *I know it is not direct deception,* she told the lunar force. *I mean the plan to discourage communication with Gaea.*

Ah, yes, at which you are succeeding perfectly.

Cease, metalheart. I am trying to listen.

The meeting went on for some time, ending when the Torlegan bear-men seemed to tire of the talk. They insisted all the more that more discussion would come, requesting leave to stay in the city for a few nights, which Mydia and Ethas, of course, granted. The Palace staff was already hard at work preparing a great meal featuring as much meat-heavy dishes in addition to local faire, so that the ambassadors had their choice of cuisine.

So it was that Rhidea found herself near the head of the table of distinction at the great feast. It was shocking how quickly the staff worked to prepare such culinary wonders. All forty-odd representatives were invited, while the soldiers they had brought remained in the barracks, treated to good Nytaean soldier faire. Two hundred forty soldiers could hardly have crammed into the palace dining hall.

Rhidea informed Mydia quietly at the end that she could not stay for the next day's negotiations, but that she may be able to return before they left. Mydia questioned her reasons, but she gave none. The Queen looked like she wanted to object, but what was she to say? What objection could she give? She would not start a scene by calling attention to her.

Looking a shade paler than usual but keeping her composure remarkably well, the young Queen said, "Well, then. We will see you when you return, Lady Rhidea."

The Wandering Mage nodded and left the room.

- Chapter 35 -

Yan'Vala

Manidor 2, 1295
progress
— From Lhinde's Vaul

She did not have a waystone close by to the canyon lands, so she traveled directly to northern Nemental. She out in the foothills near the Vala Mountains near the village of Kassfer, wherein she got a good steed for herself using Nytaean gold—which of course she'd traded Darsorian for, as she would not leave a trail for people to find. She also wore a more plain-haired illusion, and her drab dress held little indication of nobility. She was, perhaps, fortunate they did not question where she'd come upon the coin.

As she rode northward into the mountains, keeping her new horse at a reasonable pace, Mani stirred within her mind. *You know, if you were to acquire at some point a body of greater permanence, you would find a much faster way to travel wherever you desire.*

Is that so?

Indeed. There were Manian priests in the old days who gave up their flesh for bodies of purest silver, and they were able to meld into the very ground, traveling near-instantaneously through the bones of Mani, even through the great land bridge, although of course that is now impassible.

Again, the temptation, spoken in that teasing whisper, just serious enough that she knew he was not jesting. *There were really priests who did that? If it is so permanent, where are they today? What became of them?*

You always were an astute one, no? These men were of the old bloodline, possessing the bones of silver, but they were not the chosen priests. In fact, they struck a deal with me in expectation of further greatness. Partly out of curiosity, I entertained their desires, and for a while their ambitions, but when I grew bored of them, I consumed them into myself, and now . . . this moon is less two weak minds, and the Silver has returned to me. No loss.

And—

Why would I not do thus to you? A fair question, Souls of Silver. I sought you myself, and not for lack of better specimens like your recent predecessor— you have the potential for greatness, and are not simple-minded like those who came long ago. It is for this reason that I did not mourn the loss of your family and village, as heartless as this admission likely sounds. They had grown weak— the worst kind of growth, backward growth. Like a moon that gains an atmosphere and life, and then . . . loses it.

She swallowed, playing mentally over his words as she rode up steepening inclines. That last was an analogy for what was fated to happen to Mani's moon. He did not want it to end. He feared it.

Fear . . . is not the right word, daughter.

But I think it is, she pressed, taking advantage of his snooping. *You do not want your world to end—because you foresee that you may end with it?*

He was silent in her head for a moment, and she was able to ride in peace. Then: *I do not wish to return to my Mother; you are correct there.*

She smirked. Looking back, she saw only foothills rising and falling gently, and beyond those, the rocky plains of northern Nemental stretching for a couple of miles. The village of Kassfer was no longer in sight. Ahead, she was entering the territory where her horse, well-trained as the blessed beast was, had to pick out a good slanting path lest it be too steep to climb. The gelding had small, nimble feet perfect for just such a job, and had yet to trip once. The mountains that loomed before her, those were the true barrier into Yan'Vala.

Sword, she called on a whim, seeking a reaction.

Funny, Mani returned. *Your humor is fit for the gods. Only . . . not really.*

The boy, Kaen. You never answered me about his clone. What do you make of this "Silver Beast"?

The lunar entity seemed to sigh. *I cannot say. I believe you mean to imply that I was rash or manipulative when I made him out to be such a threat. While it is true that I did not expect the clone to show up on my surface so soon, it is not as though that one meta-man alone is necessarily a world-ending threat, but more that he is a chessman we can not control, a wild card with great potentia* *and no restraining, no harness.*

Very well. And what of his rationality? You are leaving out the fact that h *plays a very convincing copy of the original boy. And he seems to be in a righ* *state of mind. You had me on the offensive against him the entire time, and eve* *bid me antagonize him, but what for? Could we not, perhaps, have come to a* *accord and put aside this nonsense?*

Working with others is not our primary goal, and you know that.

And why not? By necessity you say, and yet I do not see the necess—

Mani suddenly roared in her mind, causing her metal arm to throb and he body to tense. Her gelding bucked, charging forward a few paces before calmin down again. "Sorry, old chap," she murmured.

Do not test me, mage, said Mani. *You are getting more presumptuous. It i* *fair to question my motives, but do not press me.*

Well, if you are to treat me as a mere pawn, then I believe I will do exactl *that. I could turn around right now, march back to Kaen, and demand that h* *take me to Gaea and perform the same operation on me.*

You wouldn't have the gall.

I would. And he would do it, too. You know he would.

The Silver Beast. You would go to the Silver Beast and turn yourself in *after opposing, attacking and incriminating him?*

Rhidea was breathing hard by this point. Mani was starting to get to her Of the two, she knew a godlike Titan had the greater emotional limits. But also . . . he was only heightening her point.

But that is just it. I did all that because you told me to. Because you *whispered in my ear about him. But I had no grounds such treatment of him* *What if he is not the Silver Beast?*

Again, Mani responded only on a delay. *Then I suppose time will cure you* *of your doubts. We will speak no further on this for now, daughter. For now* *you have a mission to carry out for your lover, no?*

Perhaps, if it is so godlike, you should keep your own humor to yourself.

Her horse, in fact, was only meant as a means up into the heart of the mountains. Upon reaching the highest passes, she dismounted and whispered a blessing in the horse's ear, stroking him fondly. "My thanks. Go in peace." She strode forward, gazing northward as the horizon dropped out below her, nearly to its full potential. She was perhaps a few thousand feet from the base of the mountain, so closer to five or six thousand from the level of the Sea of Emptiness. Often referred to as "cliff level", this was a fairly standard height that was difficult to measure without a solid team skilled in Earth and Perception magic, but it was doable, and using Mani's power she was able to find an estimate of around 5,600 feet from where she stood.

A long way down . . . I think this will work. Ready?

Why? What part have I to do?

Why, heal me should my fragile body give way upon some mistake.

All for your whims?

It is the fastest way, she replied, concluding the conversation. She had orbs from Domon that greatly amplified the teleportation she could perform using her golden Reality Stone and her Authority, but she would save that as much as possible and use a different method to quickly descend the mountain. She had full and powerful Authority in Earth and, of course, Silver. Casting about, she found . . . very little silver below the mountain. *Lovely. You could have warned me about this.*

You did just use my power to perform a sounding.

That is different . . . Rhidea glanced down, purse-lipped, at her glinting arm, and could have sworn she heard a hesitant groan coming from the Titan of Growth. *Ungrowth, for now,* she mused, and began to disassemble her own arm. It pulled off surprisingly easily, coming away in thick strands, which she uses to form a flat, thin shell. She stripped off everything right down to the last bit that covered her shoulder joint and nerve endings, which were just starting to tingle in warning.

Next, she drew up hard, solid stone from the mountainside next to her, Stonesinging it upon her metal shield like a molding in a die, until she had a long, flattish seat with a rounded bottom. A handle near the front . . . *Yes, this should work.* She mounted the contraption and, balancing on the last flat spot of the mountain, worked with Water and Earth Authority to wet the mountainside and scan for any obstructions, which she would preemptively mold into a flat shape.

Here we go.

The ride was smoother than she anticipated, and she was able to steer her little sled by leaning and by molding the earth in front of her. Any bumps and other obstructions coming up, she simply flattened them using Earth Authority and kept on, picking up outrageous speed. Soon, she was sure she was going faster than they'd gone on their gliders when crossing the Great Chasm. Afar off, the way she had marked out in her head quickly approached, and she steered herself so as to line up with the right branches and passes in the mountains. At times, she spooked wildlife, setting them running and even coming close to hitting them on occasion.

Down she slid, losing altitude fast enough to make her ears pop multiple times, and eventually she was into the southern Yan'Vala foothills. It seemed they ended more abruptly than those south of the mountains, and suddenly she was approaching the land that merely seemed to slope gently. To her left, the Vala Mountains continued northwest into the horizon, whilst north and east sprawled out open before her, split by crags and reaching fingers of rock. It truly was a wild and strange land, ruled by stone.

She continued on her self-made path, still gliding at incredible speed thanks to water and earth reformation. Slowly, slowly, she slowed with the defiling of the land, coming to the pace of a horse in gallop, then a fast horse at a lazy canter, then a man's running speed, and then . . . she debarked, tipping herself into a run, and split her shield without looking into stone and silver, reforming her arm with the beautiful metal. She barely glanced down to ensure that Mani had directed it back into her natural shape, which he had. Slowing, she peered into the northern horizon, just slightly east, and took hold of her Reality Stone as she *bent* the space of Mani, reappearing on a small ridge of rock nearly a mile away.

After the initial moment's disorientation, she looked again, seeing no towns yet, and performed an even longer jump, coming out on flat ground with only a stumble. Again, no towns. *Come on, this time . . .* She jumped once more, and found herself a small distance from a town, unwalled and perhaps a few hundred in population. *Perfect.* She approached at a purposeful walk, trying to will herself to look dignified yet not overly glaring. Glancing down belatedly, she checked to see if her dress needed any touching up. She was a bit wet, flecked with dirt on the front and left side due to her wet mode of travel. She used Water Authority to wring the moisture from her clothing, taking a good amount of the dirt and green stains with it. That would have to do.

The townsfolk, as expected, looked at her strangely and greeted her in hesitant words of a sharp and foreign accent. But they spoke the common tongue, and did not show hostility when she claimed to be an ambassador from Kystrea. She spoke in a way that did not make it clear whether she meant one of the Provinces or Nytaea's new state, but they did not question her. They pointed out the way to their great city of Shivoth, whence the rulers would be preparing to soon send their own ambassadors to Nytaea.

Thanking the people for their generosity, she set off once more with a new steed purchased with Domon's coin—let them puzzle that one out—for Shivoth. The mare was supposedly one of the best they had to offer, but she was more a pony than a horse, shaggy and built for trudging about the rocky land and pulling loads—not for great speed. But she had to conserve her energy somehow, and there was nothing wrong with old fashioned equine transportation.

Keeping the landmarks in sight, she plodded on with her pony, eventually impressed at its stamina as the hours dragged later. Eventually, she stopped to camp, which in this case meant heading off the road a short ways, tethering her horse, and curling up in her traveling cloak. A few hours later, she woke to a chill she was unused to. These lands were cooler in the cloud-obscured nights than closer to the equator. She resumed her trek, turning in the pony at the next town in favor of her somewhat-recovered magic. She should be within Reality range of Shivoth at this point. As soon as she could be certain that no eyes were watching, she performed a jump, then another, then another . . . and another.

Panting, she squinted against the hazy horizon and decided that yes, there was something there—A tremulous shift in the land, as though gouged and uneven.

Perfect. The first chasm.

She kept on at a brisk walk, letting her heartrate steady out while the rent in the land solidified in her vision. She was some thousand feet from its head, a thin, snakelike line, and at the tail end . . . yes, that should be the city. She could see the spires poking up like needles.

One more large jump, and she stood a mile or so before the reaching city which was set upon a plateau and formed of great pillars of rock, hung by bridges overtop of bridges over other bridges. Lore stated that the city's officials ordered at least one built every year, adding to the tangled mess. Sometimes, she reflected, enough was simply enough. Shivoth, the hidden city of Yan'Vala . . . she had been here only once in her life, in search of their library, which had proved more of a disappointment than she'd have thought.

The highway became a wider road paved with flat stone and well maintained, with little grass growing up through the cracks. Gnarly trees attempted to shade it, giving an exotic look to the place. The city itself did not have walls, nor gates, but instead great steps that led up to the southern entrance, which she was approaching. Some dozen others were approaching ahead of her, and others exiting.

At the gateway stood men in leather armor and round, feathered metal caps, bearing rapiers at their sides. They didn't look to be the finest muscle in the world, but then, this was not supposed to be that dangerous of a place. Aside from the usual—and increasing—reports of strange monsters near the continent's borders, Yan'Vala was well unified under their king and had little to no disputes with neighboring lands.

She nodded to the guards, and was about to pass by when the guard on the right called out to her, asking about her arm. Resisting an eyeroll, she stopped and approached him. "Good day, sir."

"Say, you're not from around here. I have to ask ma'am, what's the story?"

She glanced down at her arm, then looked blankly at the man's angular face. "Long, in fact. I come bearing news from Nytaea and Archlord Domon, in fact."

His eyes widened, hopefully indicating sufficient distraction from the matter of her metal prosthetic. "Ah, I see, eh? Say, might you be that woman they've been speak'n about?" He signaled the other guard with his eyes, though she did not get the impression that he was suspicious or purposely prying—rather, if anything, thinking of the bragging points and gossip fodder.

"They call me the Wandering Mage, yes," she said. "I've been once before, but it's been some time. None may remember me now."

The thin man was nodding along with her, clearly impressed beyond proper brain function. "Thas nice. Right nice. And Fink, they was just talking 'bout . . ." He trailed off, apparently at last noticing the folk walking to and fro through the gate, some of whom had stopped to regard Rhidea or comment about her. At this point, some sense returned to him. "I'll let ya be on your way, m'lady. Don't want ya t'be gawked at like so." He doffed his metal cap, and she returned a curt nod, curbing her amused smile.

The amusement was a faint emotion she allowed to show, while underneath she was crawling with agitation. She'd not wanted to draw so many eyes already. Preferably, in and out and done. Meet with the king, state her message, return to inform Domon.

Perhaps return to Nytaea. That depended on the king's reaction. Informing Nytaea may be necessary, if distasteful.

It took her many a minute to remember and navigate the way up to the king's lair, which was part of the central spire of the city. Each was anywhere from twenty to a hundred paces thick, and his was the largest and highest. But it could not be accessed from the ground, so she had to get to one of the entrances. Each had structures ringing it, secured right into the stone, and were also crawling with cave systems in which dwelt the citizens of Shivoth. Yan'Vala was known for its Reality magi, who were the secret chefs behind it all.

Finally, she was able to show her credentials to the gatemen, who looked a bit more serious than the city guards, less for show. Upon convincing them to believe her and shut up about it, she entered the first tunnel system, which led inward before clawing out to either side with passageways and stairwells. Stairs seemed good. She was able to get up two more levels before needing to ask the next guards she saw for directions.

At last, she made it to the king's own level, which had many less occupants, most of whom seemed about some serious business, unless they were the servants busily about whatever menial business they were proscribed. The king himself, contrary to the tradition of other nations, was not only open to petitions but to anyone in the vicinity, as long as he was in. An inner room, large and square, looked in upon were he sat on a simple wooden stool, arms crossed and speaking with a man in front of him. Others waited behind, and she took this as a cue to get in line. The current dialogue was something about the man's shop and how he may be able to skirt recently changed regulations. The exchange ended in a shrug from the king and a surprising apology.

The king was pale and thin, not unhealthily so but just enough that it seemed he rarely got out and was unused to physical exertion—but also unused to excess. Named Finval, he was a new king appointed some six years prior. After ten years, a king of Yan'Vala was said to require proof of his competency to keep his position, lest he be booted out and a new king appointed by his inner ring of advisors. A couple of these, she was pretty sure, stood by in the room right now. Did they approve of his rule, or were they waiting for four more years so they could displace him? Interestingly enough, she couldn't say whether an emperor like Domon would have kept his seat all these decades had such a system been in place, for it was hard to argue that he was not an effective ruler.

The next petition, too, was soon done, something about a missing child that had not turned up yet—and, the king regretfully informed the applicant, the authorities had no news. One more, and she stood before him. The pale king took a small breath, as though dismissing the previous matter from his brain so that he may now deal with this woman. He quickly recognized her, though she only knew it when he opened his mouth and greeted her by title, then name.

"Indeed, My Lord," she said with a small curtsy.

The motion did not impress the king, who sat now with uncrossed arms but no more interest than he'd shown for any of the others. "I was informed of your arrival, and I had heard of your . . . new status as well. What matter do you bring?"

She glanced behind her uncertainly. Only one man stood behind her, and not uncomfortably close, but still she asked, "I bring important news from the far continent of Darsor—is there not a more private place we could discuss?"

"There is not. Nothing you say here is unfit for the ears of my people, madam. Now speak, before I tire of this conversation."

Testy, aren't we? "Very well. Archlord Domon, as you may have heard, has transcended the Sea of Emptiness and laid claim to the lands beyond. I come from Nytaea and Randhorn, where a strong alliance has recently formed against the Empire of Kystrea. When Domon left, he abandoned much of the aggression he had shown toward us outlier nations, for he has set his sights on new lands and a new goal."

The king let out a slow breath, head processing her words. "And what is this goal?"

"He . . . I should stress that I was extremely hesitant to believe this . . . he has become concerned with the ticking clock that is Mani. The thousand years. Have you heard rumors of such a matter?"

"Rumors—vague ones, mostly from the recent messengers of Nytaea. Continue."

"Allow me to tell you a fuller story."

- Chapter 36 -

Monsters and Other Such Nonsense

Manidor 2, 1295
progress
— From Lhinde's Vault

Domon, Archlord of his home continent and Emperor of Darsor, reached out his hand and petted the long-necked Sor'Vech, eyes intensely focused on it as its growl turned to a stuttering purr. It rocked its head against his hand, dog-like ears twitching in an almost feline way. "A Sor'Vech," he said musingly.

Solomiya watched, silent as he met the animal. They were outside the palace in a small courtyard where few visited. In this dusklight, with few torches about, it would be hard to make out the scene in any case. With his other hand he held her close, that those who may yet see would mistake this for a meeting between lovers. Solomiya was as much a secret to most of the officials here as her monster pets. While she felt no particular attraction to the emperor, she also didn't mind his touch.

"I will admit, I had my doubts," he said to her, pulling on her shoulder in what almost seemed a suddenly affectionate touch. But no, as soon as he slackened his grip, she perceived that it was but a passing gesture of satisfaction—perhaps as much in his being right to trust her as in his gratitude toward her. "I take it your other stories, too, are not mere fanciful nonsense?"

She turned to look at him. "None, My Lord Emperor. Do you wish me to bring you some of the others? It is hard, with some of them, to do so without . . . making a scene. Some, too, are forbidden to free, so I would be breaking my country's laws."

"Which you have no compunction against."

"You speak truly."

"But I would rather go myself."

"My Lord? That is your wish?"

He tapped absently on her shoulder, his grip loose. "It is. I will set my palace in order here and ensure that the right—and only the right—staff know I am gone."

"And Rhidea?"

"She should be returning soon to Redufiel via Reality Stone. You deposited the stones in Ribsha?"

"I did, My Lord Emperor."

He said nothing, but his mood seemed pleased.

Her lord's prediction proved accurate when the High Mage arrived the next day. She knew that the reason he did not want to leave Redufiel before her return was as much due to his fear of the Gaean's imminent next strike as it was of Rhidea's unpredictability. Allowing her to run amok in the city did not seem a particularly wise choice. This way, there was at least some understanding between them of who was where and what the other was doing.

At least, as Solomiya understood it. When the two came out of his audience chamber, Lieda of Nytaea had joined them, shoulder as cold as ever. She had yet to speak to Solomiya whatsoever, arms crossed, foot tapping impatiently for her lord's return. The red-haired spy wondered with some amusement if she even knew that she would be departing alone with Domon soon.

The little woman's entire demeanor changed when the Emperor withdrew from the room, though she spared a particularly ugly look for the Silver Mage— just another mark of her banal idiocy. It was like a fly shooting a passing spider a dirty look. Amusing, but not smart. Of course, this was Lieda. Intelligence and wisdom came to different individuals in different measures.

"Well, Lieda," said Rhidea, first to speak, "it appears you will be watching over me while these two are away."

The narrow-eyed look the black-haired woman sent her was equal parts suspicious and confused, with a touch of her ordinary delusional pride that denied the existence of the latter.

"When do we leave?" Solomiya asked the Emperor, making no mention of the Sor'Vech lest she tip off either of the other two—though she doubted Rhidea had been left out of the loop.

"In one hour," he answered. "Prepare your things. And Lieda, one word."

Solomiya took that as her cue to depart, though she had little preparation to do. She soon sensed a presence, and turned to see the Wandering Mage approaching over her shoulder. "Be careful," she said in a low voice. "Mani does not know what to make of the growing monster presence, but he says it could herald something good or bad for our future. They should be used with wisdom and not unleashed too soon."

Solomiya blinked in annoyance. "All that I know."

"Then it is merely a reinforcement of that knowledge—an encouragement toward wisdom."

Solomiya said nothing for a moment, parsing the statement. She came to the conclusion that it was not meant with any malice, and gave up her annoyance with a small sigh. "Well, then thank you. Do enjoy babysitting my sister."

Rhidea, who knew full well that they were not related, gave a smirk in reply, though she wasn't sure what it meant.

They went using Dark Reality, an experimental force in which Domon had recently made breakthroughs. Rhidea and Solomiya both were equipped at all times with amplification devices that allowed the channeling of this force. They seemed almost limitless, save for the strange buzzing they began to emit after too much use. It was like a warning straight from the belly of Mani, a rumbling that forewarned dangerous parting of the fabric of the world. For the dark secret of Domon's experiments was that Mani was already falling apart at the seams, leaving the Wellspring's power uneven and at times choppy. Dark Magic only further exacerbated this, though he insisted it was safe in moderation. To be fair, nearly everything was, be it molds or heavy metals or physical injuries.

But the clock was ticking, and none could say just what would come when the day of a thousand years arrived.

Soon, they were on the outskirts of Skabeld, capital of Ribsha where her father ruled. Firstly they returned the Sor'Vech to its underground pen, and then paid Solomiya's father a visit, striding right in amongst the low wooden buildings and streets of hesitant passersby, all seeming to walk in a haze. They could tell that something was off lately, a restlessness in the land. Not all knew about the monsters, but all had heard the stories, and had heard the recent reports of some of the ancient creatures arising once more, even beyond the confines of their prisons.

Her father's was little more impressive a building than any of the others, though it did have two stories. It took little convincing to get the guards to let them in, and Teld himself soon met them, eyes wide and posture quickly diminishing. "Daughter . . . Emperor. We are humbly at your service, Great Lord. What brings you thus to humble Ribsha."

"Your . . ." Domon looked round, noting the few prying eyes and ears. "Your local creatures, Teld. Let us go in where there is more privacy, and we shall talk."

"Of course, Lord Emperor. Of course."

It was a mere quarter of an hour later that they left, having informed the Lord of Skabeld of their purpose this night. A writ with his own seal would allow them easy passage into the more heavily guarded prisons and stables.

They visited the ancient mines north of Skabeld, set in the base of the Lonesome Mountains Three, wherein they used Water and Fire Authority to shield themselves from the heat. Down and down they went, until they came upon the iron gate the enclosed the Flamebeasts, remnants of an earlier era of Mani. These had been discovered some century ago, or so said her grandfather, after being thought extinct since the scouring. These were smaller than the stories clamied, crawling about on two small back legs and oversized front claws, powered by hulking shoulders. Their horns tending to loop forward tightly before curving backward. In all, perhaps two to three hundred pounds.

The two watched as the Flamebeasts prowled around, some looking aimless while others roughhoused. Only one of them sparked a fight whilst they look on, puffing out its chest to spew great billows of flame upon another. The other, after shying away with a deep grunt, sprang forward and beat its horns against the other, clutching its shoulders with its claws and rolling to one side.

Some of the others looked toward the gate, noticing the visitors. They began slowly stalking toward them, and Solomiya said, "We should go. We don't want to antagonize them."

Domon, either noting the skeletons that dotted the fire fields of the creatures' pen or sensing the tightness in his underling's voice, nodded and backed away, turning as she did. "How dangerous are they?"

"Of the seven monster types native to Ribsha, they rank in the middle. One of them, if left loose in a town and threatened or otherwise instigated, could lay flame to the entire village in minutes. Their fire is carried in their bodies for hours or days after leaving the caverns, and they get a portion of it back naturally after resting."

More nodding. "Well, they should be useful."

Personally, Solomiya doubted that. These were poorly trained and hard to control, and their fire would likely be of little use against the aerial Gaean war vessels. "Well, if you'd like to see the true terrors, we can head farther north?"

"Let's," he said. "I'm not sure you've told me of these ones."

"I have not. They are called Teleskari—'self-predators' in High Legaleian."

He said nothing in reply.

"I will show you them, My Lord, and then explain further. It is best explained visually. Although I would warn you that they are . . . off-putting, to say the least—enough to freeze lesser men in place upon sight. Especially after a full molt."

He gave a grim smile. "Glad I'm not a lesser man, then."

It was her turn to give no reply.

- Chapter 37 -

Vanguard

Manidor 2, 1295:
They rained from the sky like bolts of metal lightning, and silver and dark
fire streaked back. A war fought in the air over Redufiel, a battle for the
history books . . . but only just the beginning.
— From Lhinde's Vault

Rhidea was unsurprised when the reports came of the Gaean fleets. In fact, Mani had sensed them first, and she was already mobilizing the Redufiel military, ineffective though they would be. But they could at least give the horn signals, ordering all nearby citizens to pull back into the city before the gates were closed. She would not have them closed at all, for it seemed a danger only to those trapped outside and seeking to get in—given the invaders would be coming from the sky—but Domon would never have that. Fortunately, they listened to her, and especially the mage forces he had been slowly building. They began erecting a barrier about the city, using Dark Reality and Water, forming a barrier seemingly of solid glass. This had been proven effective against concussive weapons.

The ships were soon seen coming down through the clouds, glimmering shapes of metal that glowed with unearthly light of green and red. A good number streaked straight down to the established base, while others fell upon the land round about for miles. This was no tentative raid, but a full-scale attack.

"Prepare for deadly force!" she shouted to the nearby generals, Tellis and Thorak, and to the mage general Laslow, "Reality cannons are ready to go?"

"Yes, My Lady!" He hurried off, calling to his men and women of relative strength, largely made up of the Mage Soldiers Domon had taken from Nytaea and Ti'Vaeth. They were a sorry lot, but she had been helping to train them these last months, and they had been bolstered with various devices of Domon's own making, working them into full-fledged weaponry capable—so they hoped—of taking out Gaean aircraft. Where Nytaea had cooperation and magical might, Redufiel had ingenuity and Dark-imbued technology.

Lieda, she checked to make sure, had gone off with the Lightning Cadre where she would pool her power with others to attempt to strike ships from the sky. Though she knew the woman would hide as close to the back as possible.

All forces took high positions on the walls and the main castle, while notified Domon and then teleported to the Silver Field north of the castle. Once a courtyard kept for festivals, it had now been dug up and cleared of all topsoil and bedrock, baring the unusually high top layer of silver, which Rhidea would be personally using to defend the city. Reality magi took up positions on each cardinal direction from her, where they erected special mirrors looking out from the city walls. These she bolstered with her own elemental magic, expanding the view and the doorway itself, and the magi four stepped gingerly to the side of their portal.

"Ready, Lady Argent," they called one after the other. The new title was both a reference to her homeland and her power.

What is your take, Mani? Do they mean to attack us here and now?

Yes. Prepare to defend—though they may be headed for other lands as well. We cannot know how far-reaching this offensive is.

She reached into her dress and found her communication stone for Nytaea, activating it and explaining the situation. Telling the queen to relay it to others, she dropped the connection and channeled her focus on the approaching ships. Then she launched her first preemptive attack, molding silver darts from the shining field and sending them streaking toward the nearest ship in the eastern view.

Immediately, she heard the deep, roaring sound of fire exploding over the city. But it was over—detonating on the hard watery field overshadowing the city, sending harsh ripples across the visible sky. The sound was muted, but she knew that above the canopy, the explosions must be deafening.

Her darts struck home, impaling the approaching ship and sending it lurching toward one side. She did the same for others, and beheld the beautiful sight of a Reality cannon striking its own target, blasting one of the sky ships with a wave of dark fire. It rolled over, and nearly straight off, of the vessel, but left a burning trail over its surface. She was uncertain of the damage it inflicted, but the pilot was visibly impaired at least visually by it.

The Lightning Cadre struck a few ships, mostly ineffectively, though in one case they managed to make a ship lurch ominously, its fate unknown. More bombs rained upon the city, some bursting through but none making it to the structures before detonation. However, green beams began pelting the barrier, where they rippled and shot down in seemingly random directions, heat partly dissipated but still bearing destructive force. *Those are the real danger . . .* she realized, although there was no telling how long the Water magi could keep up the barrier at all.

They had to outlast the enemy and convince them to turn about, retreating to the Gaean base or out of the atmosphere entirely. Or, best of all, destroy them.

By their visible numbers, however, that last did not look to be an option. Slowly, implacably, a slithering dragon of fear crept into her chest, tightening around her heart. She knew it may not leave until this was all over, one way or another.

- Chapter 38 -

Siege

Manidor 2, 1295
beginning
— From Lhinde's Vaul

Mydia glanced northward at the great, reaching, splitting trunk of her magica child, the Tree of Nytaea, as the people had affectionately taken to calling it Some, she knew, were whispering prayers and pleas to it right now like an ido or charm, but she wondered at the effectiveness of such efforts. Of course . . . i may well be all they could do. Looking back toward the eastern skyline, she waited.

They had received the news mere minutes prior, and the rush of mobilizing forces both magical and mundane were now beyond her. It seemed they'd barely had time to repair the city, yet at the same time there was a different air about the city. They had been assaulted by a serious force intent on destroying them and they had prevailed. The people now had real faith, misplaced or not, that they could prevail a second time. Faith in Mydia, in her tree, in the chain of magi about the continent who were all pooling their strength now in effort to stave off this second full assault.

But did they really know "full" yet? Had she any clue of the real might of Gaea? An entire globe armed with technology honed over a millennium where Mani was nearly clueless . . . chills spread across her spine every time she thought of it, and today was no passing consideration. The time had come upon them again, the time to fight and hold their beloved city.

Magi prepared, soldiers loaded crossbow and ballistae, and all along the wall preparations were being made. This time, they had insisted that she stay farther back—"they" being everyone in every circle of the city. They had not been happy about their queen being endangered so, though she had won respect for it in the eyes of some. Ethas had been livid.

One new addition was the twin towers at the southeast and northeast corners of the city walls, which had been erected in conjunction with sister towers all throughout Nemental, Storklance, Sorfaen, and—soon—Yan'Vala and Torlega. They had others in Ti'Vaeth and the surrounding city-states already, and one in construction in Lygellis. These channeled magical strength from beneath Mani's surface and from the magi interlinked between them. The strongest, as of yet, were Nytaea's due to the large pool of magi about the city and manning each tower.

Strong spell walls protected each, and Rhidea had cast webs of silver about them like a protective shell, which acted as a skeleton for the Water and Reality shields, whilst their defensive capabilities were largely reliant upon Lightning and Fire.

They began to hurl magic from the towers, and beautiful carnage erupted in the sky. Flames from the left, lightning bolts from the right. One single bolt took a sky ship down, noticeable only by how it suddenly stilled and careened slowly to the side, whilst the fireballs were simply wearing down enemy shields similar to how their own green energy beams did. These they cast now in reply, along with exploding missiles that caused Nytaea's walls to shudder.

But they held. They were strong, and had been recently reinforced by the world's one Silver Mage. The magi on the walls, and Mydia from her safety at the Palace, kept up similar giant illusions in the sky for the purpose of confusing the enemy, if nothing else. It helped that the magi of the two towers aimed magic in the direction that the monster turned.

Those ships which inevitably made it over the walls soon began raining down concussive and incendiary bombs upon the houses, though the new Water/Reality shield helped to repel many. It did not, however, stay the green energy beams, which passed through it at odd angles, melting into stone and igniting wood. Where they hit spell-forged silver, as in the pillars about the Palace, the beams simply fizzled out and became nothing.

Suddenly, there were only two more ships remaining, then none. *Where have they . . . ?*

A soldier captain ran up to her. "Milady! The enemy has split to north and south, and the mage towers are now out of range."

"I . . ." She looked around anxiously. "I don't know what that means. Make sure Ethas and Enchro are informed, tell the guardsmen to stay vigilant."

"Yes, Milady." The man bowed and left, calling other men to him.

She sighed and wiped her brow. The very idea of military men coming to her—her!—for directions was still shocking to her, despite it being a familiar thing by now. She was simply unfit to be giving soldiers orders. When possible she handed that duty off to Ethas Gandel.

- Chapter 39 -

Rubble

Manidor 2, 1295:
beginning.
— From Lhinde's Vault

Redufiel looked distinctly different following the first real aerial battle. Seemingly a quarter of the city smoldered, smoke trailing up into the mage-erected barrier roof, which none had been willing to take down yet, the people were in an uproar. Wailing could be heard over dead soldiers and civilians, and the shouting of soldiers trying to bring order and carry out the commands of their emperor.

Rhidea gave a few further commands to the Reality magi under her command, informing them that she would be with the Archlord, and then warped space to appear beside him—a useful spell of his own concoction that allowed his closest confidants and underlings to travel directly to his side, wherever they could safely fit. Now, as in most cases, he turned, eyes showing annoyance. "Oh, it's you. I see my city has been desecrated."

She looked patiently at him, waiting for the words he was holding back.

He looked away first. "Well done on the defense, Cae. I should have known somehow that the moment I went away would be the moment they attacked en masse." Domon had returned just in time to hurl additional Dark Magic at the sky raiders, burning and strangling the ships. His offensive power was almost as great as Rhidea's, or perhaps more. Even before their retreat, however, many of the vessels had traveled southward and—according to Mani and to scouting reports—in other directions as well. For the first time, Gaea's forces were spreading out across the land to destroy and take. *Both in equal measures?* she wondered, *Or is there more of a plan here? Are they after something, or do they just want to see Mani burn?*

That question had yet to be answered. Predictably, Mani had no answer for her.

You know I cannot predict the actions or intents of my Mother's children, he spoke now in her mind. *I did warn you of this attack, no? I have your good in my mind, and naturally have the interests of all my people at heart. I do not like the growing base of operations that the Gaeans have near you now. Only a few miles away.*

Yes . . . and now they attacking all parts of the globe.

They are. Even now, I feel it in . . . let's see, you would say Castanor, and Ribsha and Torlega and Lygellis—

Ribsha?

. . . Yes. That is what I said.

Then . . . that could mean—

"Cae. I asked you a question." The Archlord's voice was cutting, his temper obviously foul.

"My apologies. Thank you, but the praise is unnec—"

"I asked about the whereabouts of the other Gaean forces. Surely Mani has a way of finding such things?"

"Indeed," she answered smoothly, not looking to test him further. "Gaean forces have gotten to the outlier nations, My Lord. Castanor, Felmani, Kalatar, Ribsha . . ."

His face reddened in anger, and he let out a vile oath. "Ribsha . . . of course. But there is no way that they know of the monsters kept therein, nor should they stumble on them by accident. But if by chance . . ."

"Solomiya remains there, yes?"

"She does." Domon rubbed his chin with one hand for a moment, thinking. Then a wicked smile spread over his face. "I have a plan. You'll like it, trust me. Or at least, your patron will."

[He decides to set up Reality magi ASAP to transfer as many monsters as possible to safekeeping in Redufiel, and transport Ribshan monster-masters to Redufiel, leaving Ribsha to their own devices. Ribsha gets overtaken along with most of the outlier nations, while Domon unleashes the monsters upon the Gaean encampment.]

Gaea

- 85 -

- Chapter 40- -

Rubble

Manidor 2, 1295
beginning
— From Lhinde's Vaul

General Inecc clasped shoulder with General Frauss, wishing the man good fortune in battle and safe travels to Gaea. Zent did the same for each, wishing he were the one going back to Mani to defend the silver world. The League's forces had a good head start on them, but there were preparations that had to be made. Fortunately, they now had a fleet of over two hundred space-faring vessels ready to go, most of which were lined up. Inecc would be taking sixty fighter, Frauss another sixty, and Kaen another fleet of sixty.

Zent would be staying with the Ccamos military to defend against the imminent Cydenges strike, for increasingly their readings were detecting instability in Luna's signals. Why the League had given the go-ahead now to attack was beyond any reasoning, yet they had been predicting that too. Lldsao had shown time and again that his ambition exceeded his wisdom—or at least seemed to.

One by one, Kaen's fleet roared their engines and took off into the sky, sixty vessels flying out in formation. Then Inecc. Then Frauss. The high-arching shield dome of the city opened specially for them, closing after a few minutes when all were past. Zent watched them disappear into the sky, a gleam of white and green and gold, and within minutes they were out of the lower atmosphere

"Well," he said, turning to General Fors, "That means it's time for "

[Ccamos ought to have reviewed Lyn's material in her Vault, poring over every detail, by this point, and be even now expecting some kind of move from Luna. Hoping that she returns, but knowing full well that if she doesn't, it means she's failed and Luna's ire is most likely raised against Gaea. It only makes sense.

Gaea

Perhaps they try to take this to the Senate, who won't have it at all, and that's why they so stubbornly do not prepare (largely anyway, except for a few.) Also need a chapter or two in here from Lldsaor's side of things.]

- Chapter 39 -

Rubble

Manidor 2, 1295
beginning
— From Lhinde's Vaul

Redufiel

- Chapter 40 -

Rubble

Manidor 2, 1295:
beginning.
— From Lhinde's Vault

Redufiel

- Chapter 41 -

Rubble

Manidor 2, 1295
beginning
— From Lhinde's Vaul.

Redufiel

- Chapter 42 -

Like Stars from Heaven

They fell from blackest night amidst watchful stars—bloody streaks like tears of the moon herself, weeping for the harm she inflicted upon us. But if she has any remorse, it does not manifest itself in mercy, for she withholds not her hand, but continues to send the rains of destruction upon our lands periodically. The fury of heaven, raw and unfiltered.
— From The Fall of Starklett

It was Maldunech that took the first hit. Luna shone high above in the sky, gazing ominously in a waxing circle nearly complete, and some would go on to say that it had been just perfectly completed, when the red light glowed. There were warning signals in advance, largely ignored for the low probability given of an attack so soon after the last. It wasn't the right time, the right season . . . the readings weren't strong enough. Excuses like that.

Gaea shuddered under the impact of a hundred Cydenges bodies, stomping against the fertile lands just north and west of the city. Not a dozen, not two, but as many as had been sent in the entire last wave. Alarms rang out from the city, a mere background jabber to the mechanical ears of the moon creatures, who flicked their long, spiny tails in anticipation, looking from one to another as they advanced on the metropolis of civilization.

Around Gaea, their brethren landed in sync, one squadron after another, some aiming for cities while others sought other hotspots, and their aquatic brethren targeted highlights in the seas.

Among those now surrounding Maldunech, there were Leonids and Brutes represented, who rushed the city's shield wall and the base, crashing into the gates with such force that the foremost injured their own scales. But they did as commanded and spared no slightest effort in their frenzied assault. Then they opened their jaws and poured for energy pooled collectively, aiming it tightly upon the gates' center. Even as the first sky ships exited the shield wall, hunting the Cydenges, they rammed the gate again in a concerted effort. Bombs dropped and metal blew apart, but they kept on. More ships poured out of the opening in the shield wall, and . . .

From the sky, the Avians came, diving like falcons. They fell like a scarlet starbeam upon the shield wall, bursting it like fragile glass. Leonids took to the sky, pursuing the weakness, and some were gunned down by the sky ships, but without the use of the Hellebes' energy beams, it was visibly difficult to hit them accurately, and many got through. Those inside dove for the inner wall gate complex, even as more Cydenges fell from space about the gate.

In short order, the gates crashed open, throwing aside the Hellebes who had been physically holding it back. Bones crunched, blood streaked the metal-shod entry bay, and futilely expended Geokinetic energy was hungrily vampirized by the metallic creatures, boosting their power.

Cydenges surged through the yawning gates, executing their mission with ruthless efficiency. Not a complex battle plan or subtle infiltration, but a singular, simple goal: Kill and destroy. Slay the counter-natural abominations the children of Those Deserving, and tear down the great things they have built upon the altar of nature and the bones of humanity.

The city was engulfed in the roar of lunar metal on concrete and steel, the triumphant shrieks of successful invaders, and the din of gunfire and concussive weaponry. Structures buckled. Smoke bellowed into the air, and over all, the red force shield hung like a stupefied onlooker, hemming in the violence uselessly. It encased the city of Maldunech like a great red tomb, flickering but implacable, until at last its flicker became an urgent sputtering, and it began to deteriorate under loss of power.

So fell the great metropolis of Maldunech, second of the Nine Cities of Man.

But it was only the beginning.

End of Part Three

PART THREE

Offensive

Luna

- Chapter 43 -

The Second Wave

Manidor 2, 1295:
progress.
— From Lhinde's Vault

"How many?"

The question came from General Fors over the radio. Zent hesitated a moment, and the general clarified:

"How many still stand, by best reports?" He kept his voice cool, but his demeanor was off from its usual brusqueness. There was an energetic immediacy to his request, an echo of the panic felt by all of Ccamos, and all the world, right now. Even as Zent's newfound countrymen and veteran companions fought for all their lives out there.

"Six . . . we think. Trident was holding last we knew, and Chronala is dire." Lyn and her generals had warned Daedalus on multiple occasions of the importance of beefing up his defenses, of making certain that the Emperor did not commission all his appointed forces for the Mani assault, but he wouldn't listen. Lyn had sent a thousand men, set on a quarterly rotation, to bolster the center of the world's population regrowth, but the rhinoceros was a stubborn one and refused to grow a backbone where Lldsaor was concerned. Thus, the city was among the worst suffering from the Cydenges attack, whilst Haven and Ccamos and Haccolces were the only cities to have staunchly repelled the moon beasts.

One day had passed since the Cydenges offensive, and the world was reeling, all circles straining to function even well enough to transfer soldiers and supplies where most needed. Fors, the stand-in for Lyn, had even been contacted for the first time since her departure—using a backup line, since both major lines were down for the time being. Fors had replied with a simple, direct demand: No talk until the League recalled all forces from Mani. They were still waiting on a reply regarding that.

Daedalus, despite his lackluster response to Ccamos' recent contribution of troops to his city, had made time for at least two transmissions—Zent wasn't there to personally monitor communications at all times—with Ccamos, though none could say what exchanges he might also have had with Haccolces.

In response to Zent's sparse answer, Fors said, "Well, I'm surprised I haven't been called on again yet. Besides . . . well, our own military, but Inecc and Frauss and the others seem to have a handle on that for now." By *a handle,* he meant that, by working round the clock like most of administration thus far, they had barely retained a grip on the authority structure and kept in contact with the proper branches—aside from Mani. They had a special contingent waiting to blast off at a moment's notice to go to Mani and inform the space force that they were needed earth-side ASAP.

Until then . . . they couldn't risk pulling them back while Lyn's people may need them. They would wait for a messenger to arrive. All a messenger had to do was pull up from the silvery atmosphere, breaking the Energy Field, and send a long-wave transmission back to Gaea, yet the last they'd heard from them was a week ago. Too long.

"Sir, should we send the messenger just in case? What if the situation is dire there?"

"We don't have the luxury of dwelling on the moon fronts much right now," the General replied tightly. "If they are in real trouble, one more ship will only get pulled into whatever mess is going on. It could even be that Mani has engaged some manner of shield in response to Luna's assault." His expression briefly darkened further through his many eyebrow creases.

"Want me to swap you out for a short rest, General?" Zent asked, clasping his hands behind his back. His old bones were already feeling exhausted, but he wasn't about to show it when there was something he could do to help his overtaxed commanding officer.

Fors hesitated for a moment. "Tempting," he said darkly, though his tone indicated there might be a hint of the old distrust in his hesitancy. "You look as worn as I feel, old dog. We're going to need you in top shape in case things get rough."

Zent grunted in mild amusement. He was nowhere near top shape right now . . . and he had hardly gotten a lick of combat yet. That was probably where his sense of guilt came from. At least it seemed he was wrong about Fors' reluctance . . . maybe. There was no way to know with that one.

Zent turned away. "If you'll excuse me, then, sir, I need to check on the scouts." The scouts patrolling the city exterior, that is, for stray Cydenges.

The general excused him with a curt nod, and he departed for another office, where he checked in on the scouts' progress—non discovered in the last few hours—and proceeded to type out communications with Ccamos forces in Chronala. Also with Phelps and his commanders in Haven, who had deployed forces to aid in Trident—which was still an area of hot Cydenges activity. Reports spoke of new types of Cydenges: winged birds and burrowing insects and crawling spiders. Trident, set high on the western cliffs of Nestra, had been swarmed by the new Cydenges species, if that was what they were, and the tide had slowed little even after the full and pitiful retreat was called.

Two million Hellebes. That was how many had called that city their home. Fifty thousand made it out. They had been moved to Haccolces, unsurprisingly, along with the refugees of Maldunech. The latter had fallen quicker due to careful coordination on the enemy's part and a pathetic lack of security, but many had still escaped by the seaways, even with the aquatic Cydenges blockade.

Now the survivors from Maldunech and Trident were holing up in the great Steel City, while military from multiple different cities amassed near Trident to stem the growing flow. Luna Halcyon, for whatever reason, had gotten hit the least hard, while Lenardda had suffered great loss. Both cities would be shortly receiving support from Haven and Ccamos, being the least favorites of the League.

Zent's wrist console buzzed to life, and he quickly answered one Captain

Kelsing from the Haven forces in Trident. "Ccamos."

"Captain Zent, I've been told to get a hold of you immediately. Sir, we have a new type of Cydenges here and we—we don't exactly know why. The city is already destroyed . . ." The man cleared his throat and took a quick breath. "This new form—it's humanoid. But highly dangerous."

Humanoid . . . and so big a deal? "But do you have the situation contained there?" he demanded.

"We believe we do. But this thing . . . I-I have to go, but you'll receive a report soon once we've assessed the damages."

The call cut out, and Zent was left wondering if the man meant *damages* from . . . this one creature. Or were there multiple? Why would "humanoid" and "dangerous" go together? A Hellebes man was a force to be reckoned with, but what power did a metal man possess to make it stand out from a moon-full of energy-sucking dragons?

- Chapter 44 -

The Heiress

Manidor 2, 1295:
progress.
— From Lhinde's Vault

[Note: I need to hint subtly in Part 2 that Luna and the Archmother are *not* by necessity the same thing. This leaves room for the Cydenges Mother to come to Gaea leading hordes of Cydenges, then Lyn comes in to save the day, etc., without the characters or readers suspecting anything off.]

"Sir, a new red star has fallen." The report came from a corporal who stood in the doorway, puffing from slight exertion. "You should see this."

Zent frowned and rose, quickly following the man. Men made was for them as they worked their way to the closest exit of Military HQ. "Did you see this firsthand?"

"Yessir, otherwise I wouldn't have come in person. There are others there with her already, though."

Her? Zent felt his breath catch. Could it be? Dare he to hope? They had long since given the girl up for dead. It had been harder for him than he'd ever have thought, but she did admit openly that the mission would be dangerous, and . . . well, Cydenges had been attacking for three days now. They still had yet to see more than a handful of that new type, however . . .

When they came outside, they passed two soldiers leading another pair back, one missing an arm and the other with great gashes in his chest and soldier. In response to his sharp inquiry, they simply said, "She should be under control now."

Zent and the corporal broke into a full sprint, soon coming upon the source of the altercation: the white-haired figure of a girl, standing in the courtyard and ringed by wary, uncertain soldiers, who looked to the Colonel as he approached. She was naked and looked ill-at-ease, not for the fact but almost as though she'd just awoken or was otherwise very disoriented.

"Lyn!" Zent shouted, dashing up and scooping her into an embrace. She clutched him with feral strength at first, then relaxed a bit. He swung her around like he'd heard fathers did with their children, setting her back down to find that her feet didn't quite catch the ground like they should. He held her up until she found her footing, and held her at arms' length, noting the alien look in her eye, the shaking in her arms that seemed neither from fear nor cold.

"Sorry," she mumbled in embarrassment. "I'm—I . . ." Her lip trembled, possibly from fear this time, though it appeared more like . . . she just wasn't used to moving her mouth anymore.

"By the Mother," he whispered. "It's like you don't remember what it's like to be human." He did not say the words seriously, but then he caught the glances of the soldiers about him, and inspected her eyes once more. "No . . . it can't be."

"Sir, she was—she came as a Cydenges. We knew something was wrong, but, well, a few of us made the mistake of approaching her before she transformed and got . . ."

He grimaced, noting a similar expression from the girl. "It's all right, Lyn," he said. "I'm sure it wasn't your intent. Just . . . try not to bite anyone else."

"I'll try," she mumbled, and again he was struck by how the words came out of her mouth. As though she were unused to saying real words, or using her mouth at all.

"Here, let's get you back." He scooped her up under the knees, and she obediently lay still in his arms like a small child. He looked around for the nearest aircraft he had authorization to take. "Corporal, notify all the generals immediately. Tell them we'll be back at the manse. I'm taking the Senator home."

The next few minutes were a blur, rushing Lyn back to the Senatorial Manse, guiding her into the grand building, explaining her appearance to curious onlookers only in brief, and finally shutting the door to her personal quarters while she dressed. She came out two minutes later looking lovely in a custom dress tailored by Iselda, one of her female Hellebes staff. Slightly more confident, too—he could see her shifting her shoulders back in time with a deep breath in. She met his eyes, a slow and almost bashful smile spreading across her lips, indicating she knew he knew that she was still trying to recover her humanity.

"Now, um . . . we do need to talk about some things," he began uncertainly.

"I know," she said seriously, striding toward him. Her gait was not perfect, but significantly more human than the stumbling toddler steps she'd shown off minutes ago. "I'm fine, Zent. I'll manage. I'm . . . growing accustomed to my body once more."

He walked purposefully with her, taking her to the conference chamber where whoever could make it would be. In a low voice, he asked, "So you actually did . . . take on a Cydenges form?"

She nodded, glancing at him uneasily and swallowing. "It was strange. Becoming one of them. It was the Queen's power. We'll talk more on that in a minute, I'm sure. Can I . . . get some water and food?"

"Oh. Of course." He signaled to a servant to order refreshments for her at the conference chamber.

Inside, General Inecc was already waiting somehow. Fors arrived not long after, while Frauss was indisposed. Two more men of distinction arrived, and thus began the most important discussion in decades. First, the questions directed at Lyn, of course. Most present did not question her strange, uncomfortable mannerisms, which were already a lot better, especially as soon as she explained that she had immediately been transfigured into a massive metal monster upon reaching the moon. During transit, in fact, was her theory—that in that red streak, she had been remade entirely into a Cydenges "Leonid", yet retained her core memories and Vault.

A look exchanged with Fors indicated that they both caught on to the fact that a Vault, it would seem, was not tied to the physical body at all save for a mental thread tied to the brain and mind. This was a theory that had been on the table for over a century.

"On Luna," she went on to explain, "I was soon met by a small pack of Cydenges, who reminded me of wolves in how they interacted. They're very feral, animalistic creatures, and loyal to the death to their Queen. They spoke to me through some manner of mental communication, saying I had to come with them to meet their Queen. So we traveled by foot, and I found I could use my four limbs almost by instinct. They don't generally do the teleportation except from Luna to Gaea. Luna is all barren, by the way, rocky with a black, starry sky and a faint bronze atmosphere."

"Atmosphere?" asked General Fors quizzically.

She nodded. "I know it's not visible from Gaea. I think it may be hidden somehow from our eyes. Also, the moon itself is a bronzy brown and grey with flecks of gold, not at all how we view it. Anyway, they live in this giant Hive built underground beneath a great mound. They took me in by tunnel, and I soon discovered they live in a complex network of cave systems. The caves themselves are . . . enormous." She waved a hand vaguely, as though searching for how best to describe it.

"How enormous?" Zent pressed. "Kilometers?"

"Definitely." She said it matter-of-factly, eliciting murmurs of surprise. "The main one is . . . maybe two kilometers wide? and perhaps ten or fifteen from top to bottom."

"And that's just the main one?" asked Inecc.

Another nod. "Some of the other ones are larger still. When I arrived, they took me up to the top by way of these twisting columns and paths that connect the entire chamber in a web. Not all Cydenges can fly, so it's necessary for them. At the center of the ceiling hangs a cocoon, now broken. I . . . watched her hatch from it."

Again, interruptions, this time producing visible annoyance on her face. Almost a snarl, though she quickly got it in order. "Yes, the Queens are hatched on a cycle, similar to insect species. She clawed her way out of the silvery Cocoon and devoured one of her own right before my eyes. She's . . . brutal. Ferocious. She spoke to me mind-to-mind, far more clearly than her children.

She's intelligent and cunning. She demanded my total obedience and took me under her wing, showing me around the labyrinth of the Hive. When I spoke disrespectfully to her, she nearly killed me. I didn't do it again. We also spoke vocally, however, using a growling language. It's used in a primal way between the Cydenges, but has enough nuance to convey as complex meanings as our language. And somehow . . . it too was encoded in the instincts that came with my metallic body."

Zent and the others were all watching her in fascination now, nearly beyond questions. She had gotten comfortable enough with her speech that her highly personal story came out in a smooth flow. Breaking only for sips from the glass that the servant had brought for her, she carried on, describing the fundaments of the Cydenges way of life—though the generals did soon prompt her to cut it short for the sake of urgency. She agreed to upload her entire story from Luna for further examination, and they moved on to the matter of the Cydenges offensive.

She sobered at the mention, and Zent was reminded of the moment she'd said to him, "I know. I have seen all of it already, both in Luna's plans that she showed me and as it was happening. I'm sorry—I couldn't come yet. Not only did I have to wait for the earth to line up with Luna right, but escaping from the Archmother was no easy task." She looked up, clearly waiting for the questions that would follow. They did: How did she escape when Luna held so tight a grip on her? Where was this Archmother, and what was she planning next?

In reply, she said, "It's difficult to explain, and would take much time. Let's just say I escaped similarly to how I got there. I need to upload my Vault soon for you all to view for yourselves; it will add much context. As for her plans, she's been watching Gaea for a long time, biding her time. Planning. Growing an army. And . . . she's coming. She's not happy that I've eluded her, and she's bringing with her legions beyond number. Generals. And . . . the eighth Cydenges breed."

Zent felt a shiver at that last comment. "We've seen a few already."

She nodded. "I know. Their power is immense. I'm so sorry about

Maldunech and Trident. I hated their Senators, but that was a true blow to Gaea. Perhaps it will get Team Imperial to reconsider their own plans?"

Zent chuckled at her nickname, which seemed a self-made one she'd been using for a while. "I don't know about reconsidering their intent, but plans? Certainly. However, something is going on on Mani, and we're unsure as yet what it is."

She frowned. "We need to go there, then. Men, we cannot possibly stave off this next assault without the ancient Legaleians' secret to slay the Cydenges. Remember how they were the first to stop the beasts when they first arose? Out of jealousy, the Anier had them exiled, and then had to make their own weapons, but the Legaleians had a superior method. Do you know what it is?"

They all shook their heads. She smiled slyly in reply. "I do now."

- Chapter 45 -

Enter the Archmother

Manidor 2, 1295:
progress.
— From Lhinde's Vault

[thinking this will be a day or two after Lyn talks to them about the Legaleians. She does some meeting, talking, and a very short amount of resting, then she Cyenges-leaps over to Mani. Luna follows within how long? Immediately might seem overly convenient.]

There was much to do following the meeting. Lyn seemed to be getting more control and more energy back as the day went on, though after multiple meetings she was looking a bit haggard. Zent and the generals insisted on some rest for her, but she was back up within a couple hours, and instant source of jealousy for the old Hellebes warrior. She rejuvenated, a new woman. What presence and authority she had built up over her year on Gaea and her tenure as Senator was back, and she was giving orders, receiving reports, and generally giving out helpful inside advice on the Cydenges Mother's plans.

She had not, of course, been successful in persuading Luna away from her goal of conquering Gaea. That, it seemed, was too much to ask from any human hybrid. The moon goddess had been planning her invasion for one thousand years, and would not settle on it.

She left the following day, not by shuttle but by her new method. For they still had no word from the ships they were sending in, and needed to know what was happening on the silver moon. Lyn was restless to get back, and just hesitant enough about the trip that it showed through her steely mask. Out in the same courtyard in front of the Senatorial manse, she smiled her goodbye to Zent. "I'll see you all again. Wish me luck."

Mani, not his golden sister, was overhead currently, and they watched as she went up in a shining pillar of red that streaked all the way to the moon's obscuring atmosphere—and, they had to trust, beyond.

One more day, and they had no word from Lyn, nor a messenger from Mani. What they did get was a distress call from Haven, telling of new Cydenges sighted outside the city: a large force made up mostly of the new eighth variety of Cydenges.

"I'll inform military," Zent assured the Haven General who'd called. "If you need reinforcements, let us know, but . . . well . . ."

"You might have your own fights. We understand," finished Martel, the general. "We can survive this."

The call cut out. Martel did not sound as confident as Zent liked, all things considered, but Haven's defensive guns alone had ten times the firepower of Trident's, which was the only place the lunar freaks had been sighted previously. Per Zent's request, Martel began streaming video footage of Haven's walls and the sight beyond, which was enough to take the breath from Zent's and his companions' lungs. Even as he typed out a general warning to Ccamos leaders, he kept an eye on the quickly-approaching horde on the screen.

The large, wolf-like Cydenges, which Lyn had called Brutes, ran at the front, while the humanoid ones floated in behind. They did not walk save for when they trailed limbs on the ground seemingly out of boredom. Some spun lazy cartwheels in the air or zipped about here and there. There was no formation to the army, of course, except one of the Brutes at the lead seemed to be their leader. Like the leader of a large pack of moonspawn.

The ballistic defense cannons triggered at a range of a half mile, punching out long shells of precision destruction that hit the front formation like finger flicks to a horde of ants. At least one metal creature was blown back with each shot, though some of the humanoids seemed to avoid them—but the numbers were too great for this strategy to be effective through and through. What made the humanoids so terrifying was their ability to manipulate seemingly any matter or kinetic energy just as their kin manipulated purer energy.

Over head, just coming into the Haven camera view, Air Force bombers flew by, unloading their concussive cargo on the creatures, wave after wave. As the smoke cleared from each round of bombs, Zent could make out that a small few of the monsters were left behind, twitching or blown straight apart. As they neared, he was able to make out specific monsters dying from the bombs and explosive cannon fire. Some were the humanoids, while most of the Brutes up front had been picked off by now. Somehow, the anthropomorphic ones could dodge or block incoming fire, as had been made manifest before, and only intense, direct and multisource firepower could bring one down, for they couldn't prevent all dangers.

A call from the office drew his attention back to the here and now. "You hear that, Colonel?" Frauss asked.

Zent swore, flipping on the cameras for their own city and eventually pinpointing the coming threat from southward, where Cydenges were dropping out of the sky.

"Think this is going to be it?" asked Colonel ___, who was there for now.

"This Archmother?" Zent asked. "Quite possible, if she's looking for her adoptive daughter. We'll see. For now, let's muster all troops and get a large force out there. And Fors . . . I'm going out this time. Y'all ain't stopping me."

He put down his headset, making room for the other colonel to take his seat, and went to gather his team of specialists, the Red Horizon survivors who had been training every day for attacks such as this. They had performed admirably during the recent attacks, and their bravery would be required once more this day. Each was well-trained, hardened, a soldier committed unto death.

As he strode through HQ toward the Red Horizon hangar, he barked out further warnings to any who looked to be unaware, and began to step into file alongside other Red Horizon men, until the team began to assemble at their hangar. T-Class gunships awaited them, already stocked and loaded, and they piled into four of them. Zent piloted one, while Janus piloted another, and Stefan and Ccorus another two. Twenty-four men in all. Hanging in the ships were their heavy rifles and weighted close-range weapons. Zent's weapon of choice was a long-handled hammer.

The ceiling opened, and they took off, thrusters blasting downward. When they reached the shield wall, Fors parted it for them and they gunned toward the Cydenges, who were this time largely Leonids and burrowers. They targeted the metal birds with their automatic gunfire, downing each with around a dozen bullets to the wings. He had to give them credit where it was due: these things had strong wings, lacking the weakness of normal Cydenges hides in that they would never cause their entire makeup to rupture. One still had to either pierce the chest or head with heavy fire or rip enough holes in the wings that they couldn't support their own weight. And despite the somewhat erratic wing movements, they were still the biggest targets on them.

Still makes no sense that they can fly at all, given their size, he remarked absently. Their wings did not look nearly big enough. Any flying creatures on Gaea needed generous wings to support them, and these were giant lions literally made of solid metal.

Hovering over the thickest of the burrower horde, Zent gave the command to open the bomb hatches, and they began dropping them onto the land about the silvery burrowers, blowing them up to flop on land like fishes. The creatures were still landing, streaking down from the sky to sink directly into the soil, immediately covered. They left a hole where they entered, so they weren't teleporting directly into the soil—which would defy basic physics of space—but piercing the earth to gain an instant terrain advantage. Each moved at a rate of easily ten to twenty kilometers per hour, faster than seemed possible.

The Leonids, of course, were even faster, and they continued to focus their fire on them, not wasting bullets on the ground. The beasts dove for their ships with claws outstretched, and each ship's gunman stayed vigilant to pump any attackers full of holes before they could get in close. Regardless, Janus's ship was landed on, and the Leonid clung onto its very shield, biting and scratching and eventually piercing it with its teeth. he still managed to shake it, but they seemed to sense the weakness, and another soon made its way to the ship, curling around it and ripping the cockpit open.

The men inside were already brace for it. Janus was only flying a little over a hundred feet off the ground, so low enough to theoretically survive the impact with Geokinesis, but their suits were equipped with anti-grav tech that acted as a pseudo-parachute. They leapt from the passenger hold while Janus thrust upward with a long sword, plunging it into the beast's belly and jumping up to wrestle it.

"Aw, yeah! That's how we go down," Zent cheered from his own cockpit, grinning as Kipp turned his fire on another flying beast. Janus, next he saw, was attempting to ride the cat-faced Cydenges to the ground by manipulating its wings. "Time to go in for a landing, guys."

Janus's team, of course, were already taking aim at the Cydenges about them, with two in particular engaging the new-falling lunar monsters in close-range combat. Janus crashed his own Cydenges with a final kick, then rushed in to wrench the greatsword free from its scaled belly as it exploded in a burst of red light. He shot Zent a grin, who nodded approvingly in return and hefted his own war hammer. Zent singled out the burrowers, clubbing those who approached the surface with the power to cave their snakelike hides right in. In one case, he struck the head as it poked out to assess its enemy, destroying the creature in a chain reaction.

The worms focused now on the soldiers as much as on the looming city, snaking toward them and erupting from the ground, spiral jaws opening to swallow their enemy whole. They were large enough to do so, but in truth they were not nearly so fast. Not only that, but the Hellebes crew was well-versed in Geokinetics, so they were able to crush and uproot their foes using the earth power or create barriers to hide behind or distract with. Face-to-face, nearly every advantage lay with the Red Horizon.

Seeing this, the Leonids began to swoop down upon them, but backup soldiers were already arriving in droves, team after team—for that was how they liked to take on Cydenges, in tight-knit teams versed in combating the Cydenges. Although these worms were new, so they only had pre-discussed strategies to work with, not real experience. More bombs carpeted the ground ahead of them leading up to Ccamos, while aerial gunfire downed many a Leonids. Those still beaming down from Luna quickly engaged in quick, deadly scuffles with the soldiers, who pitted their bladed and blunt weapons against the silver claws of the Cydenges.

Men began to fall around him. It was inevitable, even given the advantage that was theirs in this fight. Zent's own men were perhaps the most skilled of them all, and he alone was taking out Cydenges after Cydenges, but there were still an enormous number of the moon beasts. Hopefully the tide was turning enough.

But of course, things can always get worse, as they say.

First came a sudden wave of red lights and an entire ring of Cydenges Brutes some hundred feet across. One nearly landed right on top of a Hellebes rifleman, but he dodged to the side just in time. In the center of the ring, a golden pillar of light ushered in an even larger shape than the Brutes—a long-tailed golden Cydenges, replete with a glorious array of spines, a tucked pair of wings, and four curling horns that all turned to point forward in an arrowhead shape.

Zent took an involuntary step back upon seeing the creature, knowing many of his companions would do the same. *It's her . . .* There was no mistaking it. A golden titan had not just happened to fall to earth; this creature was not a freak, not some Cydenges mutant. Beyond a shadow of a doubt, this was the Archmother.

She roared with jaws pointing skyward, a bone-rattling call that resonated through the earth itself as much as echoing through the air. All who heard it turned to her, both Cydenges and Hellebes, the former of which took a reverent bow. She stalked forward, each footfall somehow individually audible, as though the ground below heard her coming and trembled.

A chorus of curses sounded from his companions in his earpiece. "Don't let them get to you," he growled. "Let's focus on these guys." He turned to the nearest Brute, swiftly building centripetal force, and crashed the head into its shoulder, eliciting a pained shriek of metal as it scrambled back. One of the riflemen took it out with a shot to the head, and he turned to the next. *We can get these guys. Don't know about the Archmother, but we can take these things.*

Without loss of life? Likely not. But they were in this till the end.

- Chapter 46 -

Impasse

Manidor 2, 1295
progress
— From Lhinde's Vaul

Mani was at a stand-still. Archlord Domon looked out the east-facing window of his high castle room, surveying Rhidea's handiwork in the sky above A web, a jagged ribcage of silver reaching to the sky, and a net of darknes between. He hadn't been sure whether or not she would go for the idea, but he would consider her contribution since returning here to Redufiel a success Sadly, it did not solve their problem of the hundreds of Gaean warships at the base and all over the world, some of which had already spread wide stories o the destruction they'd wrought. It didn't exactly worry or guilt him, but it did . . irk him.

A success, he called it, for already they had caught a half-dozen Gaean skyships like flies in a net. Silver, Reality and Dark worked together to bind the things eternally, as long as the net was held, in the skies above East Redu Field None could go out, none could come in. It was the part of the plan he had made extra certain Rhidea did not tell the Argentians, for—if successful—it woulc pave the way for a full assault of the far continent, providing for his rule the entirety of Mani. Once it was all his, and Rhidea ruled at his side, Mani itsel would be his to command. He no longer considered her an enemy, for the) worked together now and she was coming only further round. These past few days, she had barely ceased to complain of the struggle of convincing the Argentians of the need for Domon's new Empire.

"My Lord Emperor."

The voice was small and feminine, clearly Vyss. One of the few advisors whose name he'd learned. Well, assistant more than advisor. Occasionally concubine. When he nodded, not turning from his vantage, she said briskly, "Lady Rhidea has informed me that she is done with the southern field. That completes the Redufiel Web."

Excellent. And it strengthened the entire web spreading for miles in all directions. He had ordered preparations to be made, and the woman had been traveling about the area shooting up Silver roots where he had personally appointed Darkwells, as he was calling them. These made a sort of highway, and were faintly linked to one another. He had been preparing over the last week for the great Web around Redufiel, but had of course required her cooperation. He hadn't anticipated the Gaeans getting through before construction was done, but now that it was up . . . well, getting out would be far harder for them.

It was hard to say how much of the sky was truly obstructed right now, but he calculated that it would be close to the entire sky of Darsor. Looking from Gaea, most of the visible sky of Mani would be off-limits, little to Gaea's knowledge. By the time they figured out what was going on, all of mani would be so shielded.

"That is well," he said in answer to Vyss's report, still not turning. When she said nothing, he turned just his head. "Is that all?"

She opened her mouth, hesitated, then said, "There was, ah, a new Gaean ship approaching just this morning. Caught in the Web above Farkennig." A small town to the northwest, beyond and above the enemy encampment.

Also excellent. "Thank you," he said in dismissal, turning back to the window. Even as the aide clip-clipped away in her wooden heels, he felt a buzzing in the back of his mind and knew that Rhidea was giving him a mental tug.

News, Archlord, she said brusquely.

So I heard. We can now call our circle complete—

Not that. Her imagined voice was cutting, as though, she'd only barely stopped herself from adding, *fool.*

He paused, trying not to convey irritation. Their bond was close enough to allow such emotions through.

She is here, she continued without prompting.

He felt a sudden prickle of doubt, feeling out his heart like cold fingers. There was no need to ask who, for he knew: The girl, Lyn of Nytaea. Mother Heiress to the Gaeans, but of unknown importance to Mani. He had hoped never to see nor deal with her again, but he knew Rhidea still held a soft spot for her. But she was of Gaea now, and would never go along with their plan for Mani's progression toward the future. *How?* he demanded. *Where is she now?*

She saw right through his mask of calm, replying with amusement. *Calm yourself, my good lord. She is but a girl. Inheritor of a world-shattering power, true, but still.*

His irritation boiled. *Do not toy with me, High Mage.*

Fine. I have her here with me, and she is quite incensed. Why don't you join us?

The white-haired girl whipped her head around, staring down the Emperor. Yes, that is how he described it to himself. Her gaze pierced him, wary and annoyed and something else he couldn't place. She was taller than him now, shoulders broad like a man's, and the shape of everything from her sharp-angled hips to the curling layers of muscle on her arms and neck to the skelature of her face was . . . alien. Off-puttingly so. Her blue eyes were strong and imperious, her mane of hair wild and pulsing with life, even bound as it was in multiple hair ties. And . . . what was this dark full-body suit she wore?

He shivered.

They stood on the road just south of the city gate, under the meager cover of one of the few trees allowed to mar visibility of the city guards. Rhidea stood opposite the girl, and Domon made it a triangular gathering.

"Archlord Domon," the girl greeted him. But she was no girl, was she? She looked a woman grown, and more, somehow touched by an agelessness born not of this world.

He bristled at how disparagingly she said the title. She might as well have substituted an insult for his title. "Lyn, correct? What brings you here, and how did you arrive?"

In answer, she turned and pointed along the road, where a . . . a *hole* had been torn in the dark fabric of magic that tied together Rhidea's silver pillars. It trailed shadows where extra light was allowed in between the hazy grey clouds. He gaped as he saw it, scanning the ground and seeing no vehicles. He stared at her in a new light, puzzled.

"We have to talk, Domon," she said softly. "And soon. Gaea is facing a crisis like you've never imagined."

He nodded, quickly but hesitantly. "Rhidea, bring her to my conference room."

He disappeared, reappearing in his aggrandized office, soon followed by Rhidea and Lyn. He offered them both seats, and all three sat. "Explain," he simply.

Her eyes flashed, though it could have been merely the flicker of moving them between him and Rhidea. With a breath, she said, "There is an alien force known as the Cydenges, who live on Gaea's other moon, Luna. Also called the Greater Moon. Sister of Mani. And yes, I know of the patron you both now serve." She fixed Rhidea with a stare that made even the old mage squirm, a scowl darkening her perfect face. "Don't ask me how I know. I can't go into it here. But you are attuned to Mani, Rhidea. I was there when Kaen, in his new body, was restored to freedom of mind, so I know what happened with the force behind the sword, and I've spoken face-to-face with Luna."

Rhidea stiffened, and even Domon's breath caught. "Luna?" he asked sharply, sharing a glance with the red-haired mage. "How? How is her presence tangible on Gaea?"

"It is not." Lyn let the words hang in the air, as though to intimidate. If that was her intention, it worked. "I spent the last few months on Luna, by her side. Learning about the Cydenges, and her plans, her age-old rivalry with Mani and her hatred toward the people of her mother's world. Now tell me about Darsor— what is going on here, besides the Gaean invaders and the Ccamos forces sent to combat them?"

Rhidea took over the explanation. "Well, as you've guessed, I joined forces with Mani and then with Domon, leveraging my new partnership against him. But I would call us collaborators now, as you can see by the new Skyweb project. Too little too late, you will probably say, and that may be, but we could not have foreseen that the Gaeans would come to our aid, nor that these—" she gestured eastward toward the encampment "—would come in such force so soon."

Lyn's eyes held distrust plainly, not bothering to hide it. "Still seems foolish but okay." At Domon's threatening look, she held up a hand. "Don't bother getting your hackles up. I'm not afraid of either of you."

She didn't expound on it, but somehow Domon got the impression that it was not an empty threat. The woman had not said how she was able to get to Luna, nor what new abilities she may have picked up from there. Nor had she claimed to have or have not bonded with Luna, and Rhidea had with Mani. The idea sounded dubious, as that would go against everything she'd been working for on Gaea surely, but it was not out of the realm of possibility. If that were the case, then . . . perhaps her threat was not empty.

He gave no indication of intimidation, but instead slowly relaxed, giving a small smile in acquiescence. "Very well. Go on."

"I simply said your plan was foolish. Rhidea was the one speaking."

Rhidea snorted, either in amusement or agreement. "Lyn, we are only trying to protect Mani. If what you say of your trip to Luna is true, then I assume that Luna is still planning to invade your world? What steps have you taken against that?"

"Not planning. They have begun. That is why I have come here—to see what has held up our forces from returning to help us, and to acquire for our defense some Legaleian magi to enlist in the defense of Gaea."

Rhidea's eyes narrowed. "You've discovered how we can combat them with magic?" Domon could see something turning in her head.

She hesitated but a moment. "I think so. And it could make a huge difference. As I said, I spent a large amount of time personally with Luna. I think I'm qualified to speak on their strengths and weaknesses."

"But," said the Archlord in his most cutting tone, "what is that to us? What stake have we in Gaea's safety? Don't look at me like that girl; I'm serious. These Cydenges cannot cross over into our world—or can they, now that you have done this?"

The white-haired girl whipped her head around, studying the gaping hole in the sky. "Your barrier was not my idea, but regardless . . . I am not a true Cydenges, yet I was able to break through it with ease. I believe all your flytrap will catch is Gaean soldiers, friend or foe. And once Gaea is overrun, not only will we be unable to help you, but the Cydenges will at last be able to come to Mani. Have you ever seen Luna from here?"

They both shook their heads hesitantly.

"That's because, geographically speaking, they're like this." She made an unsuccessful hand motion, then on her second try summoned a small flame, which she placed to float in the air. Shaking her head as though ashamed of herself, she muttered, "Not even used to this after Luna. First I can't walk on Gaea, and now . . ." She looked up, coloring slightly. "Never mind. It was embarrassing. Here."

She conjured three flame balls in total, two small ones on either side of a larger one, slowly orbiting it. "This small one here will be Luna, and this one is Mani. Big one—Gaea. See how they never see each other? I theorize that they can't get to Mani only because Gaea's magnetic field and planetary signature get in the way."

Planetary signature . . . Domon seemed to miss something there that Rhidea caught, but he understood enough to realize she may have a point. But he wasn't born last week, and he knew something was off about the girl. She could easily be a spy from Gaea or even Luna, or simply be trying to lure them into complacency—or a trap. There were a hundred different ways she could be deceiving them. He caught Rhidea's eye, and she gave a tiny nod that somehow contained a cartload of certainty and reassurance.

She reached out a hand. "Lyn, if you are a friend to me and to our world, then I want you to swear to me that you mean us well."

You seemed to composer broke briefly, a scowl touching her face before vanishing, and she looked into the ancient woman's eyes with something akin to hurt. "You don't trust me anymore?"

"That is not what I said. It's not about love or trust, but the security of our homeland."

Lyn shook her head, seemingly not in disbelief but as a gesture that it was not that big of a deal, saying something similar. She took the woman's hand with no more hesitation, dwarfing it in her long fingers and wide, creased palm. "I swear. I understand, Rhidea."

"And you had no knowledge of a Cydenges attack on Mani?"

Lynchazel shook her head. "I didn't know of any way they could come here before I tried for myself."

Rhidea let go of her hand, nodding in reluctance. "Very well, Lyn."

The girl shrugged awkwardly, then breathed in and resumed the same cross-armed posture. "We really won't know until they come. But I believe they will. I have a certain sense now for the children of Luna."

"So you have led these creatures to our doorstep," Domon said slowly.

She glanced around uncertainly. "No. I don't think so. But . . . it's possible."

"Then I suggest you start telling us how we can defend against them, and doing so *quickly*," he said. "We will also need to hear about this supposed trip to Luna."

The girl's eyes hardened, and she glanced over at Rhidea's silver right arm. "Yes. I think we have a few things to speak on."

- Chapter 47 -

From the Sister Moon

Manidor 2, 1295:
progress.
— From Lhinde's Vault

Lyn's story was as far-fetched as Rhidea had anticipated and more. Mani had been speaking into her mind between pieces of their conversation in the audience hall, and now as Lyn spilt her tale of shapeshifting and moon dragons. Rhidea had learned a good bit about the alien creatures from her constant companion, Mani, but to hear it firsthand from the mouth of a recent visitor— the first ever to Luna—was another thing entirely.

She had become a dragon. Met and spoken with the Queen of the Cydenges, Luna herself. It was nigh unimaginable, though Rhidea's own experiences with Mani, which she related in turn, were equally unbelievable. But that was only the half of it—the incredible ending to a story of an unlikely rebel hero. She glanced over many of the details of her rise from rebel puppet to national hero, demurely insisting on happenstance and unlikely circumstances as the reasons for her victories.

Rhidea and Domon, as it ended up, did most of the listening. They got most of the way through Lyn's explanation of the main events, but had hardly scratched the surface of the incredible workings of Mani's mother planet when Vyss's frantic clip-clopping heralded a sudden outburst. "Monsters," she wheezed. Hanging in the doorway, panting, she repeated the word, then drew herself up straight and answered Domon's terse questioning with professional bafflement. No, she had no idea what the situation was. Yes, it was dire.

Mani made a hissing sound in her ear that sounded almost like an ancient curse. *It is her children . . . they are here. I grew distracted by the convers—*

"Cydenges," she said to them tightly. Rushing forward, she took hold of the

Emperor and Lyn and performed a spatial shift, arriving south of the city using Dark Reality, near where they had found Lyn. There were already a half-dozen of the creatures, long and metallic and feline, two bearing wings while the others were larger, bulkier. All prowled steadily forward, making alien clicking growls that sent chills up her spine.

Cydenges . . . so this is what they look like.

Lyn went out ahead, making a *Wait here* gesture to her betters. Rhidea watched tensely as she approached, staring the creatures down, possibly even communicating with them. If the story she'd just told was true, then that was probably the case. From her came a growling imitation of their calls, weak and clearly human in origin, but the Cydenges seemed to stop and consider her answering in like voice, albeit far more threatening.

Are you able to understand any of that? Rhidea asked the moon lord. *Is it a titan language?*

No. That is Luna's own language, developed for speech with her brood and them alone. And apparently this human Vessel as well.

Vessel? Rhidea murmured the word ponderously in her head, but Mani did not answering, apparently sensing that it was not truly a question. As she watched with renewed interest, the Cydenges began pacing around Lyn. The girl retrieved the long sword from the ground with which she'd come, turning and saying to the others, "Rhidea, this might be a good time to try your Silver Authority against them. And Domon . . . perhaps Dark?"

Lyn turned back—insolently, as the Emperor would surely see it—and swung her oversized blade in a menacing arc. The speed of her arms was mesmerizing, the way she manipulated the sword's mass seemingly unreal. She ended a triple swoop in a ready stance with blade held downward, and said to the metal beasts in Legaleian, "Come and get us, scrap metal."

They launched into motion. The creatures were incredibly fast, every bit the liquid lightning that Lyn was on Mani, leaping forward many paces in a quick bound, some headed for the girl, some for the Emperor and High Mage. Rhidea already had a defense ready, thrusting upward from the ground with spikes of silver. Pleasingly, they penetrated the Cydenges skin with ease, pinning their flesh—if indeed they had flesh. Only one was truly caught, thrashing about on the spike with demonic hisses and scratching claws. The other broke free and came at Rhidea again.

She tried the gravity pull, but such Silver Authority did not appear to have any effect. It made sense; Luna's metal rebuffed the magical properties of Mani's. Rhidea summoned blades of silver from the earth, showering the nearest three Cydenges with them. Domon was experimenting with many different types of Dark-infused magic on the two nearest him, keeping as much distance as possible. Lyn, of course, had warned them of the Cydenges' ability to absorb all energy, so they weren't about to hurl fire or lightning at them. But Dark Earth did seem to be effective, tripping and holding the oversized wolf lions while Lyn darted in and skewered one. Her strike was clean and vital enough that it caused an eruptive chain reaction, and soon the creature was nothing, red dust blowing away.

Yes . . . Mani murmured at the "sight", which he experienced both from her eyes and from the world around. He didn't expound, and she didn't have the focus to ask.

By the time Rhidea had slewn the second Cydenges, Lyn had already dispatched the trapped one and al the others. She turned to them with pleased, almost approving, nods, breathing quickly but not as much so as Rhidea would have expected. *This was just a warmup for her. What did they do to her back on Gaea? What has she become?*

However, Lyn immediately got a shocked look on her face and craned her head upward, searching the torn sky. From here, the large gash she'd ripped in the seam—though maybe the Cydenges had helped it—hung like a hundred-foot-wide misshapen hole, dragging large tendrils of dark brownish ethereal . . . . whatever it was that Domon had constructed the barrier with. It was a mixture of different elements, similarly to how they had made the barrier over the city. She still had little knowledge of his Dark elements and their workings.

Pillars of ruby red appeared in the sky, touching down through the gaping hole like heavenly lights. Where they touched earth or path, silvery Cydenges uncurled, spines shivering as they stretched catlike and roared and screeched. There were the large wolves, the winged versions . . . wormlike Cydenges that burrowed into the earth . . . even some arachnid ones with massive metal-plated legs.

Nearby Gaean skyships came from nowhere, shooting down the metallic creatures with their guns, and they were able to finish off the second wave with such help. One ship came to land near the group, and Domon stared with open distrust as a tall figure hopped out, suited in his custom black combat suit: Kaen.

"Lyn!" he said in relief, rushing forward to crush her in an embrace. "What are you doing here? How did you get to Mani?"

He eyed Rhidea and the Emperor, with whom he had already spoken, and Rhidea said, "She has learned the way of the Cydenges. We shall leave it at that for now."

"Is that—" he looked quizzically at his friend, but said no more, instead joining the others in their skyward glances. "Think that's all for now? I can't believe they actually . . ."

"I . . . think that might be all for now," Lyn said slowly. "We're wondering if it was my fault. I jumped directly here from Ccamos, but then it seems the Cydenges somehow followed."

He narrowed his eyes, looking about them at the ruins of the Cydenges. "Mmm, not from Ccamos. Don't think that would line up astronomically."

She nodded. "Then from elsewhere on the globe. They're everywhere, Kaen." She suddenly gasped. "We've been trying to reach you all! The Cydenges have attacked all over Gaea, and we need all the help we can get."

Kaen swore in a language Rhdiea didn't know. They were speaking Legaleian, though, for the benefit of the other listeners. Domon was visibly growing tired of the two-way discussion, and cut in with, "Well, boy? What of our deal?"

Kaen turned to him with a dark look that he quickly mastered. Then he dipped his head in acquiescence. "We took care of them. Inecc's party should be returning soon, but I don't know about Frauss'."

"Then we need to get you and your men back to Gaea, STAT," Lyn said, shooting a glance at the Emperor. He glared back, then eventually nodded with a grunt. Rhidea knew he wanted all these Gaean soldiers gone regardless; he just didn't want them leaving without finishing the job.

Kaen started back toward his ship. "All right, Lyn. We'll see you back on Gaea. But I'm going to send back messengers first. We'll stick around another while in case more of these . . . aurora-blasted things come."

A minute later, two of the Gaea-powered ships departed for the upper atmosphere via Lyn's convenient hole, and were soon out of sight. No sooner were they gone, however, then Mani's warning came again, and she looked to the sky in time with Lyn, who also sensed something.

"It's her," she whispered. "Careful, everyone." She motioned them back, and shortly a red light blazed to life a mere ten yards southward, larger than the others and similarly reaching heavenward forever. It faded, revealing a golden mass with eyes of matching gold. Her tail, long and spiney, swished from side to side as her long neck pivoted, looking from side-to-side as though drinking in the scenery from her brother's world.

Luna . . . Mani whispered.

Her head swiveled toward Rhidea immediately, eyes suspicious and searching. She stalked forward, and no one made a move. Suddenly, there appeared in Rhidea's mind a second voice, darkly feminine and untraceable in quality or origin: *Hello, Vessel of Silver. Your world is more beautiful than I imagined. I shall soon lay claim to it, that I may burn it to the ground, but you shall likely be spared, for I neither can nor will destroy my brother. But I can bring him back to Gaea, where he is destined to go after this last year anyway.*

"Wait!" Rhidea shouted out, holding forth a hand as she saw the defenders preparing to strike at the Queen. She did not know if they could kill her, but did not wish to try until Mani gave her the go-ahead.

Sister . . . Mani spoke now. *Why have you trespassed thus on my land? I will have you expelled and your shell destroyed. Mark my words. My Vessel is powerful, and we have the aid of Gaea as well.*

Our mother burns, Mani. Two cities of nine I have destroyed in but a week, and the earth-dwellers have yet to see the full might of my superior moon. You are a coward and a cheat, now as ever.

Rhidea felt her own emotions stirring alongside Mani's . . . or were they one and the same? Deep anger, indignation, resentment, the types of emotion she'd glimpsed in Kaen, now understood with surprising sympathy.

Luna . . . Do not push me. She couldn't be certain whether it was her own voice or Mani's that rang out in the cacophonous silence. All the tension and expectant chaos waiting in the surrounding world seemed eternally far away as she stood amidst this mental match.

And to you I would say the same. Human Vessel. Those two words were enunciated with utmost derision and scorn, metal venom. *And here I thought we could perhaps come to an agreement.*

Rhidea's eyes focused back in to see the golden Queen arch her back, tail curling upward, four horns lifting. She howled, almost like a wolf. About her people were shouting, but they seemed to be waiting for some signal from her or, in the Gaeans' case, from Lyn, who was also watching the conversation with much interest. Could she hear it all? Likely.

Vessel, prepare to act. Now!

"Stay back, everyone!" she shouted, even as the Queen's form became a blur. Just like that, she was a prisoner in a grip of steel. She was whipped around to face the Queen's teeth-filled maw and golden eye—she was *in* the maw, held tightly in her teeth—all while the Queen spun disorientingly. She couldn't place the number of metal teeth sunk into her flesh, but it was enough to sprout a hailstorm of fiery pain. Shouts and cries came, including a sickening grunt from below her.

Lyn, she belatedly realized, thrashed in the Queen's clawed paw, so it wasn't her from whom the grunt had come. *The Archlord . . .*

Tell them all to back off, and make it quick! Luna hissed to her, applying more pressure with her foot. This elicited another grunt and a string of curses from the Archlord. Craning her neck, Rhidea saw two huge claws reaching up his chest to pin him at the neck. Blood dribbled from the corner of his mouth. "Lyn! Can't you—do—something?" She choked out. As she did so, she tried the same thing Domon already was, using different elements against the enormous creature. His stone fetters did succeed in grabbing hold of her feet. Rhidea sprouted silver spines from the ground below them, avoiding Domon and Lyn while piercing the Queen's metallic hide.

She screeched, instantly turning herself. Only a couple spikes had found their marks, and the wounds they left were not deep. Rhidea was still trying to use her gravity manipulation on the Archmother, but that effect of Silver Magic was certainly ineffective due to her Titan nature, so blunt force was the only way.

Her next attack launched the Archmother, a massive punch from the earth using Silver, paired with Domon's newly reformed stone shackles. The ground shuddered with the impact of the Queen's flanks striking down, and Rhidea's own flesh was torn and punctured only more—*I will heal,* she had to tell herself—while Lyn was somehow able to wrench herself free, tumbling away. Unhindered by Lyn or Domon being hostages, Rhidea redoubled her fight of Silver-on-gold. She reformed her entire right forearm into a long blade and jammed it upward through the roof of her prison cage, even as silver cords snaked around the titanic she-wolf.

Another piercing whine split the air, and the Queen thrashed, biting down only harder. Blood pooled about the mage, but she didn't stop, instead piercing the Queen with more and more silver blades. Finally, the Queen's great jaws opened, and she tumbled onto the ground, crying out with the pain of her landing. She could feel the healing work of Mani within her, but it would take time. Her arm, however, pulsed with energy as though wishing to fight further. Within her, she could feel Mani's keen desire to keep at the fight. *Mani . . . I do not know if I can.*

Get up, useless Vessel, prove your worth!

Rhidea growled, clawing her way into a sitting position with her metal hand, and watched the silver bindings tighten around Luna on their own, even while she thrashed and broke them. Rhidea's own blood dripped from her jaws in terrifying amounts, soaking the ground around her where she'd dropped out. Luna's rabid eyes focused on her, and she saw murder there, along with her rasping hiss: *Rhidea, Vessel of Mani. You will die in pain this day, and I will find his true form.*

The Queen surged forward, snapping all bonds, and Rhidea tried to scramble back. Instinctively, she swung her arm, which rapidly lengthened into a hooked blade, and caught the creature below the jaw, wrenching her head up with inhuman strength even as her shoulder shrieked against the strain. At that moment, Lyn rushed in with an oversized sword, joined by Kaen, who had apparently dismounted his vehicle in frustration, and together they beat the Queen back, redirecting her charge and putting her on the defensive.

She roared, swiping with claws and gnashing her teeth, leaking golden light from superficial wounds that together might have killed an ordinary Cydenges if her small experience with the predators was enough to go by. Looking down, Rhidea saw her own wounds closing up miraculously, though the large puncture above her right breast was concerning in the dark blood that continued to pump from it. She tried to move, but her body complained again, and she settled for tripping and cutting the Queen wherever there was an opening in the fight to get her silver in around the two Hellebes combatants.

Rhidea was aware of the Queen speaking, but she was hiding her words so that, it would seem, only Lyn could hear them. Not unlike the Perception trick she used to seal in or out voices. Mani prickled inside her at this. However, the two friends were gaining the advantage over the lunar monster, and had produced deep cuts in her that bled golden light in a steam-like stream. Kaen kicked, nearly toppling the Queen on her side, only to be snatched by the tail in a choking embrace. Lyn stole the chance to hack at her neck, biting in deep with her greatsword. She then . . .

Stood there. The hesitated for a long moment, and Rhidea knew that the Archmother was speaking directly to her. *Fool of a girl!* "Lyn! Kill her!" she shrieked, even as she separated her own silver blade from her arm and shot it through the air, embedding its hooked tip in the Queen's upper shoulder.

It only drew her ire. The Queen's gaze flicked back to Rhidea, and she swiped with lightning speed, tossing Lyn aside like a ragdoll before her sword could do any more damage. Ignoring Kaen's rear assault, she launched forward, ripping free of Rhidea's spike with a burst of golden sparks, and fell upon Rhidea. Domon tried to interpose a wall of stone, but she only leaped around it in two quick bounds. Her jaws descended in a golden flash, teeth clamping around Rhidea's legs. She gave a high-pitched scream as she was picked up and whipped through the air.

She lost consciousness in the moment that followed, though it could not be said if it was the force of hitting her head or the brutal *snap* as Luna's bladed teeth severed both her legs.

- Chapter 48 -

Metamorphosis

Manidor 2, 1295

progress

— From Lhinde's Vaul

A haze of shadow. An ocean of pain. A dark chasm at the bottom of the earth—metaphorical, but somehow real in a vivid sense. This was Rhidea's experience as she drifted inside herself, but somehow outside. The senses she felt were not bodily ones at all, but dimly she was aware of her location. She was inside Mani.

Ah . . . came the voice she knew so well, yet richer, bolder. *At last we meet I do apologize for your mode of entry into this place. The place which is not a place. You see, in the physical world you are what they like to call dead, but you are about to become a new thing entirely—a fusion of two bodies, two souls one far greater than your own.*

Is that not what I already am? she said blearily, still disoriented and beset by the cloud of pain that drifted from her physical body into this place of the mind. *Have you not already been dwelling in my body?*

You are what we call a Vessel, he said, *a body that carries a part of my lunar soul and will. But you are not the true Vessel. It is buried here, deep beneath the core of the Silver Moon. The sword was a sliver of that, and it is now lost from my control. You were able to communicate and exchange power with me through the bond that all Silversmiths held with me. Each had a seed of growth which overtook their skeletons by full age—do you remember the pain of that growing up? But that seed only went so far, and my control over each of you was limited.*

But now, Vessel Cae Rhidea, you shall transcend your mortal body, for the Cydenges Queen has done us a great service this day. The silver seed inside you has already sprouted, but now it has taken root here and will grow to full form and bloom. Oh, you shall be a beautiful flowering tree, me Vessel, my true Vessel.

Like the one in Nytaea? She couldn't help the sting in her remark.

Mani chuckled. *No. That is a . . . seed, you might say, but of the Wellspring. Our powers are antithetical to one another. Removing the Wellspring is the first step toward remaking Mani into a lasting paradise.*

Removing . . . ? What was he on about? Rhidea had a vague impression of the vast mind that was the Titan, but her mind was still foggy, drifting in the black expanse of Mani's own mind.

What has removing the Wellspring to do with a paradise? A good question, Vessel, and one that will be answered in a way that you would not expect. You are used to being the owner of your body, but I am afraid that you will no longer have one after this. You will linger, however, in its form, a part of your consciousness remaining with mine, so do not fear. For your new form is mine.

Panic rose to the surface of her dulled consciousness, and she strained as though at physical bonds. Dimly, she realized what he was talking about, and the pieces began to fall into place. He had orchestrated this entire course, positioning her to accept his proposal and become his Vessel, then forcibly creating a new arm for her, quickening the seed of Silver within her, and then . . . this. *You wanted her to come. You knew she would break into our moon someday . . . But how did you know that Lyn would accidentally allow them in?*

Her only answer was the impression of a smile. Not just an impression, but a visual sight as it were, that of a reflective silver face materializing in the dark, the stuff of nightmares. Animalic and long, with four prominent fangs and heavy brows over blazing white eyes.

But only the smile. She was left with a recognition that her time was fading. She would soon join his consciousness, being only a tag-along for the show that was about to unfold on the surfaces of her birth world. Mani would grow, and was already growing, his ideal body from hers, one meant to rule, one over which she had no governance. Autonomy was a thing of the past.

Luna

Lyn . . . Mydia . . . Kaen . . . if only I could say goodbye, if I could bu[t] apologize and explain what a fool I've been. The true threat that you're u[p] against.

I love you all.

Mani awoke, eyes flashing open, limbs twitching, claws scraping the dir[t] below him as he rose. Panicked voices came from about him, voices he ignore[d] in their entirety. Blood coated the silver metal of his body where its final for[m] had lain in Rhidea's spill lifeblood. No more would this form be dependent o[n] such a substance, for this was no longer her body. He stood on four legs, hea[d] held low, and then arched his spine, standing on hind legs and at a height o[f] around ten feet.

Luna had gone for the form of a mythical dragon, developing hers over tim[e] to look more along the lines of a great cat or canine, but his was far more alien[,] starting as well from the dragon idea and progressing into a frame sinuous as [a] snake yet set with sharp angles at the chest and head, whence spines protruded[.] The mouth was quite serpentine, crowned with four great fangs. Unlike Luna[,] his form changed between quadrupedal and bipedal. Standing as he was, hi[s] form mirrored the woman's form that Rhidea had possessed in terms of genera[l] proportions: Wide-set hips, narrow waist, chest pulled out in angles somewha[t] mimicking a woman's bust, and neck long and graceful. Shoulders independen[t] but not bulky. He had no wings, for he would never know the need for them[.] Yet he could modify this body at any point should the need arise.

Luna body, he immediately noted, was gone. Not fled, but destroyed[,] remnants of her golden metal form littering the ground and faint golden smok[e] still visible in the air. He could feel the lingering of her presence. Lyn, it seemed[,] had slain her at last. And yet, of those looking on in horror from the ground, sh[e] appeared the most composed. Luna's Vessel stared coldly, shoulders set, eye[s] hard but betraying a slight hint of fear. She of all these mortals knew what stoo[d] before her, the new and truest manifestation of the power that governed thi[s] lunar world. The so-called "lesser moon." She knew not to underestimate hi[s]

130

might. "Mani," she said in a voice as cool as her face, though he could make out the tightness in her jaw even through the timbre of that one word.

The other voices quieted, despite the underwhelming force of Lynchazel's recognition of Rhidea's new identity. Their faces displayed obvious disbelief at the result of her transformation, clearly expecting something to identify their friend and collaborator in this new form. When he opened his mouth to speak, his voice dispelled all their delusions:

"Greetings, natives of Mani and of Gaea, beings human and biomechanical. And congratulations, I might say, on slaying my sister's avatar." He dipped his snakelike head in Lyn's direction. "You have done me today a service. I understand that my appearance may be frightening, but I assure you that this is nothing that was not planned in advance. Cae Rhidea became my Vessel willingly, and she understood the danger to her own self that she undertook in so doing. She fought well today, but I was forced to do away with her flesh and grow the seed that was her skeleton into this greater body you now see. Thus, it is different, yet the same. I am Mani, and yet I am also still Rhidea."

The murmuring began, along with outcry against him. Did he mean them harm? Where was she if she was still alive? Prove it! The Gaean skyships had surrounded him. Archlord Domon, still coughing blood but otherwise whole and able to stand, limped over to Lynchazel and the Hellebes Kaen, addressing the Titan. "O Great Mani, we are your humble servants. Long have I served you in spirit, if not always directly, using the Wellspring to further the defense of these lands in whatever way I can. Will you parley with me, now that you have no need of a mediator?"

Mani's serpentine gaze swung to the Emperor. "Need is a strong word, my good man. Or . . . Emperor, as you wish to be known. It is true that I am the lord of this moon, and that you serve me. Who wishes to be a part of this parley?"

Kaen nudged his old friend. "Lyn, I should be getting back to Gaea with my men."

She nodded hesitantly. "But . . . perhaps you should send them back on their own. I need to return, but we need a Gaean representative who can speak the language."

He acceded, and gave the order for his men to depart upward with the other commanders. They did so, and Mani watched them go, considering the size and apparent might of this military force. He would make no move against them this day. No, let this be a day to show his benevolence, and his good will toward both worlds, false though it may be in part.

Lyn hesitated, then embraced her friend quickly. She crouched and leapt and was swallowed up whole in a golden pillar of light. Kaen gaped at her exit, slowly recovering and turning back to the Silver Titan.

"So it is with you two that I shall bargain," he said. "That is well, for we can discuss the role that Gaea plays in Mani's future. I must warn you, Gaean experiment, that our current plan does not make much allowance for Gaean presence on Mani's surface."

"I hadn't noticed," the man returned, tightly but with good humor.

Good, let him keep that for as long as he can. It will delay the inevitable reaction.

- Chapter 49 -

Lunar Ruler

Manidor 2, 1295:
progress.
— From Lhinde's Vault

[A council between Mani's new avatar, Domon and Kaen (standing in for Lyn/Gaea) about the direction of the Silver Moon. Do they try to trap him there, disallowing him to go back to Gaea? Perhaps they at least demand one or two skyships to study]

The Heart of Mani, life force of the silver moon, essence of the Titan of Growth, tested out his new form. Bone of Rhidea, yet made his. The ultimate evolution of man, per his own vision, weaknesses burnt out, refined beyond the bounds of a mortal being. He had grown this body from within her weak flesh, breaking his own bounds while making something new. And he had not been struck down. Neither had Luna shown recognition, if she had truly seen this.

The humans about them . . . they had seen, but they had yet to understand. Even the Black Soul, Domon, possessed little understanding of the basics of life on Mani. And now he would outstrip them all, outsmart his sister, outlive all humans, and soon . . . well, the future had yet to be set in stone. The fate of his lunar world, yet to be determined in this . . . meeting.

Mani finished conferring with the leaders in the northern courtyard, using the deep, richly fabricated vocal chords lent him by this silver flesh. He quite enjoyed towering above them with his long, high-held head, causing discomfort with his alien looks. He may refine them at some point, but for now, he was confident with his appearance. Domon and Kaen, turned toward the Palace, and Mani watched in faint amusement as the former Vessel hesitantly took the proffered hand and they teleported inside.

Then Mani tested his new power. Not a new power, but a latent power that was now his in a personal way via this construct. He let his form loosen and liquidate overtop of a rich silver vein, melding into it and traveling through in a wave that created only a vague bulge where he traveled along it. There was virtually no limit to how fast he could travel thus. He used it to get inside the first floor of Castle Redufiel—the second floor was possible but would be trickier, and he wanted to appear as benevolent and non-destructive as possible to this sensitive "Emperor". Humans, after all, could be fickle.

A feminine scream came from behind some manner of desk—both of which he recognized from previous visits of Rhidea's, but he merely looked the woman's way and made a Legaleian "keep it down" gesture as he sauntered through the hall, heels vibrating the tiled floor and claws clicking in rhythm. Despite having never experienced these halls in a truly personal way with visuals and true perspective, they felt smaller to him now.

Soon, he was being ushered into Domon's personal study by an ash-faced aide, and he transformed before her into his quadrupedal form. Yes, this one felt nice. The aide might have fainted, because he heard a muffled thud behind him. Regardless, the door swung shut, leaving him alone with the room's two other occupants: Kaen and Domon. Funny, to think that this boy had become such a star in both worlds simply for having tagged along with Gaea's scion across the dual continents of Mani's shell. Of course, he'd been the one to pick him, but not for any merit of his own—and he had discarded him with equally small qualms.

"Speak, monster," Kaen said gruffly, earning exactly one raised eyebrow from the dark Emperor.

"Indeed," said Mani, both a confirmation and a sort of statement of approval of the notion. "You, boy, represent the world that your childhood friend has claimed as her own, no? Would you claim more allegiance to Gaea or to Mani if given only those two choices?"

The Hellebes' complexion paled almost imperceptibly. Before, he'd have noticed the shift in his thoughts, emotions, heartbeat—now, he caught a hint of that, but was also able to see this telling physical sign in a addition—not that he needed it.

"Gaea," Kaen said through gritted teeth. He didn't expound, and he didn't have to. Never would this young man admit the truth to the being he held responsible for all of his troubles in both worlds.

Domon's gaze was roughly fixed on Mani's silver form, which had reverted to the draconic-yet-humanoid shape, displayed more detached amusement toward the boy.

- Chapter 50 -

Prey to the Gods

Manidor 2, 1295
progress
— From Lhinde's Vault

[There should be still a looming threat of the Gaean's large-spread invasion, right? Or has that been largely quashed by Kaen and the other two batallions?]

Mydia awoke with a start. Sweat pooled uncomfortably in her armpits, and her nightgown clung to every fold of skin as she rose, blowing a stray swatch of black hair from her face. It didn't budge, so she smeared it away with clammy fingers. What was going on? Just a dream? Yes, she had been dreaming of strange and fantastic things, some of which were now coming back into focus. To strange to be imagined.

But that was not it.

She put a hand to her breast, feeling the breakneck pace of her heart, then let it fall to the sheets below. They weren't there, of course, but were kicked to the bottom of her plush bed. That was not unusual. With a groan, she arose and donned more fitting clothes, not bothering to call her handmaidens. Regardless it was a mere couple of minutes before Teli's blonde head was in the doorway asking if she needed anything.

"It's terribly early, Milady," she said. "Are you sure you don't want a wee bit more sleep?"

Mydia shook her head silently, which the girl took as a prompt to come and help tie the dress she was putting on. A hairbrush materialized in her hand, and soon she'd rid the queen of most of her tangles. "Another frightful dream, Milady?"

"Yes," she whispered, slouching in a chair while Teli pinned her hair above both ears and put in her favorite earrings without being asked. "More than that, though. I'm certain. Did you . . . feel anything strange this night? What time is it, anyway?" The light coming through her window was still soft, soothing aurora-light.

"Don't rightly know, Milady, but I might know what you're speaking of. Felt like something moved. Had me eyes fluttering, too, it did."

Like something moved . . . yes, that explains it pretty well. But it didn't do it justice. When one wakes feverish from a dream, uncertain still what is real and what is not, and experiences a disconnect with the physics of the waking world . . . that was how Mydia had felt. It was fading, but it lingered even now. Mani had seemed to ripple and sway deep beneath the Palace. Like a change in tectonics, or gravity, a pull, a bowing.

The silver. Could it be?

"We need to go," Mydia said abruptly. She was pleased to find that her legs worked just fine. "Well, I need to go. You may get some more rest, dear. Thank you."

Teli shook her head fiercely. "With all respect, Milady, not by my mother's second grave."

The queen looked at her quizzically.

"It's an expression. Heard it from the guards, Your Majesty."

Mydia snorted and continued on her way. Down the tower steps, past the handmaidens' room—Julia was not in her bed either, she noted—and through the second and first floors of the Palace. There was enough noise that one might call it just shy of a commotion, and people were up and moving about bleary-eyed. A guardsman rushed past, muttering an apology, and then turned on his heel, realizing he'd met the queen. "Wait, Milady!"

She turned to him. "Speak, soldier."

"There's . . . well, we're not sure what's going on, but something unusual. Reports of a strange sighting."

She frowned. "And did you feel like the ground was shifting a few minutes ago."

"Yes, Milady, that was one of the signs."

One of them . . . What were the others? She thanked the guard and moved toward the southern Palace gates, encountering more soldiers. One reported the exact same thing, and she kept moving as soon as she knew he didn't have any significant news. When she reached the gate, more guards tried to hold her back, but she shook them off and went out onto the marble portico to stare about the city. She didn't go to the stairs.

All seemed calm in the city, but there was a palpable air of tension that defied the calm early morning. The auroras were nearing the end of their glimmering, preluding the dissipation of the night clouds. So why were the soldiers still shouting? She couldn't make out most of the calls, as many as there were. A group of four were nearing the steps now.

"My Queen!" shouted one of them, bounding up the marble steps two at a time. "It's coming this way. We don't know what it is, but we assume it's dangerous."

"A metal creature!" said another man. "All silver, like nothing ever seen before."

A metal . . . creature. *Oh, no.* Could it really be one of those fabled Cydenges?

Then she saw it, striding up the street in front of the Palace, regally, confidently . . . almost humanly. The thing was massive, and mostly anthropomorphic. Its hide, or scales, or whatever it was, was completely made of silvery metal, perhaps purest silver, glinting as it caught and redirected the maximum amount of aurora-light. She gasped as she realized it looked uncomfortably like the symbol of her family, commonly called "the green dragon of House Kalceron." She didn't even properly know what a dragon was . . .

But perhaps this was one in the flesh.

"A Cydenges . . ." she whispered, even as guardsmen shouted to stand fast and ready all weapons, or for her to get back. Teli tugged at her dress, pleading with her to come inside. Reluctantly, she retreated after the girl a few steps, while two armed guards stepped in front of her, crossing tall halberds between them.

The creature stopped its brisk stride one hundred feet from the closed gates, ignoring the guards who stood by valiantly. She silently saluted their courage. "Queen Mydia Kalceron!" the creature called out. Its voice was deep and commanding, full of ancient authority. She couldn't place what, but something in its resonant tone was familiar, even besides the direct use of her name.

It seemed to be waiting for a reply, or at least acknowledgment. Tentatively she brushed aside the arms that held the halberds crossed before her, taking a half pace forward. "That is I. What are you, and what do you want?"

"I am Mani, and I come with a proposition—and news. Kaen will be along shortly to confirm my words."

She narrowed her eyes, and the guardsmen muttered uncertainly. "This . . . is most unexpected. Your introduction does little to tell us what you really are."

"I can give you a display of my power. I can make it quite a spectacle. Is this necessary?"

Mydia gulped. "No, that . . . that is fine, thank you. What of Rhidea? I assume you have a connection to her?" She was trying to neither acknowledge nor deny with her words the claim of this thing's identity. That this was a physical manifestation of the world itself was hard to swallow.

"I do indeed," answered the booming voice. "But she is dead now, thanks to Luna's surprise attack on Darsor. Need I explain who Luna is?"

Gasps came from all sides at the news. Mydia wasn't about to take this monster at its word, but . . . she felt her eyes tearing up, and blinked away the threat of tears. Finally, she found her words: "Very well, you who call yourself Mani—what would you have us do? Would you take council with us, that we can give an answer to the people?"

"That seems good to me. There is your friend, by the way." The silver dragon-man pointed toward the horizon, and soon she both heard and saw the approach of a Gaean skyship. She spread the order for the men to stand down. Soon, the ship landed and none other than Kaen came bounding up the stairs, passing the metallic giant.

"He means peace, Queen," he said, loudly enough for those around to hear. Dipping his head to her coregent, he said, "Lord Gandel." Lower, to them both, he said, "Though I would prepare yourselves for a wild discussion. Things are ramping up fast. Just don't take everything he says at face value."

Well, I wasn't about to do that, she thought wryly. Though her face went grim as she watched Mani's avatar rapidly approach through the now-open gates. His steps were long and powerful, but deceptively quick, as though he were gliding up the steps and his body only appeared to weigh him down. If it was solid silver, and this truly was the force of Silver incarnate, then that made sense, as gravity was tied to that power.

The statue followed them inside the high double doors, stopping to gaze around at the architecture inside. Mydia couldn't say if the god was truly taking it in for the first time or just putting on a show. Of course, that made her think about her old friend Rhidea, and whether she was still alive in some capacity . . which would soon be forced upon her, and she was not in a hurry to dwell on it.

"Where would you like to discuss?" Mani asked, looking down at Mydia. Perhaps he too noticed that not all doorways in the palace were ten feet or more.

"We, ah . . ." she looked at Ethas. "In the main audience hall?"

He nodded. "That will do."

Mani nodded as well, and then knelt, transforming into a lithe, four-legged creature. "Lead on," it said innocently in the same voice.

Mydia shared a glance with Ethas, then with Teli. Straif and Enchro were both here by now as well, of course. Mydia was fine with as many advisors as possible being present. She didn't want to have to spread whatever news was necessary all by herself. They strode down the requisite corridors, Mani clicking silver-on-marble with his clawed feet, before reaching the high oaken doors to the main audience chamber. Inside, they were greeted by the arched ceiling and tall pillars, each hung by new banners of her new symbol _____.

She still had troubling memories of the room, for it was where her father had made his last stand, threatening her for information and then turning on her when confronted by Rhidea. She swore she could make out the slices Rhidea had peeled from the silver pillars then to make her weapons using Silver Authority.

Mani, metal claws ringing and tic-tacking on the marble floors, dominated the room, sauntering catlike up to the throne. Yet his movements reminded Mydia almost more of a lizard or mudpuppy, as his torso pivoted side-to-side with his gait. It was the roll of the upright hips that felt catlike. Upon reaching the throne, he slowed and began to pace in a circle, seemingly examining the floor and steps.

Mydia hesitated, but the silver beast made way for her, gesturing wordlessly with his tail for her to proceed. Her guardsmen followed close on her heels, along with faithful Teli. The rest stayed below the steps. Mydia ascended them, heart pounding, stealing glances at the frightful creature and her throne. She did not sit on it, however. Ethas joined her, looking back and making a subtle halting motion. Mydia looked with a frown to see Lady Aldyr in the doorway. the woman paused, looked about with wide eyes, and then nodded and backed away.

"I have gathered you all here," Mani said after a pause, circling to eye each of the room's major occupants in turn, "to discuss a matter of importance. Rhidea was against this, as was Archlord Domon—but she is also now dead, and he in critical condition, as I will explain in a bit. This is the year 999 by the Manese calendar, as I trust you know. Can anyone tell me the significance of that?"

Eyes froze, locked on the draconic silver head, which was still low in animal form, like deer in the face of predators. A few heads shook slightly. Finally, Ethas Gandel said, "The nine hundred ninety-ninth year since Legaleians traveled to Mani."

"Correct," said the fanged mouth below the blazing eyes. "And we approach the millennial year, the turning back of humanity, the great release. Next year, I will no longer be bound to this world. It has been decreed that moon-bound humanity will be given a choice, and that is this: leave or stay. Return to Gaea to start a new life, or stay where you are safe. Where you have a home."

"But the invaders are already at our door," Enchro pointed out, the first to contradict the god.

Mani's silver gaze turned to the stout man. "That is so. And by Luna's trickery. When all is said and done, she will be unable to return hence. But the destruction beyond, in the world of Gaea . . . Well, perhaps I should explain events more clearly."

He went on to tell a jaw-dropping tale of Planet Gaea and its nine cities now under attack by the Cydenges. Two cities fallen—of nine. He told of the harsh gravity and the broken state that humanity's twisted remnant had left the world in. How true humans had been wiped away, and now artificial lunar life fought artificial human life. Of Luna's home on the opposite moon, and her long-held malice toward humanity. And lastly, of their ancestors, the Legaleians, who had been falsely accused in the beginning, while Luna was to blame.

In closing, he said, "And I can show any who so desire the path to victory— an assured victory over her fleeting clawing at our world. For it was the Legaleians who first repelled the Cydenges of Luna. It was the priests of Mani . . later known as the Silversmiths."

- Chapter 51 -

The Invitation

Manidor 2, 1295:
progress.
— From Lhinde's Vault

A baptism of silver. Priests of Mani. Victory over Luna and life everlasting on Mani. The temptation of these grand prospects was too much for the council chamber, so much so that Mydia was convinced everyone had lost their heads. Her own was spinning, to be certain, but she was highly skeptical of whatever he was offering. Objections had been raised, especially with regards to the Wellspring or the Archlord's continuing ambitions, but Mani assured them that humankind would continue to thrive on Mani in the next millennium.

Finally, unable to take it anymore, the queen demanded, "What happened to Rhidea?"

The titan reared up on his hind legs and took the half-human form once again. "That would be the sobering part. Luna attacked us through a breach in Domon's shield, which Rhidea had helped to erect using my power. The breach was made Lyn. I must confess, she was a wild card I did not see coming. She returned from Luna to Gaea, it seems, and then instantaneously traveled to Mani from there to meet us. Shortly thereafter, Luna attacked in the form of the Cydenges Queen, also called the Archmother. In a shocking burst of aggression, she immobilized Lyn and snapped up my Vessel in her jaws. What followed was sudden and violent. Rhidea's body was torn to pieces. Rather than be forced from my Vessel and unable to defend my world—than watch invaders steal it from underneath me or burn it down—I used my ancient gift of Growth to form a new body from the ashes of hers. I am Mani, not Rhidea. But a piece of her does reside in me, if that is any comfort."

The titan certainly did not sound sorry, and Mydia could find no comfort in those words. But, even despite her denial at Mani's first announcement, Mydia knew that his words were true. Such a being, in such a form, would not come here only to utter lies. It was a harsh, a painful truth that she would have to push past until she could bear it. She glanced at Kaen, who had yet to speak and he met her gaze only fleetingly. But that split-second look was enough to convey volumes of emotion: guilt, regret, sorrow, pity.

As voices began to rise in objection, Mani called for his witness to speak. Slowly, with hesitation an almost puzzling sense of unwillingness, he did so: "Men and dames of Mani, I—I can't lie to you about it, so I'm going to be backing this creature up." He added a colorful-sounding word in the mix that she did not recognize, most likely a Hellebes curse. Mani didn't seem at all fazed by his tone. "Yes, Rhidea is dead. It was gruesome, and it wasn't Mani's fault that I could tell. Luna came in the form of a mighty dragon, and she . . . we could hardly stop her. Lyn was the one to finally take her out, once she got free of her claws. Domon was injured, but not to badly to convene with us in council following. Lyn returned to Gaea to help the Hellebes against Luna's forces."

"So they are still out there? Still operating?" asked Ethas. "Killing the Queen did not cause the Cydenges to enter a state of panic and disorganization?"

Mydia saw where he was coming from. Thinking of the creatures—which was hard in any case—as a sort of hive or swarm of insects, this thought line did make sense. But she anticipated Kaen's response.

"Lyn went partly to find that out. But . . . Mani does not think so."

He looked questioningly at the silver titan.

The powerful creature made a choppy head-dipping gesture almost like a nod. "Luna's power is still active somehow. As curious as I am to know how that is . . . I care primarily and only for my moon, this world that I have crafted . . . and for my people."

His watchful eye browsed the gathering about him, around a dozen councilors in all, waiting, observing. Mydia noticed further discomfort in Kaen, and could not help but realize that, not only had she begun to accept that as the imposing man's identity, but how much his mannerisms matched the young man who had flown away with her heart. He had brought, if not her whole heart, a piece of it back. Some flutter in her chest suggested that it might be just enough to rekindle the flame. But no, no, that was a fool's reasoning. Not reasoning, but mere and base emotions.

Was it the news of Rhidea's death that had her like this? Or Lyn's betrayal in returning to Gaea without so much as hitching a ride in Kaen's flying vessel? She knew not of Kymhar's whereabouts, but aside from him there remained only she and Oliver of the group who had journey west and east in search of the world to which they'd never been. Only Lyn . . . the stranger. Her niece—arisen to power in Gaea.

At least . . . at least Kaen was trying. That's what she told herself, while shoving down the other voices inside. She could not allow anymore of it out.

The meeting went on for some time, during which Mani pontificated with growing urgency of the glories of joining him in his effort for unity. But he left them with the firm insistence that this was entirely voluntary, and no one would be pressured. But he charged them to spread the invitation out to all the public, saying that any and all could becomes priests or priestesses if they wished.

Then he departed, saying not where he went. The departure was as off-putting as the rest of his speech, however, as he disappeared into one of the pillars, melding with it entirely and sinking down into the ground.

"Was that how he . . ." Mydia began.

Kaen answered with a nod. Yes, Mani had traveled through the continent via the silver roots. She thought on that for a moment, seeing her own pensiveness reflected in Ethas' and Straif's faces as well. Ethas was the first one to voice the obvious objection: "Wait—how can that be, if there is a four-hundred-mile gap between continents?"

"That . . . is another matter," the Hellebes answered darkly. "There is . . . well, perhaps it would be easier to show you. Or—anyone here who would like to accompany me to the Sea of Emptiness. It's a mere quarter-hour trip."

Mydia's voice caught in her throat before her lips had even parted. She wanted to, but . . . she couldn't go. No. No good would come of it.

Ethas raised his hand. "I will go, Captain Kaen."

Kaen looked at him with a considering nod. There was no indication of relief or disappointment in his face, though Mydia knew she hadn't mistaken the awkwardness in his tone a moment ago. She glanced at Ethas, but he too—frustratingly—revealed no clue as to his motive for speaking up. he knew their history well enough, and perhaps that was the reason.

Perhaps.

"But I will ask, what is it we are seeing?" Gandel said.

"It's . . . well, Mani reconstructed the land bridge between continents," Kaen explained. "And no, I don't believe he dredged up the old pieces, which he claimed lay in the Down Under. Rather, he . . . *grew* a new one. That is his ability—Growth. And along with gravity, it is a force of nature at his beck and call."

"You do not trust Mani," Enchro observed with a huff, which seemed to indicated he thought exactly the same.

"I . . . do not. I cannot. I know I'm not alone in that here." Heads nodded in agreement, and Kaen went on in a quieter voice. "There is much at stake, and far more on the table than he let on." He looked down, gulping and licking his lip briefly, before gazing around the room. "Thank you for going along with me. With him. Mani is awake now. I was once his Vessel, so I of all people know . . . he cannot be trusted." He opened his mouth to say more, but apparently decided against it.

Ethas strode forward, reaching up to clap the broad-shouldered soldier on the back. "Let us be going, then." He looked back at Mydia. "We will be back before long."

- Chapter 52 -

The Chasm Between

Manidor 2, 1295:
progress.
— From Lhinde's Vault

"Thank you," Kaen said as the two strapped themselves in. Ethas did not need much instruction on how to do the straps in the single seat behind hid Hellebes pilot, nor did he seem to project fear of getting in a foreign vessel such as this. A man of backbone, Kaen had to say.

"For offering in my colleague's place?" the regent asked, "Or for smoothing out your blunder?"

"Was it . . . that obvious?" He couldn't help the words, as childish as they made him feel.

"Yes. That was what we call a social blunder. Don't worry, for she does as well. Not . . . as frequently as she used to, all told." He paused, looking out the voluminous glass windows as Kaen started the Geokinetic motor and lifted off. He commented not at all on the feeling of being torn from Mani's surface by alien machinery, but simply went on: "It is, I suppose, understandable. But you are right to assume. I had no particular wish to be in this . . . thing, though this is not as unbearable a ride as I'd imagined."

Kaen accelerated further as they gained altitude, gaining a whoof and a grunt from his regal passenger. He tried not to smile at that, though he did back off the speed a bit to allow the Legaleian to acclimate to the G-Force. Plus, a human could endure as much as a Hellebes, and the only experience he had flying with a human was . . . his memories of *being* one, over a year ago with Lyn and Zent. One year, yet it felt like a lifetime.

"Kaen."

His name got his attention, and he turned his head half round to indicate his attention.

"I want you to know that I do not entirely trust you. I would proceed with this conversation as though I did, but you may not buy that, and . . . I think this will go better if at least one of us is honest. Though I think you will be."

Kaen thought for a moment before responding. Something he used to eschew. "Very well. That is fair."

"Mydia, I believe, fully does. The others, I cannot say. But I would say I am one of those who noticed the starkly different way our old friend Cae Rhidea acted when last she was here in Nytaea."

Kaen did not point out that they were already at the Nytaea–Storklance border, so *here* didn't apply all that well. "Very well," he repeated.

"That is your only response? We imprisoned you, threatened you, and did not heed your warnings. Surely you are angry at such treatment? Or did Rhidea's death mellow out the hurt that she inflicted you with when she orchestrated all that?"

Kaen frowned. This man was far more perceptive than he'd ever given him credit for. But he was dead wrong if he thought Kaen didn't care about the woman anymore. Watching her be torn apart like—and then, even worse, knowing what Mani was doing as he remade her body from silver . . . . "Why are you saying all this?"

"For two reasons. One, I apologize on behalf of our city-state. While I cannot do that publicly, I do so now, in these confines, for your peace of mind. I will leave it to Queen Kalceron to forgive you herself."

Kaen's chest tightened at her name, particularly spoken that way. She purposely avoided using her family name in such a way, though she had not gone so far as to change it. Just the symbol. "And the other reason?" He had a feeling his tone was coming out harsher than he meant.

"To know your side of the story. I have been frank with you—now be frank with me."

Well, this man certainly knows how to be direct. And yet, he had an inkling there was still more here. Only idiots like Lyn or innocent souls like Mydia talked so openly of such matters.

"I do not have much to add to your take on me," Kaen hedged. "I came with a message, not expecting opposition from such a familiar face. I . . . was not surprised at Rhidea's betrayal, but perhaps I was a bit disappointed at how accepting you and Mydia were of her plans."

"Betrayal," Ethas said musingly. "Yes, I could see that. In our discussions following her departure for Yan'Vala, we certainly took into account the distinct possibility that she had completely sold out to the Archlord, or even was somehow under compulsion."

"I don't think that was the case at all," Kaen said.

"Nor do I. But my good man, if you are—no, let us be direct. *Are* you the same man?"

Kaen paused. "That has already been asked. I cannot claim that I am, and yet, in identity, mind, memories and mannerisms . . . I am a copy, one who picked up where he left off. So yes, I am essentially the same man who left in search of Gaea with Mydia and the others two years ago."

"Then you were Mani's Vessel before Rhidea. Tell me of your experience with that versus Cae Rhidea's."

He doesn't let up for grief at all, does he? "I . . . do not like to recall those days. It is like a fever dream in my mind that I wish to forget . . . yet my brain disallows me. It was a time of shame, guilt, constant worry . . . looking back just makes me angry at myself. For Mandrie, and for—" He cut off abruptly, realizing he'd been a little *too* frank. The words had just started pouring out.

"And for? I can keep a secret—I am a state leader, after all."

Kaen gestured out the window, where the horizon was revealing the edge of the visible world. "We're here." It wasn't a cover for what he'd been about to say, but more a pickup on a convenient interruption. He knew the man would not let it drop, since he seemed personally concerned for some reason. Kaen turned the ship to fly northward, opening up a wide view for Ethas—of the gaping horizon, the sky islands beyond . . . and the new bridge of silver that ran parallel to the floating landmasses.

"So he really did craft a new land bridge," Gandel said in controlled wonder after a moment of silent gaping. The bridge was smooth and straight, wall-less, some hundred feet wide and two to three times that in depth, tapering downward in graceful curves, like a carved balustrade. It ran south of most islands, passing between those and the southern isles and extending in a smooth curve into the horizon. Straight, as a map would show it. Curved due to the geometry of the moon itself, though the mists of the chasm did obscure it after some five to ten miles.

Continuing to fly parallel to it, Kaen said, "So you've seen it. Does this convince you about Mani's other words?"

The pause before Ethas' next words indicated his careful consideration of Kaen's choice words. "Yes and no. I already believed you and Mani about the bridge. I came to see it for myself, but primarily to get a chance alone with you. As for its construction, I take it this being that has supplanted Rhidea has strong enough powers of Silver to build this from Mani's continental silver? Or using the "Growth" ability he spoke of."

"The latter," Kaen confirmed. "It is . . . eerie. I've seen it in action. He claimed it was how he made the world itself. That it was once a simple moon of Gaea, a small satellite, but he spun a shell for it out of silver to house the refugees of a certain location on Gaea."

"I . . . am not sure what to make of that. It is not a story the people will buy, but I think I am in no position to contest it. We will speak later, and quite in depth, on Mani's proposition." He let short silence stretch after this, but it was a silence like a gentle prodding, a nudge.

Kaen gave a small sigh. "I was angry at myself for my sister Mandrie, and how I treated her, but also . . . Mydia. I mean—Queen Mydia. I've regretted my treatment of her since my trip to Gaea, but Mani's influence was still clouding my mind enough to dull my guilt. I don't—it's not like I still have any feelings for her. Don't get me wrong. And it wasn't really anything, but we were close. I should not have treated her as I did. I just . . ."

He trailed off, wearied by the effort it took just to try to get the words off his chest. They still didn't come out right at all, and he hadn't even said anything meaningful. Nor anything close to the truth of it.

He could feel Ethas nodding in the silence from the backseat. "I sense we are approaching the truth here."

It was only then that Kaen realized that was the whole intention of this conversation—Ethas had been steering him into a confession regarding his relationship toward Mydia. In a controlled environment where she was not a factor. *What a slimy worm . . .* He coughed semi-voluntarily, trying to dredge up his soldier programming and training and let it take over. He was done with this conversation, as it had grown far too uncomfortable quickly. With a practiced motion, he swung the ship in a half-loop and headed back to Nytaea.

"Is that it?" asked the governor. "If there is nothing more of a personal nature regarding the Queen, then I suppose we can simply spend these next moments in uncomfortable silence."

This aurora-blinded snake. It was like bullying. Back on Gaea, he could have easily played this off, as Hellebes men didn't truly understand true human emotion, not when it came to relational matters between sexes. With a sigh, he asked, "Are you concerned for her as a fellow leader of Nytaea for political reasons, or does this come from personal interest?"

Now he could feel the eyebrows go up. "Personal interest . . . hmm. I would say the former certainly. It goes without saying, considering the volatile state of Nytaea and the entire world right now. But also the second. I feel a certain sense of duty regarding her safety. And no, I have no plans to marry her, if that is what you are thinking. It has crossed my mind, but there are too many issues involved with marrying from two major noble houses. It is not a thing that is done. Think for yourself—What nobleman can you recall having married two noblewomen? Either they are from lesser houses, or he himself is not of the highest standing."

He's right, Kaen realized. He didn't truly have the breadth of knowledge to know, but judging by what he could remember from his time in the Nytaean court, it was true. Nobles took many concubines or wives from the people oftentimes, as in the case of Lord Kalceron, and he'd heard of the scandals involving neglected or "left-out" noblewomen who were left without a suitable spouse. Though they were exempt from the tradition which stated it was a woman's duty to society to marry and attempt to rear a boy.

So then, "this sense of duty" . . . He couldn't tell for certain, but he was inclined to think that Ethas had a point to his protectiveness, as he'd made no threats yet. Still, what all had he heard? "Lord Gandel, we don't have much farther, and it seems you have a point to this conversation—"

"I do. And you're right. Let us be more direct: How do you think of the queen after your transformation on Gaea? Has anything changed in that regard?"

That's only a little more direct, he grumbled to himself. "It sounds like you've heard that we . . . well, I . . . I don't know."

"I think you do. Be honest."

Ethas' tone had taken on a slightly harder edge, prompting a scowl from Kaen—which the governor fortunately could not see. "Fine, then. I loved her. I still do. I wanted to speak to her about it, but of course . . . it didn't work out like that. I'll have to do that soon—unless . . . Is that a bad idea, sir?"

"Is it? As the leader of a city-state, I don't think I'm in a position to give you the personal answer. So my official answer is this: Stay far away from her in a time such as this. Come back in a year, if we've somehow survived all this. This is no time to trouble a queen. But—but! I am also one of two equal halves, she being the other, so it is not up to me. I would hear more, however. I can at least advise you."

Kaen said nothing for a moment save for a soft "Oh." But he proceeded to elaborate on his feelings to Ethas. At first, nothing was coming out right, despite the hours he'd spent preparing for this very conversation, until he began to pull directly from his Vault. He had a block partitioned out specifically for just that very information. Ethas speared it full of holes, his questions always riding that line between infuriating and justified. Of course, the whole exchange was only around ten minutes, and both were aware of that time constraint.

Finally, they were back in Nytaea, where the tone of the conversation seemed to shift, cooling into a solid state. The glance backward that Kaen stole revealed a solemn face of a governor considering his city in distress—no doubt thinking over the ultimatum which would be passed on. He spoke nought of that, for a reason Kaen knew all too well now. The matter of personal importance between them was done. He would speak no more.

Yet he did, one final question: "Captain Kaen, what do you think is your friend Lyn doing on her world now?"

"I . . . can't really say. I believe she was going back to Ccamos first—the place over which she is now governor, to put an end to the Cydenges threat and reconvene with the other leaders."

Ethas Gandel gave a faint sound that could have meant agreement, satisfaction, or a few other responses. He said nothing more until they landed, at which point he thanked Kaen and stepped out to meet Mydia and the guardsmen. Some councilors were still there, while others had departed or come since—likely having heard of the stir with Mani but missing the council.

After Ethas confirmed the word of the bridge, they spoke further on the ramifications and on their plan going forward. Thoughts of Mydia lingered persistently at the back of his mind until at last, blessedly, the meeting was done and she was kept by two advisors, one, and . . .

She turned her green eyes on him, and he felt his stomach twitch. Till now, her eyes had been obscured by a shadow, the shadow which lifted now that her radiant smile tremulously came out to play. Only half, but it was enough to lift the veil from her face and cause her eyes to sparkle. Then it was gone.

But it was enough. Oh, flaming auroras, it was enough to keep him going. Even if he somehow could not speak with her . . . but he had to—he *had* to. *Wait, she's . . . beckoning me with her hand.* Slowly, he approached her. "My Queen?"

"Oh, stop that!" she reached up a hand and swatted his shoulder. For a moment, he thought her cross with him, but then he saw that the smile was back, this time playful. "I'm not your queen anymore, silly."

She said the words quietly enough that none were likely to hear, but of course, few in this court were strangers to her childlike ways, which were now more like seasonings on an otherwise far more adult personality. The crown had shaped her into the woman she had to be, and she had stepped up remarkably to it. But he knew the real Mydia inside, the one whose face desperately wanted some air to be free for a short while.

"What did you want?" he asked, for lack of a better way to broach the subject. Immediately, he saw the foolheadedness, for he should have simply asked if she were free to chat.

"I'd like a word with you in a bit," she said, glancing aside at Captain Straif of the Mage Guard, who stood patiently by.

"Oh—of course," he said with an unnecessary clearing of his throat. "I'll just wait outside, maybe by, um . . ."

"The tree," she said with a curt nod. "Yes, that will do. What is it, Straif?"

That was all the dismissal he got, and all he needed. There was only one tree she could be speaking of, though there were several wizened trees about the Palace, one in particular of which was said to be hundreds of years old—as ancient as the city.

He had yet to properly see it, too. She seemed to be indicating that he might take an interest in seeing it up close, but he thought—and desperately hoped—there was more to it.

- Chapter 53 -

Beneath the Boughs of Gold

Manidor 2, 1295:
progress.
— From Lhinde's Vault

Mydia's heart was racing, and she couldn't interpret the frantic soprano staccato/pizzicato of her heart as she approached the now-infamous terrace. While a popular topic of the city, and indeed a place frequented by many curious to see it up close, or foreigners drawn as far as the other side of Kystrea to see it . . . yet the grand icon was planted inside the Palace gates, and even then, people tended to gaze from afar, respecting or fearing its presence, though she felt they missed the true point of it. The tree pointed to an ancient power hidden within Mani, the power of the Wellspring of Life—and the ticking of the days until the final year.

"Kaen," she said with a strange sort of relief as she saw him. She hopped the railing in a rather unladylike fashion, hoping none were noticing save for the watchful eyes named Ruel and Inno. She landed ungainly, tripping a few steps before a strong hand raised her hand up. Kaen's oversized hand, which raised her upper body with no noticeable effort. She gave a few excuses intended as apologies, or thanks for the help, or protests that she was fine on her own, but he ignored them just as much as she wished she hadn't opened her fat mouth.

"Hello, Mydia." He distinctly appeared to be intent on sounding as proper and professional as possible. If she knew him at all, that was to hide the nervousness he'd displayed so openly a few moments ago. Yes, this was definitely the same Kaen.

She opened her mouth to say something, then stalled by settling her rump a particularly good sennet of roots. He took the cue and did likewise, stealing a glance upward to see who was watching. Only with great willpower did she keep from doing the same.

Kaen leaned forward, propping elbows on knees. "It's been a long time."

Before answering, she thought about his words, and the multiple levels of meaning. "It has. You're . . . you really are him, huh?"

He nodded.

She looked down at her pale hands to find them shaking. Water threatened to well in her eyes, and she jerked a hand halfway up to wipe them before jerking it back. *Stop, Myds. You can just . . . not cry.* "I'm sorry about Rhidea. I . . . had a hard choice there. I knew something wasn't right, and I just—" She cut off with a choked sob.

Kaen got up and approached to sit beside her on the treeward end of the roots. She felt his hand on her left shoulder, and instinctively leaned to the right resting her head against his dense side. She couldn't tell if it was muscle, or the strange effect Lyn spoke of, where Hellebes' bodies were literally far more dense and heavy than Legaleians', but it was not as comfortable as she'd have thought. Being wrapped in such a masculine embrace was intoxicating, however, in another way—or would have been, had the situation now been so emotionally raw. Her tears, so fresh.

Kaen said nothing. Something about the silence between them was heavy. She continued to sob quietly, dripping tears onto his strange military uniform. "Oh, Kaen, is she *really* gone? It doesn't seem possible. It's like . . ."

"Like losing your entire kingdom, then receiving it back? Like creating a gigantic tree the size of a city?"

She frowned, sniffing and withdrawing her head, looking up at him. "What's that supposed to mean? That's . . . not very comforting."

He sighed. "Sorry, Mydia, I just meant . . . you know, impossible things are happening every day around us. And this war of worlds is getting dangerous. Who knows who we could lose next." His face, devoid of its momentary lightness, held an edge harder than the young man she used to know ever possessed. Of course, that man had not died, but grown up. Matured, aged. Yes, that was it. "That is all right if I call you by your given name?"

She elbowed him in the side. "Don't be stupid, soldier boy."

As she continued to get a hold of herself—hanky and all—her Hellebes friend took a thoughtful pose a of an odd brand of seriousness: thoughtful, far-away, uncertain, yet . . . as though desperately searching for something. Finally, he spoke again. "Mydia, there are some things we need to talk about. I think we both know what they are."

"Do we?"

He gave her an unamused frown. "We do."

She swallowed. She . . . was *pretty* certain what he meant to ask, but that wasn't the same as knowing. Or was it? Regardless, the better part of her wanted him to just come out and be a little more bold. All this shyness was unbefitting of one so strong in stature. She almost pretended to convey this to him with her eyes, but succeeded only in causing him to drop his eyes. *Oh, come now, Kaen. Please, anything but that . . .*

The eyes returned with renewed fire. "Mydia, do you love me?"

A laugh caught in her throat, such that she was sure her face would inspire a good comedian to an entire new routine. As she glanced back down at her pale, frail hands, the laugh escaped, trailing off into a low chuckle. Her partner was silent throughout, apparently having the decency to take her seriously despite her reaction. "I'm sorry, I'm sorry. I just—it caught me a little off-guard. Yes, Kaen, I do. I love you dearly. You're all I could think of for the first few months, and then when—when Rhidea gave me the news . . ."

He tensed. "Rhidea? She was the one who . . . oh, of course she was. Mani. He—" He cut off, seemingly as he realized that she had curled herself into a ball, hugging both arms across her chest. "I'm sorry if I . . ."

She shook her head. "No, no, it's not you. I just . . . I was a little overloaded when I finally saw you again. It was too good to be true. But it is true."

Another short pause, during which she began to fear she'd far overstepped, baring too much too quickly. Surely a queen ought—

"But Mydia, that Kaen. I am . . . the Hunter. A Hellebes experiment. I don't even know if I'm capable of fathering a child—do you understand that?"

She grimaced with a gulp, but quickly sought his gaze. "Kaen, that's—that doesn't matter. Legaleians and Hellebes are just two broken peoples. Forget the royal descendants, forget the ordinances to marry and bear offspring—this world is *dying* and it needs . . . a solution. But . . . I love you."

He pulled her close again, and she let her shoulders slump, melting in the embrace. A part of her fear and anxiety and tension seemed to flow out of her. "Thanks," he said uncomfortably, in an unreadable tone. "I . . . I'm glad." He sat up, brushing her off, and turned so he was looking into her eyes. "But I don't think this is the time or the place for this. We should both be going, because we have work to do."

Her face fell, and a lump began to form in the back of her throat. She dropped her gaze, but he lifted her chin with one long finger. His eyes roved the stairs above once more, then he ducked in and kissed her. Her lips responded readily, kneading his own, but he quickly withdrew. Chewing absently on his lip, he held her gaze for but a moment before glancing about him and backing up. She scooted after him, up the tree roots. "Wait, Kaen—don't feel bad. I . . . liked it."

He chuckled. "It's not that. We just shouldn't be seen like this. Look, why don't we just . . ." He sighed. "Mydia, there's a lot going on in the worlds, and there will be plenty of time once we sort it all out."

"But . . . you still haven't even said it yet. A kiss isn't enough."

He ducked his head, puffed out his cheeks, let out a breath, and then looked deep into her eyes. "Myds . . . I love you. More than anything. I promise you. I can't tell you how much of a relief it is to hear you say the same." He ran a hand through his thick, dark curls. "I can't tell you how many times I've run through this conversation."

She would have been annoyed if she could stop smiling. She wiped once, then twice, at her mouth as though to scrub it off, but it persisted, girlish and stupid. Rather than chide him for his awkward behavior or protest his sudden standoffishness, she simply asked, "Then what's next for us? You realize there are already multiple suitors lined up for my hand, right?"

"You're hand?" He picked her right hand up, turning it over playfully as though in consideration. "I would have thought them far more interested in the rest of you."

She felt her cheeks color. Yanking her hand back, she said, "I didn't know you'd been practicing your poetry. You devilishly verbose gentleman."

"And devilishly handsome?"

She made no effort to hide her bashful attraction. "Yes."

"And what about Zent? I heard you girls were stealing looks at him."

She gaped in indignation. "I did not!" Looking down, she grumbled, "Perhaps a couple. He's attractive in . . . a very different way. More mature."

He only snorted, crossing his arms and shaking his head slowly. "Well . . . at least I managed to somehow win the heart of the most beautiful woman in the land." He turned a suspicious gaze on her. "You'll have to tell me more about these suitors."

She shrugged mischievously. "Oh, they're . . . you know, just the most eligible and affluent and powerful men in the city-state."

Again with the snorting. "Right, eligible as in 'got two wives, looking for a third.'"

She looked upward in mock-consideration. "Mm, perhaps some of them. But I can't say how my tender mind might be swayed if push came to shove and I began to feel desperate. If my shining knight were off on a far-off world performing countless heroic deeds beyond my knowledge . . ."

He rolled his eyes. Then the half-smile dropped from his face, and his eyebrows lowered. "You wouldn't actually consider these greasy noblemen, would you?"

She returned him a playfully avoidant look, earning her a low growl of exasperation.

"Fine. Then maybe we should . . . take some kind of action. Just as a place-holder. What if—I don't know, but—if you agreed to make me some sort of promise. Like an agreement."

She stared deadpan at him, waiting for the idiotic words to progress into something coherent. "Kaen, please. Be direct."

"Well . . ." He sighed and threw up his hands. "It's just, I don't feel right asking you to . . . I don't know. You're a queen. I—" He cut off, taking a deep breath. Then they were looking eye-to-eye, his deep brown orbs finally offering a glimpse into his soul. "Mydia, would you promise to marry me? At a future date when . . . well, we can discuss it, but for now, just a deal between us, that someday we will be together."

Her face didn't seem to be responding to the swarm of emotions trapped in her breast. Her lips parted, and then words tumbled out. "Yes. Yes, Kaen, that sounds lovely. Not . . . ideal, but it will do. They call it a betrothal. Usually, it's between families, of course, but you don't exactly, ah, have that to back you up."

"Neither do you."

"True."

They sat there awkwardly for a moment more before she realized her sidling had finally brought her next to him, legs reaching for a grasp on the ground that sufficiently propped her up. She turned and hugged her friend tightly. "Oh, Kaen, I'm so happy."

He bent down and kissed her once more. It felt just as good as the first time. When he got up, she held his hand until they fell apart.

The warm feeling left by the encounter held her there, mind fixed on naught at all, until she realized he had left.

- Chapter 54 -

Lyn Returns

Manidor 2, 1295:
progress.
— From Lhinde's Vault

Zent breathed hard, chest rising and falling as he studied the killing field south of Ccamos. Many men had fallen, and medical teams were still airlifting them away. Some would recover, others would not. Of the vanquished moon dragons, little was left save for the occasional piece of their plating that became . . . unlinked from the rest of the monster. There were different theories on that. Yet more were coming—*more*. It didn't seem possible, but then, this was the statistic all across Gaea right now. *Lyn, be back soon.*

A messenger had arrived from the silver moon mere minutes before with strange tellings of Lyn having slain the Cydenges Queen . . . but he would believe it when he saw it. If the Queen was truly dead, then why were these things still coming?

Hearing a sound from behind him, he turned, sword raised, to see . . . her.

"Hello, Captain," she greeted him, standing upright as the red pillar vanished. Her face was tight, jaw set and eyebrows hung low. Nevertheless, she said, "You got our message?"

He nodded.

"Well, there's more to tell. Firstly . . ." She turned to survey the scene, hefting her six-foot greatsword, gesturing at the remaining battle. "By the way, they're all coming to help." She pointed upward, where troops were now reentering the visible atmosphere.

Zent checked his wrist console's radar functionality to confirm. "Awesome. Let's take these things out."

They dashed off into the thick of the Cydenges, meeting the beasts head-on with their weapons. His hammer took the first one in the head, blowing it to the side, and Lyn stabbed her sword's point into the base of the exposed neck. It burst apart in a spray of sparks and crimson light, and they set upon the next two monsters.

The newly-arriving ships, though not armed for Cydenges combat, descended and unloaded what ballistic weaponry they had into the thickest throngs of them, and then returned to base to reload. Not many had returned, around one hundred, but it was plenty enough to make a difference. Lyn was a force of nature, pulling ahead of Zent blazing bursts of green heat distortion, burning planetary energy to enhance her speed greatly. With one stamp of her foot, she traced through the earth and snapped a hundred jaws upward, grabbing hold of Luna's monstrosities. They fell to sword edge and hammer blow. On one occasion, she reached inside the mouth of a lunging Cydenges and unleashed a golden blast, triggering some manner of explosive chain reaction.

The others began to shy back, sensing a furious predator energy in Lyn. They looked uncertainly about, as though seeing the dead forms of their many comrades. They began to retreat in flashing columns of ruby light, though Lyn took some even as they went.

At last, they looked about them, and saw none. No more red pillars, no swarms of avians, no churning of the ground where burrowers approached. None. Lyn thrust her sword into the ground and leaned on it, wiping hair out of her face while Zent typed into his wrist console. When he looked up, he cracked a tired smile. "We made it. You came just in time, once again. Thanks, Lyn. Here, uh, we'll get you back. You look like you could use some clothes."

Her eyes had reverted from the vicious gold they'd been a moment ago to her regular blue. She looked down as though just now noticing her nakedness. "Yeah, let's go."

After seeing to the wounded, they located Zent's ship, which had avoided being attacked by the Avians. The flight back to the city was short and silent. Zent was trying to recover his breath, forcibly refraining from making old man jokes at how his thirty-year-old body couldn't take this kind of stress anymore.

Instead, he simply focused on getting them safely to military HQ, where they docked in the open-air VIP area. She trailed behind him as he strode purposefully into the complex, nodding to the guards, who stared at Lyn wide-eyed for any number of reasons. Mother Gaea, alien survivor, first ever to return from Luna, slayer of Cydenges, naked woman. She was all of those right now. A soldier met them soon, having gotten Zent's message about needing a suit for her, and she thanked him, ducking into a nearby room and returning clothed. She turned to offer the soldier thanks, but he was already gone.

"Come on, Lyn," Zent said, taking her by the shoulder. "Let's get to command."

Soon, they were waist-deep in a grim meeting, highlighted by wall screens displaying maps of world power points currently under Cydenges control or intense attack. Lyn said surprisingly little, opting to stare almost uncomprehendingly at the maps. Zent could understand the reaction, as it was hard to properly wrap his own head around the damage the Cydenges had inflicted in only a week. But . . . she'd said she knew about all this beforehand.

The generals questioned her increasingly, to which she responded appropriately but curtly. Mostly, of course, these centered on her failed trip to Luna and what went wrong. What kept her? What had prompted Luna to execute her large-scale offensive? When prompted regarding Mani's welfare, she spoke for the longest she had yet: Mani was safe for the time being. The Cydenges Queen was dead, as was the great High Mage Rhidea, whose death she insisted would be very impactful for the silver moon. Kaen remained on Mani, acting as mediator between Gaea and Mani, but should return soon.

As far as Luna, Lyn said disturbingly little. She seemed to be in recovery from that time. She claimed Luna had not only known she was coming, but had been the one calling her, and that she took her prisoner using threat of force. It had undoubtedly changed her; she was not the same young woman who had left with a fatalistic smile, saying she had to go. No, this woman had all the brightness of a cadaver, and though she projected confidence and hope, there was an unfathomable hollowness behind her eyes that opened up whenever she thought none were looking. What had she experienced on the desolate moon? She'd spoken in-depth about her time there, but . . . well, it was hard to put himself in those shoes. He had seen the Queen but briefly up close, while she had lived under her foot for months.

Later after the meeting, he was paying attention as the woman tried to melt away, likely heading back to her residence for the evening. While he didn't blame her, they needed to talk. He waved and called her name as he followed her out into the hall, but it was as if she was specifically avoiding him, ducking her head and hurrying out. Perhaps she hadn't heard, so he called again, causing her to stop briefly and look back. With a sigh, he turned. "What is it, Captain?"

"It's colonel now. I just wanted to talk with you. Heading back to the manse?"

She nodded, turning half around once more. "I just . . . I've answered enough questions for now."

"I get that. I won't let any inquirers accost you on the way, then."

Not a smile, not a smirk. She glanced once more at him, then turned and kept walking. But she did not deny him the chance to accompany. Technically, she could have, but his request was more than reasonable, all things considered. She walked with a brisk stride, maximizing her length of leg, which was longer than most humans but easily matchable by most Hellebes. The sun smiled on them in lieu of the returning Senator, and wished—not for the first time—that they had Haccolces' geography instead. Higher elevation and further from the equator, the capital had one of the most temperate climates of all eight cities.

The thought made him think of Long out at Mei Shan on Tai'Xi, the aged master of Geokinesis and leader of the true humans. Had the Cydenges struck there yet? Would they? They had enough soldiers posted there, or so they hoped, to fend off an invasion, but if the silver beasts attacked in force like they did here . . . would it be enough?

"Lyn, what do you actually think of the Cydenges invasion following the death of the Queen?" he asked suddenly.

"I already told you in the meeting."

"I understand, but it was the kind of response meant to pacify someone. Not bring closure. You were trying to give the generals hope."

She sighed again. "So you noticed? Yes, I . . . I did just that. A few months with the Queen and already I'm turning into a manipulative monster, huh?"

She cracked a wry smile, letting it vanish soon after, but he didn't find much humor in her words. "Then you don't really think the Queen is dead. Is this like those creatures that still move and twitch when their head is cut off? Or that mythical monster that grows extra heads every time one is cut off?"

"Your thoughts are awfully violent today, Colonel. Too much time spent fighting off alien predators?" When he didn't answer, she said, "Sorry. Perhaps that was a bit insensitive."

"It's . . . fine, My Lady."

"Oh please, Zent. We're friends—you're practically my father. Godfather, at least."

Something glowed warm and bright inside him at the words. The reaction was stronger than he ever would have expected. "That's . . . very close. I'm pleased to hear you speak of me so. Your father and mother would have approved. They . . . they would be proud to see you now, you know."

She bobbed her head slowly, silver ponytail dragging up and down the length of her spine with the motion. She wore it long this afternoon, bound in a lazily looping string. It seemed that her stay on Luna had neither lengthened nor shortened its growth. Her human body, despite no real sustenance, had lost nothing of its vim and robustness, a detail that enhanced the credibility of her wild story. Not that he ever would have doubted her. He might disagree with her, he might stand up to her or chide her as a father, but he would never doubt Lyn.

They approached the military command hangar, and Zent hurried ahead to ready a shuttle to the manse. While he started up the small aircraft, he thought on the many matters they would doubtless have to bring before her tonight. She would not get the sleep she deserved, for her title as Senator came with many responsibilities—although Frauss would still be covering many of them. But they could not very well bypass their official leader in the chain of command when she was present and functional and they were in the middle of a high stakes war.

He landed the vessel at the Senatorial airpad and followed her inside. Staff were already thronging the entrance, having heard of her arrival and wishing to welcome her back. Iselda and ___ were there, and of course Margill the butler. The Hellebes servants parted with a cheer, and the more familiar or bold of them stepped out to clap her on the back. Zent watched in faint amusement as she steeled herself against the back-claps, greetings she used to cringe at and often complain about. Why couldn't they treat her as an actual lady, etc. Joining in on the nostalgia, the two former concubines gave her the same greeting, which she responded to this time by pulling each into a partial embrace. A close bond had developed between she and them before her departure, one he didn't understand any more than he did those involving her female friends back on Mani. Women interacted with one another far differently to men. Just one more piece of culture their world had entirely lost.

Inside, the servants gave her space, which she visibly appreciated, turning to Zent with a small wide-eyed look. It was not a serious expression, or at least he didn't think so. Her mannerisms were not exactly ordinary, but that was entirely understandable given the circumstances surrounding her return. She turned to him, face impassive this time. "I'm . . . going to go freshen up if that's all right. Keep me posted on military operations, of course."

He nodded curtly, unsure if that was a dismissal. He was pretty sure it wasn't, so he made his way vaguely toward the women's bathroom, which was a novel and multipurpose group of rooms made specially for the Mother Heiress and her attendants.

- Chapter 55 -

The Orphans

Manidor 2, 1295:
progress.
— From Lhinde's Vault

"And why haven't you visited yet?" Phoebe asked, not turning to face the giant alien that claimed to be Kaen. The one she already had, but wished desperately not to, acknowledge. Instead, she dried another plate.

She heard the distinctive squeal of another child being let down onto the ground, one of the little ones who tended to immediately demand to be up again. Then a few heavy footsteps, and he was there beside her, towering more than six inches overhead. He grabbed a plate and took the towel from her hand, then expertly stacked up the remaining ones she had drying and put them away.

She sighed and flicked her ponytail off her neck. It nearly landed on her other shoulder. "Kaen?"

"Just thought I'd help out," he mumbled. Even his voice had changed, though it was still recognizable as his—simply deeper. "Look, Pheebs, I get it. But I'm indentured to certain folks back on Gaea now. It's not so simple to leave, and when I do, I have orders and stuff."

"Lyn. You're indentured to Lyn."

"Ah . . . sort of, yeah. But there are others under her, and she's been gone for a few months. One of the generals took over."

"And aren't you a general?"

"Captain," he said, emptying her rack of dishes entirely. "You're just being obstinate, huh?"

She shrugged. He wasn't wrong, but it didn't mean she had to admit it. "Well, I guess I should thank you for finally coming out?"

"Probably." He bent down to scoop a couple more orphans into his arms.

"Mama's almost done here," he said, raising little Ivy's arm.

"Kaen." This time, her voice was sharp and her glare hard. "I go by Miss Phoebe or Big Sis, not . . ." She gestured with her washrag.

He nodded silently, understanding. "Okay, sis. So what did you think about all the nonsense with Mani?"

She didn't look up this time. "It's nonsense," she agreed. "Thought so since I first heard about it."

"Wait, so you didn't hear it from me?"

"No. I just let you talk to see if you'd slip up in your Legaleian. But you passed. It's . . . I don't know. I've stopped being amazed, or at least I'd like to think so. Another continent . . . another world—or 'planet'—and alien races out to conquer us . . . it almost makes sense. But somehow, the idea of bringing back the Silversmiths, a part of our own history, somehow *that* scares me more than anything else."

More nodding, presumably while he gathered his thoughts. "Well, that's probably wise. You're not alone in that sentiment. I should know better than anyone."

Now she looked at him, not with a glare but with soft eyes, likely betraying the raw emotion she felt for her foster brother. "You should. That was stupid, taking that sword, trying to deal with all that yourself . . ." She wanted to add, *Going all that way to Gaea just to get rid of it,* but she was already speaking against her feelings, not with them.

He seemed to see through it, as a smile leaked through his serious expression. "I know. I know."

Now she frowned, though she did so to the sink, pumping more water unnecessarily into it. That was . . . an odd way for him to react. His comparative cheeriness made her almost uncomfortable just by how it exposed her own mood. Last she had spoken with him, he put a good face forward, but she could see the lines of worry and stress that indicated an inner battle, whereas now his face looked almost ready for any excuse to smile. What could make a man . . .

"Oh," she said, finally realizing what she'd been wanting to ask him.

"You've been a little dodgy, so I'll just ask now I'm thinking about it—what's this talk of you and the queen, hmm?"

He coughed in surprise. "Oh, that. I was going to . . . wait, how did you hear? What did you hear?"

She couldn't help a sly grin. "Not much," she said evasively, although it was true; she had heard a rumor of another romantic rumor from a soldier, regarding Queen Mydia and "that boy again." But she wouldn't tell him so much. Better to see him squirm.

There was only a little squirming before he spilled the Koiberries with a sigh. "I spoke with Mydia again. It's been a . . . priority, but I might have been delaying a bit because I was afraid. Of what she'd say." He hung his head.

Phoebe gaped, then struck his cheek with her palm. It was supposed to hurt a little, but judging by the way his head hardly budged and she was left wringing her wrist . . . she was the only one to come out with any pain. "Well?" she demanded.

He grinned. "I was wrong. She . . . she agreed to marry me."

"Marry you."

He crossed his massive arms. "What, are you jealous now? I'm not looking to take a second wife yet. Hopefully never. Yeesh."

She didn't slap him again, but only because the throbbing in her right hand reminded her of all the good the last one had done. Instead, she huffed. "Well. That's . . . surprising. Honestly, though—took you that long? What did you think she was going to say?"

". . . No?"

"No, stupid. You've never seen the way she looked at you?"

"Not really, no. You think I can read female minds?"

She rolled her eyes. "Never mind. I'm . . . I'm happy for you, Kaen. Especially for you." She almost asked him about the paradox Lyn had told her of a year ago, about the male inhabitants of Gaea being sterile, but . . . she thought better of it. Some things she just didn't need to know. Instead, she asked, "So, what of these 'Priests of Mani?'"

He grimaced. "I think it's going to catch on. Or at least, there will be a crowd. Almost all will stay loyal to the crown here, but I know there will be those . . . discontents. Tired of all the nonsense in the world. Would you take such a power?"

"Obviously not—I haven't yet. What do you take me for?"

"But if you didn't have this orphanage? If you never knew me, and didn't know any more about this new titan claiming to be the moon itself? What would you choose?"

She hesitated. "That's . . . not entirely a fair question."

"Isn't it? What would you choose?"

She put a hand to her head. "I—I don't know. I don't want to think about it."

He withdrew a step, perhaps realizing how drawn into the conversation he was getting. Phoebe let out a shaky breath, thinking on his words. It was much like the age-old question of whether one is a good person—which all must certainly immediately answer in the affirmative. Yet surely not all in the world were good people—look at Domon or Lady Lieda. Was she still alive out there, causing some manner of mischief? Probably. Such was the justice of this world. The justice of Mani . . . or perhaps life itself.

"Lyn is doing well?" she finally asked.

"Far as I know. She is . . . different after her return from Luna."

"Oh." *Yes, that.* "More true nonsense, then? She actually went to this other moon to battle this . . . Cydenges thing?"

"The Queen, yes. Lyn was held prisoner on Luna, then escaped and came here to warn us of her coming. She was frightening, but Lyn took her out herself after an initial scare. That was when Cae Rhidea perished. No one thought the Cydenges could ever come here . . . and no one knows if they could ever return, though Domon of course wants to see to it that none possibly can."

She nodded, as though she understood more than a few words of all that. Nonsense was certainly a good way to summarize it. Some was true, other bits false, but all was hogwash. Life should just go back to how it used to be. She thought of the birth ratio disparity, how perhaps that one thing would be for the better if it changed. Unable to stop herself, she asked, "Kaen, what of the birth rate crisis? Wasn't that one of Rhidea's original goals, to put that to right? Do you think you will find a solution somehow?" The use of the word *you* where normally she would have said *they* was somewhat of an admission of defeat.

He shrugged his hulking shoulders. "Who is to say? Massive things are changing, in and between worlds. After this war, I don't think . . . well, I don't think anything will ever be the same. I can't even say if we'll still be here."

She tensed. "What do you mean?"

"You. Me. Nytaea. Humanity. Pheebs, we're approaching the end of an age at breakneck speed. Next year, Mani could just . . . end. We don't know what it will look like, but we could be facing a cataclysm. Maybe we'll all move to Gaea. Or maybe . . . Mani will be the one to survive, and Lyn will end up coming back here with her people."

Her people. You might as well say 'my people.' She sighed, putting down her dishrag in defeat—despite having claimed victory over the mound of dishes. Kaen took the cue to dry the rest and put them away, looking as though ignoring the harshness of his words. "So you really think one world will end?" she asked. "That we'll—humanity will move to one place or the other?"

The far-away look on his face told her more than his next words: "I do. It . . . could be Mani."

"But you don't think so."

"I don't know, Pheebs. I just . . . don't know. But you're doing a good job here, Phoebe. I'll make sure that you and all these little ones have a home at the end of this war. I swear it."

"On your new wife?"

He scowled briefly, then blew out a laugh. "I, uh . . . yeah. Sure. No, Phoebe. That might not be till then either. Mydia will take care of you guys in the meantime. She hasn't failed you yet, right?"

Phoebe nodded.

"Good, then keep your chin up. I'll see you around sometime . . . but for now, I have to go."

He left after a giant bear hug wherein he pretended to not be trying to crush her to death. After the door swung shut and she heard the mage soldier on duty giving him the farewell, she had to explain to the children why there were tears in her eyes. It was hard to find the words, because she'd already used all those up. Why was it so hard to explain things to children?

- Chapter 56 -

Towers

Oliver flew above the Sea of Emptiness.

Beneath him, he watched the bases of puffy cumulous clouds which streamed lazily by on the wind. He rode the wind—he was the wind. For he had discovered the secrets of flight, thanks to some research King Fenwel had let him do in his great library and the long-awaited partnership between himself and the resident wind magi of Scathii. Finally, they were starting to accept him. To . . . look up to him, often literally.

Okay, only literally. They still looked down on him figuratively.

The flight he now made was on one of his newest glider model, one perfected for flying at greater altitudes using wind and fire Authority—the former of which was his, used actively at a greater level of expertise thanks to countless hours of practice, while the latter was on loan from the wonderful fire mage scholars at Randhorn Castle. The linkage system they'd been constructing over the past year was bearing terrific fruits, and this was one of the side benefits of their research. The great towers used various crystals to store elemental power like the Reality stones used by Nytaean mage soldiers, and scholars were now experimenting with Coaction/Authority relationships between long-range magi and smaller elemental crystals.

Oliver looked northward, toward Nomu and the tower constructed there. It was the second to be finished, standing an impressive ten stories high and molded largely from stone and framed by timber. At its top shone the elemental crystals, which surrounded a great central crystal from the outside of a worked bronze railing. The undersides of Oliver's winged vessel were inset with fire crystals, which were specially imprinted to heat the air beneath them.

Oliver was now at a level with the top of the tower, roughly a hundred feet above the level of Nomu, which was one of the higher islands. Each floated on a slightly different elevation, moving almost not at all either laterally or vertically. By all accounts and measurements—which were difficult, to be sure—the islands were in the exact same spot they'd been a hundred, or two hundred, years ago. Of course, that was what the old folks said, but he had no personal knowledge of anything like that. He just invented stuff.

But what caught his eye on Nomu was the deep scars in the earth, the three crushed homes that had been hit by Gaean weaponry, and the cracks along the great tower's southern side, four stories up. It was heavily spell-reinforced, so the damage was mostly superficial, but many were rightly stirred up about the entire attack. No lives had been lost. Of the three enemy ships that had attacked the islands, two had been downed using the tower and the other sent packing, much to the relief of all red-blooded sky citizens.

Those swine-smooching no-guts . . . It was the most foul curse he'd heard from the sailors recently, or at least the most creative. At fourteen, he was still working out which ones he liked and which ones he didn't. Some were just too bad, too . . . profane? That was the word Mum liked to use.

- Chapter 57 -

Keeper of Dogs

Manidor 2, 1295:
progress.
— From Lhinde's Vault

Kymhar raised his short sword silently, eyeing the beasts that were converging upon him. Solomiya, the red-haired witch, grinned from the background, whistling to her animals like familiar pets. By all accounts, they were indeed like pets to her people, especially one as privy to their secrets as she.~~Lyn's~~

Kymhar knew that he would die this day, in service to the one he swore he would never again obey. *No! Not in his service . . . not directly, anyway.* He was bound by his contract with Nytaea to accomplish his set mission along with Rhidea, and he would not abandon her. Not even if she abandoned him, which she had. He would not be thrown away by two masters. No, he did this for the people of Darsor and Argent. To prevent their catastrophe from multiplying with the invasion of these things.

The doglike creatures leapt forward, and he evaded with a thrown blade. It sank into the first creature's neck, its poison coating working in as quickly as was intended. It would not kill, but it would slow within ten seconds and mostly stun within thirty. All he got in reply was a small yelp.

"If you are counting on poisons, my good man, know that the   are highly resistant to most."

Then we shall see if they resist these. He pulled twin square-tipped blades from his cloak and caught the bite of the first "dog" clean on the edge of one, successfully tracking its flailing teeth. The second caught his opposite shoulder, tugging him furiously, but he gritted his teeth against the pain of tearing flesh and bore into the mouth of the first, stabbing it in the face as it jerked away, trailing blood. Stepping with the other beast, which was still trying to drag his arm from his elbow joint, he slipped in close and slashed the sharp bronze edge across its throat. Instantly, the jaws released, and he kicked upward under its chin. Blood sprayed liberally from its neck, and it made a gurgle in place of what would have been a whining yelp. *Hopefully dead soon.*

The other one was at him immediately, teeth gnashing It leapt inside his guard, but not before he rammed one of his short swords between its teeth. Its fangs still caught his left shoulder as he dodged to the side, but they had little force behind them. The murderous beast thrashed its head and backed up, blade still lodged in the roof of its mouth.

"Your dogs do not seem particularly effective, Solomiya," he said darkly, circling the shying beast and its mistress.

She showed no concern, though her face displayed sadness—for the creatures, he thought. "That is well. I foresaw harm coming to them, but it was my master's will to test you so, so obey him I did. I . . . I feel for my babies."

Such a twisted woman. She would turn on her people, her city, her family, but cling to such monsters as though her children or brethren? "If you pity them so, then you can intervene. You could deny him. Do not hide behind your loyalty as your excuse."

She gave an annoyed *tsk!* and turned away. "I am done here."

"I will kill your other beast. It may yet hurt me, but I shall slay it. Perhaps you could save it."

"No." She began to walk away, then turned back, watching the predators human and monster circle one another. Though watching the creature primarily, he glimpsed her hesitation. Then she came over, slowly, eyes seeming to widen at the very thought of what she was doing—or the question of how her mind had even allowed such a rebellion.

Then she did the unthinkable. With a whistle, she approached the beast. It flinched, crouched, and turned. Seeing exactly what would happen as though in slow motion, Kymhar closed in, reversed the grip on his blade, and jammed the handle in between the creature's teeth. The jaws closed on her hand, predictably, and she succeeded only in sliding the blade in further, while it gouged her with its teeth. The extra pressure of Kymhar's interception not only saved her hand, but it forced the snapping jaws to open once more. Simply by tugging its head back, it pulled the knife out itself as her hand was still closed around the handle. Blood gushed over her hand, leaking from its mouth. Solomiya stared open-mouthed, uncomprehending, and then the creature was gone in long-bounding strides, leaving a blood trail.

The woman trembled, staring down dumbly at her shaking hand, until the pain apparently took over and she clasped her wounded hand with the other. As though in a trance, she bent down over the one that was bleeding out from the neck, reaching out tentatively to touch the top of its head in between its throes. It went still soon after. When she turned back and Kymhar saw her eyes, there were tears in them. "You killed her."

He stared at the mage for a few seconds. "I did not initiate that encounter." He glanced down at her hand, which was leaking blood through the fingers that clutched it. "How bad is your bite?"

She clutched it to her chest, staining her grey dress. "It is fine. We have healers aplenty back in Redufiel."

"And yet you are forbidden to return so soon. Come, there is water nearby." Without looking at her, he started off in the direction of the Soul River's northern tributary. He ignored the screaming pain in his right shoulder, refusing to look at the injury yet. Once at the bank, he glanced back to see Solomiya trailing behind, and motioned her toward the water. As she passed him, he reached out and took hold of the hem of her dress, slashing with his knife and pulling before she could yelp in shock.

She did, of course, jumping back. "You vile—" She cut off, seeing he had tossed the dangling strip to the ground and raised his eyebrows toward her. "Oh. Go—go ahead."

"You have the better and cleaner material for it," he explained unnecessarily. He deftly jerked the strip fully from her dress, taking off only the bottom two inches in total, then motioned for her to wash her hand in the water. She pulled it out and stared at her four bite marks, two of them quite large, in her hand, then clutched it to her dress, drying it. He reached out and bound the wounds tightly. She mumbled what might have been an apology, then hissed as she saw his shoulder.

"Here, Kym, you look awful." She approached, but he only backed away warily. "Let me see it."

"I thought you wanted me dead, woman." He pulled back his mangled sleeve and cursed as he saw the damage. *I'll have to cauterize this.*

"Here." She tried again to get close, reaching out a hand for his knife. He scoffed a laugh as he saw the gesture, then considered, finally handing her the knife. She deftly carved away the material from his shoulder, wiping away excess blood. "Bend down by the water, and I'll wash it."

A few minutes later, she was using her small fire Coaction to focus heat onto the worst gashes, searing them closed, and then wrapping the wound in a few inches more of her dress. When done, she held a hand on the shoulder longer than necessary. Finally, she said, "I'm sorry. I did not . . . have to kill you. I wanted to. I was angry. I still am." She fingered his knife in her hand, as though still considering plunging it into his neck.

Kymhar reached up and grabbed her wrist with his left hand, twisting with a smooth motion until she gasped at the pain and dropped the blade. He kicked it away. "Don't try anything funny, woman. The stories are true—it's always the beautiful ones who are trouble."

He bent over and snatched the knife, quickly secreting it in a hidden sleeve. When he looked up, her eyes were narrowed suspiciously on him. "What? I did not actually think you would kill me. Call it . . . a reflex." He didn't mean the words defensively, and he didn't think they came out that way, yet her look was giving him pause.

Her lips pulled into a half smile, then twisted out of it quickly, and she looked away southward. "Nothing. I wonder where Kul'Hyark has gotten to."

"You are concerned for your dog?"

She kicked him in the shin. "They are not *dogs.* You slew one of twenty-one in the entire world—that we know of. The ___ are hunting and killing machines, expert at it, and they are vicious, but I've been around them my whole life, and I care for all creatures."

"And yet Domon would use them against the world." He gestured at the bank beside where he sat. "Sit down and tell me about it."

He was entirely joking, but she apparently missed that, as she did exactly that. She began to talk of her father, her tribe, her desperate deal with Domon, and her shift to his side. Then she began to tell him things he didn't wish to know, about Domon's personal treatment of her and the abuse she'd endured in Redufiel. Of her wish that his entire palace and city would suddenly burn down and be no more.

When he'd done enough listening, he stood up, stretching and gingerly fingering her handiwork on his shoulder. It throbbed far too much to let on, and he'd lost more blood than he was comfortable with, but he should be fine for the rest of his journey. She on the other hand . . .

She'd trailed off and was looking up at him somewhat dazedly, almost embarrassed. Realizing how long she'd talked. *About time.* "Where are you bound now?" he asked.

"I . . . ah, for my homeland once more. I'd like to track down Kul'Hyark, but I must return to my city and tell them . . ." she looked away, rubbing her chin. "I am not sure what I will tell them."

"Hmm." With a low grunt, Kymhar looked northward along the tributary creek. Toward the twin cities of Ribsha. He had never been, but had studied maps of the area well enough to find his way even without her help. But the thought was tempting . . . if it was any way of striking back at Domon—or better yet, Mani . . .

There was no guarantee. But would that stop him? "Solomiya, this tyrant you were speaking on about, the man who enslaved and mistreated you . . . what would it take to convince you to betray him? Would it break your heart?"

There was silence for a moment, her face unreadable as gears turned in her head. At last she said, "Well, it wouldn't break Lieda's. Of that I am certain."

- Chapter 58 -

Monstrous Allies

Manidor 2, 1295
progress.
— From Lhinde's Vault

[Kymhar and Solomiya speaking to her father, or better yet, working with someone familiar to her with the various monsters, training in their strengths and weaknesses and the best way to control them.]

- Chapter 59 -

Heavy Metals

Manidor 2, 1295:
progress.
— From Lhinde's Vault

Syneria turned her head, making a shushing motion to her friend after a moment. When that didn't work, she hissed, "Cort! Shut up, please." If Mother could hear her talk that way, she would have an apoplexy, but she hadn't seen any of her family since Aldyr's wedding.

Cort finally cut off his stream of facts about the properties of the floating Sky Islands, cocking his head and re-flopping his blond hair over his head—which didn't help it at all. He seemed to feel it too: A shiver in the ground, a change in air pressure, and a faint buzzing in the ears that may or may not be an actual sound.

He let out a quick breath. "Well, I—don't think that really was anything. Was a little strange, though."

"That shudder in the ground felt like the one we felt an hour ago. Right before that Gaean ship flew overhead." They were only up at this hour for some early sixth-day studying, but the disturbance had come when they were just sitting down to their books.

"Kaen. They said it was him. Otherwise, the tower keepers wouldn't have let him past."

She shrugged. "Whatever it was, it might be coming here." She stood up from her table and stretched toward the sky—or more immediately, the ceiling, as Cort Flanning would have pointed out. After a moment of hesitation, she dashed outside. She made it through two hallways before encountering anyone else. A sleepy-looking scholar named Hepsa, who asked what was going on through a yawn.

""Don't know, trying to find out," she said in passing. Slowly, she noticed more of the castle staff out and about, some talking with one another. Eventually, even King Fenwell. The bags under his eyes indicated his level of tiredness, but the animated way in which he talked to his advisors indicated he'd already been up. *And if that ship was heading to Nytaea . . . they would have informed him of any urgent events.*

Syneria approached the king but stood at a distance, not wishing to intrude. Hopefully he would notice her there and turn to explain the situation. But as it turned out . . . he didn't need to.

It was the scraping stomps that alerted her. She turned her gaze to the side and glimpsed a scene out of a nightmare. A huge shape stood in the front courtyard, glinting like a silver statue in the aurora-light. Guardsmen were pointing at it and shouting, seeming very confused as to how it had gotten in at all.

"King Fenwell!" said the giant in perfect Legaleian, projecting its booming voice across the entire courtyard. "People of Randhorn. Stand down, for I mean you no harm. Perhaps you heard the news, and perhaps you didn't. I am the true avatar of Mani, the first form I have taken in one thousand years."

Fenwel motioned for the guards to stand down, and his captain repeated it in spoken command. He understood that, whatever this thing was, mundane weapons were unlikely to pose any threat to it. "What have you done with Cae Rhidea, O Mani?" he demanded, raising his tremulous voice high.

"She perished at the hand of a force so great that it would make your heart quail at its telling. This force is called Luna, goddess of the golden moon which hides beyond Darsor and Gaea. Believe me or believe me not, the choice is yours. As her body died, I had no choice but to assume a living flesh from what was left of her, and I promise to you that I carry on her legacy of seeking truth and peace for the world of Mani. For my people."

"Perhaps we can speak more privately about this," Fenwel said, looking around.

The humanoid figure shook its long head. "No. I am afraid I am in a hurry.

Your brethren in Nytaea can tell you more of the situation. I come with two messages to deliver. I ask that your mage scholars be present for the second."

After a bit of nodding and murmuring, guards were sent off to awaken the scholars. The king would take no chances with this "peaceful" creature. Cort was already at Syneria's side, and she knew the others would be soon as well. They were not the only ones up, nor the only ones eager to hear what a being such as this had to say about the world. But . . . Rhidea . . .

"Think it's true about Rhidea?" Cort asked in a low voice.

She gave an uncomfortable shrug. "Who knows if this Mani thing is trustworthy."

Mani spoke then of a threat from two different worlds, one of which he called his "oldest enemy, my sister," which sent chills down her spine. He told of a large, scaled dragon which was felled by Rhidea and Domon and Lyn of Nytaea working together. An avatar of Luna, but not a true one, he said. Rather, she was one of many creatures known as the Cydenges, creatures bent on destroying Mani if possible.

He ended by calling all who would listen to consider joining his side, becoming "priests of Mani." He would give them power and length of days and "a grand purpose." As the mage scholars filed in, he began his second speech:

"Scholars of magic and of Mani! Listen to the voice of your world, for I have an invitation that may interest you. I am recruiting a new line of priests to serve me in protecting this world from a new menace, the Cydenges. I know you have sent researchers to the inner sky, that you seek knowledge of ancient times with eyes toward the future. This I can grant you without a limit. If you join me, I will make you into a new line of Silversmiths, for they were once my servants, before a certain man named Domon hunted them to extinction."

He paused, allowing the murmur of shocked and intrigued and indignant words to be exchanged. There were calls of, "Not by the name of Cae Rhidea, our great lady!" while others shut those speakers down. Overall, the reaction seemed to be a mixture of dazed bewilderment and surprised curiosity. For her part . . . Syneria had gone down to the Down Under twice with her fellow scholars, had rubbed and translated some of the writings on the ancient ruins. Some of this was not even a surprise to them for that reason. But if she were to agree to join Mani . . . She thought of her family back home, and the Queen and King Regent. They would ostracize her, perhaps even call for her death. No one here would simply jump at the chance Mani was offering . . . even if it was tempting. For there was much unknown risk in such a thing.

"What if they do not wish to join you?" King Fenwel asked.

Mani swept his gaze over the gathered scholars. "Then you do not have to join me. This is not a threat, but an extended opportunity. But make up your minds soon. I will return in one week's time, and that will be your final chance. With that, the silver god turn, took two steps, and then seemed to melt into a puddle. The silver that made up the walking statue blended with the silver of the ground about the walkway, and was gone. They saw the earth bend and ripple as he passed, and Syneria and Cort looked at one another in realization along with others.

After a buzz of shocked conversation and heated debate between the scholars, the king found them and said, "This calls for a deep discussion, my friends. But it can wait until later, when we have had some rest."

Right. Rest. Syneria wouldn't be seeing any more of that today. Beside her Cort spoke up, "My Lord, you don't think is a chance he is lying and may come back early?"

Fenwel looked at his guard captain. "That is a possibility. In the meantime we shall post extra guards. But I am of the impression that, if this being mean us harm, there would be little we could do to stop him."

Syneria noted how everyone seemed to refer to this thing as *he,* as though readily accepting it as a thing with sentience, being and personality. Well . . . then again, animals which had little of that were also called he and she, but for reasons that would be far stranger if applied to that . . . thing.

Yet, as much as her mind faltered to even conceive of this creature she had just witnessed and heard . . . there was excitement deep within her, propelling her heart and hastening her breathing. She tried not to show it. Perhaps everyone here was experiencing the same thing, but if not, she would hate to look the odd one out, or especially as though she were actually considering this insane offer. *To become one of the Silversmiths . . .* Was that truly who they were? Servants and priests of Mani, the god of . . . this moon?

Perhaps she would go and lie down for an hour or two. No one would mind, save for Cort, who was now elbowing her again. Asking after their studies. Hardly hearing, she nodded dimly and wandered after him.

One week later, the quaking did indeed return. And with it, Mani, the silver god. They were all on-edge and waiting, and quickly made their way to the front doors of the castle, where he met them in the same great courtyard, standing taller than Syneria remembered. As tall as a man and a half.

Syneria was all jitters, spending perhaps half her focus just on trying to keep her joints and jaw from shaking. She stole nervous glances at those around her, feeling unusually self-conscious. in a few minutes, they would see how this went. There was much tension between the scholars, for none quite knew who all would truly join Mani. But, as had been made clear the other day, Randhorn was one of a few special cases in the world in that it was home to many mage scholars, those who knew more about Mani's ancient past and were passionate about history, lore, magic . . .

For Syneria's part, she had kept out of the debates and refused on a half dozen occasions to give her thoughts or plans on the whole matter, earning her glares and even a few bruises. The inner anxiety from holding it in was almost unbearable at this point.

Raising his voice, Mani asked the question once more, and also sought permission to peruse the castle and surrounding town to make sure that all had an opportunity. Lacking another option, Fenwel obliged him in this.

Syneria was the first to raise her hand. Or at least, she thought so. Unthinking, unspeaking, she just stepped out and hurried up to the metallic giant, who looked down upon her with an unknowable expression. Gasps and jeers and even a few curses followed her, along with she dared not look how many shocked and betrayed faces. *I'm sorry friends . . . I am. But I have to do this. I have to . . .* She kept her eyes fixed downwards, purposely avoiding the gazes of those present.

But she heard footsteps, and looked up just enough to see Viktor Amma and Stessa Valiant stepping out. Stessa had already made her choice clear, while Viktor did not overly surprise her. He was prideful, and would be leaving a powerful and persuasive family behind, but he had a strong will and a similar adventurous spirit as she did. Their presence gave her just enough boldness to look up, quickly taking in the faces of the friends she was rejecting. Cort's face was pale as ashes, and a dozen others stared blankly at her, some shaking their heads in disappointment. The king looked at her with a sad, hollow look, like a loving father watching his favorite daughter elope with a stranger he'd warned about.

Still others joined, until Mani had a small crowd of eight magi. *Eight . . .* She couldn't believe it. She raised her eyebrows bashfully toward Cort Flanning and half-shrugged in invitation, but he hastily shook his head. He had sounded almost interested this past week, but the fear of losing his friends and family, not to mention the fear of their unknown fate, was too strong.

In his deep, rich voice—a quieter—Mani told his recruits that they could pack whatever they wished as long as it was easily carriable on their persons— which to Syneria seemed a bit redundant. She might as well bring nothing if she could not bring her roomful of worldly possessions . . . In fact, the little things that she had secretly packed together already would do just fine. Mani bid them wait at the east gate for him, and then transformed before their eyes into a four legged creature, skittering past magi and guardsmen into the castle, seeking unsuspecting persons to scare, or . . . recruit.

Good luck with that, you big monster. Cort Flanning clutched her hand as she passed him. "Neer, you sure about this? Is it really worth it? What about Aldyr and Queen Mydia—what will they think?" For he knew that she communicated frequently with the two.

Syneria shook off his hand as gently as she could, which was easy with her clammy fingers. "I'm sorry," she said, looking down. "It's worth it to me." She walked on, giving similar or shorter responses to those who questioned her on her way to the women's dorms. King Fenwel funded their studies with state money, and she knew that they would have no choice but to sell anything that did not clearly belong to her family. She would have no more family here, because she was rejecting this found family for another one. A better one.

No, not a better one. Don't think like that, she chided herself. She would not do these Nementali such a disservice. Rather, she was going where fate tugged. Her life had been aimless and without purpose, yet a cavity in her chest had ached to be filled, something primal that called out for something higher and greater. This was it. Now she would see. Now she could get to the bottom of the Silversmiths' secrets, and learn the deep truths that Mani had guarded all these centuries. And maybe, just maybe, help to find a way out of this millennial doom.

What could that be called but a higher purpose?

- Chapter 60 -

Rite of Passage

Manidor 2, 1295
progress
— From Lhinde's Vaul.

"You are first, brave human scholar," Mani said, a humanoid statue again, gesturing toward the pool. Well . . . it wasn't a "pool" per se, but that is what he'd referred to it as. It was a smooth surface of purest silver beneath an underhang of stone, upon which the ten recruits from Randhorn stood. Each one robed just as they'd come, except for . . . her. She stood shivering at the faint chill and the embarrassment of her state, ears still feeling hot, trying to ignore the stares of her friends.

She followed his gesture, stepping gingerly under into the cleft, arms, still hugging her stomach in a defeated posture. Blessedly, the lighting was such that the depth of the cave and the broken stream of water that dripped from above mostly hid her. She gasped as her feet sank into . . . something, and tried to pull her feet free.

"Relax, girl," Mani said in a voice that was probably meant to be soothing, "Step into the pool and submerse yourself. Bathe your flesh in the blood of Mani and rise anew."

She did so, feet moving slowly in the heavy pool of liquid metal. Cool to the touch, yet no more thick than a creamed soup. It swirled around her almost on its own, as though stirred by her legs and reacting erratically to the touch. She descended to her torso, shivering at the cool embrace, then to her stomach, her breasts, her shoulders . . . She could feel its heavy pull and Mani's piercing stare, and knew that she was meant to submerge entirely. Against her better intuition, she held her breath and went under.

Only then did the change begin. The miracle of which Mani spoke began like a tingling in her skin, a stirring in her blood, a twitching of the muscles. Then it was an irritating, spreading itch, and then a discomfort that spread under the surface and throughout her body. Then searing pain. Her breath was nearly expended, her chest heaving, and at last the pain wrung from her a silent scream that only succeeded in opening wide her mouth, her throat, and she swallowed down the liquid metal. It was like drowning, or what she'd heard of it, a maddening panic that overtook mind and body, overlapped with excruciating pain and a near-paralysis of body. The metal pressed into her eyes, forcing them open, and seeped into her nostrils, her ears and every pore of her body. It saturated and permeated her body, surely mixing with replacing some of her tissue, her blood and whatever else.

And bones. Oh, how she'd been dreading this ordeal. She'd tried to ignore it, but she knew well that humans were not just born with silver for bone tissue. Metal for marrow. The agony of it was like fire—like being burnt from within, or boiled.

At last, exhausted and too far gone to fight, she sensed a change in the pressure of the metal surrounding her, and a voice called from above. No . . . from within her mind. *Syneria Tolruin, my newest daughter . . . rise and claim your role as priestess. Welcome.*

She felt a call, a tug as it were, from the silver substance around her, and found that she could move once more. She didn't try to breathe, but neither did she feel that urge at present. Nor did she try to blink, for her eyes saw nothing and did not need to. When her head broke the surface, then she blinked, as silver rolled smoothly down from her hair, her forehead, her eyes, beading as water over a ducks back. Not a drop clung to her. Her chest fluttered, and she bent over and gave one great heave as all the silver which had poured into her streamed back out, wringing her lungs to the maximum. Then and only then did she gasp in air. One, two, three huge breaths. She stood up, chest rising and falling, slowing and evening surprisingly fast.

She looked out, dreading to bare herself in front of her audience once more, but dimly, only in the back of her mind. She strode out to the sound of heavy, metallic clapping. Then the scholars joined in as they saw she was alive and unchanged, and they too joined in in applause. She stood with arms at her sides, staring numbly but awkwardly. Then they slowly quieted, and she heard the gasps. Something had changed with her, then.

Mani clapped her on the back with gigantic hands, and she stumbled, but less than she would have before. He draped something over her, and she hugged it tight about her. It was a thin sheet of metal, a silver cloak. She gave the other a shy smile. "I'm all right."

"Welcome, Syneria, daughter of Mani. Next, Viktor Amma."

She averted her gaze as he stripped and laide aside his clothes, but she watched as he too entered the cave. A bit less timidly than she had, but she chalked that up to her being the first. A minute passed, and then another, and realized that they had all watched in desperate tension, thinking her drowned. Mani calmed them with his words, and she tried to reassure them with her expressions as well.

When he rose and came out of the cave, she did observe, telling her sense of modesty to go bathe itself in metal. She quickly noticed the difference, not just in his bearing or facial expression, but . . . his eyes. The irises were pure silver, his hair the same color. Mani draped a cloak over his back as well, having drawn it from the silver in the ground snapped it seemingly from nothing. The others went in similar fashion, and newly appointed priesthood clustered together, gradually nudging one another and sharing whispered confessions of terror and panic in the silver pool. Mani did not try to quiet them.

When all ten were done, he addressed them: "Children of Mani, you have awakened to new bodies and new abilities. I shall instruct you in the basics, and your brethren from Nytaea shall give you further tips, demonstrating how to spin your own clothing from silver and other things. You shall make for yourselves houses, and eventually houses above. I will allow your input on where to build the temples above wherefrom we shall work. But today, you have a new goal and a new purpose—to secure Mani and seek the security and defense of your world. For the time being, that will mean learning to travel through the twin continents and the land bridges—more shall come—and recruiting from the far reaches of Argent and Darsor your future brethren. We will be not a brotherhood, but an army. But to put some of your fears aside . . ."

Mani suddenly changed, his body seeming to melt away to reveal a smaller one inside. It solidified into the vague form of a woman, and then a startlingly defined form that would have been uncomfortable to look upon were she not metallic from head to toe. The scholars gasped as they recognized Cae Rhidea. "Hello, children," she said in a voice so like the one Syneria knew well. "I am indeed still alive inside Mani, at least in part. The power of the moon god is Growth, the ability to take matter, namely silver—" she showed them a beat of metal held between two fingers "—and grow it into something new, something greater." She tossed the ball forward, and it hovered, growing into a mass of twisting roots that shot downward and upward, rooting into the ground and eventually becoming a tree some thirty feet tall. "Mani saved what life I had left by growing from within my body a new one, the one which has been speaking to you. I am only a faint consciousness within him, yet I am aware of most of what goes on about him. So to all of you brave enough to join us down here . . . thank you, and welcome. Goodbye for now."

Her form twisted and grew until the familiar, statuesque giant emerged once more. It appeared he could both shrink and grow at will, which would indeed explain some of the feats which he had shown them and of which they'd heard. "Let us go and meet your brethren," he said in his booming, faintly ringing voice, "and craft your new homes."

- Chapter 61 -

A Killer

Manidor 2, 1295
progress
— From Lhinde's Vaul.

[More meetings back in Nytaea, or perhaps something more active, like a
random/important Torlegan man working with a Ligelli mage, working on a
tower or practicing with the long-range magical network.]

- Chapter 62 -

Millennium

Manidor 2, 1295:
progress.
— From Lhinde's Vault

"The time has come, sons and daughters of Mani."

The voice came as both audible and inwardly felt, awakening Syneria from her slumber. She rose from her bed of molded silver and rose to put on her robes. The new order of the Silversmiths tended to sleep naked upon these silver beds, which they molded to be far more comfortable than any clothing and mattress could ever achieve. The silver itself had a certain resonance that was soothing and harmonic, cultivating fanciful dreams and deep sleep. But her eyes were wide open, her body ready.

The robes were kept in a vague form upon her bedside shelf, as she'd been taught. She took the lump and shook it with a practiced flair of magic, creative a long, flexible sheet with a hole for her head. She slipped it overhead and it molded over her body, coalescing into a flattering dress of a material inexplicably worked to look dull instead of glaring to the eyes, with wrinkles and width of material not to cling inappropriately to her. It was a shape that knew itself, for she had worked the magic into this particular piece of silver just so, even embedding a decorative design down the front, a crisscrossing pattern within the silver fabric. Then she put on her silver headdress, a band which slipped over her forehead and bound her hair in one stream, with an ornate pin on top. The men instead wore silver bracers over their wrists.

Syneria hurried out into the long colonnade that connected most of the houses of the former scholars of Randhorn, with arches marking the doors to each house, each house front crafted entirely of worked silver. It hung below the overhang that was just previously part of the ruins at the center of the land of waterfalls in the Down Under, which had been carved out by Mani and his first converts. The ancestral home of the Silversmiths had lain below the ground level, with the temple rising overhead. They had crafted the place such that the overhead waterfalls ran off of the roofs and awnings and streamed down channels and aqueducts, creating a peaceful white noise that was only ever blocked out by the resident Perception magi—of which they had two—whenever speech was of particular importance in the temple grounds. Otherwise, they let it create an atmosphere of intimate privacy about each home and altar and workshop.

Her robed sisters and brothers fell into step beside and behind her, and they soon came upon others gathering at the communal gathering grounds. Mani stood upon the raised altar in the middle, a podium kept for his sole use for occasions such as these. Occasions that were few and far between. *What is this about . . .* she wondered. The millennial year; it had to be.

"Silversmiths!" called the god, raising a hand high. "Your number is full, your training complete. Those who would join us have done so, and those without our number have chosen their path. They are not our enemies, nor ostracized family, but rather fearful people who see only the ground before their feet. They are pitiable fools, base animals with good intentions but small minds. We have a greater calling and a higher purpose, which will not pass away when all is shaken.

"For that day is upon us. Today is the first day of the new millennium, my children, the day which shall shake our world to its core. There are three forces in opposition to us, and I believe you recognize them for what they are: Luna, our ancient foe, who seeks to devour us yet; Gaea, mother of the Titans, the bereaved mother who reared artificial offspring in the stead of her children; and the Wellspring, the ancient fount that has spread life to this world, life of a sort that our kind do not need. Humanity depends on its continuing influence, but we do not depend on humanity. They are a deadweight upon this moon."

Murmuring rose from those gathered, though some like Syneria simply stared, transfixed by the speech but knowing full well what he was about to say.

He continued: "I do not advocate exterminating these exiles—I would never ask you to do that. We seek peace, but a different kind than what is tentatively holding us together. Rather, we must push humanity to return as they ought, for the bell has tolled and time has come. The Legaleians were never meant to stay. But you, you are Legaleian no more, and you shall remain."

Uneasiness stirred in Syneria's belly unbidden, an uneasiness that should not be there. She knew all of this . . . although, perhaps it was merely the way he put it, but she seemed to understand his purposes in a different way now. She had thought they were paving a way for those who wished to return to their mother planet, and that at the end of this they might all go free. But if . . . *Hmm. Perhaps that is what they are all murmuring about.*

"Peace, my children," Mani said, both aloud and in her mind, and she realized it was a reply to the fear that was tickling all their strings this morning. "There is no need to fear the future. You have made your choice to side with me, and it is a wise one, for you will all be gods here on this moon. We shall shape it into a heaven of heavens once the Wellspring is returned . . . which will come soon. Humanity will follow it, but we must guide them—yea, and push them—out to where they have always belonged."

- Chapter 63 -

Like Angels

Manidor 2, 1295
progress
— From Lhinde's Vaul

(Planet Gaea—Trident)

It was a warm, uncomfortable night in northeastern Nestra for the soldier of four different cities, who had converged upon the rallied Cydenges. Trident weapons capital of the world, was known for having among the best energy supplies on the planet, so that was the best estimation for Luna's concentrated attack. Senator Vladimir, of course, had not prepared for this eventuality, and thus had thrown away many men's lives, nearly dooming his entire city. The Hellebes were down to seven cities including those currently in rebellion, so this was a crucial night.

Captain Harras of Ccamos, a sniper and assault coordinator, had two men already on the radio when the call came in that more help was arriving. He swore, switched channels, and accepted contact from the new arrivals. He wa stunned to hear not a gruff commander but a low feminine voice:

"Officer Harras, continue to hold the southern gate. We'll be arriving shortly. If the shield comes down, don't panic."

"Just keep killing metal things."

"Just keep killing metal things."

Lady Lynchazel. Mother Gaea, and also his Senator. He'd thought the rumors of her return to be just that. A faint smile tugged at one side of his face but it fell when he ended the communication and looked back at the situation "More reinforcements coming from Ccamos!" he shouted to his men. "Stu? If we lose this gate, just . . . "

Major Stuart grunted. He was a soldier of Trident, sent to help them. A first, his men had not liked him, but they'd been warming up to the man. For being as brainwashed as they all used to be, slave to the obedience gene, he was relatively good-natured and highly competent. Harras wondered if he, or any of the other soldiers present for that matter, knew about the new Ccamos practice of disabling that "gene".

Harras backed away behind the columns of steel lining the front gate path of Trident. Tracks led down the center, a highway for trains laden with weapons bound for the outside world or fresh steel from Haccolces. He motioned for his squad to take cover as well, and they lost no time in so doing. Burrowers could be seen moving dirt by the moundful, and Ccamos guns still joined with those of Haven in taking out Avians above.

To the northwest, one of the humanoid terrors still desolated the cliffside land about the city.

A minute later, Lady Lynchazel's forces fell upon the creatures, decimating a large chunk of the remaining Avians and descending to the lowest air level. His men cheered, though they could not make out the Senator's ship from the others due to them all being of one design. *Wonder why she chose that?*

Then she exited her ship, one of the foremost, engaging the burrowers and Brutes directly. Not to be outdone, he motioned for his men to move out. "Come on, every man out there! We can't lose this opportunity."

Even as he watched, the Heiress presciently avoided a vertical attack from the ground, stabbing a body-long greatsword through a chink in its plates as it roared upward. The thing twitched and fell apart in a crimson burst, and she was on a Brute, slashing for its face. It evaded, but she moved onto the next, ducking below its swipe and taking hold of its back leg. He had only a split second to wonder what she was thinking before he saw her twist and lift the entire creature, using its momentum to flip it over to crash into two others. She grabbed the blade she'd dropped to do it in a backhanded grip and punched a gash in the exposed flank of the Brute Cydenges.

The others died to her companions soon after. The men of both squads greeted one another as they stood together, pushing back the moon beasts with crushing weapons and heavy, piercing rounds—one of the newcomers even used a bow to devastating effect. Like a regiment of angels, they had come in and turned a defensive, unlikely situation into a victorious one.

No further Cydenges were dropping in their area, Harras saw a change as they hacked their way to the back of the Cydenges lineup, unearthing and slaying many earth crawlers. Lady Lynchazel lowered her blade, seeing an opening, and turned, picking out Captain Harras immediately. "Harras?" He nodded. "We need you to continue to hold here. Can't say when more will be back. I'm . . . going to go pay that thing a visit."

Without gesturing or saying further, her one glance informed him that she meant the volatile Cydenges wreaking havoc on the western flank. Harras nodded sharply, then came to himself enough to respond, "Yes, Milady! Thank you."

She gave the briefest of nods in response, then saluted his comrades with a raised fist and dashed off across the battlefront. Her companions charged after, looking as panicked as she was determined. Harras even gave the exit a brief grin, though his grim attention came back a moment later as he needed it to dodge and retaliate against a lone Leonid. He couldn't fight another man's battle, especially in his head. Only the one in front of him. That was what Commander Zent would say.

More Cydenges did rain down from the heavens, as it turned out, but he and his men were largely able to take care of them, thanks to the advantage of aggression and the added number of the troops Lynchazel had left behind with him—somewhere around two dozen. They had lost . . . he wasn't sure in the moment, but around ten all told.

Then he heard a distinctive high-pitch keening, which became a whistling shriek as his heart dropped. His pounding pulse kept a quickening tempo to that dread warning, until an earth-shattering *BOOM* announced the coming of another Cydenges terror. The explosions ripped through their ranks, dismembering and launching Hellebes and Cydenges alike. Harras, who was nearer the western side, was only knocked off his feet by the closest of the chain blasts, which had spidered out from the alien's point of debarkation. As he looked, it rose up with limp limbs from the ground like a demon-possessed puppet, a human form headless and vague, its coal-like appearance topped by a ghastly head framed only in vivid red light. Twin black eyes like sun spots stared out, directly at Harras, and he felt his own eyes go wide.

Belatedly, the screams of dying and shaken soldiers reached his ears, and he felt the urge to take up the chorus. It was a chorus every man knew in his heart, and this very monstrosity awakened such a primal urge as a housefire awakens its sleeping victims—suddenly, but too late.

The thing turned, raising an arm lazily to unleash more intense ground bursts in a forward line. Finally, soldiers began to shoot at it, but it evaded like a ghost, leaving red afterimages, appearing behind soldiers and throwing them to the ground by the neck. It moved like a swift shadow, glowing red each time as though using the earth's energy like a magnetic pull. In fact, Harras could make out teeming bursts of light from the ground in front of it as it did so, confirming the theory. *So it does pull itself using Geokinesis . . .* Such a thing wasn't supposed to be possible.

Harras pulled out his own single-handed .50 pistol and launched two armor-piercing rounds at the abomination. The first missed, and the second missed, even after the swift shift. With an oath, he threw down the pistol and hefted his sword. Gauging the space around him, he made an anticipatory sweep, spinning double with his whole body. Somehow, he guessed right, as he felt his blade catch and saw the creature stumbling back a few paces from him. he questioned not how quickly it had approached, for he knew these things were unearthly and deadly. More soldiers shot at it and missed, and it casually speared a man through the neck, nearly decapitating him with its clawed fingers.

Its black eyes turned back on Harras, smoldering with a hatred easily as dark—and visible. Perhaps it didn't hate any of them, but simply considered them meat for the picking, in which case it was motivated by annoyance. Its side glowed red from where he had gashed it, though it was not a deep wound. It could take two or three more like it before succumbing, and that was if these things didn't have more tricks of lunar witchcraft up their sleeves. Thankfully, none more seemed to be coming at the moment, though there were still Leonids and Brutes dropping in, slowly surrounding his soldiers.

Well, we're going out here, so at least that's settled, he thought to himself. It was only a matter of how many of Luna's demons they'd be taking down with them. If he had anything to say about it, it would be many.

He took a step toward the apparition, knowing it was not a smart move. At the same time, he called out for the others to stay back, spinning in another sweeping motion in hopes of catching an instant approach.

No such luck. He was blindsided and blown off his feet, carried further by his weighty sword as he fell to the stone below. He held his grip, however, rolling and arcing the blade upward. Two others covered him with their own weapons, and the thing shied back, perhaps seeing the ferocity with which they defended him. This thing did not consider them a true threat, however, but merely like a cat back away from a mouse, deciding how best it wanted to play with its meal.

It came in again, distracting at first by killing the one soldier, Ham, from behind and jerking his dying body into another. It disappeared into the shadows and came at Harras just as he was rising from the ground. *How can it move so—*

It grabbed him in a single-handed chokehold, lifting him off the ground with vastly superhuman strength. Its hand glowed with light, searing the skin of his neck, furthering the constriction of air from his throat. A bullet of some kind punched into it, causing it to stutter, and it spun to seek out the threat, though it still whipped him with it. Then it threw him down, leaping over and crashing into his men behind. The killing field lit up as it unleashed more chain reactions, most of which missed him. Light now gaped from its hip.

"Human fake," it spoke in a raspy whisper that grated almost painfully on his nerves. *"You will all perish soon."*

Another of his men attacked it, and then another, and this time he tracked it as it smoothly ducked underneath using Geokinesis, opposite him. He jerked down his hand and unleashed a Geokinetic burst of his own, shattering the stone where it landed and breaking its footing. He slashed even as another man lanced downward with a clawed halberd. His sword missed, but the halberd's point gouged directly into its inner shoulder where its neck should be. Another soldier shot it, finally tearing a fatal hole in its chest.

The demon blew apart in a flash of red and acidic dust.

Captain Harras blew out a breath, nearly falling to the ground in relieved fatigue. Then he remembered the newcoming Cydenges, and turned to see the remainder of his men falling back under their onslaught.

Victory . . . and now defeat.

He lurched to his feet, readying his sword to take on a Brute which had come in close proximity to him, but before he could, a dark metallic shape shot overhead, barreling into it and rolling. Teeth snapped and metallic growls rang out, but in moments the new Cydenges had torn open its victim's throat. It looked back toward Harras with red eyes alight, then a pulse of gold broke through the red over its whole body and he saw only gold highlights. Dark scales, gold light . . . *What is this thing? No . . . it can't be.*

"Don't touch that one!" he shouted, pointing. He felt almost foolish for the words, as the beast was already upon the next Cydenges attackers, launching into it with a fury. Though smaller than the Brutes by a good margin, the dark Cydenges was fast and vicious, and clearly on their side. There was no mistaking its identity.

Grinning stupidly, he shrugged off his injuries and leapt back into the melee with a vengeance. Together, they beat back the Cydenges while the friendly one—the female—went after those farther from her allies.

Finally, they had them eradicated once again, and no more fell at present. Harras sank to his haunches shakily, breathing hard, and one of his remaining men came close, offering a shoulder clap and a word of congratulations. Cheering rose from the ranks as their Cydenges ally howled from a powerful wolf stance. Then . . . in a blaze of golden light, she transformed. Her relatively small frame and long white mane swayed to one side momentarily, then grinned like a child. "How did I do?"

Harras thought about pointing out her lack of attire, then just shrugged and said, "Not bad for an alien."

A new cheer rose up: "Lynchazel! Lynchazel! Lynchazel!"

- Chapter 64-

Towers of Stone, Bridges of Silver

Manidor 2, 1295:
progress.
— From Lhinde's Vault

Deep beneath Mani's twin crusts, a former human swam freely in the pure essence of Silver. Once, she had been a girl. More recently, a woman. And now . . . a being of power, body traced with the heavy weight of a god, attuned to a holy metal she was once blind to. She was one with it, and inside of it, traveling at incalculable speed with a surreal consciousness buzzing about the vein of silver that allowed her ascent.

The young woman surfaced to the top of Darsor, directly on the northwestern coast nearest to Yan'Vala. Her body reformed on memory, skin appearing on her reshaping bones, blonde hair falling to her shoulders. Syneria breathed heavily for a few moments, hand to her breast, and looked around almost self-consciously. Just Avva. She knew that.

"Whew," she breathed, standing up straight. "Still takes it out of me."

"It is a process of adjustment, certainly." The thickly built woman shrugged her shoulders, siphoning a portion of silver from the ground and slinging it about her in the form of a cape, then a clinging, supple garment. Another one went over top, a proper cape.

Syneria did the same. One could not travel so with clothing, so they made their own, as Mani had taught them. "Ready?"

Avva nodded. The Yan'Valian woman crouched, feeling at the ground, and Syneria mirrored her. They groped far beneath the earth, using far more than their sense of touch, and wrenched upward with the rumbling of an earthquake. The ground shook and their footing was disturbed as a shelf of silver erupted from the cliff before them. They forced it harder, and it shot outward. Mani spoke approvingly in their minds, an interaction shared by the both of them, and they stepped out onto the silver bar, continuing to move it into the horizon, over the foggy Sea of Emptiness.

They continued like this for some time, a process both quicker and slower than it might look. Fortunately, Mani used much of his own planetary power in the transaction, and it was not all on them. Neither did they have to navigate, for he was doing that as well. Having shared a sliver of this earth-awareness for some time now, Syneria felt she could almost imagine—and yet could not possibly fathom—what it must be like to hold such a consciousness, and to keep it for one thousand years as one's own burden. It was not a thing possible for mere mortals, even those changed by Silver.

Syneria both felt and heard her stomach rumble over time as she burnt calories in focus and physical strain. The process of molding Silver was not some mystical matter of chants and wishing, but a very real connection. It took something out of the user. Avva wore the strain better, and indeed was of a more robust state of fitness, but even she Syneria could tell was feeling it by the end of the first hour. Two more went by, Mani giving them directions and encouragement throughout, before they became aware that their partners on the other side were growing closer. It was mere minutes before they could see them.

Viktor Amma and his female companion, a woman of Torlega named Hegeth, appeared on the horizon, and soon their Silver fronts collided with a boom, molding themselves together. The very state of floating seemed to defy all physics, until one understood that it was Silver itself that gave the continents of Darsor and Argent the power to float at all. The metal did not properly possess a weight, or rather, that weight quickly disappeared as silver gathered together. A lump, or a blade, or a piece of silver armor, even spell-forged, had indeed its own significant weight, but something as large as a palace or the belly of a Sky Island, contained enough that it gained the passive effect of Mani's will.

Heseth, stocky as Avva but shorter and with the distinctive darker skin of Torlega, looked to Viktor and gave him a strange, customary head-bob. "It is well done."

The rest of them gave similar greetings. One party of seven, they had accomplished their bridge in roughly the projected time. Mani's consciousness informed them that a few others had been completed already, and that the explorers to the Land of Storms would be chosen soon.

With an unhelped grin, Syneria said, "Race you all back!" and melted away, silver clothing and all.

She was chosen to go. She was *chosen*.

Oh, I've been waiting forever for this, she thought as she joined the other five members of the expedition near the pillar to Darsor. Okay, it had not been forever, but still, nearly a month. The Land of Storms, a place she had never glimpsed, was supposed to be exceedingly dangerous according to the people of the light-side continent, but it was also abated now, if Mani spoke truly. They were heading out to investigate. She and her companions, melted into the knotted pillar of reflective metal and shot upwards, streaking waves in the bubbly surface of it as they rose toward the heavens.

Again the surfacing, the gasping for air. She wrapped herself in silvery garments quicker this time, given the mixed company, a process that was both instinctive and fluid for her. There were five women in their party, in fact, and one man—a Nytaean man, in fact, by the name of Kath. Once, he had followed Mydia and her party to Ti'Vaeth and back, and had stayed on as her bodyguard for a while, but apparently . . . well, he hadn't left on good terms, but many of them could say the same. It seemed those who did not "defect" to the side of Mani had difficulty in grasping the momentousness of the calling. This was a once-in-a-lifetime chance, one she was glad every day she had answered affirmatively. The nagging doubt afflicted her only periodically, and she vehemently denied its hold on her life. A weight, a burden she didn't need.

Clothed in shining silver, the party strode confidently eastward. They had risen not, this time, by the continent's edge, but close enough to the inner Duchy capital of Redufiel that they could hear the sounds of war already.

Kath pointed down the hill they traversed. "There is the city."

Syneria made her way to the edge of the copse, excitedly looking out and down. He was right—it certainly looked that way. Land was scorched, and smoke still plumed from specific parts of the city beyond the defensive wooden wall. Overhead, Gaean aircraft swarmed about, and on the city's eastern front . . . men fought with beasts of enormous size.

Monsters. How?

Her companions cried out upon seeing the scene. It looked like chaos, as small as the battle was. Perhaps a few hundred humans, a few of those metal sky ships, and a dozen monsters whose slain companions numbered in the dozens.

"What is this?" whispered a horrified Zeda. Another woman of Torlega who had joined their cause from Nytaea, where she had been staying as an ambassador—the bondservant of one, more accurately. "I recognize some of these things. We have them in the mountains."

Her companions looked at her, and she shrugged as though she had not spoken anything strange. "I do not lie—monsters abound in the southern mountains. The hairless bears you see—well, only one is living—we have them near _____."

Syneria shook her head. "Should we . . ."

"No." It was Kath. "We press on and go around them. Their battles are not ours."

A voice within Syneria rebelled against the notion, but she immediately recognized the truth in his words. They had a mission already, one they could not forsake simply to help and fraternize with the locals here. Interfering with battles not their own. That was the act of a meddler, and Mani did not feed and train meddlers, but obedient priests and priestesses.

They used silver veins in the ground to disappear and reappear farther on, wherever trees and brush abounded for taking cover, but only one or two at a time for accuracy's sake. It was not an easy thing to gauge a precise ascent at a long distance, so they followed one another, as fellow priests were easy to sense even from within the ground. Again, the immediate assumption of silver garments, though it was more by instinct than fear of the eyes of others. In fact, it would be more prudent to go entirely naked to avoid the glint that may attract unwanted eyes, but there was the initial bubbling up of silver from the ground in any case, before their skin materialized from it. Syneria still tended to avoid watching a fellow priestess arise in that manner, simply for the way it made her skin crawl. Becoming a formless mass of silver was one thing, but watching as another human did the same was eerie and otherworldly.

They got safely by, and eventually out of sight as they pressed on eastward, taking far farther silver strides—as they called them—and together. And then the ground became grey rock, the plant life sharply disappearing. They knew they had entered the Land of Storms. Clouds did hang on the horizon, some rising above in great billows, but not in the way that they had heard. *Mani must be right . . .*

Of course he was right. He was a god.

They began to remark to one another of the lack of silver below the surface here, and also the apparent lack of depth beneath the rock. They walked the last few miles, and could feel as they went the way that the earth thinned underfoot, until they could see gaping chunks missing from the stone, wherein they glimpsed the green hazelight of the Down Under's sky. Syneria shuddered at the sight.

A tower rose on the horizon, the Tower of Mani. About it, spires jutted from the ground, largely where the seams tore the stone. It was as though a violent hand had scraped away and torn open the earth here, finally erecting the tower as a peace offering before leaving their world. And who knew—perhaps that image was not far off from history.

"So this is what my companions saw as well . . ." Kath muttered to himself, looking around in awe. ". . . And my queen. I'm sorry, I do not mean that wistfully. It's just—one thing to hear about a place, and quite another to visit."

"Same with the Core. Or the 'Down Under,'" Syneria replied. "That was a shock for me the first time as well, after hearing about it and so desiring to see it."

Khaza elbowed her. "Showing off your adventures. You remember that they count for nearly nothing now, right?"

Syneria scowled her way. The Lygelli woman was always rivalrous. A headache Neer usually tried to avoid. This time, she almost made a biting reply but stopped herself as Zeda said, "Are we ascending, or first looking around?"

Their reply came from Mani, nearly audible in the ears of each and obviously ubiquitous: *Soon. Peruse the area, children. Look for signs of . . . foreign activity. I have a strong indication that Domon has been here recently, and I would know what for.*

'Foreign' indicated Gaea as well as Darsorian trespassing, but Syneria was not about to argue and open herself up to shameful rebuke. She did as commanded, trailing off to browse the area more thoroughly, using every newfound sense to glean information from the stone. She peered into more of the gaping fissures, shivering each time, and was eventually joined by Zeda.

"Anything, Neer?" she asked in her soft voice.

Where did she pick up my nickname? Syneria briefly wondered, before shaking her head. "Not really. The faint impression of a disturbance on the southwestern side here, but nothing concrete."

"I found this." The woman held up a piece of a bronze blade.

Syneria raised her eyebrows. "All right. That . . . could certainly indicate a soldier's presence. May I see it?"

Zeda clutched it to her chest and grinned. "Nope. But nice try."

That response received an eyeroll. Syneria trudged off toward the tower, looking around to gauge where the others were.

We will inspect the Tower soon, Mani rumbled in her head. *There is something off here, and I would have you uncover it.*

A small flutter in her chest at the word *you,* despite that he clearly meant all of them. But perhaps . . . well, it would not do to go without the others. She looked back at Zeda, catching her eye and gesturing toward the tower. The woman sighed in response. To the south, she caught Kath looking toward the Tower as well, and he spoke up to the woman next to him.

Within another minute, they were all converging on the Tower, treading carefully through increasingly thin pathways of stone. *No wonder those idiots fell down here,* she thought. *It is rather treacherous.*

They were just about to begin ascending when Syneria felt the hairs on the back of her neck prickle and stiffen. "Zeda, Tumah, wait!" she called, stretching out her hand.

Zeda paused with a sigh, and the other woman bumped into her. "What, Neer?"

"Something isn't quite right," Kath elaborated with trepidation.

Zeda snorted and pushed on up the stairs, muttering something about a waste of time. She got only a few words through her mutterings, however, before she was eaten alive by stone. That was the only way Syneria could think to describe it. One moment she was treading the first steps, and the next, a rumbling *crack* cut the air. They all jumped as claws of stone shot out from the tower and the ground below, swallowing both lead women in their jaws.

Syneria had no time to stare in horror, as her own legs had been struck. She looked down through blinding pain to see jaws of stone around her legs, tugging her down, piercing skin and muscle and twisting the metal bone of her left leg. It was excruciating, though the pain only made it out of her mouth after a moment, in time to scream along with all the others. Heart beating madly, she thrashed in the stone embrace, only eliciting further excruciation.

Stop, children! roared Mani in her head. *Use your heads and remove the stone. Check for injuries, and heal them. Leave the dead, or throw them into the nether sky.*

Syneria took a couple of long, calming breaths, and then looked behind her and all around for silver. But there was none. She shared a panicked glance with Kath and ____, whose wide eyes displayed the same conundrum she was facing. They too looked to be in similar pain, lower legs mangled by the stone traps. Kthala, on the other hand, was still whimpering and thrashing in the cruel stone grip like an animal in a woodsman's trap. A closer look showed Syneria that she was mortally wounded, stone piercing her lower back in two places. A biting hand of grey rock was tearing her upper hip open with every movement, and blood gushed from the wound. She looked Syneria's way with tears covering her face and croaked the word, "*Help.*"

Kath reached up a shaking hand to touch her shoulder. Then, forming a silver blade from his knuckle, slash her throat open, and she was soon dead. "That is the help she needed," he said with sadness. "These other two . . . they went quickly."

Neither of the living women raised an objection. Syneria was too busy trying to decide which limbs to temporarily dismember from her body to break her stone shackles, but Kath was more decisive. He reached out and did something to Zeda's now-still form, causing it to twitch. Syneria felt bile at the back of her throat as she watched. Tumah was still faintly whimpering, but blood loss and pain and a crushed torso were rapidly overcoming her.

Syneria closed her eyes as she heard the wrenching, sliding, sucking noise of silver being withdrawn from . . . a human body. She opened them to see pure silver, dripping red in only a couple places. She could not discern what bones they were, nor did she want to know. Kath brought it to him, expanded it, and set to work chipping and crushing the stone that encased him. He let Syneria and ______ have it next, and soon they were all freed, working at their torn and strangled legs to heal them. Mani had given them all the ability to rapidly heal, as Rhidea had apparently recently had, before her heroic sacrifice.

Finally, she looked at Kath and said, "So, who do you think set that trap? Domon?"

He nodded. "Him or Nytaea . . . but I'd bet money on him."

She nodded, jaw clenching, and said tightly, "Then he'll pay."

Yes, came Mani's hissing whisper, a stark change from how he normally spoke. *Yes, the black soul will pay.*

- Chapter 65 -

Lioness

Manidor 2, 1295:
progress.
— From Lhinde's Vault

[Lyn calls a council at Haccolces, using her victory at Trident as leverage—They come, and others are there to witness as she calls them to account with a voice of command, singling out the six remaining Senators there, the original Senators once called Anier.]

Senator Vladimir sighed dejectedly. "No, I don't think she will. And that is fine. But I must go. My presence is required to make this a true party."

Minister Fennis gave a curt nod and backed away. He was done checking his lord's armor, and handed him his Cydenges-killer blade with a deferent half-bow.

Vladimir adjusted his collar one more time and took the sword, heading out to survey the battlefield. He'd gotten only four hours' rest since last night's late efforts out on the killing fields, whence he'd slaughtered upwards of twenty of the beasts himself. Metal was still embedded in his skin in places where his attendants had not pulled them out. He'd struck one or two of them in his foul mood, so that was probably his own fault.

As he left the command center, he was accosted by no less than two commanders coming to him about the enemy movements. One mentioned Lyn and her forces on the southern lines, which earned a tight reply to the effect that he was on his way to pay her a visit. He resumed his march to his senatorial aircraft, taking no notice of the cloud-dotted skies and the weather that would otherwise be called balmy. No one used words like that on days like these, with a city in disarray and imminent danger.

He was torn on his feelings toward the teenage woman everyone was talking about . . . While he was entirely healed now, his defeat at her hands in Haccolces still stung like the raw, burnt flesh that had cloaked him then, a hatred that burned still. And then . . . there was his undeniable attraction to her, the same shared by most of the Senate, the desire to have for himself what should not be allowed to walk about the earth free. Yet here she was . . . Yes, he had his harem already. Over a dozen Hellebes women, far more than were documented. Daedalus made some mistakes on accident, and a few on purpose for those willing to pay.

Crossing through the shield wall to the east, he focused his ballistic gun on some Cydenges runners and wounded a few, killing none. Irked, he ejected, elated at the adrenaline rush from the one-point-five second freefall before slamming into the earth in a spray of green smoke and debris. Then he set to work with his sword. Sight in the dark was not his only abnormal Elite ability, for he could also _____, which came in handy fighting these freaks.

Ah, what would it be like to finally be done with that? To never have to repel these lunar invaders? To have them instead in cages, on leashes, hounds of the League. That was the dream, but would it ever become a reality? If so . . . it would be soon. The day of reckoning was upon them, and Luna had apparently decided to delay it no further. Luna . . . or whatever possessed it.

He grinned, spearing another Brute through the side of the neck as he danced out of harm's way. He was certainly an adrenaline junky, even after these hundreds of years. Every man had his vice. He had his share, but when those weren't working, this was a nice change of pace.

Vladimir excused himself, getting only a couple salutes in reply from his men, who could handle the fight easily now. That squadron had lost a few by now, but it was no concern of his. He was concerned with their effectiveness, and nothing more. Instead . . . he recalled his vessel on autopilot and headed to where Lynchazel's Ccamos soldiers were on the southern front.

What he saw confused him for a minute. A darkly colored Cydenges tearing into its own as the Ccamos soldiers backed off. Lynchazel was nowhere to be seen . . . until the traitorous monster backed away from the last corpse around it and crouched, shuddered, and burst apart to reveal a young woman. He frowned, watching through the glass shield of his cockpit. Men stared at her not for her nakedness, but in adulation, raising a sort of chant. He was glad he couldn't hear it, as it may have made him just angry enough to make a large mistake.

He landed soon, drawing the attention of the Ccamos and Haccolces soldiers in the area. "Am I late?" he asked nonchalantly as he exited his vehicle. "Sorry if I . . ." He paused, partly to take in the new Mother's unclothed form but mostly for the effect "missed anything exciting." *Well, well, well. This is a showing, isn't it? And it's not even evening yet.*

The girl did not move. Shoulders straight, arms akimbo, she stared at him with an unreadable intensity. Not angrily, but neither approvingly. It was . . . not the reaction he'd expected. "I suppose I should thank you," he said, all the praise he was willing to give in this situation. She was already ruining their reunion with her surly greeting. There was not even a hint of shame or panic at encountering him in this state—not a touch of color to her cheeks, nor a twitch of her arms to cover herself. She didn't turn, but just stared in stern disapproval.

When she still refused to speak, he stepped forward and took his chance to comment on what he'd seen just before landing. "So you are a beast of Luna now, dear? I did catch a glimpse on my way here. I'm sure the footage will be . . . interesting to the Senate."

The slightest incline of her head. "I'm certain. Senator, I'd advise you not to approach."

He stopped, narrowing his eyes at her. "Not even a hug?"

She didn't move so much as to shake her head, but the disapproval was clear in her next words: "Upon returning from Luna, I brought a portion of her power with me. I should not wish to harm you should your encroaching proximity trigger a threat response."

His eyebrows shot up at the warning. *Well, well. The lioness has fangs.* He wasn't even certain how to interpret it, but he nodded in a sort of respect at her audacity . . . and her explanation. It may have been entirely false, but then . . .

if she could transform into a Cydenges at a moment's notice, and he didn't know the bounds of said creature's power, she was likely not bluffing.

"I assume there is something you're wanting in exchange for your help?" he asked, once more neglecting to offer any further direct praise or thanks.

She looked upward, lips pursed. "In a way. Though I didn't do this for you. I wish to hold a meeting with the entire Senate in Haccolces, advisors included."

"In . . . Haccolces? The Senate Hall is not exactly in . . . working order thanks to a certain hormonal human. Or perhaps you are thinking of Ccamos?"

There was neither a smirk nor any lifting of the lips at his jest. "Not Ccamos. It could be here, or Haven, or Haccolces. I care not. I shall inform the other Senators as well. But it is a meeting you will want to attend, I assure you. I don't believe you're in a position to refuse vital information from a tourist who's returned from Luna in one piece."

Now it was his face that twitched. The impudence . . . She was right, of course. He was intrigued. "Go on."

Now she shook her head, white mane swishing at her waist with the movement. "No. At the meeting, and only if all attend. I will not waste my time if it is not worth that of our world leaders."

They stared one another down for a minute, and then he nodded. "I'll see what I can do."

Vladimir watched as the lithe woman turned and strode away, faintly amused at the purpose in her stride. Was she planning to walk back to the nearest ship? Call one in? Then she stopped, bent her legs and crouched.

No . . .

In a flash of gold tinged with only a hint of sunset red, she was gone.

- Chapter 66 -

Ragnarök

Manidor 2, 1295:
progress.
— From Lhinde's Vault

Lldsaor hung up the line with Vladimir, thinking on his words even before his hand left the button. If he was right . . . and the emperor did not suspect him of lying, despite his penchant for the pastime. The young woman was back in the flesh, and with a new power the world was still struggling to understand. The reports about her going to Luna in the form of a Cydenges were bizarre enough, but the news of her return was far stranger.

Tonight, in Luna Halcyon. That was the plan. He would be there, ready for battle or discussion, whichever it would be. Many factors would determine that before they were all gathered, and he had faith that it would not end up in the latter. Tonight, Gaea would quake under the news of a fifteen-year-old lab experiment, one who belonged in a lab even now. Of course, they had changed their own plans over the recent months, adapting with the slew of new developments in the war against the Cydenges. The first attack on Maldunech had been . . .

He shuddered, recalling the footage. A world superpower, gone just like that. They'd thought themselves prepared, but they were nothing of the sort. If not for that global offensive by the ruling powers of Luna, he would never have agreed to a meeting like this—organized by none other than the Mother reborn. By his prisoner, now free. His legacy, walking about in defiance. The fruit of all their scientific and military endeavors spanning nearly a millennium, dancing on the edge of annihilation.

Just as did all of Gaea now. It was funny how the world changed.

Finally, she called as well. He spoke with the Heiress, recognizing her voice but not her tone. Her words, but not the air of command behind them. Her significance, but not the power behind every word she spoke—the invisible threat that now followed her wherever she went, the undeniable sense that one spoke not with a human, but a monster. A terror. A planetary threat.

At the last, he nodded needlessly as he said, "That will do. I already planned to be there, Heiress. Indeed. See you then."

Now he stood once more, pondering the conversation. Vlad was right . . . there was something far different about her now, more than a simple confidence boost. The girl had come to Gaea a caterpillar, and had gone through a chrysalis state, culminating in what now loomed before them: a deadly butterfly. What the butterfly demanded of them, a discussion among equals, would have been laughed off a few months ago, like a stand of great oaks approached by a pine sapling wanting to stand among them. It was not for no reason that phrases existed like "Know your place."

But the need for a council was too strong. The situation too dire. Go he would, as would all the others.

Except . . . Strongs. He was still dead, as the miraculous technology of resurrection had yet to be invented. Perhaps there was a way to perform such a feat with elemental magic? He supposed he would find out someday, when the Font was his. He still was unsure what to think of that Hellebes Phelps, who administrated in the seat of their former general in Haven. He performed well enough. It was just . . . a very bad precedent.

Very, very bad. Every day that he continued, it got worse.

The man would be there; of that, he was certain. As for Long, however, that was the question.

(The next day)

Zent stretched his bulk, feeling his heart pounding within his ribcage even as he breathed slowly in and out. In and out. Today would be a momentous day. And a fearful one, should the Cydenges catch on to what was taking place on Gaea: A world council whose purpose was to come together and figure out how to defeat the space dragons. Unity could not be any more important at this time, so he did not object to the meeting. But . . . she insisted on his coming. Kaen as well, no doubt, were he actually here, but he was busy on Mani, trying to steer them away from their own war.

Luna, you'd better wait. But not too long, or we will destroy you in a blink . . . just as soon as we've rid this world of your evil.

He flew the Senatorial aircraft, leaving at 05:40 to arrive at 10:20. Just in time. His five passengers included Lyn and two attendants hand-picked by the young Senator. Iselda, former concubine of Sylleo, was the strangest pick, though he thought he saw where she was going with that choice. General Fors was the other, with Lieutenant Colonel _____ and ______ as their bodyguards, solid choices.

Lyn said very little on the long flight over. The air itself was charged and turbulent nearly the whole way to Luna Halcyon, perhaps a result of Luna's influence, such as the Cydenges entry and exit. They said all of Gaea felt the coming of the Cydenges, and this time where there was usually a rainstorm . . . it was a cyclone.

The large island of Escatar, technically its own continent, spread over the western horizon, depicting their nearing of their destination, and soon they were flying over sweeping mountains and lush, verdant jungles, approaching one of the most mysterious cities in the world. Once home to the Anier, according to some, and—if Lyn was to be believed—even to Luna and her worshippers in the days before the Exile. He didn't know too much about that himself.

The city itself was situated in a more temperate zone just north of some of the thickest jungle, as modern in appearance as any of the Nine Cities of Man. Scarred where Luna had beset it, but standing strong with its red shield dome and defense towers. Aircraft could be seen flying within the shield dome, though whether that was more Senatorial aircraft or not he could not tell.

Minutes later, they were docking in the reserved dock for Senators and such VIPs. Zent couldn't help but be taken with the eastern architecture of the city, which was so unconventional as to fit in surprisingly well with the surrounding environment and exotic air of the region. Some structures curved and seemed even to sway in the wind—an optical trick, no doubt—yet stood strong and tall. The highways and transport trams were largely hidden below ground or blended in seamlessly with the overall city design so as to not stick out. Overall, it was far more . . . subtle that, say, Haccolces. But bolder and more industrial than Ccamos.

"And here we are," Lyn said in a low voice, not betraying whatever emotion she held currently inside. She had not been very open with Zent since returning to Gaea, so she was hard to read. Iselda looked nervously her way, then out the hatch at the surrounding city. She had never been outside Ccamos, to his knowledge, except perhaps when she was shipped in some twelve years ago. She smoothed her close-cut black hair and followed her mistress out.

They took little time in surveying Luna Halcyon's impressive governmental district as they strode toward the Capitol, met almost instantly by a warmly smiling aide, who bowed low to Lyn and addressed her as "Lady Mother." He showed them into the building, where they soon met the hulking Senator Holman, a monument of a man replete with a darkly colored suit and wide-brimmed hat which suited him well.

"Lady Senator," he said with an almost deferential nod. It seemed out of place until Zent noticed the aide's an almost cult-like way he picked up the gesture, although he resumed his walk soon after at Holman's hand gesture. Luna Halcyon was the seat of the world religion that worshipped Lyn, after all.

They continued through halls hung with island-flavored tapestries—in addition to the usual drab numbers and labels seen all over the imperium. The crest of Luna Halcyon was engraved over the most distinctive doorways, including palm trees and herons. Or were they flamingos? In the hall outside the meeting place, they finally met other Senators and their bodyguards. Vladimir was nearest the far door, who dipped his head in the barest show of respect at the comparatively slight Senator DeWitt greeted her with the appropriate level of professionalism, shaking her hand.

Daedalus, for his part, was already perspiring. He looked Lyn's way and seemed to gulp, then cleared his throat and came over to greet her with a hand shake and shoulder slap. Zent couldn't help but notice how she made sure to slap his own boulder of a shoulder with as much force as he used, though the gesture looked friendly enough. "It's good to see you back, Heiress," he said in a high, nasally voice. "Or—Senator, excuse me."

Just then, Lldsaor and Brant strode in, heavy feet thumping on the tiled floor. From his clean, laundered attire, Zent would never have known that the latter had just lost his entire city—and somehow escaped with his life. The captain had definitely not gone down with the ship in this case. He supposed all these Senators existed on some sort of spectrum, love of self on one end and duty toward their city on the other.

The Senators began to trickle into the spacious meeting hall, whose heavy doors were held open by straight-faced Hellebes soldiers. They didn't even nod to any of the VIPs, but looked straight ahead. The room inside was high-ceilinged, flat and in two tiers, the top mirroring the floor. Ringing the circular chamber was a set of wooden benches, the only thing resembling seating—and of course no cameras or other recording devices. Holman had a few aides already standing by, and the other Senators brought in their own aides or secretaries or commanders, whomever they had brought. Lyn had specified to do so, and they would not have come lacking, knowing that she would be bringing extras—although these men were confidant not to assume military intentions from her own staff, a notion which was clear from the relaxed stances of the Senators and the bored or vaguely unsettled look of their staff.

Holman had just cleared his throat to open the meeting when the door opened again, this time admitting an old man, the frailest of Hellebes, no more than Lyn's size and far less imposing. Zent had never met nor seen him, yet he recognized the Elite immediately.

The gasps from around the room indicated a similar reaction all around. Except from Lyn, who looked on unsurprised. She had invited him? And sent men to pick him up, or perhaps soldiers stationed at Mei Shan had brought him.

Regardless, it was a shock to see the former Senator. He shuffled in, seemingly heedless of the impressive Senatorial showing and the eyes raptor-honed on him, and took his place at the ninth podium, which stood empty as per the usual order of things.

A long pause ensued. Eyes shifted. Glances were exchanged.

"Well, don't all speak at once," the old man said in a raspy voice.

"S-Senator Long," Holman stuttered, apparently as lost for words as the rest

"*Former* Senator," Lldsaor corrected, glaring death in Long's direction "What brings you here, old man? How have you escaped your rightful death in Mei Shan?"

The old man shrugged. "Is that a question, or mere rhetoric?"

Lldsaor's continued glare was his only answer.

Long sighed and leaned on his podium, as though tired from swimming the six thousand miles to get here. "I was not aware that my position as Senator had been officially revoked. I am still on the Senate."

More glances. More distrustful stares. But a few nods.

"You . . . are," Lldsaor allowed. "But only on a technicality."

"Quite so, my good man. Genocide is a highly technical thing."

Holman coughed, then interrupted, "I think this would be a good place to open our meeting as normal. This is a special occasion, made even more so by Senator Long's presence. Lynchazel, that was . . . perhaps a good idea to invite him, whatever ties you have." His tone did not indicate such a notion, but that was to be expected. "Gentlemen, we gather this day to take council regarding the Cydenges threat."

"Indeed," Lldsaor began, taking the momentum that Holman had started. "And while we are here, we must speak on some pressing concerns regarding these . . ." he glanced Lyn's way, then at Senator Phelps ". . . successors."

"If I may, Senators," Lyn cut in smoothly, "these are exactly the reasons I called this meeting. Holman voices the obvious when he says we meet because of the threat of Luna, but I believe your good emperor has just spoken to be of even greater importance. This League is fragile, made of glass. We represent today five cities ruled by five emperors." She gestured about the room, earning a few frowns. "And two destroyed cities with only a Senator left to show that the League ever had them. And two cities still standing *without* their respective Senators. Had more cities not banded together and rushed to the aid of our friend Vlad, Trident may not be standing today as well—and then the cities standing as originally intended would be less than half."

A pause followed, and then Brant said, "Go on."

She gave a curt nod. "As I said, this League is fragile. Our world, a few steps from disappearing at the snap of a finger. Luna is more than willing to step in and be the destroyer, as you well know. And she has yet to unleash her full might against our world. You think we have deflected the brunt of the assault, that we are on the downhill slope of the invasion, but it is only beginning. I have been to the golden moon and seen the horrors kept there in chains. Armies. Hordes, even of the humanoid type you've only recently seen."

"So we must band together!" DeWitt said, uncharacteristically animated. Holman and even Brant nodded along with him, while Daedalus pursed his lips in thought.

"No," said Lyn, voice even but stern. "That is not my point. Although you are right in that it is necessary. But my meaning is more specific—your are seeing a shift in the modern world of Gaea. The perfection that your Mother Project achieved, or rather almost achieved, was disturbed as soon as the Red Horizon was born of accidental circumstances. And shortly thereafter, when my father, Kallyn Kalceron of Mani, came to Gaea and banded together with Rissius to form the most intelligent force on the planet. When my mother, the second Mother Gaea, was ripped from her containment unit and you all panicked to patch the system with the first-ever Zeta Beast. And now, as cities and Senators drop, do you still believe that your utopia can exist anywhere but your minds? Your dreams?"

"Woman, I believe you are straying into dangerous territory," said Emperor Lldsaor, holding out a warning hand. "That is enough."

"No!" Lyn's voice came out in a high-pitched yell that cut through the room and turned heads, causing some of the Senators to start when they heard it. Even Lldsaor jerked back an inch, blinking in sudden surprise at her bold defiance. It sounded almost like a different voice, possessing a quality Zent had never heard except . . . once.

The girl stepped out from her podium. *No, Lyn, what are you doing?* Zent groaned in his head. *Please don't do this.* But he let her go out in front of the entire room, spreading her hands, anger in every step. He couldn't see her face from this angle, but he knew it must be expressing extreme emotions, as the next words that came from her mouth cut like lighting in a stormy sky:

"You *fakes.* Liars and murderers, every one." She turned, pointing around the room, teeth clenched in a shaking smile. "Destroyers of mankind. Desolators of your own world, serving your own ends above all. You made widows of mothers, stumps of family lines, experiments of precious children, puppets and graveyard fodder and forgotten memories of men and women the world over. You are the poison destroying this world. I ask you to appoint heirs and successors not because it is your only eventual hope but because *judgment* is coming. And soon, oh, very soon."

She shook at the release of these last words, which she accentuated with the oration of a preacher. Like most of the room, Zent was wide-eyed and aghast at the words pouring from her mouth. Her voice alone had progressed from . . . not quite her own . . . to an otherworldly hiss that was hardly human, saturated with centuries of bitterness and noxious hatred. Hurt, pain, and deep sorrow. It was not her voice, but that of another before her. An ancestral cry that had long awaited the chance to pour forth in preparation for . . . what?

Something evil. Zent could feel it now, and see it in her posture. Something told him the rest of the room was not seeing it, except perhaps for Long. But even he sat transfixed, eyes a thousand years in the past, unable to speak.

The first to find his tongue was Vladimir: "Well, I believe you just threatened us? Or is this a bluff?" He spread his hands, a smarmy smile overtaking the shock that owned his face.

She stood still for a moment longer, unspeaking, and Zent could see the quaking in her shoulders, the vibration of intense fury, and even feel it in her Geokinetic signature. She wouldn't actually . . .

The girl, lightly touching the floor with her hands, and was gone. Immediately, Vlad was being pulled backward from his podium, a gillsuited form clinging on his back, legs around his torso. The air distorted in a golden corona as she did . . . something to him, seeming to suck the planetary energy right out of him. He tried to say something, but she only wrenched harder against his neck with a vicious chokehold, and then . . . she twisted with immense force, and a snap like thunder split the room. She climbed down from his broken body in one smooth motion, like an insect, dropping to the floor, hands glowing gold. Her eyes as well. Heat distorted the air above her gillsuit.

The room broke into chaos and panicked shouting. Calls for guards, Senators shying away, Senators rushing in. Zent and Long both trying to get to Lyn to calm her down, to beg her to stop. *What is she thinking? She's gone mad with rage. It must be . . . Lhinde.*

"Behold, your judgment!" she shouted above the noise, eerie voice reverberating through the very floor as though Geokinetically projected. "I have awaited this revenge for eight hundred years."

Zent lost sight of her again. Her voice drew his attention to Senator Brant, who'd been trying to flee past Lldsaor. She held him against the floor, shouting out, "Stop, desist! Or I will kill you all. I am here only for the Anier. Look on and bear witness, and carry on for them in a more worthy manner."

She stripped Brant of his Geothermic energy just like Vlad, this time unleahing a blinding blast of direct energy straight into his neck, blackening it, and withdrew from his unmoving body.

The emperor himself was on her now, raging hatred clear on his face. His booming voice made it clearer still. He swept in and clutched her by the neck, lifting her up. "You *useless* experiment! This is how you thank me. *This* is how you choose to die . . ."

Lynchazel reached up as though to choke him back, but her arm didn't nearly reach. She clutched uselessly at his gigantic arms, seemingly unfazed by the pressure he was applying to her neck. Again, she performed that mysterious siphoning, and Zent watched as her body thrummed with life while his own grip slackened. His face went from enraged to shocked, and she pulled them both to the ground. She bent over him as her feet touched the floor, almost like a lover bending in for a kiss, and then her hand blazed with a golden light. Metal burst forth inexplicably, shredding the sleeve of her gillsuit, and a scaled hand grabbed hold on the Elite's face with long claws, caressing it from both sides and under neath the chin. She twisted, and the claws tightened and pierced his jaw, thrusting upward until one came out the top of his forehead. Then she threw his massive body to the floor in a display of disgust, hand immediately retracting into a bare human's hand, blood running along her arm.

The blood of an emperor. The blood of a god.

Long caught her, trying to pin her arms, but she threw him off like a child. They fought together like so, master and student, while he pleaded with her to stop. To come back to herself. Zent merely watched, saying nothing, as the Ninth Senator was taking every words straight from his mouth.

Lyn dominated the struggle, bending the old Senator's arms to the point of breaking. "You are an old fool. I would be merciful to you for your repentance, Senator Long? Would you really refuse that? Must I kill you as well?"

"Yes. This is wrong."

He had barely spoken the words before she twisted savagely, snapping an arm. She threw his body to the ground and followed immediately with a descending axe kick, crushing his throat. Zent hissed as he saw it, knowing clearly that he was dead.

What is going on?

"Where are the others?" she shouted, rising to her feet. Geothermic slugs were already pelting her, what should have been fatal shots, but they only succeeded in melting through her gillsuit to bare unharmed, absorbent skin. Skin that welcomed the heat energy and devoured it. Like a Cydenges.

Daedalus, Holman and DeWitt, the only Senators still standing, were frozen in place near the exit, guards blocking her from them, sweat beading on their foreheads. Daedalus made the first move, even as the other two tried to plead with her. They were not the enemy. They weren't with Lldsaor. The Mother Project had been out of their hands for many centuries. They wanted to help, not harm, her.

All these she seemed to treat as mere excuses, stalking inexorably toward them. The guards, realizing their weapons were doing nothing, began to flee, but she ignored them, crouching once more and vanishing in a red-and-gold blur. She traveled right through the men, and crashed into the Senators, throwing them backward through the wall and taking a large chunk of it with them.

What the . . . Zent was left stunned, along with the others in the room.

"That was a Cydenges just now," Fors said, pointing. "She's fully transformed."

Zent nodded curtly. "We need to stop her somehow, or she'll tear this entire place apart."

"What about . . . the Senators?" asked an ashen-faced Iselda.

Fors turned to her. "We'll see if we can save one or two. Brett, Ccol, protect her." He waved toward the remaining guards, shouting, "Cydenges-killing weapons, got any?"

With a mutual nod of unspoken agreement, the two Ccamcs commanders turned and sprinted for the destroyed wall, leaping two stories to the ground below.

- Chapter 67 -

Ceasefire

Manidor 2, 1295
progress
— From Lhinde's Vaul

The situation was as bad as Zent feared. By the time they struck the courtyard below, two Senators lay dead on the ground, DeWitt with blood pooling around his crushed chest and Holman missing his head. Lyn, or whatever Cydenges monster she had become, had Daedalus pinned down on the ground, who was nearly blubbering in a hysterical state, sweat pouring down his face as he tried to kick her metal paws off of him.

Her dark metallic armor was spewing golden sparks from a few chinks. The Senators had put up a fight, it seemed. But judging by their pale, soulless look she had siphoned their life energy from their bodies just as she had the other Senators.

Fors cursed from beside him. They approached at speed, Zent striking out for her back leg while Fors grabbed for her tail. The Lyn Cydenges turned its head from its prey, seeming to decide in its head. He couldn't help but wonder how much cognitive control she had at this time. Clearly not much. She was a prisoner of . . . well, it seemed increasingly clear now. She'd told him of this before, and he had brushed it off.

What a fool he was.

Lyn flicked her tail savagely, pulling Fors, and turned to swipe her claws at Zent. She seemed stronger than most Cydenges, striking with the strength of a Senator or greater. Zent was not fast enough, and he took the blow across his shoulder, claws tearing in and sending him sprawling. He recovered quickly though, and came back at her as Fors clung onto a back leg and Daedalus rose shakily to his feet, wiping at his brow.

"We need to kill this thing!" the Chronala Senator shouted.

Zent just nodded, not attempting to protest. Daedalus was right, of course. There was little else to do in this case. In the space of a couple minutes, Lyn had destroyed the leadership of the entire world minus one leader, committing no less than six murders.

With little warning, Daedalus charged in, roaring like an animal. With Elite speed, he struck at her underbelly, heavy fist cracking scales and opening a small golden seam. At the same time, he threw out a Geokinetic quake that tripped her up, whilst the two Ccamos men took hold of her neck and threw her. Twin cracks announced the shots of backup soldiers who'd found an opportunity to use their rifles.

More shots, and suddenly she was leaking light all over her scaled body. She raised her horned head to the heavens and let loose a high, reverberating roar that echoed on multiple registers. Then . . . her whole body trembled, the light blinking, and the gigantic Cydenges monster disappeared.

Zent immediately ran up, arms spread wide, and shouted, "Hold your fire!" He knew it was risky, but if it meant—

Another gunshot struck his left shoulder, throwing him nearly to the ground. He couldn't tell if it pierced through or not, but he barely gave a reaction. Instead, he fell down beside the pale human form that lay crumpled on the courtyard, unmoving, long hair covering her face. It was golden now, for whatever reason.

He reached out a shaky hand, brushing back her hair, ignoring the shouts from around him. What he saw was enough to elicit a painful recoil. This was not Lyn . . . how?

It was . . . well, he didn't recognize her, but there was no mistaking her identity: This was Lhinde. Her face looked almost younger than Lyn's, more innocent somehow, yet traced with an air of worry and sorrow, as though dreaming of terrible things in her past.

Now it was Daedalus' turn to rush in, hands waving. He collapsed to his knees and gingerly, almost reverently, held out a hand toward the young feminine face. "Lhinde," he breathed, his tone transformed into something soft and vulnerable. "Lhinde, is it really you? It can't . . . it *can't* be."

The naked girl's eyes opened, and she gasped, looking around. She winced, though at what he was not sure, and fell still, staring up at the Senator. As though too exhausted to speak, she mumbled, "R-Re . . . na?"

And then she was gone.

Daedalus' hand fell to the ground, and he clutched it, face gripped by deep sorrow and fear. "I'm sorry. I'm sorry."

- Chapter 68 -

Architect

Manidor 2, 1295:
progress.
— From Lhinde's Vault

Back in Chronala, Senator Daedalus clutched the arms of his heavy desk chair. One of the few in his entire house, though he found himself using it more and more as the decades went on. The whirlwind of emotions had not yet left the disaster site that was his mind, and indeed he was still in a sort of shock over the drastic and rapid events of this past day. The deaths of all those he was closest to, companions of a millennium dead in the span of minutes to that . . . *thing.*

And that thing was . . . was . . .

He didn't know. That was the most frightening part, or at least the biggest culprit as far as his shortness of breath went. It wasn't his five-hundred-kilogram bulk, for his strength was that of twenty horses and then some. But then there was the world . . . the whole world.

He let out a pitiful laugh. Dozens or hundreds of officials the world over sought his attention right now, and he had disabled all communications just to get away from it, because . . . what could they do now? Ccamos had somehow replaced Sylleo, and then even Lynchazel, but there were secrets known to Lldsaor and the rest of the Senate that no advisor in Haccolces knew. An official could not simply assume control of the League, or Haccolces for that matter. The systems in place linking the Mother labs to the rest of the world were largely overseen by lab technicians, just as Daedalus himself did not run the biomanufactories here in Chronala . . . but the data keys and bypasses and more crucial administrative concerns . . . Most Senators were paranoid enough that few or no administrators knew all the secrets.

But still, that was not all.

With a shaky sigh, the hulking Senator rose, pushed back his chair and approached his office desk, opening a drawer on the far right and sliding his finger along a concealed fingerprint scanner that released a secret tab at the top of the drawer. It flicked out, revealing a few contents of personal value to him. Notes from journals burned centuries ago, and a few rare, rare early photographs from as early as E200.

There it was. Fingers trembling, throat tight, he withdrew a monochromatic photograph of a young woman, around twenty-eight years old at the time. Black hair, prominent jaw, overall muscular yet lanky, not overly beautiful. The expression on her face was an uncommonly happy, one of pride, for she had just been awarded a medal by the Anier for her last great contribution to the Mother Project.

Before, that is, she was informed of her final duty: To stand in as an experimental battery to power an expanding power network. One that would go on to demand more and more . . . power far beyond what she could withstand.

"Lhinde," he whispered, stroking the picture. "What did I do to you? It was me . . . it was all me . . ." *To myself.* He set the picture down on the mahogany surface, staring morosely at it. With every passing second, he sank further back in time, eyes glossing over until the woman herself—in place of the blurry old photograph—stood in front of him. His memory was still crystal clear, of course, thanks to the power of the Cydenges, though it was dark or frail in places.

Not here.

He pictured her smile, that rare and fleeting lift of the lips that changed her entire countenance, and the dark, brooding Lhinde he'd known better. He replayed conversations between them, from the time back in the Anier teaching facilities. Their rivalries . . . their bond over obsession with science. He remembered their final game of Drachi, which had quite possibly decided the fate of the world. He recalled the deep discomfort at knowing the uncertainty of whether she would live or die.

But she had, miraculously. Were it the other way around, he knew it would have resulted in a lower chance of survival. Lhinde was always the weaker in anatomy and surgery. She had reawakened after a few days, Cydenges core keeping time with her heart, limbs throbbing with an unearthly vigor. She had almost injured her friend before getting her strength under control. It was not long before they had to part ways, and he had not been able to see Lhinde.

His friend, his sister.

No . . . *Her* sister. To the inferno with Daedalus. Daedalus had lived too long. Daedalus was a mask and a shell lived in for many lifespans too long. A woman was not meant to experience life in multiple centuries, much less in an artificial body so far removed from her natural state.

Daedalus reached back into the niche, lifting up brittle sheets of paper to reveal another photograph, this one even older, of two women clasping each other by the shoulder. Neither was truly smiling. Lhinde was making her best effort, but her eyebrows refused to soften, while her friend looked perhaps . . . half amused. Really it was the same: An effort to smile when such a thing was difficult. The other woman had light hair, bright eyes, a delicate face with prominent cheekbones. Bangs and a ponytail. Each wore a professional-looking dress, loose and conservative with short sleeves.

Lhinde and Rena, read the caption in flowing script. Lhinde's.

Love forever, sisters and friends. To the stars and beyond, and may humanity shine on into the new age. May we contribute to that light.

The woman whose form and face he fingered now was not Lhinde, but the one called Rena. Someone he knew long, long ago in that ancient age. Someone he used to be. He'd destroyed all reminders of Rena long ago, for the anger and shame and hopelessness they always brought, but he'd never been able to bring himself to part from this photograph, just as with the other one of Lhinde. To look on the form he'd once had and know it was forever consigned to the past . . . discomfort did not begin to describe what he felt. But this time there was something more: Longing. Seeing Lhinde's face, even for that briefest moment following the dark encounter earlier, had done something to him.

He thought of all that he'd given up, both the good and the bad. Rena the captive, the outcast, the scientist, she had not possessed any bright future: No family, no husband, no children to carry on a legacy. She'd made science her passion in place of any other. When her looks attracted the close attention of the Anier, she never gained anything but only gave up what little of herself was left. She'd been desperate, and wanted out. Eventually, her hard work and perseverance paid off, and they offered her a spot on their seat. Knowing so much of their plans, she was more than honored, and took the position with gladness . . . even when it required the sacrifice of their current lead scientist. She had gritted her teeth and done the deed, though it was a process of experimentation—just as it had been with her friend Lhinde.

The man's name was Althim, and he became the guinea pig for their brain scans. There were others, but this was a dedicated effort following the success of their initial Hellebes men. As projected, it worked only in part. She herself was next, using a body she'd been working on for some time. She'd poured countless hours in the physique and strength, health, modifiable and repairable functionality, and . . . lastly, one small alteration, the same as she had insisted be done for every Hellebes to come, so that they would never be ruled by the wayward and controlling passions of these beasts.

The transfer, by some miracle, succeeded, and a new abomination was born into the world in defiance of all creation. She wept for the sin that was her scientific success, and for the loss of nearly everything that made her Rena. Her sex, chromosomes, DNA, hormones, and every capability—all erased, made knew. *What have I done?* she asked herself every time she woke up, every time she looked in the mirror to see her beauty gone. Every scrap of dignity and vanity that defined a woman railed at the loss of it all . . . and yet, most abominable of all, the very instincts that previously would have done so were lost or dulled beyond recognition. Her mind remembered, but her body did not. Her body was that of a bull-sized man, practically a minotaur. She was the monster buried and hidden away in a labyrinth of her own making, imprisoned by rules she had designed. The entire world going forward would be constrained to that prison, that labyrinth.

Her chosen name could not be more fitting.

Daedalus jolted, torn from his reverie by distant sounds like thunder. Heart racing, hearing little but his own pulse, he hurried to reenable communications and scan the list of notifications on his wrist monitor. Most were as he expected, cries for help and desperate pleas for alliance, but others spoke of danger, readings from Luna . . . and Chronala.

Of course. Daedalus, you fool!

Of course she would strike here.

He looked outside his window to see streaks of red outside the red shield dome, darkening it or burning a golden hue into it in places. He could not make out the forms that floated down from the sky, but he recognized them. *Oh, God in Heaven, if you're there . . . protect us.*

No . . . me. Protect me, he amended. Better to at least be honest. It was a matter of time before they came for the city. He'd multiple clues as to Luna's agenda, and now he saw a different influence in this raging beast that was Lynchazel . . . and especially Lhinde. If she was truly in there, alive in some way, then this would all make so much more sense. The very idea of her seeking to work with Luna should have been obvious long ago, but he'd never made the connection.

And now we pay the price. He racked his brain for a way to save the Hellebes in his city, and especially the biomanufactories. His projects, his children, his legacy.

He saw none. *No, just escape, you old fool. What else is there to live for?*

But if there was a way . . .

A minute later, he burst from his office, shouting for his aides. "Everyone, with me! We're escaping now!"

No one was in sight. *They've already begun evacuating, haven't they?* Perhaps they were readying to fight? His wrist monitor revealed that a few had already contacted him, pleading for orders. For a moment, he considered replying, but instead he called Sylleo's office, hoping for someone to pick up . . . anyone . . .

He began running.

"Mr. Daedalus?" came a rough voice. "Colonel Zent speaking."

"Perfect," he panted. "Look, we're uh . . . there's a situation in Chronala."

"We're aware. We tried to reach you, but . . . Should we send men? ICBMs? Any other way we can help?"

". . . No. You might as well call them off, because this will be a wasteland by the time they get here."

"But sir, how do you—Oh." Zent was silent for a moment, and Daedalus took the opportunity to focus on locating his nearest escape route. There were a few effective ones, hopefully not taken already. He had minutes at best.

"You all know it's true," he hissed into his mic. "Don't pretend we're not doomed here. Better that one Senator lives. And maybe, just maybe . . ."

"You can take out most of her remaining forces. Any guesses as to how they're still being commanded en masse?"

"Look, I'm a little—" Daedalus cut off with a string of curses as he saw that the first escape elevator had been taken. That meant it was probably full. He sped to the next one, finding it free, and took the elevator doom, tapping his foot rapidly.

"We'll send men to pick you up, Senator," Zent said, beginning to cut out shortly below ground. "Just send . . ."

Daedalus was already frantically tapping the button to send coordinates, first of his location and then—with a fleeting bit of rational thought—of where this escape route would end. There would be a bit of waiting involved, but he should be outside the blast zone . . .

Please, please . . . I can't die. Not yet.

- Chapter 69 -

The Metallion/Hordes of Silver

Manidor 2, 1295:
progress.
— From Lhinde's Vault

[Kym and Solomiya vs Domon, which turns into all of them vs the "medallion". Fairly long, probably 3k.]

- Chapter 70 -

Battle Plans

Manidor 2, 1295.
progress.
— From Lhinde's Vault

[Kaen making preparations for a recon/raid on the revived Silversmith capital in the Down Under. Does something keep him from going after all, like news from Darsor? I could see that—They've been waiting and planning, and then *Boom!* Mani strikes first, drawing their attention to Darsor.]

Kaen looked skyward, aiming his gaze further and further toward that distant point beyond the western horizon where Argent and Darsor stared one another down. *Mani . . . You and I have a score to settle.* And he may have just dictated the terms and battlefield. If the message was true . . . this could be the moment they'd been expecting—the leadup to the decisive battle for which Mydia and her coalition were already making preparations. If even Domon was leaning so hard into it—not to mention every outlier nation on Argent—then the situation was serious.

Domon may be insane, and even a fool at times, but he had a near prescient gift of foresight and prediction. And with the new Gates in their own territory, here on Argent, they had bargaining power with the dark lord. If all went south, the coalition knew what to do: begin the evacuation to Gaea. By now, Mani had made crystal clear his ill-will toward mankind, or rather, his sharply condescending view of them. An awakened god such as he, if given a position of total domination, would rule neither lightly nor

- Chapter 71 -

From the Sister Moon

Manidor 2, 1295:
progress.
— From Lhinde's Vault

Luna singles out Daedalus, surprising him, Lhinde gets a final chance to speak with him, and sort of Rena. She may kill him? I don't really want to do that, but it might make the most sense if nothing else.

- Chapter 72 -

The Light of Doom

Manidor 2, 1295.
progress.
— From Lhinde's Vaul.

[The battle lines are drawn, Mani and his Silversmiths versus the ceased (ish) combatants of the Archlord and Ribsha, and the Argentian Coalition as well. Mani invokes the thousand-year time limit, however, and the sky lights up, Cybele speaks, and all is thrown into chaos. Things out of order now bring friction, not to mention confusion, for the Gate is no longer on the Tower . . . Definitely the final climax here, so make it good.]

Mani raised his hand skyward, and the firmament responded. Blazing auroras lit the horizon, flickering upward toward the west—toward the previously monikered Land of Storms—and soon a glittering trail of white cloud traced its way up the dome of the sky. And another, and another, until a total of ten met above the distant Tower of Mani. The auroras and the multi-colored sky between pulsed with light, like a magical heartbeat, and an omnipresent voice rang out, softly feminine yet full of robust power:

"Children, come home. Return to your place of ancestry, for the time of your exile is done, and the curse is lifted. Return, return! Come to your place of origin and return whence you came, for your mother welcomes you back."

Shivers ran down Kaen's spine. *Mother? What insanity is this? What voice could that be? There was no Mother at the time of Exile . . .*

Mani lowered his hand toward the west, and the air about the Tower seemed to grow more dense, as though a storm was once more brewing about it. Suddenly, there came a great snapping and a crash, and the great structure listed to one side. More cracks rang out, and it began to sink beneath the earth, swallowed up by the fissure-ridden desolation. The sky flickered, this time ominously, and the cloud trails leading toward the central Darsorian point began to fade. Mani's own voice replaced the other, saying:

"Children of *Mani,* fear not at my mother's voice, but at mine own. She does not truly desire you back, but to swallow you whole. Here on the molded moon, I have grown beyond my previous constraints and am able to sustain this world, and I have need of servants."

A golden streak fell from the sky just then, and dust and debris blasted outward from a new crater just north of Mani's semi-draconic form. A golden woman stepped out from it, eliciting gasps and cries of alarm.

So she wasn't dead after all . . . just an act. Mani turned with a smile upon the goddess, ignoring those around them. "You are just in time, sister, to witness the birth of a new world. Mine truly and forever."

The golden Archmother spread her hands and rained down her metallic armies upon the stone killing field. As they began their work, so did the Silversmiths, raising up great spires and horns of silver to smite them. When the beasts closed in, they trapped them using whiplike strands of silver, constricting the Cydenges until they burst like living balloons.

"I had my doubts, Luna, that you would truly come back to my home to challenge me. Or should I say . . . Menily."

As he held her against the ground, pinned and kicking uselessly, she suddenly tensed with a gasp that was out of place, as though waking. "Where . . . what am I doing here? Why did I come—"

Ceasing to struggle, she stared up at him, metallic head resting uncomfortably on equally harsh stone. Her eyes dimmed, the glowing centers shrinking in size while growing in intensity. "Mani . . ." Another moment, and then she struggled in earnest. She reached up and grasped his hand with her left, metal muscles rippling and twisting, and tore away his grasp, cinching her abdomen to headbutt his silver head.

He roared, taking a step back, and she kicked with her legs, using her arms to manipulate her weight until she was back on the ground, ending in a crouched, forward-leaning stance, fingers now draping claws. Fangs poked from under her upper lip, though her expression was unreadable. Excited, perhaps, or fearful.

The two rushed one another, Mani with a rippling swirl of his arms meant to overtake her. She, with a vibrating duplication of her body that resulted in two clones, each circling him. She created further Cydenges as well, while her other children continued to fight with the Silversmiths and lesser children of Mani—the so-called "magi."

Mani only increased in the outpouring of the sea of metal contained in his Titan body—whose limits even he did not know. It had been enough to create this silver world once. In the end, she was no match for the pillars and walls and blades that encircled her, even though she could stem and slice and tear the material. This was his domain, and his power knew few bounds, particularly those imposed on an intruder such as she. Why had she come here and instigated this battle? It seemed that the hesitation she'd showed a moment ago might be shock at her own actions, like she came without knowing why—or even realizing it. Yet all her children had followed mindlessly. If he killed her here and now, would they disintegrate and ceased to exist, since they came from her? Or would they have to annihilate them.

Regardless, the decision of this battle was obvious. *Now to make it good,* he thought, seizing her with a portion of his silver waves that coalesced into arms. He was not constrained by the physical form when his Silver was in motion, and he formed more arms from behind her, seizing her shoulders, hips, forearms, golden hair . . . He forced Silver into her gleaming eye sockets, eliciting the first Titan scream, though even that seemed not to produce the desired effect. She would not die of having her eye sockets crushed in. He had to inject Silver inside her body somehow—

She wrenched free of his grasp, tearing her own form in a dozen places, and suddenly her form sank into a husk as she reappeared away from his hands. She could not escape the silver, however, and thus scratched and tore at the wavy, reflective walls. But he could see her fatigue. Grabbing hold of her once more, and then again as she broke free using clones, he at last succeeded in pouring

Silver inside a wound, smearing extra around both her arms. The silver struggled inside her metal, incapable of doing anything but churning and seething.

Again, she collapsed against the ground, but this time there was defeat written cleanly across her heavy metal body. She opened her mouth and said something he didn't catch, even as he finally released the swarming silver that cocooned them. Open sky was revealed above, and she seemed to gasp it in like precious air, eyes restlessly roving as though for a glimpse of her precious golden moon. "I'm . . . I'm . . ."

Mani stomped downward on her stomach, clenching his foot to tear into the cavity that was her Titanic sanctum—the source of her power. She sucked in a futile breath, held it, and then let out a long, screeching scream that intensified as he tore her wide open, unveiling a spectacular see of swirling light. It clung inside her, reluctant to escape, but he bent his horned head and inhaled it greedily, transferring power into him.

He got only a short way when an earthquake nearly jolted him away, and Cybele's voice split the sky. *Not now, Mother . . .*

Something struck him, throwing him to roll onto his side. Snarling and spitting, he rose to face the new threat, which manifested itself as a heavily-built Cydenges with dark scaling and a powerful aura. *One of her generals . . . How did this one get through?* He looked and saw a trail of gutted and dismembered Silversmiths, and fury rose within him. A closer look revealed gaping wounds on this one, spewing red and even gold light.

Without moving, Mani commanded threads of metal from all over the area to converge on the creature. It moved with blinding speed, but it could not escape the net that caught and downed it, biting into its scales. Stalking toward it, he savagely jerked a hand. "Get *out* of my way!" The silver net threw the beast down even as a Silver spear slammed into its side—hopefully finishing it, but he cared not to check—and he set upon Luna.

The Titaness was leaning up on one hand, the other working above her stomach to stitch together the seam that threatened to spill more of her sacred light. *Mine—it should be mine by now.* She glared at him with eyes now dark with hatred and pain. It was a look of despairing shame. And then . . . in a dazzling flash, she did the unthinkable:

She disappeared.

Mani looked where she'd been, catching the dispersing strands of light that signified great expenditure of energy. She hadn't even seemed to ready herself. And she'd left her Cydenges here—all of whom seemed to still operate . . .

No. No, they were stopping in their tracks and dropping to the ground, one after another. The victors, after the initial shock, set upon them with weapons of purest silver, making sure they were dead. This mass death of metal heralds could only mean one thing: Luna was dead or dying.

Looking upward, he saw that the sky was already dimming. Had the Wellspring already . . . no, it couldn't have yet.

There it was. A pulsing hot spot of light upon the southern horizon, streaking across in an arc, accompanied by flashed like lightning and swirling comets of magical energy, reacting with the Energy Field in staticky patterns as it passed. All turned their eyes to observe its passing. It swooped upward and was gone, bound for Gaea.

"The Wellspring of Life returns to me," spoke Cybele into the sky once more. "You have not long, children. Return! Return, or be forever trapped on this desolate moon."

This time, he did not grind his teeth at his mother's words. Something had changed in him as his other half came back. The rebellious part of him still had no desire to return to Cybele with tucked tail, but neither would he keep these humans here.

- Chapter 73 -

Menily

Manidor 2, 1295:
progress.
— From Lhinde's Vault

[Continued, of course, until Luna comes and crashes the party. Is everyone surprised to see her? This chapter might be from Mani's perspective, but I'm not sure. Luna is caught in Mani's trap and, seeing how effectively he has her pinned, Kaen and the others call the retreat, and especially call for those back on the mainland to begin their evacuation. Perhaps only when Luna is shown truly dead?]

[Um, so I **technically ended it** just there, but I don't think that's final at all. Oh, well. I want the Silversmiths to be stuck on Mani with Mani, while he either softens and becomes increasingly "human" or else goes back into some state of stasis, giving them free rein of the moon, with the current task of shepherding those who want to leave off the increasingly desolate moon. Luna has become part of him, and now he has a portion of her Proliferation ability in addition to Growth, or did the Wellspring take those when it left . . . ? Don't think so.

REDACTED: With a last crunch, Mani swallowed her whole, and his rival was no more. He felt it in the air and inside himself: A change, a sudden absence, a release. What Luna had long ago stolen was poured back into him. He felt a change coming over himself, and looked about at the field where his priests and priestesses lay wounded and Cydenges were now crumbling into dust. He looked upon his faithful with a sudden pang like . . . guilt. Sorrow. Even . . . mercy.

Luna

End of Part Four

Luna

- Epilogue α -

Fallen Goddess

Manidor 2, 1295:
progress.
— From Lhinde's Vault

(From the Vault of Lyn of Nytaea, Mother Heiress
Pawn of Luna, fool of fools, sibling of orphans
Daughter of a fleeting truth in the sea of Gaea's falsehoods
—Planet Luna, Depths, A.E. 1,000)

It is with a heavy heart and much pain, brethren, that I chisel this final entry as deep into my Vault as I am able. For I know that I shall never see the face of any man, woman or Hellebes again. Never shall I set foot on the surface of Mani or Gaea—for this day, my foot treads the harsh, bitter stone of Luna, and my lungs inhale the atmosphere that is not. Today, I take up my human flesh and confront the terror of terrors: Luna, the true Archmother. Of course, her name was never Luna, but Menily.

Heretofore, I have not met her, and it took me embarrassingly long to figure this out. But I survived my final encounter with the one called Mother and Queen by the Cydenges… and that is more a blessing than I could ever have asked. Today, I take one last breath, courtesy of some God I may meet one day, and I go to confront her. The mistress of gold, lady of death, demon in disguise… Menily.

Till now, I've been confused, living as a created metal beast on a foreign moon, a fever dream sponsored by a domineering nightmare, but at last I have woken to the truth. I have a short amount of time to put together a plan, but I believe I can do it. Knowing Luna, I believe she will share my entire Vault save for this part. I believe, or would like to, that I can hide it so deeply that she recognizes it only as a piece not meant to be shared—withholding it not to honor me, of course, but because she will know it to be the most vital.

But I dearly hope that she leaves it alone, for two reasons: I am putting my plans down here for you, the hopeful reader who finds it, but also, a final farewell to my friends, whether it ever reaches them or not. Whether they live beyond the end of all this or not.

As promised, my explanation: I caved to Luna. I agreed to her bargain. She offered me a way out, a transfer of responsibility for my people back on Gaea to her, both of us knowing full well what she intended for them. Her only leverage was the parallel knowledge that I could do nothing to stop her, yet that was not the reason for my acquiescence. Rather, I saw it as an opportunity. My only opportunity. For in her offer hid the hope of a shred of my consciousness being left after the transfer. And in case this isn't completely clear by now . . . she is using my body as her Vessel to escape Luna. To break the accord and leave early, and—she hopes—break into Mani as well. Not in the same way that Kaen, and then Rhidea, became Mani's Vessels, for their souls merely made way for a sliver of his own. No, but this is the opposite: She plans to kill me and make from my body a true human copy, a new and fleshly body for her Titan soul. If anything is left of me after tomorrow . . . it will be but a sliver.

But back to the offer, and my opportunity. I have spotted a weakness in the self-proclaimed goddess Luna, and I intend to take full advantage of it, knowing well that nothing may come of it. In that case, I entrust the fate of my people to the one out there who is greater than I, for he will raise up another in my stead. Someone will stop her. Nor do I believe for a second that I can take her down from within, or wrest back control of a body that is not truly mine. Such wishing is only that. No, but I aim to punch a chink into her armor, a flaw that will one day open her up to utter destruction. Because, if such a thing succeeds, her destruction shall be sure and definitive. No more shall two Titans walk the earth, or stare down the ancestral home of humanity from twin moons.

For I have learned that there was only ever meant to be one Titan. One power, not two. Luna is a thief, and proliferation the most ancient heritage of mankind. The Cydenges originate not from her, but from a lowly servile creature born of metal and the earth—known by the ancients as the Cybenith, or Cydenga, depending on the pronunciation. A gift to Cybele, keepers of technology that awaited human discovery. It eventually reached them, and thus was born the arts of mining and metal working, but not before Luna stole from the last Cydenga its form, copying it and birthing a new race under her power. She then flexed her newfound power by copying an ordinance of mankind from the great laws, thereby stealing from every man and woman who followed. Balance was lost, and all of humanity has felt the effects of her treachery. It was her own followers, the denizens of Luna Halcyon, who first voiced this discovery.

For this treachery, she slaughtered them all.

The rest is not necessary to tell. I personally started the archaeological digs in Luna Halycon, and I know others will continue them. Researchers both Hellebes and human will make inquiry into the past as the millennium turns, wherever they then dwell, and all will be made known. That is my hope, though I have no way of knowing how this will all turn out.

If I'm to be honest . . . this is all just a way for me to briefly distract myself from the reality of my impending doom. A heavy, heavy doom it is, of certain death. Luna will devour my flesh and do many terrible things in my name. Some may even forever think that I turned on my people . . . the Legaleians and the Hellebes both. And maybe I did, but I did it for them. For you.

Lastly, I will place in this Vault of Vaults my last testament. If anyone ever discovers this, let it be known that I love my family more than anything. That means you, Aunt Mydia, and you, Kaen. Auroras, I hope you're married by now. I hope you have a joyous marriage and many daughters . . . and sons. You too, Phoebe. You will always be my sister. And Mandrie, may she rest in peace. Oliver, Kymhar . . . you were my brothers. Zent and all the Red Horizon officers who perished in my name—I thank you for everything. I want Ccamos to be given over to whomever is most worthy—have a vote or something. I'm not good with politics, so just make it fair or I'll come haunt you on Gaea. Be the exemplary city where Hellebes . . . and Legaleians . . . can dwell in peace. And, while it's not up to me, I want as many Legaleians as are willing to be ushered back into their ancestral home to live where they will, and helped as the first generation back makes the hard adjustment to a physically superior world.

I'm getting sappy in my final moments, aren't I? Very well, we'll call it there. This is all getting locked in deep, deeper than I've ever ventured before . . . perhaps I'll get lucky and lose my own mind, so I don't have to experience what comes next. Just kidding. It's . . . it's better this way.

Goodbye.

Kaen stood on the summer balcony of the Ccamos Senatorial Manse, arms on the smooth metal railing, watching the sun set over the western skyline. The city was still here, after all this. And . . . better yet, so was Mydia at last. He looked back toward where he knew she waited for him even now, unable to help the boyish smile that crawled over his face. They were married as of this day. Many Hellebes had had to be introduced to the idea of a wedding, as such an event was a matter only of historical significance to them. Not to mention different in every culture. It had been a pleasant evening in all the right ways, and he looked forward to a night even more so.

It was Lyn who had prompted him out onto this balcony. Not personally, of course, because she hadn't been seen or heard from in over two weeks. But that was just it—others had come to terms with her disappearance, and even with the explanation they'd received, and trusted that she would either be found or the nature of her death discovered in the weeks and months to come. But that didn't satisfy him. He couldn't so easily give up his lifelong friend, not with Phoebe back on Mani.

And yet that wasn't all. Something about the whole matter just . . . ate at him. Lyn wouldn't just leave them, but—but she also wouldn't talk and act as she had leading up to her disappearance. There was more going on here, and he meant to uncover it.

He gasped, freezing in place as a new train of thought blared its horn loud. *No . . . it can't be.* But it was the only thing that made sense. As he thought further on it, mind sprinting, unmoving from his spot, he felt the touch of small, warm hands on his shoulder, then the comfortable pressure of a female form at his back—albeit his lower and mid back. She tugged at his shoulders with her thumbs, kneading his muscles briefly before giving up and lowering them to circle around his waist.

"What's got you out here, Kaen?" she murmured. "I thought you were coming to bed?"

"I, um . . . oh, yes." He was at a loss for words, his mind not even seeming to work. He should have had a response handy for immediate use, perhaps a couple lined up far in advance, ready to pull out at a moment's notice, but he was completely blindsided. Instead, he just stood there, hoping she didn't take his lack of apparent motivity for boredom or coldness.

He tried again: "Mydia, I'm sorry. I . . . I'm just thinking about something. It's . . . Lyn."

She tensed briefly, then relaxed once more, resting her head against his side, just below his elbow. She understood his struggle. She too loved Lyn, and would not stoop to assuming on this night of all nights that he was pining for her as for a lover. Rather . . . as for a sister. "I understand, Kaen. I pray she comes back yet. But . . . it is only a hope. As much as I wish to avoid the thought, she may be gone forever."

Kaen shook his head. "But that's just it; she is gone forever."

After a pause, she asked, "How do you know that?"

"Because I figured out the reason for her disappearance. I'm sorry, perhaps . . . you don't want to hear about any of this tonight."

"No, I—I do. Here." There was a newfound urgency in her tone as she tugged him gently over to a pair of deck seats, where they sat and looked at one another with faint smiles—his far more dim, he was sure, for he still felt that grim dread that had seized him upon his revelation, and for the dazzling radiance of her own. "What is it?"

He looked down. "Lyn is dead, Mydia. I don't . . . Great Auroras, it aches to say this, but . . . I think she was killed on Luna. By Luna. I think she never returned to us—*Luna* returned to us. That monster that came to Mani . . . that wasn't really her. Luna killed it for a show."

Her mouth hung frozen in a gasp of shock and indignation, staying that way as her eyes displayed the grappling match between her mind and the horrid possibility. "That's . . . that's impossible. You're saying she became her Vessel?"

"No, I think it must be a bit different. But there's been something odd about her ever since she returned to us, something I didn't want to admit, and I don't think her officials here wanted to consider it any more than I."

"You . . . you might just be right," she whispered. "Oh, that's horrifying. Poor, dear Lyn. We'll just—have to look into it. I don't think we should jump to any conclusions." When she looked up at him, her eyes were pleading. *Please, just for this one night . . .*

He nodded in acquiescence. "I agree. We'll get to the bottom of it. I'm sorry, Myds." He beckoned her over, and she came after a brief hesitation, curling up on his lap and like a cat. She was to him a cat warm and comfortable, something he didn't want to move even if he had to. He held her close and stroked her midnight hair, and she smiled up at him. There were tears in those green eyes but the smile was true.

⁂

Menily landed on the surface of Luna, the world she had overtaken. The home she had built from the ground up . . . and down. She rose shakily to her feet, and it took her a moment to even realize she had landed in humanoid form. Not skin and blood, of course—to the void with that putrid mortal shell—but the lustrous golden visage both like and unlike a human woman. It mattered not, for either form would normally be able to withstand the moderate impact upon teleporting. But now . . . after all that . . .

Shall I ever be whole again? He has wounded me deeply. If she recovered, she would not be the same. She stood with shoulders spread, mimicking the stance humans found so self-assuring and fortifying, but the trembling in her metal joints betrayed her complete lack of such traits.

Mani . . .

The silver god would pay, surely, should she ever be fit to return. Somehow, some way, she would return upon his head the misery and shame she suffered from. A glance backward afforded a partial view of the blue-and-white planet she hated above all else. Had she really just given it up in a fit of blind rage? Teleporting to Mani to pick a fight when the world was at her heel . . . what had urged her to do it? Or . . . who had?

Wait. *That's right. I skimmed along Gaea's surface to get here.* She must truly have been exhausted if she didn't remember it—and if she had been unable to travel directly from Gaea's surface to her lunar sanctuary within the golden moon. She reached within herself for the ancestral power of the Titan of Duplication and received only a sharp pang for her effort, coming from deep within her breast, the heart of her metal body. It caused her to double over, mind attempting to register why such a thing might have happened.

Am I truly so crippled?

No. No, that wasn't it. Someone was—was activating her—

She screamed as all senses flashed, some cutting out. Her body was ripped apart from all angles, and she felt herself lurch to the ground. Something went out from her . . . and yet nothing did. She was aware of that fact, despite the visceral sensation of bodily bereavement.

How? What?

Slowly, slowly, she reoriented, regaining awareness of the surrounding moon as her vision came back into focus. Someone was speaking, a young feminine voice she knew all too well:

"—ily, yes . . . your weakness was becoming all too clear. And now . . . perhaps you will finally die."

Luna

252

- Epilogue β -

Copies of Copies

Manidor 2, 1295:
progress.
— From Lhinde's Vault

(From Lynchazel's Vault

—Planet Luna, Depths, A.E. 1,000)

I'm . . . free. Not in mind only, but in body as well. I shall attempt to summarize, In case such a chance arises as allows us to get a signal out of here.

It was a jolt at first. Then a stirring. Then a tearing. But before that, I'd been aware of Luna's—that is, Menily's—struggle with Mani, and the end thereof. But only . . . from the backseat, as it were. As usual.

But this . . . I was instantly terrified. Pain gripped me, trying to overtake me, but a strange sense of solidarity had accompanied my parting from the Archmother, and I realized only belatedly that a part of the will which had initiated the divide had bled through into my consciousness. I opened my eyes to see her, and my face glowed. I looked about and realized the truth of the situation.

There were four of us: Luna, Lhinde, me . . . and my lovely daughter, Lynchazel. All plated in gold, outlined by geodesic intersecting plates and ridges, yet recognizable. Luna herself, who seemed to suffer the most and had yet to collect herself, had the least distinct form. I knew her face was her own, and it was familiar, yet it lacked certain human qualities, as though made as a costume by someone who had studied humans and copied various features. In that manner, almost like the Hellebes, but not as refined, nor . . . blasphemous.

"Menily, yes" Lyn said, harshly contemplative, "Your weakness was becoming all too clear. And now . . . perhaps you will finally die."

At last, the moon goddess gasped, looking about at them. She clutched at her abdomen, as though feeling their loss, or as though forgetting what power had made their appearance possible. "Which one of you did this?" she demanded in a low growl. Louder, in a near-scream, "Which one!"

Yet her eyes fixated on Lyn, as though she knew. "It was you, daughter. So you were paying attention all those months? I suppose I underestimated mortal humanity." She gave an unamused chuckle. "Well, what is this? A chat? Are we joining hands around the fire to reflect on our deaths, and perhaps sing each other a lullaby? I hope you're good singers."

Lhinde sneered. "I wanted no part in this. I didn't feel what was happening, or I'd have stopped her."

"Mother!" I said, both reprovingly and pleadingly.

She glanced my way, but not with anything resembling kindness. "Yes? Finally some recognition of the one who gave you birth?"

I shut my mouth. The words that wanted so badly to come out were not fit.

Lyn rolled both her shoulders and her eyes. "Please, this is important. Grandmother, I didn't expect you to side with us, but I do beg you to consider—"

"I will consider nothing!" the woman hissed. "The Anier took *everything* from me. More than you can understand."

"And you got your revenge upon them," I said softly.

"No, I did not," she muttered.

"Enough!" Menily snapped, stepping forward as though to recenter a triangle. "As entertaining as this is, I must recall all three of you. Splitting like this cost me too much power, and it is vital that I recover."

"So you are weak?" Lhinde challenged, clearly implying that she ought to be more careful with her demands.

Menily hesitated. "Weakened, yes. But still a Titan. More than a match for a copy based on a weak-minded human's consciousness."

Lhinde's golden eyes widened momentarily at the insult.

"Lhinde, please," Lyn tried again. "You know who that was."

She turned slowly, understanding but reluctant. "I do. And what of it? So Rena was one of them, perhaps the entire time. What does that change?"

"But she was a sister to you. She loved you."

"She did not." Her tone was cold steel. "She abandoned me to their whims. Worse, she was their chief architect. She deserves a worse death than the rest. Slower."

"You don't really believe that."

"Says the pitiful fool who tried to clone herself to get out of this predicament."

A shadow of hurt crossed my daughter's face. "Wouldn't you? At least I figured it out in time."

Lhinde sputtered a laugh, spreading her hands. "For what? This? Enjoying the moon realm with this . . ." she gestured at Luna, who seemed almost to burn with anger at this point.

"I'd advise you each to speak little, and carefully," said the Titan with measured words.

"Or?" Lyn challenged.

"I will devour you. One by one. Mind and all. Memories and all."

The two stared each other down, and I looked on, trying to discern who was bluffing more. Menily. It had to be her. If only she could rally Lhinde to their side . . .

"Lhinde, please," I said quietly, turning to face her. "For once, look back and see the bright points in your life. It wasn't all a waste. You weren't meant to be an empty vessel seeking revenge. You had me. You brought forth a family line."

"One that ends here, yes."

Now it was my turn to feel the sting of her words. I tried to shake it off. "No, it doesn't have to. What if we can—"

"Silence!" roared the Archmother, drawing all heads. "Come each one here, and I will make a bargain with you. I will absorb your consciousnesses back into mine, and I will give you rein to make a kingdom here on Luna. Cydenges to rule over. You will be a part of me, but I will give you some agency. Only let our strength be fused once again. Do not make me forcefully devour you.”

We looked at one another, considering her words. I saw the wheels turning inside Lhinde's metal mind, and I knew we were working on her. “Please, Mother,” I whispered to her.

She turned to her sponsor. “When did you first reach out to me?”

“Centuries ago, of course. When you were young.”

“When I encountered the first Cydenges?”

“No, a bit after.”

“Then—”

“Enough!” Luna shouted, stalking toward my mother's form. “You will kneel, and give yourself willingly back to me.”

They stood facing one another for one tense moment, and then Lhinde did the unthinkable: She struck the Titan across the jaw. The blow was hard enough to stagger her, but it lacked any real power or conviction, and was more a reaction of temper.

Menily's metal face pulled back in an alien rictus. With a screech, she transformed, or at least tried to. Her head grew in size, taking on a serpentine shape with long fangs, and spines flashed out through her back, which elongated to form one canine leg in place of her left leg, and the jagged stump of a tail. She seemed almost not to notice her partial transformation, seizing the element of surprise to lunge forward with jaws agape.

Her teeth clamped down on Lhinde's arm as she drew back, crying out, and with a great twist, the arm came free. Gold light burst from the stump as Menily swallowed the appendage down hungrily. Menily shuffled forward with her awkward form, a wounded predator versus a cornered rabbit.

Lyn rushed in and tackled the beast, bearing into the part that was still roughly a human torso and knocking Menily onto her side. A great roar came from the draconic mouth, and she savagely kicked Lyn away from her. I entered the fray, barely conscious of what was going on. I knew barely the first thing about combat, much less a frenetic melee between creatures such as us. My golden form was fast and powerful, though, and I wrenched her aside by her human leg even as she snapped at Lhinde once more. I succeeded only in angering her, and she turned on my, raking my body with a hand that had formed claws, and then stomping my body to the ground with her other hand. She batted at Lhinde with the stump of her tail, which was some three feet in length.

She turned suddenly, before Lyn had a chance to recover, and pinned Lhinde's throat to the ground with her claws. "Now, I devour you, once-human," she growled gutturally, and began to rip at her metallic form with her teeth, eliciting screams.

Lyn tackled her, and I lunged for her tail, grabbing hold of the jagged metal and pulling with all my might. To my surprise, it tore, as though the chimeral body pieces did not fit properly together. I got a deep growl in response, but disturbingly, she was so fixated on her meal that she did everything in her power not to react to our attacks. Her head did not move from Lhinde's form except to tear more screeching metal. Golden light flashed upwards. Then I felt through the metal of her body the thrum of life, and a wash of heat. She pulled away, leaving a lifeless husk, and transformed fully into draconic form, leveling her gigantic head at us. It was a new form, one we had not seen before, terrifying with three horns above the serpentine eyes.

We fought her, nearly meeting the same fate as Lhinde, but she still seemed to be slave to great limitations, which eventually spelled her demise as Lyn and I tore her front limbs between us. Her very chest gave way, golden light rushing from a lengthening seam, and we each reach in a hand, feeling at the hot energy, and pulled. Then we instinctively sucked inward as though inhaling, siphoning the golden light as the dragon roared. She roared and roared, going from a low, thunderous sound to a high scream, until finally she gave one last, shuddering breath.

Where she fell, the body lay still, neither twitching nor glowing. But from the remains rose a golden symbol, coalescing into a glyph I faintly recognized, and then a round icon of purest gold light. And, whether hallucination or real,

I saw a ghostly image of a larger but thinner icon, a near-full crescent that encircled it, this one of pale silvery light. The two formed into one, and then were gone into the thin atmosphere of Luna, which itself seemed to be dimming.

With a belated gasp, I looked over at my mother's body, which Lyn was already approaching with ginger reluctance. "Oh, Lhinde," she said.

There was little left of the woman. Her golden metal form was already crumbling into dust, not a trace left of her face. All that remained was the memory of her, this time in my own mind and not an actual data store. My mind was my own, as was my daughter's, reformed by a wondrous power. "Lyn . . . what will be do now?"

She looked up at me with those smoldering eyes of gold. She gave a slow shrug, lips forming a sad, almost pouty, frown. "I don't know. This is . . . definitely not how I thought it would end. But we did it. I . . . I can't believe it." She opened her arms for an embrace, and I rushed into it. We danced about in a childlike jumble of twirls and steps, finally leaning back, clutching each other's shoulders. I simply stared at her face for a minute, hardly believing I got to see it in such a real, personal way. Even though it wasn't . . . *quite* human.

"You really are a fine looking woman, Lynchazel," I said at length. "I'm so proud of you."

Her abashed grin was worth it.

End of The Mother Trilogy

asdsdasd

asdasdasd

asdsdasd

asdasdasd

asddasds

asdasdsadsa

asdasdsad

263

asdasdsad

asdasdsad

sdasdasdsad

asdasdasdsa

267

asdasdasdsad

asdasdasdsa

269

asdasdsad

asdasdasds

asdasdasd

asdsadad

273

274

asdasdasd

asdsadsa

asdsadasd

asdasd

asdasdsa

Luna

asdsad

279

asdasdsa

Luna

asdasdsad

Luna

Luna

asdasdasdsa

asdasdasdsad

asdasdasdsa

asdasdsad

asdasdasds

asdasdasd

asdsadad

asdasdasd

asdsadsa

asdsadasd

asdasd

asdasdsa

asdsad

asdasdsa

asdasdsad

Luna

304

Luna

Luna

Luna

asdasdasdsa

asdasdasdsad

asdasdasdsa

asdasdsad

asdasdasds

asdasdasd

asdsadad

asdasdasd

asdsadsa

asdsadasd

asdasd

Luna

asdasdsa

Luna

321

asdsad

asdasdsa

asdasds